KISMET AND KARMA

Part Two of

THE BLACK GLEN

trilogy

KISMET & KARMA

Part Two of
THE BLACK GLEN
trilogy

by

Elizabeth Burton
Scotland

Author of: 'The Life and Times of Thomas of Ercildune'
(The Rhymer)

A story of fiction

Based (very loosely) on fact

In memory of Floss

ISBN 978 1 861431 72 1

KISMET AND KARMA

The Black Glen

The continuing story of Isobel Ferguson

In 1965, Isobel Caldwell, now twenty three years of age, has everything she's ever wished for. Married to her soul mate and expecting his child, her childhood dream of staying at the remote croft in the Black Glen has come to fruition.

Real life though, is a world away from the one of fairytale endings - fate has a habit of dropping bombshells when least expected. Not long after moving to An Gleann Dubh, Isobel is beset with a sequence of tragedies, one in particular that alters the course of her life forever.

During her subsequent times of torment and desolation are brief moments of happiness, which in turn, bring hope and optimism for the future. But pleasure is fleeting and fickle. Life's journey, plagued with trials and tribulations.

All names have been chosen at random and bear no relation to anyone who may, coincidently, have a similar name.

Acknowledgement

Debra Garside

True North Fine Images

www.sableislandhorses.ca

Kismet and Karma, alias fate and destiny, play an important role in the life of Isobel Caldwell, as indeed they do in everyone's. They are also the names of two Highland ponies that are woven into the story. With this in mind, I began my search for an image to use for the front cover of the second book in the 'Black Glen' series.

Having always been an advocate of fate, I truly believe that this amazing photograph was taken especially for this purpose. Not only does it capture the essence of the story, but also, it is precisely the image I had in mind. My Kismet and Karma had come to life.

Consequently, I hereby express my sincere thanks and gratitude to Debra Garside, True North Fine Images, for allowing me to use her photograph, 'Light Contact', as my front cover. This is one of many taken by Debra on a photo shoot of the wild horses of Sable Island in June 2012.

The cover photograph copyright belongs to "Debra Garside Photography"

Chapter 1

Christmas Day 1965 was one of the happiest days of Isobel's life. Not only had her pregnancy been confirmed, but so too had a long held suspicion. Rob, with whom she'd had a special bond for the past thirteen years, was indeed her long lost sibling.

The following day, she came back down to earth with an almighty thump. After the initial euphoria of having her pregnancy confirmed and the feeling of jubilation that she'd finally found her brother, the reality of her present situation hit her like a thunderbolt. For a start, she was in the early stages of pregnancy following a recent miscarriage. Then there was the little problem of being stranded without transport at the virtually inaccessible croft in the middle of nowhere. Worst of all though, was the realisation that she wouldn't be able to do any manual work around the croft for the foreseeable future. Before they'd taken on the tenancy of the croft in the Black Glen, both she and John had given Rob their solemn promise that it would be run efficiently. They'd also assured him that the livestock, his champion Blackface rams in particular, would be in safe hands. However, in light of the present situation, it would be impossible for them to run the croft without help. For a start, John knew little or nothing about crofting, and in a very short time she would be unable to tramp the hills or be of much physical help.

That evening, Gordon and Mairead, their nearest neighbours from the farm at the other end of the three mile track, paid them a surprise visit. They'd come to collect the chairs and crockery Mairead had lent for the Christmas Day lunch party. Isobel looked upon Gordon and Mairead as her two dearest friends. In fact, both she and John thought of them as their adopted parents and always welcomed them with open arms. They never came empty-handed and as if by magic, Gordon produced a large bottle of malt whisky from a pocket deep within his threadbare, tweed jacket. His work-worn fingers appeared to be welded to the bottle and anyone would have been forgiven for thinking it contained liquid gold, which, in his opinion, it did. Mairead's contribution was

1

slightly more appealing as far as Isobel was concerned. She carried a basket filled with home-baked goodies. During the course of the evening Mairead happened to mention that their son Calum had completed his course at the agricultural college and was looking for a job. Isobel could hardly believe her ears. Once again, Lady Luck had smiled upon her. Or, was it just another quirk of fate that had tossed the ball into her court?

'Mairead, that's wonderful news,' she cried out joyfully. 'John and I are in desperate need of someone to help us out during my pregnancy.'

John's scowl didn't go unnoticed by Isobel. She was left in no doubt that he didn't share her enthusiasm about the prospect of Calum coming to join them. No sooner had Gordon and Mairead left for home than he voiced his irritation about there being a threesome at the croft. Isobel's response was one of anger and frustration. As far as she was concerned, it was the ideal solution to their current problem. John however, remained unconvinced.

The following week, Calum duly arrived at An Gleann Dubh to work alongside John in his relatively new venture of running the remote hill croft. Calum was delighted to have found a job so close to home, and besides, he'd always had a soft spot for Isobel. John, on the other hand, regarded Calum as nothing more or less than a necessary evil. It had nothing to do with the fact that Calum and Isobel's friendship spanned many years. Nor was he jealous of the relationship they once had, but somehow, he just couldn't stop his feathers getting ruffled when he saw the two of them sharing nostalgic moments. In an ideal world, he would have preferred it to be just him and Isobel sharing the first few months of their new venture at An Gleann Dubh. He accepted though, that there was no such thing as an ideal world. On the plus side, he was overjoyed at the prospect of fatherhood and accepted that the present circumstances necessitated an extra pair of hands.

As it turned out, Calum's presence during the first few

months of 1966 was a godsend. The snowstorms during their first winter as tenants of An Gleann Dubh were the worst Isobel had ever experienced. Rob had already told her about the atrocious winter conditions of the previous two years, but she hadn't seen them for herself. This year, the blizzards began in January and didn't let up until April. For some of that time the croft had been inaccessible by road and Calum had to move into Isobel's old room in the loft. During this time, vital provisions had to be flown in by helicopter. Isobel had been frustrated by the fact that, due to her pregnancy, she hadn't been of much help, but, ever pragmatic, accepted that there was absolutely nothing she could do to change it. What she'd found much harder to accept however, was the fact that a large number of sheep had died during the first few months of the year. The poor beasts had either perished in the freezing conditions or been buried alive under several feet of snow. The situation had been caused by the powers of nature though, which, Isobel had to concede, even *she* couldn't control. Thankfully, Rob's prized rams, having been brought in from the hill to the safety of one of the barns, had survived. Recalling the time she'd had an extended holiday at the croft due to the severity of weather, Isobel had to concede that had been nothing compared to the conditions they'd endured this year. John, on the other hand, being raised in the city and having no previous experience of such extreme weather conditions, had suffered something of a culture shock.

'Never in my entire life have I experienced such Arctic conditions,' he'd remarked one night when the temperature plunged to fifteen degrees below freezing. 'If I make it through the winter, I'll survive anything.'

Despite the life-threatening conditions and the fact that they'd lived like hermits for several weeks, not once had Isobel regretted her decision to swap her old life in the city. At one point, the thought did cross her mind that they'd no means of summoning help in the event of an emergency, but somehow, she'd had a gut feeling the need wouldn't arise. Thankfully, there had been no climbers on the mountains this winter, and therefore, no casualties. The dearth of

3

intrepid mountaineers was mainly due to the fact that the mountains had been completely inaccessible for most of the winter months. Now though, Isobel was filled with a sense of optimism. Not only was she more than half-way through her pregnancy, but spring was just around the corner.

****

Chapter 2

On awakening one morning to feel the warmth of the sun's rays streaming through the bedroom window, Isobel's heart leapt with joy. Spring had finally arrived. At long last she could emerge from her state of hibernation and venture from the sanctuary of the croft. Despite having provided a haven of refuge during the ferocious, winter storms, it had also become something of a prison as far as Isobel was concerned. Her months of longing for a girly chat had suddenly become an obsession, and on impulse, she decided to pay Mairead a visit. Her only means of transport was the old Ferguson tractor; however, since her destination didn't involve driving on the main road, it would be fit for purpose. John had made her promise not to drive the tractor during her pregnancy, but if she was to escape from here for a couple of hours, there was no alternative. Since the onset of the big thaw, many of the improvised bridges had been swept away. This had resulted in gushing torrents of meltwater cascading through the gullies, rendering the track impossible to traverse on foot.

Despite being springtime, an icy chill hung in the air and Isobel donned a thick winter coat on top of several layers of woollen clothing before leaving the warmth of the cottage. She'd picked up a cushion from the sofa on the way out and as she placed it on the metal seat of the little grey Fergie, a mischievous smile crossed her face. While acknowledging that negotiating the track in such wintry conditions would be something of a challenge, she was relishing the thought. The downside was that John would probably be furious with her when he found out. Throughout the winter months, especially during the time they'd been cut off from civilisation, he'd been overly anxious about her welfare. If truth be known, Isobel, not one to enjoy being mollycoddled, was beginning to feel rather stifled by his fussing.

Despite it becoming something of an antiquity, Isobel had a great affection for the little grey Ferguson tractor. In fact, her first experience of driving it would remain one of her most treasured memories of all time. She was twelve years old at

5

the time, painfully shy, and worthless - at least - her parents and peers looked upon her as being such. Learning to drive the tractor had been her first major achievement in life. It was her beloved brother Rob that had taught her to drive the tractor. He'd also shown her the correct way to milk a cow, speak the Gaelic, and most of the other facts of life she'd learnt as a child. Until their fortuitous meeting, she'd known nothing about anything. It was also Rob, not forgetting her devoted collie Meg, she had to thank for the formation of her indomitable character.

Isobel pressed the starter. Although the tractor hadn't seen the light of day for several months, the rickety exhaust pipe shuddered and rattled before spewing forth puffs of black smoke as the engine spluttered into life. The smell of diesel oil filled the shed. How she revelled in the memories it evoked. Moving at little more than a snail's pace, Isobel made her way across the yard, at the same time, glancing around for any sign of John returning from the hills. After manoeuvring the tractor between the narrow gateposts she pushed the throttle lever forward. The little grey Fergie responded by belching forth a column of thick, black smoke, before lurching forward like a thing possessed.
Although well accustomed to driving the tractor along the winding three miles of track that led to the farm, today, Isobel found it to be a bumpier ride than usual. Not only were there lumps of compacted, frozen snow to contend with, but she also had to dodge the debris that had tumbled down the mountainsides. Despite feeling like a floppy rag-doll as the old tractor bounced and rattled along, her mood was one of elation. She was living in the place of her dreams and married to the love of her life, she was also carrying his child. The mountains were bedecked with a topping of pristine white snow and the infinite space of clear blue sky overhead only added to her sense of wellbeing. As Fergie and heavily pregnant passenger slowly snaked their way through the glen, a chill, north wind was beginning to sting Isobel's cheeks and bring tears to her eyes. For the past twenty minutes or so, her hands had been tightly clenched round

6

the metal steering wheel and it was hard to tell if her fingers were still on the ends of them. None of these minor discomforts could quell her soaring spirits though, for the first time in ages, she was free. Now, she'd reached the wooden bridge that crossed the river and, with the farm in sight, couldn't stop the word, civilisation, from escaping her lips.

The tractor had barely come to a stop when the farmhouse door flew open and Mairead strode down the garden path with a look on her face that would have curdled milk. Her forehead creased with deep furrows, she bellowed, 'Isobel, what's wrong?'

Despite shivering like a wobbly jelly, Isobel managed to say, 'Nothing's wrong Mairead,' while at the same time thinking it wasn't exactly the greeting she'd been expecting. As they met on the path, Isobel informed her that she was in dire need of some female company.

Mairead's relief was displayed in her warm, if somewhat bewildered smile and Isobel placed a friendly arm around her shoulders as they entered the farmhouse. As Mairead bustled about in the kitchen, Isobel could hear her muttering in an agitated tone.

'Speak up,' she urged through chattering teeth. 'I've got cloth ears from the racket of the engine.'

While lifting the steaming kettle off the stove, her voice now having gone up a few decibels, Mairead responded by saying, 'The very thought of you being stranded away up the glen in your condition made me sick to the very pit of my stomach.'

'There's no need to shout. I'm not deaf.' Isobel then patted her growing baby bump and added, 'We've all survived the storms. I just wish I could say the same for the flock.'

'It's just one of the hazards of running a remote hill croft,' Mairead responded. 'Rob wouldn't have fared any better if he'd been there himself.'

'I know, yet I can't help feeling we've let him down.'

'Don't talk nonsense,' Mairead reprimanded while handing her a mug of steaming hot tea.

By now, Isobel's frozen fingers were beginning to thaw out, but her teeth were still chattering. After taking a few sips of the hot, sweet tea, she gazed imploringly at Mairead and said, 'Can I ask a favour?'

Nodding her head, Mairead replied, 'Isn't that what mother's are for.'

Isobel positively beamed with delight. She was aware that Mairead now regarded her as the daughter she'd always longed for, and for her part, Isobel looked upon Mairead as her guardian angel. After all, had it not been for Mairead and Gordon's arrival at the croft on the night she'd suffered the miscarriage, she wouldn't be here today.

'It's just a small favour,' she added. 'I'd like to make a couple of phone calls.'

Isobel's first call was to Helen, her favourite sister. Although their homes were within an hour's drive of each other, due to the atrocious winter conditions, they hadn't spoken to one another since Christmas day. Once the two sisters began to chat, they found it hard to stop. After all, they had five months of news to catch up on. During the lengthy conversation, Isobel learned that Stella had given birth to a daughter just two weeks earlier. Naturally, her second call was to her step-mother. Stella was delighted to hear from Isobel and told her they'd named the baby Annabelle, but she was to be known as Anna. It suddenly occurred to Isobel that, since Stella was now her step-mother, Anna was her half-sister. These were changed days from her lonely childhood years when she'd assumed that her entire family consisted of just her and her parents. Isobel had always longed to be part of a large, happy family, and now, her wish was coming to fruition. Not only had she been reunited with her three siblings, but she also had a husband, a step-mother, a newly born half-sister, and, in a very short time, her own child would be making his or her way into the world. How she longed for that day to come. She could hardly wait to get rid of her cumbersome bump and get back to running the croft. Just then, Mairead entered the room and interrupted her pensive state.

'I'm so grateful for the use of the phone...... ' she began.

Mairead however, stopped her in her tracks with the words, 'Why do I get the feeling that the word "but" was on the tip of your tongue?'

'Can I make just one more call?'

While dialling the now familiar number, Isobel was filled with a mix of apprehension and excitement. The dialling tone stopped and a deep, formal voice boomed out from the earpiece, 'Good Morning. Inverculden Estate'.

Isobel's voice, in complete contrast, was high pitched with excitement, 'Hello Rob. It's me'.

Rob's tone changed immediately to one that always filled her heart with joy. 'Hello Bella, it's so good to hear your voice. I've thought about you constantly during the past few months. How are things at the croft?'

'Our first winter has been quite a challenge,' she replied solemnly.

'I sincerely hope you and John are not having second thoughts about moving there.'

'Not for *one* moment,' she replied adamantly.

Isobel went on to tell her brother about the many obstacles they had faced, and overcome, during the winter months. The last thing she mentioned was the large number of sheep that had perished during the first few months of the year. The two siblings chatted, mainly about the croft, until Mairead called out that tea and freshly baked scones were laid out on the kitchen table.

Later that afternoon, Isobel climbed aboard the tractor and made her way back to the croft. After parking the Fergie in the shed, she went to the cottage to get Floss and the pair then made their way to the byre. Fly was asleep in his kennel and didn't stir as they approached. He was now almost fourteen years of age and the harsh winter had taken its toll on his health. Isobel knelt beside him and stroked his greying muzzle, saying as she did so, 'For as long as I live, I'll never forget our first meeting.'

Two glazed eyes tried to focus on her face. Nonetheless, as his tail swished back and forth among the straw, there was no doubting the fact that Fly knew it was the voice of his beloved mistress. He'd come a long way since the day Rob saved him from being put to sleep because of his aggression, and over the past few years he'd been worth his weight in gold as a working sheepdog. The winter conditions this year had been much too severe for him to work the sheep though and Isobel knew that, very soon, he would have to be replaced. His frail, work-weary body was trembling with cold and Isobel made up her mind there and then that he would spend the last few years of his life in the warmth and comfort of the cottage.

****

Chapter 3

Being the loyal and obedient dog that he was, Fly followed close to Isobel's heel as they made their way towards the cottage. Since his entire life had been spent as a working dog, he'd never set a paw inside a house before and he paused before entering. With Isobel's encouragement and Floss's reassurance he slunk inside and cowered in a corner. After much coaxing and cajoling he reached the kitchen, where he spent the next few minutes pacing up and down. He sniffed each item of furniture and every nook and cranny, before deciding that no danger lurked here and flopped onto the mat beside Floss. A few moments later, the door burst open and John stormed into the kitchen. Isobel could see that he was agitated and the furrows on his forehead deepened upon seeing Fly fast asleep in front of the range. His foul mood was totally out of character and, while finding it both puzzling and unsettling, she was determined not to let it show. In an effort to make light of the tense atmosphere, she remarked with an undertone of sarcasm, 'Hello dear. Have you had a bad day?'

'Let's just say, it's not been a good one,' he replied sharply. 'How was yours?'

Smiling sweetly, she replied, 'I've had an absolutely wonderful day. I paid Mairead a visit, had afternoon tea and made a few phone calls.'

'I sincerely hope you didn't walk all the way to the farm,' he said in a solemn tone.

'No. I *drove*,' she retorted.

Knowing that the tractor was her only means of transport, John glared at her before launching his tirade. 'Didn't I forbid you to drive the tractor in your condition? Have you no thought for our unborn child? Or are you just plain stupid?'

'My *condition* is that I'm pregnant, not incapacitated,' she retaliated. 'And furthermore, having recently qualified as a vet, I would say that I possess a small degree of intelligence.'

A forlorn smile crossed John's face as he gathered her in his arms. 'My darling Isobel,' he began. 'I love you more than life itself. I couldn't survive without you.'

Isobel's frustration subsided as she draped her arms lovingly around her husband's neck. She kissed his mouth and a quiver of excitement shot through her body. John was her soul mate, her other half, and despite being pregnant, her desire for him was still rampant. John also had the unique ability to calm her fiery temperament and she melted into the familiarity of his loving embrace.

'I love you with all my heart,' she responded lovingly. 'And furthermore, I have no intention of putting myself, or our baby, at risk. Talking of which, Stella has given birth to a baby girl. They've called her Anna.'

'I'm counting down the weeks 'til we have a little girl of our own,' he replied dreamily.

'I hope you're not going to be too disappointed if it's a boy,' Isobel teased.

'Much as I long for a son, I have a feeling we'll be blessed with a daughter. Perhaps next time,' he added with a grin. 'Now tell me, why has Fly been brought into the cottage?'

In a tone that was in complete contrast to her beguiling smile, she replied, 'Because the winter has taken its toll on his health and giving him some comfort in his retirement is the least I can do to repay his loyalty.'

The nature of her reply was such that John knew it was the end of the discussion.

With the track now negotiable, Calum had returned to stay with his parents and for the first time in ages, John had Isobel all to himself. During breakfast the following morning, he asked in a casual tone, 'How would you like to spend the weekend in Dumlocher?'

'Oh John, that would be absolutely wonderful,' Isobel responded eagerly.

Not only was she longing to see her step-sister, but six months had passed since she'd seen her father and Stella. Since John's parents were now staying in their house in Dumlocher, they would be able to pay them a visit too - perhaps even stay with them. Isobel suggested that she would go down to the farm later in the day and make a couple of phone calls. John's response was as swift as it was abrupt. 'Indeed you won't. I'll go.'

12

Despite feeling aggrieved and frustrated, Isobel knew within her heart that he was right. Until the bridges had been replaced there was no way she could reach the farm. Although enjoying her role as tenant crofter of An Gleann Dubh, the feeling of complete isolation was beginning to irritate slightly. With John refusing to allow her to drive the tractor for the last few months of her pregnancy, it was time to think of another means of transport.

****

Chapter 4

John and Isobel's weekend in Dumlocher doubled as a family reunion and recharging of their batteries, following which, they returned to An Gleann Dubh. Even though she'd enjoyed the family reunion, meeting her half-sister for the first time, and dining out at her favourite restaurant, Isobel could hardly wait to get back to the peace and solitude of the croft. Despite being born and raised in Dumlocher, she'd never felt any connection with the city, or city life for that matter, and now that motherhood was imminent, that feeling was intensified. City life was being lived at a much faster pace these days and she had no wish to be drawn into its decadent culture. Neither did she wish her child, or subsequent children, to be influenced by the new, "liberated", generation. An unsavoury culture was rampant in certain parts of the city and the housing scheme where James lived as a child was notorious for fights among rival gangs. Fortunately, Mary and James had recently moved to a quieter, suburban area. Although the decade of the Fifties had seen many changes, the Sixties was a time of even greater, faster, and worst of all, irreversible change. The giant leap in the standard of living during the past two decades was unprecedented, and previously, inconceivable. Those from the "lower classes", as Isobel's mother used to call them, were now employed in tedious but well-paid employment and had cash in their pockets for the first time since the war. Their ethos was to work hard and play even harder. As for the younger generation, they were embracing the innovative and outrageous music revolution. One pop group after another was topping the charts, each trying to outdo the other with their weird attire and even weirder music. To accommodate the demand, dance halls were opening up in all the major towns and cities. It was a time of constant change, teenage rebellions, and unbridled progress. For the youth of the decade, it was time of liberation from the oppression and outdated values of the "older generation". And yet, Isobel couldn't help feeling a sense of regret that those very values, the ones she'd held in contempt and rebelled against as a child, were slowly and surely disappearing forever.

There had been no time to visit James and Mary during their brief, city visit, however, Isobel's father had informed her that he frequently spoke to James at work. Apparently, their baby was due in July, the month before theirs'. Isobel couldn't think of a time in her life when she'd ever felt remotely maternal – not even when Mary had announced her teenage pregnancy - however, since cradling her tiny, half-sister, she could hardly wait to hold her own infant in her arms.

In the spring of 1966, time was beginning to weigh heavily on Isobel's hands. She'd never taken kindly to being idle, and now in the latter stages of pregnancy could neither take the dogs out onto the hills, nor do any manual work around the croft. John steadfastly refused to allow her to drive the tractor - in fact he would hardly allow her to lift a finger - and she was becoming increasingly bored. Mairead's unexpected arrival at the croft one day prompted her to pursue an idea she'd had up her sleeve for some time.

'Mairead, can I ask a favour?' she began.

Mairead sighed.

'I was wondering if I could hitch a lift to the farmhouse and make a phone call.'

With an expression of unconcealed relief, Mairead replied in the affirmative.

Isobel's plan was to call Rob. She'd never forgotten his words to her long ago: "If you need anything, at any time, all you have to do is ask."

After dialling Rob's number she waited with a degree of apprehension until the receiver was picked up.

'Hello Rob,' she began hesitantly. 'I'd like to ask you a question?'

Before he spoke, the sound of hearty laughter could be heard down the line. 'If I'd been given a pound each time you said those words, I would be a millionaire by now.'

Rob, having inherited the fortune of his adoptive parents, was now a multi-millionaire and Isobel joined in the laughter before replying, 'Keep working on your jokes. Seriously though, I was wondering if you could lend me some money to buy a horse.'

Rob was still laughing as he responded by saying, 'For a moment there, I thought you said a horse.'

'I did,' Isobel replied in a solemn tone. 'I've no transport at the croft and I need a pony and trap.'

Isobel was aware that Rob had kept a few of his mother's thoroughbred racing horses, but her equine requirement wasn't for pleasure. What she needed was a sturdy, working pony.

Following a brief silence, Rob responded by saying, 'There's a horse sale at the auction mart at Culbeg next Wednesday. I'll pick you up at ten thirty.'

That evening, Isobel broke the news to John.

Glaring at her with an expression of disbelief, he began by saying, 'You can't be serious?' While slowly shaking his head, he added, 'You are serious, aren't you?'

'Yes, of course I'm serious. Why shouldn't I be?' she retorted.

'For a start, you're seven months pregnant. You're forgetting another slight problem, you can't even ride.'

Isobel giggled, before replying indignantly, 'Don't be silly. I'm not going to *ride* it.'

Rob and Isobel returned from the Culbeg horse sales with an addition to the livestock at the croft. In a horse-box attached to the pick-up, was a pony. As always, Rob had insisted on his favourite sister having her heart's desire, at his expense, and the decision had been made in the space of a heartbeat. The mare she'd chosen was a three year old Highland Pony. She was brimming with spirit and character and Isobel had bonded with her the minute she set eyes on her. Never having owned a pony before, Rob had just fulfilled another of her childhood dreams.

'How can I ever repay you?' she'd asked on the way back to the croft.

Rob's reply had been: 'Finding my family is all the payment I need. If it hadn't been for you, it wouldn't have happened.'

The pick-up had no sooner come to a stop before Isobel went to the rear of the horse-box and began to lead her pony towards one of the small barns, where she'd prepared a loose-box. Her smile stretched from one ear to the other as she and Rob watched the young mare investigate her new surroundings.

'All I need now is a trap and I'll be mobile again,' she remarked optimistically.

'That could prove to be more difficult than acquiring the pony,' Rob replied solemnly. 'First of all, we'll have to locate a trap, then, you'll have to train the pony to pull it.'

'You find the trap and leave the rest to me,' Isobel responded boldly.

Just then, John sauntered into the barn.

'What do you think of Kismet?' Isobel asked as he came to stand beside them.

'Kismet?' he repeated, frowning.

'Yes, I've just named her,' Isobel began. 'Kismet, destiny, fate – they're one and the same. I now truly believe that the paths we take in life are predetermined. I also believe that I can teach Kismet to pull a trap,' she added with an air of arrogance.

John and Rob exchanged glances that expressed their mutual sentiments - a combination of frustration and futility.

'In your pregnant state, that's going to be more dangerous than driving the tractor.' John responded scathingly.

'I hope you fully appreciate the dangers,' Rob added in a solemn tone.

Shaking her head in frustration, Isobel said sharply, 'You men are all the same. No sense of adventure.'

Rob left the croft to return to Inverculden and John announced that he was going out with Ben to check the flock on Beinn Ghlas, calling as he left, 'I should be back within the hour.'

Isobel was secretly delighted to be having an hour on her own. She planned to use the time to get acquainted with her new pony and had already decided to take her for a short walk on the lead rein. With the idea of killing two birds with one stone, she went to the cottage to get Floss. Their long walks had been curtailed recently, with the result, Floss was over eager to get going. Unknown to Isobel, Kismet hadn't seen a dog before.

Floss was now barking excitedly and Kismet, regarding her as an unfamiliar threat, reared up on her hind legs, yanked the lead rein from Isobel's hand and bolted. Given her heavily pregnant state, Isobel could only stand and stare as the pony high-tailed it into the distance. Standing forlornly in the yard, she was in a state of disbelief, helplessness and complete devastation. With John out on the hills and Rob probably half way home to Inverculden by now, she was also completely alone.

'How could I have been so stupid?' she muttered under her breath.

Her vulnerability in this remote and ruthless environment suddenly hit home. With their baby due in a matter of weeks, and no way of accessing the nearest telephone, she now realised the true extent of her isolation. Just then, she heard the sound of a vehicle coming through the glen. As it got closer, there was no mistaking the familiar sound of the farm Land Rover. It cut through the deathly silence like a knife and was sweet music to her ears. A short time later, Mairead pulled up in the yard.

'Why the long face?' she asked.

Despite the seriousness of the situation, Isobel couldn't stop herself from smiling at Mairead's opportune choice of words.

'Kismet has bolted,' she replied.

'Is Kismet the new pony by any chance?' Mairead enquired with a wry smile.

'Yes,' Isobel muttered dejectedly. 'She took off the minute Floss barked. It never crossed my mind that she'd be spooked by a dog.'

'They say you learn something new every day,' Mairead remarked with a knowing grin.

'And I was foolish enough to believe I'd learned all there is to know about animals,' Isobel replied glumly.

'What way did she go?' Mairead asked.

'Towards the Black Glen,' Isobel replied.

'Jump in. She may not have gone very far,' Mairead said while starting up the Land Rover.

With Isobel and Floss as front seat passengers, Mairead drove slowly and cautiously over the rough terrain that led towards the Black Glen.

'What made you come up to the croft?' Isobel asked as they bumped and rattled over the uneven ground.

'I can't explain,' Mairead began slowly. 'Except that, I had a feeling you needed me.'

Isobel was deep in thought. This had happened before, when she suffered the miscarriage. It was as though there was some kind of telepathy between her and Mairead. Passing the big meadow, Mairead pointed straight ahead and called out, 'That's a pony if I'm not mistaken. Either that, or it's an enormous sheep.'

With a sigh of relief, Isobel cried out, 'It's Kismet.'

To avoid running the risk of spooking her again, Mairead stopped the Land Rover. Then, she and Isobel began to creep stealthily towards the young pony. Kismet lifted her head and eyed them warily. The last thing Isobel wanted was for her to bolt, and, being no horse expert, was on unchartered territory. Acting on pure instinct, she did the first thing that came into her head; she called her name. Almost immediately, the futility of her action dawned on her – the pony had only been given her new name that day. The leading rein was trailing on the ground and Isobel was tempted to lunge forward and grab it, however, having already learnt a swift, harsh lesson, she resisted the urge. Instead, she extended her arm and Kismet took a faltering step towards her. Her hand was empty, but the pony's curiosity had been aroused. While Kismet nudged her hand, Isobel slowly moved her other hand towards the trailing rein.

'You and Floss head back to the croft, I'll walk back with Kismet,' she said softly as Mairead joined them.

'Are you sure?'

'Absolutely, I would like to spend some time alone with her.'

As Mairead drove off in the Land Rover, Isobel continued to stroke Kismet's neck. She wasn't too daunted by the thought of walking back to the croft; after all, they'd driven less than a mile. Although well accustomed to walking, Isobel was beginning to feel twinges of pain in her lower back by the time the croft became visible. She thought nothing of it and put it down to the jolting around in the Land Rover on the outward journey. By the time she'd reached the yard however, the dull ache in her back had become almost unbearable. Mairead, who'd been waiting in the yard, took one look at her, snatched the reins from her hand, and said, 'Get into the Land Rover.' She then marched off in the direction of the barn - with Kismet submissively trotting behind her.

'You're in labour,' Mairead said while starting the engine.

'I can't possibly be in labour. I've still got a few weeks to..........'

The sound of an agonising scream could be heard long before Isobel had finished the sentence.

****

Chapter 5

Late in the evening of May 28th, 1966, Isobel gave birth to a daughter. She was six weeks premature and weighed little over five pounds. Isobel was given only a brief glimpse of her newborn infant before she was whisked from the delivery room and placed in an incubator. When finally wheeled from the delivery room to the ward, Isobel and John were reunited for the first time since he'd left in the morning to check the flock. The nurse had no sooner left the room when he leaned forward and said softly, 'Don't do this to me.'

'Do what?' Isobel enquired wearily.

'Scare the living daylights out of me. It's the second time in the past year I've been summoned to your hospital bedside. I could scarcely believe what I was hearing when Gordon arrived at the croft to tell me that Mairead had taken you to hospital.'

Isobel, now sobbing quietly, said, 'I'm sorry. I don't do it on purpose.'

John buried his face in his hands. 'Losing Jennifer was bad enough, but if I lost you, I would lose the will to live.'

'We've already lost one child,' Isobel sobbed. 'I'll lose the will to live if our baby doesn't survive.'

John took her in his arms, saying, 'If she's anything like her mum, she's a born survivor.'

'If she dies, I'll blame myself for the rest of my life.' Isobel replied solemnly.

The nurse returned and politely asked John to leave. The second bell had gone, visiting time was over, and apparently, Matron insisted that the times were strictly adhered to. Once he'd gone, Isobel asked the nurse about her newborn infant's chances of survival.

'She's doing as well as expected,' she replied gently. 'For a six week preterm baby.'

As on many previous occasions, Isobel drifted in and out of a troubled sleep that night. At one point, she even imagined it had been a bad dream, until she placed her hands on her flattened stomach and realised the awful truth.

Early next morning, the nurse entered the side room and

21

greeted the new mum with a smile. 'Would you like to see your baby daughter?' she asked.

Isobel, still suffering from the effects of gas and air, not to mention, lack of sleep, asked drowsily, 'Is she going to be okay?'

'She's not out of the woods yet,' the nurse replied, 'but the initial signs are looking good.'

Isobel was helped into a wheelchair and taken to the special care baby unit, where she saw her baby daughter for the first time. Gazing at the tiny infant she and John had so lovingly created, once again, her emotions were in turmoil. For one who'd never worn her heart on her sleeve, Isobel couldn't stop herself from displaying her immediate and intrinsic love for this tiny scrap of humanity. A whole host of emotions ravaged her mind as she gazed in awe at the tiny form - the overwhelming one being guilt. Their new-born infant was clinging to life by a flimsy thread – and it was all because of her. If not for her impatience – and pig-headedness - her pregnancy would have gone full term. The nurse left the room, giving mother and baby a few precious moments alone. Isobel sat beside the incubator and gazed in wonder at the delicate, but perfectly formed, scrap of humanity. Never before had she experienced love this intense - not even for John. Once, she'd vowed she would never love anyone other than her beloved animals, and Rob and John apart, this had been the case, until now. This alien and slightly disconcerting maternal emotion had come as quite a shock to her. After squeezing her arm through the hole in the side of the incubator, she removed the cotton mitten from her daughter's tiny hand. The perfectly formed fingers, like the rest of her frame, were minute. Just then, Isobel felt those tiny fingers wrap themselves around her forefinger.

'Màiri,' she whispered. 'Welcome to the world. One day, you and I will tramp the hills together.'

She and John hadn't chosen a name for their first-born child, yet the name Màiri had just rolled off her tongue. Isobel could offer no explanation, other than it being the Gaelic name for Mary, and, second to Meg, Mary was her best friend.

The nurse returned and explained that the first forty-eight

hours of her baby's life would be critical. Once that time had elapsed, her chances of survival would continue to increase.

'You may even get to hold her,' she added.

While the nurse had been talking, Isobel was conscious of another voice telling her that Màiri was going to be just fine. This one had been inside her head.

Isobel and her premature infant remained in the hospital in Drumevie for the first three weeks of Màiri Elizabeth Caldwell's life. Then came the wonderful day when the family returned to An Gleann Dubh.

'My life is complete,' John remarked later that evening. 'Right now, I am the happiest man in the world.'

Isobel frowned as she gazed lovingly at the sleeping infant in her arms. Although overjoyed that Màiri, now weighing a healthy six and a half pounds, had finally come home, something was troubling her.

John looked anxious as he asked, 'Are you all right?'

'I'm fine. Just tired,' she replied softly.

'Isobel, I know when you're not telling the truth,' he said tenderly.

'I can't explain the way I'm feeling right now,' she responded in a forlorn tone.

John was puzzled, but more than that, he was concerned. While fully aware that his young wife had come through a traumatic time, and her sombre mood could be down to post-natal blues, he knew her well enough to realise that her melancholy mood was completely out of character. Although thrilled to be reunited with his beloved wife, and more especially, the fact that their infant was now out of danger, he went to bed that night deeply troubled.

A few weeks had now passed since Isobel returned to the croft with baby Màiri. She was growing fast and Isobel was able to resume some light duties around the croft. She'd fashioned a type of baby carrier out of an old sheet and carried Màiri with her wherever she went, whether it was to milk Daisy the cow, or feed the poultry. Mairead visited daily, mainly to check that Isobel was coping with motherhood, but if truth be known, she enjoyed fussing over the new arrival. One day, Isobel asked her if she would look after Màiri while she took Kismet for a short trek.

Isobel hadn't ridden before, and recalling the disastrous consequences of her first outing with Kismet, left Floss behind. After leaving the cottage, she made her way to the small meadow with the intention of becoming reacquainted with the pony she'd seen only briefly before Màiri's untimely birth.

Much to her surprise, Kismet began to walk towards her as she approached. It was a good start. She extended the hand that held the carrot while gently stroking the pony's neck with the other. Rather deftly, especially for one with no experience, she fitted the halter around the pony's head. The first task duly accomplished with relative ease, the pair then sauntered back to the croft. Although Isobel's intention had been to use her as a driving pony, due to her daughter's premature birth, that hadn't materialised. She couldn't even be sure if Kismet had been ridden before – but was about to find out. With the saddle now in position, she gingerly placed her foot in the stirrup. Without warning, Kismet reared up. This time though, Isobel was ready for her. She kept a tight grip of the reins and began to talk in a calming tone. Kismet was trembling. She was a very young pony and Isobel knew very little about her past – or about ponies for that matter. This time, instead of placing her foot in the stirrup, she pushed each stirrup to the top of the leathers and led Kismet from the yard. The pair then continued to walk side by side in the direction of the Black Glen. It was the first time in months Isobel had ventured this far, and just as the ruined cottage came into view, she paused for a few moments of quiet reflection. The cattle, mere dots in the distance, grazed contentedly on the lower hillslopes. A huddle of old ewes moved stealthily among the waist-high bracken. The silence was broken only by the distinctive and intermittent call of a wheeling lapwing, but that apart, the deathly hush, unique to the Black Glen, was almost tangible. Kismet's timely, but unexpected whinny jolted Isobel back to reality. The young pony turned her head and eyed Isobel with a look she took to

24

be a challenge. It's now or never, she said to herself while sliding the stirrups down the leathers. Like it or not, I'm going to ride you back to the croft.

Kismet moved off long before Isobel had time to fling her right leg over the saddle. Holding on to the pony's mane for dear life, and by a feat of ingenuity - or perhaps just good luck - she manoeuvred her right foot into the other stirrup. Now seated securely in the saddle, she gathered the trailing reins and eased them back towards her body. Never having so much as sat on a horse's back before, her actions were purely instinctive. Kismet was now moving in a fluid canter and Isobel's body quickly adjusted to the steady rhythm. By now, she'd gained a degree of confidence – not to mention, a rush of exhilaration - and urged the pony on. After a short canter, she pulled gently on the reins and sat down in the saddle. Almost immediately, Kismet slowed her fast gait to a trot. Isobel smiled. Despite the fact she hadn't ridden before, and suspecting that Kismet had only recently been broken, it was obvious they had established a mutual bond. Horse and rider then approached the yard as if they had ridden out together many times before. As she led her young pony to the meadow, Isobel positively glowed with self-satisfaction; another hurdle had been overcome with relative ease. It was at that moment she recalled Rob's words from her childhood: "You have an uncanny way with animals. It's almost as if you can read their thoughts."

****

Chapter 6

Each day during the summer months, Isobel rode Kismet to the foothills of the mountains. Over a short period of time she'd introduced Floss and Kismet to each other and Floss now accompanied them wherever they went as a matter of course.

Now, it was autumn. The days were growing shorter, the nights were drawing in, and the grim prospect of winter was already giving Isobel cause for concern. One day while out riding, she met a group of mountaineers. Although there had been no casualties on the mountains during the past year, the thought crossed her mind that it was time to put her plan regarding the radio link into action. The cattle were grazing up ahead, and, catching sight of the young bull, another thought crossed her mind; soon, he would have to be brought indoors for the winter months. Seumas, one of her many animal friends from childhood, had sadly passed away, and his successor Torcall, was a bull with attitude. Since Floss was with her, she gave the cattle a wide berth, before riding deeper into the glen. As always, the beauty of her surroundings left Isobel feeling humbled. The rowan trees were laden with crimson berries. The heather clad lower hill slopes reminded her of a luxurious, mauve coloured carpet. The sun was shining down from a cloudless, blue sky, yet she felt ill at ease. There was no rational explanation for her feeling of gloom, given that everything in her life was perfect - perhaps too perfect - she mused.

The following week, Isobel drove to Drumevie. For many years she had wracked her brains over a means of communicating with the outside world. Due to the distance from civilisation, the installation of a telephone at the croft was out of the question, today though, the need to explore other avenues was at the forefront of her mind. She'd been told about Citizens Band radios but knew they weren't readily available in Scotland; she'd also been told they were illegal. Another option was a two-way radio, and her intention today was to make further enquiries. More than an hour later she left the only shop in Drumevie that could have given her advice on any such radios with a feeling of frustration. She'd been advised by the shopkeeper that they were only available in the city stores. The problem was that the nearest city was an hour's drive away and she didn't have the time to spare. Besides, Mairi, now almost five months old, was beginning to get fractious in the back of the car. Isobel's mood, as she drove back to the croft that day, matched that of her wilful, young daughter.

'How was your day darling?' John asked as he entered the kitchen in the evening.

'Don't ask,' Isobel replied tetchily.

'Didn't you get what you wanted?' he added in a sarcastic tone.

John idolised Isobel. She was his life and his reason for living, but he also acknowledged her failings – one of which was – she liked to get her own way.

'No.' she snapped. 'The small shops in Drumevie are useless compared to the department stores in the city.'

Isobel prepared their evening meal, venting her frustration on pots and pans, and anything else she could make her feelings known with, in the process.

'How would you like to spend the weekend in Dumlocher?' he remarked - a mischievous glint in his eye. 'We could catch up on all the family news and combine it with a shopping trip.'

'Oh John, that would be wonderful,' she began. 'But we have too many commitments here to be able to just get up and go on a whim.'

'Leave it to me,' he replied. 'You need a break and, after all, it'll only be for a few days.'

On Friday morning, Mairead arrived at the croft in the Land Rover. John had driven to the farm on the tractor the previous evening and made all the necessary arrangement to allow them the luxury of an extended weekend break.

'This is going to be more trouble than it's worth.' Isobel remarked grumpily as she loaded everything but the kitchen sink into the Land Rover.

'Don't be so negative,' John replied cheerfully. 'It'll be worth it

27

in the end – especially if it makes you happy.'
Isobel was angry with herself. Here she was, living her dream at An Gleann Dubh and putting John to all this trouble to take her back to Dumlocher – the place she couldn't wait to get away from. But then, John had always gone out of his way to make her happy. Anyhow, her visit to the city would be different this time, because that's all it would be. In a few days time, she would be returning home. While transferring the luggage from the Land Rover to the Mini, Isobel began to reel off some last minute instructions to Mairead. Her response left Isobel speechless.
'Just get into the car and go,' she barked in frustration. 'The croft, the livestock – and the dogs - will still be here when you get back.'

The many recent improvements to the roads meant that the journey from the croft to Dumlocher was completed in less than two hours - Máiri having slept for most of the journey. They had now reached the outskirts of the city and Isobel was surprised to feel a tiny twinge of anticipation. She'd received a letter from Mary with the good news that she'd given birth to a daughter in July and was excited at the prospect of catching up with her childhood friend, not to mention, enjoying a family reunion. Recalling the happy times spent here with John, she was overcome by a feeling of nostalgia as they reached the drive that led to their old house. The car had barely come to a standstill when the front door opened and John's parents rushed outside to greet them.
'Welcome home,' Mildred called, her arms outstretched as John met her on the steps. 'It's so good to see you.'
Behind him, Isobel was cautiously making her way up the steps with Máiri in her arms.
'I can't wait to hold my first grandchild,' Mildred gushed while reaching out to take Máiri from her arms.
Once inside, John and Isobel were taken to the guest room and, after unpacking, joined John's parents in the lounge. Mildred was still cradling Máiri and acting like a besotted grandmother as she greeted them with the words, 'I'm sure

28

you young ones must be in need of some time to yourselves. As for us oldies, we would just love some time alone with our granddaughter. Why don't you go out and enjoy yourselves this evening?'

John and Isobel exchanged glances. It was a tempting offer. What with Máiri's premature birth and the pressures of work at the croft, they'd almost forgotten what enjoyment was. Therefore, with some reservations, they accepted the offer.

That evening, John and Isobel dined at their favourite restaurant. They followed it up with a visit to a dance hall in the centre of the city, where one of the top pop groups of the time just happened to be playing. For the first time in ages, Isobel let her hair down. She felt like a teenager again - happy, carefree - and deeply in love.

That night, for the first time in many months, she and John made love. As on her very first experience of intimacy, Isobel wept uncontrollable tears of passion. Basking in the serenity of his tender embrace, she felt euphoric, fulfilled and cocooned in love. Pressing her lips lovingly against the small facial scar that remained from his horrific accident, she whispered, 'For as long as I live, no-one will ever take your place in my heart.'

Máiri, who'd been fast asleep when they returned, stirred and brought them back to reality.

The following day was Saturday and John and Isobel's plans were to go into town. Before leaving, the morning paper dropped through the letter-box. John picked it off the floor and read the headline out loud:

"Dumlocher Bank Raiders Escape With A Large Sum Of Cash".

The article went on to say that a bank in the city centre had been held up at gunpoint the previous afternoon. A teller had been shot and seriously injured and the gang had made off with their loot.

'We made the right decision at the right time,' Isobel remarked almost inaudibly.

'I beg your pardon,' Mildred remarked with a questioning frown.

29

'The city is no longer a safe place to stay,' Isobel continued. 'During the war years, it was deemed safer to live in the countryside. I fear the situation will come full circle and it'll be the case again very soon. Although living in the back of beyond brings a few disadvantages, at least we can go to bed at night and sleep easy with the door unlocked.'

Their shopping trip was successful and Isobel ticked another box on her list. Following their trip into town, they visited Isobel's father, step-mother and their baby daughter. Anna was just six weeks older than Máiri and Isobel had laughed out loud at the sight of her father on all fours, attempting, rather unsuccessfully, to put a nappy in position.
'Changed days,' she managed to say between sniggers. 'I'm quite sure you never changed my nappy.'
'I'm one of the "New Generation",' he replied with a straight face. 'I'm a modern father now, and furthermore, sour grapes will get you nowhere.'
'In that case,' Isobel began with a hint of sarcasm, 'you can perfect your technique by changing Máiri's nappy.'
That afternoon they visited James, Mary and their baby daughter Jessica. She was two months younger than Máiri and both sets of besotted parents took great delight in discussing and comparing their offspring. Mary and Isobel also revelled in the joy of being together again and playing "catch up". As they were leaving, Mary took Isobel's hand in hers, squeezed it and said, 'I'll never forget your loyalty in my time of need and I will always regard you as my best friend.'
With a smile, Isobel replied, 'And you will always be my second-best friend.'
As children, Isobel had told Mary that her beloved collie Meg, was, and always would be, her best friend. For her part, Mary had always been, and would continue to be, happy to settle for that.
John and Isobel spent Saturday evening with Robert and Stella at their favourite restaurant. John's parents had offered to babysit both Anna and Máiri and, as the foursome chatted over dinner, the last few years seemed to roll away.
'This is like old times,' Robert remarked with a smile.

The jovial atmosphere changed to one of solemnity as Isobel responded in an anxious tone, 'Let's leave the old times where they belong, in the past.'

Robert frowned, as did John, before saying, 'It's not like you to be so melancholy.'

Isobel couldn't begin to understand her morose frame of mind. After all, at this moment in time, she had all she'd ever dreamt of - and more.

That evening, she was consumed by an inexplicable and frantic need to be close to John.

'Just hold me tight and never let me go,' she whispered as their naked bodies made contact.

'I told you once before, I don't intend to ever let you go,' he replied. 'I will love you until death us do part.'

John was now kissing her with a frenzied passion and Isobel responded with a similar urgency. Their bodies were now saturated with perspiration - their frantic need for one another borne out of mutual passion. John tightened his arms around her pulling her ever closer, before letting out a rapturous groan. Isobel was powerless to do anything but yield to the primal desire he had aroused. While lying in his arms, as on many previous occasions, silent tears ran down her cheeks.

The following afternoon, Isobel, John and Máiri left Dumlocher to travel back to An Gleann Dubh. Although she'd enjoyed her time in the city, and more especially her weekend of passion with John, Isobel could hardly wait to get back to the croft. It was early evening by the time they reached the farmhouse and Isobel, weary from travelling, flopped into an armchair in Mairead and Gordon's kitchen. She was eager to find out if all was well at the croft, but before she could say a word, Mairead beat her to it.

'We heard about the bank robbery in Dumlocher on the news,' she gushed.

'We read it in the newspaper,' Isobel responded nonchalantly.

'Read it in the newspaper,' Mairead exclaimed. 'Were you not there? The young girl died from her injuries this morning.'

'I'm sorry to hear that,' Isobel responded sympathetically, 'but we didn't see it'.

'Dumlocher is a big place Mairead,' John began, 'and besides, we had other things on our minds.'

His remark had momentarily silenced Mairead, giving Isobel the chance to ask Gordon about the radio link.

'It'll do the job,' he remarked with a nod, before leaving the room.

A few moments later he reappeared with a bottle of malt whisky in his hand.

'Will you take a wee dram for the road?' he muttered, while pouring equal measures into four glasses.

In the meantime, Mairead had been bustling back and forth laying an assortment of hot food on the kitchen table.

'Supper's ready,' she called.

'Mairead, we didn't intend to stay for supper.......'

'Be quiet woman,' she interrupted, glancing in Isobel's direction. 'Just sit down and eat up.'

There was no point in arguing with Mairead - or Gordon for that matter. As far as they were concerned, John, Isobel and Máiri were now a much loved extension of their family.

****

Chapter 7

Máiri, having slept soundly all through supper and the sampling of Gordon's single malt whiskies, was now awake and making her presence known.

'It's about time we hit the road,' Isobel said wearily.

'That may be closer to the truth than you intended,' Gordon said with a chuckle as he struggled to rise from his chair. He then staggered towards the door, slurring his words as he spoke. 'I suppose you'll need me to take you up the glen.'

'You're right there Gordon,' John replied in an equally inebriated state. 'Otherwise, it'll be "Shanks' Pony".'

After offloading the luggage from the mini, John went to park it in one of the sheds, while Mairead, Gordon and Isobel shared the laborious task of loading the suitcases and other paraphernalia associated with travelling with a young child, into the Land Rover. John had once suggested that they replace the mini with something more suitable for the terrain now that they'd moved to live in the back of beyond. At the time, Isobel, who loved the tiny car, had been against the idea - however, at this particular moment, she was deeply regretting that decision - Gordon was in no fit state to drive. In fact, as she rattled around in the Land Rover on the way to the croft, she was beginning to wish she'd never agreed to spend the weekend in Dumlocher. I just wish I was home and tucked up in my bed, she kept saying to herself, while thinking they would be extremely lucky if they made it home safely. Despite her concerns, Gordon successfully negotiated the hairpin twists and turns of the precariously narrow track, and eventually, by the light of the harvest moon, the croft became visible. As far as Isobel was concerned, it wasn't a moment too soon. The Land Rover had barely come to a standstill before she dashed into the cottage, ran past Floss and Fly, who had come, tails wagging in unison to greet her, made a beeline for the toilet and immediately threw up.

'Damn Gordon and his whisky,' she muttered while splashing cold water on her face.

'Are you okay?' John called from the other side of the door.

'I am now,' she replied quietly, emerging from the bathroom

ashen faced, 'Just a bit too much Uisge Beatha.'
'One day, you'll learn to say no to Gordon,' he chided.
'Perhaps', she muttered under her breath.

Isobel spent the following day catching up on all the chores that had been neglected while they'd been in Dumlocher. Gordon and Mairead had seen to the dogs, the poultry and the milking, but the stock out on the hill hadn't been checked since the day before they left – four days ago. John had left at first light to make sure all was well with the sheep and cattle on the hills beyond the Black Glen and as yet, hadn't returned. It was almost mid-day but Isobel wasn't unduly concerned as he always carried a knapsack containing a flask and sandwiches. With Máiri now settled in her cot, she sat down at the kitchen table to have lunch on her own. With a spoonful of soup mid-way to her mouth, the door burst open and John strode past without uttering a word, before collapsing into one of the armchairs. Isobel noticed that his face was drained of colour as he sat there staring blankly into space.
'Are you all right?' she asked with trepidation.
'Can't you tell I'm not?' he replied tetchily.
Isobel was both confused and concerned by her husband's uncharacteristic response. Having prior and personal knowledge of climbers succumbing to the hazardous conditions on the mountains, she asked sympathetically, 'Did you find a corpse?'
John didn't respond. He couldn't at that moment. Instead, he was staring at the floor, reliving the horrific events of the morning in slow motion. When, finally, he began to speak, his voice was shaky and hesitant. 'After checking the stock on the foothills of Beinn a Bhròin, I began to make my way back to the croft. As I emerged from the Black Glen, I heard the most horrendous, blood-curdling commotion.'
Isobel recalled the day in the glen when she'd witnessed a terrible commotion - that of Highland Warriors charging towards her in full battle dress - but remained silent. Until now, John's tone had been quiet, calm and subdued. Now, he spat the words out in anger, 'It was a dog.'

'A dog.....' Isobel repeated in bewilderment.

'It appeared out of nowhere and began to chase the sheep. I didn't have my shotgun and was powerless to do anything but watch as it grabbed first one and then another. There's worse to come,' he muttered, a look of sheer anguish on his face. 'Ben lunged at the dog and tried to stop it...........'

He paused for a brief moment. 'The other dog was twice his size and had tasted blood. It was in a frenzied state, and..........'

Isobel's cry of anguish stopped him mid-sentence, 'Please don't tell me Ben is dead.'

The look of utter despair on John's face made her heart skip a beat. Rising from the table, she ran to the bathroom - and threw up again.

'Are you sure you're okay?' John asked on her return.

'I'll be fine,' she snapped. 'Ben's welfare is much more important than mine. Where is he?'

'I carried him into the shelter of the ruined cottage.'

'And the other dog........' Isobel asked, her voice faltering.

'He was injured in the fight with Ben and slunk away to lick his wounds.'

'I'm going to hunt him down and shoot him.'

Isobel had already risen from the table and was making her way towards the gun cabinet.

Returning with the shotgun and a full belt of cartridges, she added with a look of defiance, 'And I won't return until I do.'

'I forbid you to go there on your own,' John said sternly. 'It's far too dangerous, and besides, you've never fired a shotgun before.'

Isobel flashed a look that left him in no doubt about her tenacity, before she spoke in a calm, clear tone. 'I'm a vet. My first priority is to tend to Ben and the injured sheep. Once that's been done, I'm going after the dog. I need you to stay here and take care of Máiri.'

John was powerless to stop her. Besides, he knew that if anyone could save Ben's life, it was Isobel. He was also aware that she would have to humanely destroy the sheep that couldn't be saved.

It was early afternoon when Kismet trotted out of the yard

35

with Isobel on her back. Knowing that the killer dog would be in a savage frame of mind, Isobel had left Floss and Fly in the cottage. She urged Kismet into a canter and before very long they'd reached the old ruined cottage. The sight that greeted Isobel was one of sheer carnage. Her brain couldn't quite comprehend what her eyes were seeing as they flitted over the bloodied carcasses. After staring in disbelief for a few moments, she finally acknowledged the grim reality of the scene in front of her. Kismet tossed her head and snorted loudly. It was as if she too had been traumatised by the sight of such a cruel and pointless slaughter.

Sheep had grazed these foothills in peace, safety and solitude for many centuries. Today, in the space of a few minutes, their sanctuary had been violated by an alien killer in their midst. Isobel dismounted and led Kismet towards the graveyard where she looped the reins over one of the metal railings. Although her intention had been to prioritise Ben, the sight of the mutilated sheep made her stop in her tracks. The lucky ones lay completely motionless, their suffering over. Others were in the throes of a painful death – throats and stomachs gaping open - spindly legs kicking out spasmodically and aimlessly. Since her very first visit to the croft, Isobel's compassion had been first and foremost towards animals and their pathetic bleating tore at her heart strings. She went round each one in turn, ensuring as she did so that all with their hearts still beating were put out of their misery. Knowing the gruesome task that lay ahead, she'd put the necessary syringes and phials in her saddlebags before leaving the croft.

'Please don't let me have to do his to Ben,' she kept repeating while making her way to the ruined cottage.

Tending to the sheep had been traumatic enough, but this was part and parcel of her chosen career. Ben was different though. He was Meg's offspring. Her beloved Meg, who, even after all those years, still brought tears to her eyes when she recalled their wonderful times together.

Ben lay on the moss-covered ground with his eyes wide open – rigid and motionless. His tongue, an odd shade of blue, hung limply from the side of his mouth. His throat had been ripped open and crimson blood was staining his white ruff. Isobel knelt beside him and whispered his name.

'Ben. You mustn't die. I won't let you.'

Ben responded to the familiar voice he trusted implicitly by moving his tail. Even though it was just the merest fraction of an inch, it lifted Isobel's heavy heart.

'Thank God you're still alive', she muttered.

She rummaged frantically in her knapsack. It was imperative to administer a combination of antibiotics and barbiturates to stabilise the trauma and help fight the inevitable infection from his wound as a matter of urgency. It was obvious that Ben's throat wound would have to be stitched, but she didn't have the necessary equipment to hand. Somehow, she would have to get him back to the croft. Fortunately, Kismet had long since lost her fear of dogs, and Isobel led her into the ruined shell of the burnt out croft. Very gently, she lifted Ben's now comatose body and placed it across Kismet's back, before roping it to the saddle. The trio then slowly began the long trek back to the croft.

On their return, John was in the yard.

'Is he alive?' he called out.

'Only just,' Isobel responded solemnly, 'but I'll need some help with him.'

Despite having qualified as a veterinary surgeon, Isobel had no experience of dealing with real life emergencies. In her opinion, Ben's life was far too precious to risk anything going wrong due to her lack of experience, therefore, she asked John to test the new two way radio system and try to make contact with Gordon. It was essential to get the help of an expert, and the nearest vet was in Drumevie. While John ran towards the cottage, Isobel lifted Ben's body from Kismet's back and followed some distance behind. Before reaching the back door, she could hear the sound of his agitated voice.

'Come in. Come in. Are you receiving me?'

'Receiving you loud and clear,' Gordon answered.

'Call the vet,' John yelled into the mouthpiece.

'Why are you shouting?' Gordon asked, in a tone that had gone up a few decibels to match John's. 'Isobel's a vet. Why would you need a vet?'

'Just do it. No time to explain,' John snapped impatiently.

'Will do - over and out,' a rather confused voice responded.

Knowing that help was on the way, Isobel began to prepare Ben for surgery.

'We'll have to use the kitchen table,' she muttered while spreading large, white cotton sheets over the entire table.

Once that task had been duly accomplished, she and John gently lifted Ben onto the table. Since being brought into the safety of the cottage his condition had stabilised and Isobel could do nothing more than monitor his breathing and heart rate until the vet arrived. Eventually, the back door opened and Gordon, accompanied by a young man, dashed into the kitchen.

'I've brought the new vet,' Gordon mumbled, while staring, wide-eyed at Ben's motionless body lying on blood-soaked sheets on the kitchen table.

'Move aside and let me take a look at the injuries,' the young man muttered as he strode towards the table. Although very young, his tone of authority had taken Isobel by surprise, and, rather grudgingly, she allowed him to take complete control of the situation.

'Ah yes, quite a few sutures needed here,' he muttered, as if to himself. 'What happened?' he added, glancing at John.

'A dog fight,' John replied.

The vet glanced, rather accusingly in Isobel's opinion, at Floss and Fly lying quietly in front of the range, and she couldn't stop herself from snapping, 'It wasn't one of our dogs.'

The young vet ignored her reply, just as he'd ignored her presence, before redirecting his words towards John. 'I'll need your help.'

'Isobel would be of more help than me,' John responded. 'She's a vet.'

Despite the seriousness of the situation, Isobel couldn't help but feel a sense of superiority as he exclaimed, 'A female vet! What next?'

After administering the anaesthetic, he set to work stitching Ben's wound. Isobel meanwhile, monitored his heart rate and

38

other vital signs, as well as watching the young vet intently as he worked. Despite having ruffled her feathers, thus putting her on guard, she had to admit to being in awe of his expertise and dexterity. She recalled having had the same feeling when the vet from the practice in Drumevie saved Moss's life many years ago. Moss was the mother of Meg, her beloved collie, and Meg was the mother of Ben. The continuity of that line lay in Ben's progeny; therefore it was imperative that he survived. Whether he did - or did not - was well and truly in this young man's hands. Isobel glanced at him briefly and saw that he looked about the same age as her. We probably went through vet school at the same time, she was thinking to herself while watching him work. He though, was totally engrossed in the task of saving Ben's life.

Despite having immediately formed the opinion that the young vet was cold, aloof, and apparently looked upon females as being incapable of doing "a man's job", Isobel couldn't help but admire his surgical skill and professionalism. Just then, he caught her off guard by looking her straight in the eye and uttering the words, 'His life is in your hands now. I've done all I can.'

'Thank you so much,' was all she could say, before turning her head to hide the tears. The vet meanwhile, with Gordon following at his heel like an obedient sheepdog, beat a hasty retreat from the cottage.

Isobel was rooted to the spot as she gazed helplessly at Ben lying there, barely breathing, on the kitchen table.

'You can't do any more for him,' John said quietly while taking her in his arms. 'His fate is now in someone else's hands.'

'I have to go back to the Black Glen,' she whispered.

Realising there was little point in trying to stop her, John urged her to take great care, adding, 'The dog is extremely dangerous.'

Isobel's expression was one of dogged determination as she replied, 'I'll deal with it.'

Despite her show of bravado, Isobel's heart was thumping against her ribcage as she and Kismet rode deeper into the Black Glen. Her emotions at this moment were wide-ranging -

desolation, frustration, apprehension - fear even – but mostly, anger. Adrenalin was pumping through her veins and every fibre of her body was on high alert. They were now in the narrow pass, surrounded by towering mountains and Isobel couldn't stop herself from shaking. Apart from the steady clip-clop of Kismet's hooves, there was complete silence. Each and every time she'd come here she'd felt a presence in this part of the glen - a spiritual presence - but today, it was another, more sinister one that prevailed. Her shotgun was within reach, but her quarry right now wasn't human, but canine. Emerging from the narrow pass, the mountain peaks known as Beinn A Bhròin and A Beinn Gheal reached high into the sky on either side. It was here she'd had the vision of the Highland Clansmen many years ago. Lifting her head to gaze upon A Beinn Gheal - "The White Mountain" - she was entranced, as always, by its serene, silent, and beguiling snow-covered peak. Turning her head to the other side, she gazed upon Beinn A Bhròin - "The Mountain of Weeping". The mountains had claimed many innocent victims over the years, and at this moment, Isobel was forced to acknowledge that they would continue to do so for many years to come. Never before had she ventured this far from the croft - there had been no need - neither sheep nor cattle could graze here. The landscape for miles around was one of precipitous mountains - their austere, jagged rock faces almost perpendicular.

"A mountaineers dream", were the words uttered by the young man she'd rescued many years ago. So barren and unforgiving was the landscape here that she was certain the dog wouldn't have come this far. She'd also noticed that the sun was sinking lower in the sky by the minute. Soon, its burnished light would disappear over the horizon to be replaced by twilight. It was time to head for home. Kismet cautiously picked her way between colossal, randomly strewn boulders. Isobel couldn't help thinking to herself that they were probably still in the exact spot where they'd come to rest following the last ice age. Never, in all the times she'd frequented the Black Glen, had she felt afraid; today though, was the day that changed forever.

40

Now it was dusk and Isobel could scarcely see more than a few feet in front of her. Kismet, though stumbling at times on the uneven ground, kept plodding along at a steady pace, As horse and rider emerged from the gloomy murk of the Black Glen, Isobel was heartened to see that a hunter's moon had appeared low on the horizon, its amber glow shining out like a welcoming beacon amid the gloom. The vicinity of the Black Glen had many corries - including the one where, on several occasions, she'd heard the sound of weeping and had sensed a mysterious, paranormal presence. While cautiously approaching one such corrie, the sound Isobel heard was neither paranormal, nor mysterious. It was the spine-chilling and unmistakable sound of an animal whimpering in distress. She slid from the saddle and positioned the loaded shotgun against her shoulder. One of the many lessons Rob had taught her as a child was the correct way to use a shotgun in an emergency. If the sound she'd heard was from the killer dog, this could prove to be her first such occasion.

Approaching the corrie with cautious steps and pounding heart, Isobel knew that if she were to stumble, the gun could go off and lead shot would ricochet off the surrounding rocks. The whimpering sound had stopped and a deathly silence hung in the air. Dark clouds scudded across the night sky, now and then obscuring the moon. They cast fleeting shadows and imaginary forms, which in turn made Isobel's finger squeeze the trigger just that little bit more. Just then, her foot made contact with an object that was in complete contrast to the unyielding rock. It was soft, and warm, and made Isobel stop in her tracks. Almost afraid to look, she cast her eyes downwards and recoiled in horror. In her path, blood-soaked and motionless, lay the body of a dog. Her head was telling her to point the gun at its head and pull the trigger. Her heart though, was stopping her from doing so. In the past, she'd always followed her heart. When asked for advice during Rob's dilemma over tracing his biological parents, she'd told him to follow his heart. Therefore, she couldn't be a hypocrite and ignore what her own heart was telling her to do. After releasing the catch and breaking the barrel of the shotgun, she gently placed it on the ground before kneeling beside the dog. Its body was still warm. This in itself wasn't an indication the dog was alive, but only a short time had elapsed since she'd heard the sound of whimpering. A shaft of moonlight allowed her to see that it was a large, powerful breed, but painfully thin and undernourished. She saw also that it was a bitch. Now, she had to determine whether it was a corpse or a critically injured patient she was dealing with. Running her hand gently over the dog's chest, she detected a faint heartbeat. The quest for revenge she'd felt earlier in the day was rapidly diminishing. Due to her five years of studying veterinary medicine, her prime objective at this moment was to save the dog's life.

With the dog now lying across the saddle, Isobel couldn't help but notice that, although its frame was massive, each and every rib was visible. The poor beast looked as though it hadn't eaten a decent meal in a long time.

Eventually, she reached the croft in a state of weariness and complete exhaustion. It was early evening and now completely dark. After looping Kismet's reins through the ring on the byre wall, she went to fetch John. Upon seeing the dog's apparently lifeless body slung across Kismet's back, he called out in delight, 'You shot it.'

'No I didn't,' Isobel replied glumly.

'Then how.......why...... what happened?' he stammered.

'I found it like this,' she muttered almost inaudibly. 'It's still alive.'

'Not for long it won't be,' he barked, grabbing the shotgun from her.

Tugging frantically at his arm as he made his way towards Kismet, she called out, 'I won't let you shoot it.'

'After the carnage it has caused. Ben... the sheep.....' he bellowed, his face like thunder. 'Have you lost your mind?'

In all the years she'd known him, Isobel had never heard John raise his voice, lose his temper, or question any of her decisions.

'The dog was only following its primal instincts,' she began imploringly. 'Look at it, it's obviously starving.'

John glanced briefly at the dog's emaciated frame, before

42

continuing to rant in a raised voice.

'That's completely irrelevant. We've lost at least half a dozen sheep and Ben is at death's door, all because of this killer dog........and you want to save its life!'

Shaking his head in disbelief and still muttering under his breath, he began to walk towards the cottage, leaving Isobel to carry the dog into the byre. After gently laying it on the floor of one of the straw bedded cattle stalls, she made a start to treating the wounds Ben had inflicted. The dog had lost a lot of blood, and given its state of malnutrition was in no fit state to fight the infection that would have set in. After sedating it, she began to clean up the open wounds. Most of them weren't serious enough to need stitching, but two in particular, in her professional opinion, would heal quicker if drawn together with sutures. Despite having practised inserting sutures many times at vet school - under supervision – she found it to be a whole new experience when doing so on her own. She'd been watching intently as the young vet stitched Ben's neck wound and had gleaned some tips from her observations. I'm sure that, unlike me, he wasn't treating his first patient, she mused after inserting the last suture. Once the necessary antibiotic and anti-inflammatory drugs had been administered, there was little else she could do but let nature take its course.

****

Chapter 8

Isobel could hear Máiri's high-pitched screams as she crossed the yard. Inside, she found John frantically pacing up and down the kitchen in an effort to pacify her. Even before he spoke, she could see that he was still angry with her.

Snatching Máiri from his arms, she snapped, 'What have you done to her?'

In the same tone, he retaliated, 'It's high time you got your priorities right.'

'I beg your pardon?' she retorted.

'As her mother, your role is to be here for Máiri. My role, as crofter and tenant of An Gleann Dubh, is to tend the stock. That includes hunting down and destroying any predators – be it foxes, carrion crows – or stray dogs.'

Isobel was in no doubt about the reason for John's foul mood. She hadn't carried out her promise of shooting the killer dog. Not only that, but she'd brought it back to the croft and attempted to save its life. In fairness, she had to admit to seeing it from his point of view, but she would never let him know that.

Máiri was teething and all that was needed to pacify her was some gel rubbed on her inflamed gums. With her now happily settled in her cot, Isobel returned to the kitchen to check on Ben. He didn't stir as she knelt beside him and gently laid her hand on his head. Gazing at the blood encrusted throat wounds the young vet had so deftly closed, the tears began to fall.

'Oh Ben,' she sobbed.

At the sound of her voice, he opened his eyes and lifted his head the merest fraction of an inch.

While aware that Ben's recovery would be a slow and lengthy process, Isobel was now confident he would recover. Whether the dog in the byre would be so lucky, was anyone's guess.

It was now very late in the day and neither John nor Isobel had eaten since lunchtime. With very little enthusiasm, and a great deal of effort, she prepared their evening meal, and as they each sat in silence toying with it, wondered why she had even bothered. Isobel couldn't deny that she and John being at loggerheads made her sick to the very pit of her stomach. In all the years they'd been together, they had never disagreed about anything. Probably, she had to admit, because John, like Rob, had always given in to her. That said, something was telling her she'd done the right thing by saving the dog's life, and no-one, not even John, could convince her otherwise. Despite feeling this way, there were times such as this when she wished she wasn't quite so dogmatic. John had gone to bed without saying goodnight, and, with a heavy heart, Isobel picked up a paraffin lamp and left the warmth of the cottage to check on the stray dog in the byre. There was no change in its condition and she walked away wondering if, perhaps, it would have been better for everyone if she'd just put it out of its misery in the corrie in the Black Glen. Overcome by a feeling of nausea on her return to the cottage, she was also tired, frustrated and desperately unhappy. Her eyes began to fill up with tears of self-pity. She'd dreamt of spending the rest of her life here with John - an idyllic life - the two of them working together in harmony from morn 'til night, just as Rob and Helen had once done. The reality though, was entirely different. Due to her pregnancy she'd been unable to work alongside John, and now, if her suspicions were correct, it would be a long time before she would. After nursing a mug of cocoa for almost an hour, she made her way to the bedroom in the early hours of the morning. During that time, her mind had been spinning around in circles with conflicting thoughts. While accepting that she'd developed a fiercely independent, headstrong, and resolute character, she knew for certain that no-one, not even John, would ever change it. I can't help the way I am – or the person I've become – she thought to herself while flopping, in a state of sheer exhaustion, into bed. That night, for the first time ever, John and Isobel slept with their backs to each other. Before drifting into a troubled sleep, she said to herself: He'll come round in the end.

John wasn't in the bed when Isobel awoke next morning. This concerned her slightly until she saw that it was nine o' clock. With a groan of annoyance she leapt from the bed. Her feet had no sooner touched the floor however, when she was overcome by a feeling of nausea. Emerging from the bathroom ashen faced and trembling, the sound of Máiri whimpering in the nursery next door forced her to throw on her dressing gown and slippers instead of going back to bed. As John had so fervently pointed out, seeing to Máiri was her priority, but Ben and the dog in the byre also needed tending. 'If only I didn't feel so wretched,' she muttered while carrying Máiri to the kitchen. The sight that greeted her there made her gasp with delight - Ben was up on all fours - albeit rather shakily.

'Good boy,' she said encouragingly as he attempted to take a few steps towards her. 'I'll warm some eggs and milk for you.'

Ben was all alone in the kitchen, which meant that Floss and Fly were with John. "The blind leading the blind", was the quote of her father's that came to mind at that moment. Floss would only work to Isobel's commands, and even then, she didn't have much herding experience. As for Fly, he was a geriatric of the canine variety. Neither dog would be of much use to John in herding or rounding up the sheep. At this precise moment though, Isobel had enough on her mind without concerning herself about John's problems. She popped Máiri into the playpen and went to make up the lambs milk supplement for Ben. Knowing that the dog in the byre would be ravenous – if still alive – she made enough for two. While Ben lapped up the raw eggs and warm milk, Isobel finally got round to feeding Máiri.

John has a point, she thought to herself as Máiri suckled at her breast, I should be putting her first above all else. With Máiri now fed, changed and strapped into the pram, Isobel made her way to the byre. What awaited her there was anyone's guess. After parking the pram in the yard she picked up the small milk churn that contained the remainder of the egg/milk mixture and entered the byre. Inside, as out, there was complete silence. Torcall was still out on the hill, and apart from the injured dog, the cattle shed was deserted. With a degree of sorrow, she assumed that the dog had died overnight. Nevertheless, she made her way towards the pen and peered apprehensively over the top of the make-shift gate

46

she'd rigged up the previous night. To her surprise and delight, the dog was cowering in the far corner.

'It's okay, I'm not going to hurt you,' she said softly.

With Ben's feeding dish now filled with beaten egg and warm milk, Isobel returned to the stall at the other end of the byre. She was aware that the dog, although injured, was still capable of attacking should it feel threatened. It had already killed the sheep and attacked Ben after all. Yet by some means as yet unknown - be it intuition, sixth sense, telepathy, or just an optimistic guess - Isobel was firmly convinced that there was no malice in the dog's head. After removing the gate that stood between them, she slowly approached the dog with the dish in her hand. It made no attempt to move. The minute she placed the dish on the ground however, it began to creep forward on its belly. Two almond shaped, fear-filled amber eyes flitted between the dish and Isobel as it inched towards the food. Then it began to lap the mixture. Isobel smiled - her first for some time - it was one of satisfaction. Not only had she saved the dog's life, but it would appear that there had been some reason, at present unknown, for its previous savage aggression. Noting that some of the dog's wounds were open and raw, she decided to come back later and clean them up.

Since there were no urgent chores to attend to, and if she were honest, none she felt like doing, Isobel decided to take Máiri for a meander down the track. Before very long, her doleful mood was replaced by one of optimism. It wasn't easy going pushing the pram on the uneven surface and she'd already made up her mind to turn around and head back to the croft, when a vehicle appeared in the distance. This in itself was unusual, since no-one ever traversed the daunting three miles of treacherous track through the glen. As it got closer, she could see that it was a police Land Rover and by now, her feeling was one of unease. Eventually, the vehicle caught up with her and pulled up alongside.

'Good Morning,' one of the two officers began. 'We're making enquiries with regard to a missing person. I don't suppose you've seen anyone on your travels?'

'I've seen no-one, apart from a dog,' Isobel replied warily.

'What breed of dog?'

'It's a big dog, an Alsatian, I think.'

'Would you mind if we have a look at it?'

'Well, I'm not too sure about that,' she began slowly. 'It's a long story, but to cut it short, the dog is badly injured.'

'Apparently, the missing man never went anywhere without his devoted Alsatian by his side, and, according to his family, it was with him when he left to go hill-walking.'

'We really need to see it,' the other officer added solemnly.

Things were slowly beginning to fall into place as far as Isobel was concerned. Both she and John had been mystified by the dog's sudden appearance. Now though, the mystery deepened. There had been no sign of a person, dead or otherwise, on any of the terrain they'd searched.

The two police officers insisted on coming to the croft to see the dog for themselves; if only to log its description as part of their ongoing enquiries. The Land Rover continued on its way towards the croft and by the time Isobel returned, John and the two policemen were chatting in the yard; John having apparently filled them in with the details she had purposely omitted.

'You should have shot it,' said one, glaring accusingly at Isobel as she approached.

'Probably better that it's still alive,' his colleague argued.

'Where is it?'

'In the byre,' Isobel replied dryly.

'I hate dogs. I'll stay here,' the other said.

Isobel rolled the big, wooden door along and, with the policeman following close behind, entered the byre and made her way towards the pen. The big dog immediately rose to its feet, tail wagging. The moment the uniformed stranger stepped out from behind her, it snarled menacingly through bared teeth.

'Okay, that's enough evidence for my report,' he muttered, before making a beeline for the door. 'I'll forward the dog's description and its whereabouts to the relatives of the missing man.'

Once they'd gone, John spoke for the first time since their slanging match the previous day.

'I have to admit, you made the right decision.'

'How gracious of you to admit you were wrong,' Isobel replied with a hint of sarcasm. 'What made you change your mind?'

'Circumstances,' he muttered.

'What circumstances?' she probed.

'Who knows how long the dog had been wandering around on its own,' he began. 'It's obviously been a much loved pet at one time.'

'What do we do with it now?' Isobel asked.

'We'll have to keep it here until someone comes to claim it. Or until the missing man turns up,' he replied.

****

Chapter 9

John left the croft to check the stock on the foothills of the Black Glen. Since this was where Torcall and the cattle were grazing, he'd left the two dogs behind.

'Even the gentle slopes of Beinn Ghlas are getting too much for Fly. Besides, I'm not sure how Torcall would react to the dogs. Probably best if I go alone,' he'd remarked before leaving.

While knowing his logical thinking made sense, Isobel couldn't help but worry about him going out all alone. Not only that, but his task would be so much more difficult without a sheepdog. It was evident that finding a temporary replacement for Ben, one that would double up as a permanent replacement for Fly, was now top of their list of priorities. The problem was that ready trained working collies didn't come cheap, and their bank balance, which had always been in the black, had gradually changed to an undesirable shade of red. There had been very little income during their first year at the croft and numerous unexpected outlays. Instead of two, there were now three mouths to feed. The unexpected and extremely unfortunate incident at the graveyard with its disastrous consequences, had incurred even more unforeseen expense. Not only did they now have an extra dog to feed, but there would also be a hefty vet's bill for Ben's treatment. This annoyed Isobel greatly; after all, she was a qualified vet. She was beginning to regret ever having summoned that ill-mannered young vet from Drumevie. She'd been expecting the kindly old vet to attend, and besides, if she'd had some experience, she could quite easily have carried out the procedure herself.

After feeding Máiri and settling her in the cot for her afternoon nap, Isobel went out to the byre to check on her other patient. Since the dog now regarded her as a friend, it was obvious she had gained its trust.

'Look at you,' she remarked joyfully upon noticing its bright eyes and wagging tail. 'You've made a remarkable recovery.'

After placing the bowl on the ground, she watched from a safe distance as it devoured the food. Its speedy recovery is as much down to the fact that it is receiving nourishment again as to my prowess as a vet, she thought to herself after examining the various wounds. She had observed too - with a degree of irritation - her sutures were not quite as neat as the ones the young vet had inserted into Ben's neck wound. While deliberating over her next course of action, the sound of a vehicle entering the yard took her by surprise. Her first thought was that the missing man had turned up and the police were here to collect the dog. Upon stepping outside however, her jaw dropped a few inches as the young vet, the one she'd been thinking about only a few minutes ago, stepped from his van.

'You look surprised,' he remarked with a deadpan expression. 'But then, I don't suppose you get many visitors just turning up here unexpectedly.'

He looked around with an expression that Isobel took to be disdain, before adding, 'Come to think of it, I don't suppose you get many visitors at all.'

Despite her rising anger, she managed to suppress it, for the time being at least. The fact that he was here was nothing short of a miracle.

'I came to check on my patient,' he remarked drily while making his way towards the cottage.

'Actually, I'd rather you checked on another, needier patient first,' Isobel replied in an equally offhand manner.

Now, it was his turn to look surprised.

'Two casualties in as many days,' he sniped. 'Perhaps you should have considered a career in veterinary medicine.'

Isobel, knowing full well he was patronising her, was seething. She was finding it increasingly hard to be polite to this young man - A City Slicker - her father would have called him.

'Don't bother,' she snapped. 'I'll see to it myself.'

'Ah, a fiery temperament to match the flaming hair,' he began. 'Are you always this zealous?'

Isobel had heard enough. She responded by saying angrily, 'Get off my land and don't ever come back.'

'I'm sorry,' he muttered, his face softening. 'I've often been told I have a rather strange sense of humour.'

51

'Nothing you've said so far has had *me* in stitches,' Isobel replied with a straight face. She then smiled at the unintentional wit of her words.

'Can I share the joke?' he asked; his expression one of confusion.

'Stitches,' Isobel repeated, a dazzling smile now replacing her frosty facade. 'I would like you to check the dog's stitches.'

The hint of a smile played on the young vet's lips, though it didn't escape Isobel's notice that it hadn't reached his eyes. He's a troubled young man, she thought to herself as they made their way towards the byre.

While walking alongside, she gave him a brief account of the injured dog's attack on the sheep and about it being Ben's opponent in the fight - although in truth - the word should have been, antagonist.

Following a meticulous inspection of the bite wounds, he stood up, and, without making eye contact, muttered the words: 'You did a good job in the circumstances. Just continue with the treatment and they'll heal in time.'

Not another word was spoken as they crossed the yard to the cottage. After examining Ben's neck wound, he left the kitchen, saying as he went, 'I'm quite sure you'll be able to remove the sutures when the time comes. It'll save me the bother of a return visit, as well as saving you some money.'

On that note, he departed, leaving Isobel completely flabbergasted.

What an extremely rude young man, she said to herself. He obviously has an issue with females - or perhaps - just female vets.

****

Chapter 10

The young vet returned to Drumevie in time for evening surgery, following which, he went back to the boarding house where he rented a room. Deep in thought as he sat in the antiquated and extremely uncomfortable armchair, he was pondering over the impending mission of house hunting. But that wasn't the only thing on his mind. He was also analysing his emotions. The position he'd acquired here in Drumevie was his first since qualifying as a vet. It was proving to be a steep learning curve, both professionally and personally, with each day presenting a new challenge. Tonight, it was the personal one that was concerning him most. In fact, it was the first time since his early childhood that anything, other than his studies and career, had affected him so deeply. It was then that his entire life to date began to flash before him. Born at the height of the Second World War in 1941, he'd been christened Tormod Seumas MacAlister. An islander by birth, he'd left the family home in his early teens to further his education in the nearest mainland town. Until then, his childhood had been happy, carefree and relatively unaffected by the war. At the end of each school day he would run home to lend a hand on the family croft. He'd had no interest in lessons at school, until that is, the day something happened to change it forever. He could remember it as clearly as if it were yesterday. This particular day, he dashed home from school as fast as his legs would carry him. He was eager to change out of his school clothes so that he could help his father with the peat cutting - a job he loved. No sooner had he arrived at the croft than he was met by his mother, who said in an anxious tone, 'Your father's not cutting peat today, he's out on the hill trying to calf a cow.'

The time Tormod took to change out of his school clothes and into his dungarees and wellie boots broke all records to date and it was only a matter of minutes before he ran from the croft in search of his father. He was easy to find, the sound of the cow bellowing in distress pointing him in the right direction. Upon reaching them, Tormod stopped dead in his tracks. The distressed cow was lying like an upturned turtle and his father's face was the colour of a beetroot as he tried to yank the calf from its rear end. Tormod, on the point of throwing up, turned on his heel and began to make a beeline for home. Too late...... his father had spotted him.

'Tormod', he roared. 'Run to the village as fast as you can and bring the vet.'

Tormod took to his heels just as fast as his wellie-booted legs would permit and didn't stop running until he'd reached the village. After locating the vet, he jumped into the passenger seat of his old van and accompanied him back to the croft. He then looked on with a combination of awe and disbelief as the vet separated calf from cow. He'd never been present at a birthing before.

Later that day, his father told him that neither the cow nor its calf would have survived had it not been for the vet. From that day forth, Tormod's vocation in life was to study veterinary medicine. He was fully aware that his chosen profession would mean dedication and commitment, not to mention, many years away from the island. Although determined to see it through, his tenacity had been tested to the limit. He'd simply detested living in the city. "A fish out of water", was the phrase of his father's that came to mind. Despite this, he was determined to realise his lifelong dream. That dream was to return one day to his beloved island and establish a veterinary practice of his own. However, lack of experience – and finance – had necessitated him finding a job on the mainland first. This would be no easy task he'd thought to himself; veterinary practices were thin on the ground. But Lady Luck was smiling on him. He'd heard on the grapevine that the vet at a small country practice in a town called Drumevie in the Scottish Highlands was looking for "young blood" to fill his shoes in his impending retirement.

He'd duly applied for the post, part of him hoping he wouldn't be successful, but fate, luck, or "sod's law" as he'd called it, had played its part and he got the job. Tormod had conflicting emotions about his success in securing the post. Although keen to step on the first rung of the ladder to success, it meant spending another few years on the

54

mainland. After fifteen lonely years of feeling like a square peg in a round hole, all he longed for was to board the ferry that would finally take him home for good. All his friends lived on the idyllic island - or at least – they did. Dolina would be sure to welcome him home with open arms. From the time they were both knee high to a grasshopper, she'd been his best friend and confidante. He could still see her standing on the pier the day he'd left home all those years ago. Her hair, the colour of burnished copper, was fluttering in the breeze like demented streamers. She'd always been a bit of a tomboy, preferring to rough and tumble with the boys rather than play with the other girls in the class. He'd been slightly surprised to see her sapphire blue eyes fill with tears as he boarded the ferry that would take him away from everything he'd ever known and loved. And then there was Fergus, his sparring partner in the playground. He wore a grin on his freckle-dotted face that stretched from ear to ear as he stood with a comforting arm around Dolina. Neither he nor Dolina was clever enough to attend high school and, when their school days were over, would most likely find menial jobs on the island and remain there for the rest of their days. He couldn't quite understand the reason for the queasy sensation in the pit of his stomach when he'd thought of the two of them staying behind on the island. Many years later, he'd realised it was because he envied them.

Now aboard the ferry, he dodged the holidaymakers and ran upstairs to the vessel's upper deck, making his way to the railings as the ferry's hooter sounded that they were about to leave port. The boat had just begun to move when an easterly breeze sent the less hardy passengers indoors, but Tormod's hands clung to the railings until his knuckles turned white. His eyes were firmly fixed on the pier as the vessel picked up speed. Soon, the expanse of foaming, blue water between them quickly transformed his parents, and his two best friends, into minute, indefinable specks in the distance. Then the island itself disappeared from sight and that was the last time he'd set eyes on his beloved homeland – and the only people he'd ever loved. By a cruel twist of fate, his parents had been killed in a freak accident two months later. Tormod was an only child – and following their deaths - a very lonely child. He had very few relatives, and none that were willing to take him in. The outcome was that he was placed in foster care in a town on the mainland.

Right from the start, he was made to feel different from the other kids. Not only was he an orphan, but also an islander with a strange name, which rendered him an object of ridicule. His mother tongue was a foreign language to most of the kids in school and his peers picked on him relentlessly. While accepting that he was different from the local kids, he resolved not to change the habits of his short lifetime just to be accepted into the clique. The way he saw it, there was no need. He had much to be proud of. He was proud of his island heritage, proud of his language, and proud of his achievements to date.

Tormod retreated into his dismal, solitary shell and immersed himself in his studies. By doing so, he acquired the necessary qualifications to enable him to progress to university, and thereby, finally achieve his goal. Throughout his life he'd found it hard to interact with his fellow man. Animals though, were entirely different. He'd always had an innate and unique ability to communicate with them. Today, he'd observed that the young woman at the croft appeared to have a similar rapport with animals. He'd also been bemused to feel a degree of admiration for the way she'd handled the situation with the two dogs. Not many folk would have spared, not to mention, saved, the life of a savage, killer dog. But then, not many females could carry out manual work on a croft in the back of beyond and retain such charming femininity, he mused. The remote hill croft, though on the mainland, had reminded him of home. It was as though he'd taken a step back in time - to happier times. Perhaps that was my reason for being so abrupt and offhand with the woman, he thought to himself. In a way, I envy her. There was also something vaguely familiar about her. Come to think of it, she reminds me of Dolina - actually, the similarities were uncanny - the sapphire blue eyes, tomboy appearance, and hair the colour of burnished copper.

Despite having perfected the technique of treating his fellow

56

man, or woman in this case, with complete indifference, Isobel Caldwell, unwittingly, had managed to get under his skin. While appearing callous and aloof, she was at the same time, warm and receptive. There wasn't a shadow of doubt in Tormod's mind that her brawn could match that of any man, and yet, her physique was undeniably feminine. Judging by the character displays he'd witnessed to date, she was indomitable - and yet - he sensed that the real Isobel Caldwell was quite naïve and extremely vulnerable. She and I have much in common, he concluded.

****

Chapter 11

Isobel popped her head round the door of Máiri's bedroom and saw that she was still fast asleep. The days were rapidly growing shorter and Daisy was due to be brought in from the meadow for milking. With a hint of annoyance she realised that if John didn't return soon she would have to go and fetch her before darkness fell. Normally, this wouldn't have bothered her at all. Isobel enjoyed all aspects of work on the croft, especially when it involved the animals, but today, for some unknown reason, she was feeling very downhearted. It was time for a comforting cup of cocoa. No sooner had she sat down on the mat in front of the range, than the kitchen door opened and Mairead walked in with a grin on her face that would have banished even the darkest of moods.

'Ah, good timing,' she remarked, eying Isobel's mug of steaming cocoa. The smile was then replaced with a frown as she followed it up with the words: 'A wee birdie told me that the boys in blue paid you a visit today. What have you and John been up to?'

'It's a long story Mairead,' Isobel replied wearily. 'Make yourself a cup of tea and I'll tell you all I can.'

Returning from the pantry with a mug in her hand, Mairead informed Isobel that she'd been in Drumevie for most of the day and had heard snippets of gossip about a missing person in the area. Back home, she'd found Gordon pacing up and down like a lion with the toothache; apparently, he'd seen a police vehicle making its way through the steading. Curious to find out more, she'd jumped into the Land Rover to hear the truth from the horse's mouth - the horse in this case being Isobel.

By the time Isobel had explained the truth as she knew it, Máiri was awake and demanding attention.

'I'll see to Máiri, you bring Daisy in for the milking,' Isobel was taken aback by Mairead's words, and more especially, her bossy tone; nonetheless, she was aware that, if not for Mairead she and John would have struggled to cope during their first year as tenant crofters at An Gleann Dubh. Not only that, but in her self-imposed role as her "Guardian

Angel", Mairead was worth her weight in gold as far as Isobel was concerned. She was also one of the few people who could bring her to book.

It was dusk when Mairead left and John still hadn't returned from the hill. Although concerned for his safety, Isobel could do nothing but wait. Eventually, the outer door opened and John entered the kitchen. Under normal circumstances she would have welcomed him home with a hug and a kiss, but tonight, a frosty atmosphere lingered between them. Although John appeared to be enjoying his new role as carer of livestock at the croft, Isobel could tell that he didn't share her inborn love of animals. He, on the other hand, thought she should be spending more time with their young daughter. Judging by the look on his face, it was obvious that something was amiss.

'Don't tell me there's been another problem with the sheep,' she remarked with a look of concern.

'It took me ages to dig a pit deep enough to bury the sheep carcasses,' he began. 'And then, while passing the graveyard at the ruined cottage, I noticed that one of the young rams had become trapped in the railings.'

'Did you manage to free it?' she asked anxiously.

'Eventually,' he replied solemnly. 'I had to go into the graveyard though, with the result, I forgot to lift the spade.'

Isobel could feel herself breaking out in a cold sweat.

'Oh no,' she gasped.

'It's just a rusty old spade. I'll pick it up tomorrow,' he responded casually.

'It's not the spade I'm concerned about. It's the fact that you were inside the graveyard.'

John's tone, as he replied, was one of frustration. 'Isobel, I know what's going through your mind. You think that because I've stepped on "Hallowed Ground", as you believe it to be, some tragedy is going to befall me.'

'Don't disparage me. It's happened before.'

Isobel's angry outburst was replaced by a subtle, sardonic undertone, as she added, 'Although some folk treat it with ridicule, the curse of the Black Glen has been proven to be more than just a myth.'

'Never, in my entire life, have I met anyone as superstitious as you,' he responded irately. 'Believe me when I say that the curse of the Black Glen is nothing more than a tall tale.'

The following few weeks went past without incident and Ben and the stray dog, which Isobel had named Dileas, continued to make steady progress. She had patiently nursed the big dog back to full fitness and removed the sutures from the wounds of both dogs. If truth be known, she was extremely proud of her achievement as far as the stray dog was concerned. In light of its physical condition, it certainly wouldn't have survived without food for much longer. With regard to its temperament, during each of the many times she'd treated it, the dog had been the essence of placidity. She couldn't help but wonder where it had come from and the reason for it becoming separated from its master. The policeman had told her that, until they'd become separated, the dog was the faithful and devoted companion of the missing man – hence her choice of name - Dileas was the Gaelic equivalent of loyal.

The dog hadn't been outside the pen since the day it had been brought to the croft almost three weeks ago, and Isobel was aware that would have to be rectified, and soon. For one thing, it was Torcall's pen and he would be coming in from the hill to spend the winter months indoors. As for Ben, he was a working sheepdog and would soon be swapping the comfort of the kitchen for his kennel in the byre. Dileas, being an Alsatian, would also require regular exercise, and, given her past history with sheep, would have to be kept away from the livestock in the meantime. Living on a croft isn't quite the idyllic life I once imagined, Isobel thought with resignation.

Another problem, which had nothing to do with living on a croft, was that her previous suspicions had now been confirmed. She knew, without the shadow of a doubt, she was pregnant again. This time, she'd decided there was no need to have it confirmed by a doctor, and, for some bizarre reason, couldn't bring herself to share the good news with John.

****

60

Chapter 12

The morning of 23rd November 1966 started like any other. John had left the croft to check the stock, taking Ben and Floss with him. Although still recuperating, Ben seemed keen to get back to work, and Floss, well she was still a sheepdog in training. By early afternoon, John hadn't returned for his lunch and Isobel was beginning to get slightly anxious. She was aware there could be many innocent reasons for his lateness, but a voice in her head was telling her otherwise. She chastised herself for thinking the worst and tried to rationalise her fears. To be honest, what could possibly go wrong? The only danger facing John on the foothills of the mountains was the bull. Torcall was still out with the fold and should have been brought in long since, but the young bull wasn't as placid as old Seumas. Isobel had once suggested to John that he ask Gordon or Calum to help bring him in, while at the same time knowing he was extremely independent and didn't like troubling anyone. Just then, a harrowing thought crossed her mind. Surely John wouldn't try to bring Torcall in by himself. The sound of barking interrupted her thoughts. Isobel dashed to the back door to find Floss in a frenzied state. After circling her legs a few times, Floss ran off down the yard yelping furiously. Knowing that something was amiss, Isobel radioed Mairead and asked her to come to the croft straight away, there was no time for explanations. A short time later the Land Rover screeched to a halt in the yard and Isobel jumped into the driver's seat as Mairead ran indoors to stay with Màiri. Floss had run off in the direction of the Black Glen and Isobel followed in the Land Rover at a speed that was at best, reckless, and at worst, downright dangerous. By the time she'd caught up with her, Floss was still running flat out towards the ruined cottage. Isobel's heart was now thumping against her rib-cage. She felt physically sick - not that this was unusual these days - but what was more terrifying - she had a vivid image in her head of John lying on the ground near the ruined croft.

The grim reality was that the image wasn't confined to her

head. Just outside the graveyard, in the shadow of the ruined croft, John lay on the ground in the foetal position. He was rigid, motionless and blood-stained. Now looking down on him in a state of shock and bewilderment, Isobel was rooted to the spot. It was almost as though she was a casual bystander watching someone else's inconsolable grief. Even the piercing scream that escaped her lips seemed to have come from someone else. She knelt in the shadow of the blackened ruin and cradled her husband's battered and bloodied body. John was dead, that was agonisingly obvious, and yet, the awful truth just wouldn't sink in. Her hands now stained red with his blood, she cried out, 'John, please wake up.'

Gordon, Mairead and Calum were pacing up and down the yard when Isobel and the dogs returned to the croft. Isobel made a vain attempt to speak, but the words wouldn't come out. Her face was a mask of sheer terror and her legs were like strands of string. Stepping from the Land Rover, she promptly slumped to the ground.

'Isobel, for pity's sake, tell us what happened?'

Such was her pain she couldn't tell which one of them had spoken. The pain was mainly in her chest, but it was also in the pit of her stomach. She'd felt this pain before - not just the unbearable ache in her heart - but the excruciatingly painful one in the pit of her stomach.

'John is dead,' she cried. 'Please, please, don't let me lose his baby.'

The events that followed would remain a hazy memory in Isobel's head until the day she died. Apparently, Gordon had taken control of the situation and made the necessary arrangements to bring John's body back to the croft. Mairead meanwhile, had taken Isobel to the doctor's surgery in Ardbuie, from where she was transferred by ambulance to the hospital in Drumevie. Calum had contacted Helen, and she in turn had made contact with the other family members to break the devastating news of John's death and Isobel's admission to hospital.

For four days, Isobel lay sedated in her hospital bed in the hopes of saving her developing foetus. During that time, she was completely oblivious to the events that were taking place at An Gleann Dubh. When, on the fifth day, she was gradually brought back to reality, apart from the agonising concern over her unborn child, she was numb with grief. No matter how she tried, she couldn't erase the image of John's blood-soaked body from her mind. That same day, the doctor came and sat by her bedside.

'Mrs Caldwell,' he said softly. 'The good news is that you still have your baby. But from now on, you must rest as much as possible.'

"Rest". The word hit her like a slap across the face. At this moment in time, Isobel felt sure she wouldn't have a moments rest for as long as she lived. Closing her eyes, in a vain attempt to blot out reality, did nothing to stop the silent tears from falling onto the pillow.

On Isobel's discharge from hospital, Helen had said that both she and Mairi should move in with her and Ruaridh, at least until after the funeral. Mairead had suggested that she stay at the farm with her and Gordon. John's parents had even offered to drive north and take her back to Dumlocher to stay with them, but Isobel had insisted on going home. It was where all her happy memories were; memories of Meg, Rob, and of John.

Despite her decision to return to An Gleann Dubh, never in her entire life had Isobel dreaded seeing the croft as much as she did today. And yet, something much stronger than her powers of reasoning and utter despair and heartache was controlling her actions.

Helen was driving her home and had offered to stay with her for a few days to lend moral support. In the evening, once Mâiri had been settled for the night, the two sisters sat down side by side on the sofa. Although they'd always shared a close bond, the atmosphere was tense, with neither of them knowing what to say. For her part, Isobel didn't really want to talk to anyone, even her beloved sister, and as far as Helen was concerned, she'd been dreading this moment since the day John's funeral arrangements had been announced. Since Isobel was in no fit state, either physically or mentally, to

63

organise a funeral for her husband, the arrangements had been taken care of by his family while she'd been hospitalised. It was at this moment Helen broke the tense silence and shattered the precarious peace.

'Isobel, I know you won't want to hear this, but there's something of great importance you need to know.'

Isobel merely glanced at her sister with a blank expression and replied in a monotone, 'There's absolutely nothing of any importance I need to know right at this moment. All that's important to me is that John will never again walk through that door, and it's all because of me.'

'Don't talk such utter nonsense,' her sister rebuked.

'John came here because of me' Isobel sobbed. 'It was what *I* wanted, not what *he* wanted.'

Helen embraced her young sister and whispered in her ear, 'John was devoted to you Isobel. He would have followed you to the ends of the earth if you'd asked him.'

'I'm so glad you're here,' Isobel sobbed.

'Rob and I will always be here for you,' her sister replied.

Rob had been out of the country on business when news of John's death was broken to the family, but he was due to return later in the week.

'I've missed Rob,' Isobel said between sobs. 'I can't wait to see him.'

Helen rose from the sofa saying 'I'll put the kettle on and make some tea.'

Returning with two mugs, she handed one to Isobel and sat down on the sofa beside her. It was then she dropped the bombshell.

'John's family have made arrangements for his body to be taken to London for burial.'

Isobel's mug fell from her hand and boiling hot tea splashed across her lap, ran down her legs and onto the floor.

'You'll be scalded,' Helen cried in alarm as she dashed to the sink to get a wet cloth.

Isobel stood up abruptly, her face displaying no pain, only anger, as she retorted, 'I'll be damned if I will allow my husband to be buried in London.'

****

64

Chapter 13

Isobel spent the next few days in a world far removed from reality. News was spreading like wildfire that the crofter at An Gleann Dubh had been found dead. Not only that, but a climber was missing in the same area. Speculation and gossip was rife within the local community that "The Curse of The Black Glen" had something, or everything, to do with both tragic events. Isobel's once idyllic life of isolation in the remote glen was transformed almost overnight. The daunting, three miles of hazardous track was traversed many times by neighbouring crofters and acquaintances eager to offer help in any shape or form. There were others who risked the perils of the unknown purely for self-gratification, curiosity, or downright ghoulishness. For whatever reason, Isobel was besieged by a steady stream of visitors in the aftermath of John's death, including reporters from local and national press. In complete contrast to her wish for anonymity, she was thrust headlong into the spotlight through no wish, or fault, of her own. Isobel though, was safely cocooned inside her self-imposed bubble and completely detached from reality. It was as though she was watching from a safe distance as the drama unfolded in front of her eyes. Or to put it another way, she'd been chosen to play the lead role in a production of amateur dramatics. The role she'd been given was that of a grieving widow. As such, her first duty was to arrange the funeral of her dear, departed husband. Rising to the occasion like a true professional, an idea was already forming in her head. Her next task, this one perhaps needing a little more effort, was to consult her deceased husband's parents to ensure they were happy with her request to have his body interred in Scotland. It was only fair to ask - he was their son after all - but then, she argued with herself, she was his wife, and as such, should be allowed to have the final say. She was adamant that John's final resting place wouldn't be in London and was determined to remain unyielding in her decision.

Isobel played her role as the bereaved and bereft widow to perfection. She'd even been given permission from John's parents to proceed with his funeral arrangements as she saw fit. At this point in time however, she'd only revealed part of the plot.

With only one act remaining, the finale was now imminent. All that remained to be done was to arrange the service in the small church in Ardbuie - the one where, only a few short years ago, she and John were married - then, she would take the final curtsey, leave the stage, and return to obscurity.

Since the day of John's death, a police presence had been maintained at the croft and Isobel was accustomed to seeing the local police Land Rover pull up in the yard. Usually, it contained another search and rescue team and they headed into the hills without coming anywhere near the cottage. At other times they would spend hours checking the various barns and out-buildings for any signs of human habitation.

Since no-one had come to claim the dog, and the police hadn't told her otherwise, Isobel could only assume that the missing man hadn't been found. One day, Isobel heard the sound of a vehicle entering the yard, followed by a loud rap at the back door. Upon opening it, she was slightly concerned to be confronted by two police officers, one of whom asked if she could spare them a few moments of her time.

'We've come for two reasons,' he began as Isobel ushered them into the kitchen. 'As you'll no doubt be aware, the missing person hasn't been found, but at least some progress has been made in that regard.'

He went on to say that his car had been found with a note on the dashboard detailing his route.

'Apparently, his intention was to reach the summit of A' Beann Gheal. The other reason we're here is to inform you that your husband's body is soon to be released for burial.'

Isobel sat in silence for a brief moment as the words sank in.

'Released for burial?' she repeated.

Wide-eyed with bewilderment, she gazed from one to the other.

'As with all sudden and unexplained deaths, forensic tests are carried out to rule out foul play,' one explained.

'Foul play!' she exclaimed, her expression now one of utter

66

confusion.

At that very moment, the door burst open and Rob stormed into the kitchen.

'What's going on?' he bellowed, his eyes darting between Isobel and the police officers.

'It's a long story,' Isobel replied, bowing her head to hide her tears.

The police officers left, but not before promising to keep Isobel informed of any further developments.

'I sincerely hope you're going to tell me what's been going on here.'

Rob's tone was one Isobel had seldom heard before; the few previous occasions being when he demanded to be told the truth. He knew nothing about the episode with the sheep, Ben being attacked, or the fact that the perpetrator was in the byre. He knew nothing about the dog's owner being missing, or that there was an ongoing search for him. Neither did he know anything about her recent spell in hospital following a threatened miscarriage.

Isobel shook her head in despair. 'I don't know where to start,' she murmured.

'The best place would be at the beginning - when things started to go wrong,' he said softly while taking her hands in his.

Isobel gazed into his face. She was still coming to terms with the fact that Rob, Laird of Inverculden, her best friend, confidante and former fiancée, was her older brother. Yet, even if they'd not been siblings, she'd always felt closer to Rob than anyone else in the world – apart from John.

'Things have never gone right since the moment we came to stay at An Gleann Dubh,' she began in a solemn tone. 'The worst part of it all is that John and I had been arguing over trivialities just before his death. Until we moved here, we had never argued about anything.'

'Can you elaborate?' he asked softly.

'It was all because of a dog.'

'A dog?' he echoed.

'And Máiri.'

'A dog and Máiri,' Rob repeated the words slowly while

67

shaking his head in utter confusion.

'John was angry with me for leaving Máiri with Mairead so often, and the dog attacked and killed some sheep – as well as attacking Ben. I went looking for the dog with the intention of shooting it - but I couldn't bring myself to do it. She's in the byre.'

'Hold on a minute,' Rob began. 'Have I got this right? You've got a dog in the byre that attacked Ben and killed some sheep?'

His expression was a mixture of confusion and disbelief as he went on to say, 'If so, I don't regard that as a triviality – if that's what you and John had been arguing about.'

'There's more to it than that,' she went on. 'Apparently, the dog belongs to the missing man.'

'Missing man......?' he questioned.

'A man has vanished into thin air somewhere in the hills,' Isobel began. 'The police officers came here today to inform me he'd intended to climb A' Beinn Gheal. John and I had a short break in Dumlocher, so neither of us had been out on the hills for a few days – still haven't actually – given the circumstances.'

'Where's Kismet?' Rob asked abruptly.

'She's in the small meadow,' Isobel replied, mimicking his brusque tone. 'Why do you ask?'

'I'm going to tack her up and go as far as I can on horseback,' he muttered.

Isobel shook her head. 'You're wasting your time,' she began. 'The hills have been searched thoroughly by volunteers, not to mention, squads of police.'

'I'm not going out to look for the missing man. I'm going to check on my livestock.'

With that, Rob turned on his heel and left the cottage.

Isobel was left on her own, feeling even more disconsolate than she'd been before his arrival. She'd let her brother down. After all, she had assured him that she and John would be the ideal tenants for An Gleann Dubh. They would have been - if only circumstances had been different. Circumstances, which they'd been powerless to change, had worked against them since the day they'd moved to the remote croft in the Black

Glen.

Since Máiri was still fast asleep, Isobel went out to the byre to check on Dileas. Many questions were forming in her head as she walked the short distance from the cottage. Why hadn't she been told that John's body was being detained for forensic tests? To be fair, she argued, she had been hospitalised in the immediate aftermath of his death. Then another question popped into her head. Why would they have any reason to suspect foul play? Here, of all places, in the most isolated and peaceful place on earth, where nothing out of the ordinary ever happens........

It was at this moment she recalled the deaths of the occupants of the cottage many years ago. Then there was the strange vision she'd had of the charging highlanders. Not to mention, the unfortunate climbers she'd found close to death in a corrie on Beinn Ghlas - the ones who just happened to have been inside the graveyard – and later died from their injuries. And how could she ever forget the extraordinary vision she'd had of the cottage intact and its occupants alive and well - or the Will o' the Wisp?

'What is going on here in the glen?' she said aloud.

But this time, there were no answers. Nor was there anyone she could ask - not even Rob. Judging by the way he'd reacted today, it was as if he was blaming her for all their misfortune.

Isobel had now reached the byre door. Apart from the big dog she'd named Dileas, the large shed was empty. Torcall, who'd been blamed for killing her beloved husband, was still out on the hill, and Ben was becoming accustomed to being a house dog rather than a kennel dog. Now that he'd almost fully recovered, Isobel knew she would have to harden her heart and return him to his working sheepdog status – which meant him being relegated to the byre.

Isobel entered the byre and Dileas began to yelp with excitement. Her delight at seeing the person she regarded as her saviour was displayed by her frenetically wagging tail and jubilant body language. Recalling how Meg used to greet her in exactly the same way, she unclipped the leash, giving Dileas the freedom of the byre. It was the first time the dog had been out of her small pen since being brought inside. She'd now

69

fully recovered from the trauma of the bite wounds Ben had inflicted and was gaining weight. Watching her in motion, Isobel couldn't help thinking she was a stunning looking dog.

'I do hope I'm allowed to keep you,' she whispered as the big dog came to sit beside her. She knew however, that should her owner turn up safe and well, he would almost certainly want to reclaim her. After spending some time with the dog, Isobel returned to the cottage. Máiri was awake and she spent the next hour savouring her only link with John. She began to think about the developing foetus in her womb, their third child, taking account of the one she'd miscarried. I hope it's a boy, she said silently. John always longed for a son.

Just then, the kitchen door opened and Rob walked into the kitchen. For a fleeting moment, she'd expected it to be John. It was then that the grim reality finally sunk in. She would never see John again.

'Oh Rob,' she sobbed hysterically. 'I'm not sure if I can live here without John.'

Taking her in his arms, he whispered, 'Isobel, listen to me. You can, and you must. You were sent here for a reason.'

Rob's words prompted her to recall the time when John had told her she'd abandoned her dream of living at the croft and returned to the city - for a reason. Now, Rob was telling her there was a reason for her having returned to the Black Glen. Though what possible reason there could be for her heart having been broken in two, she couldn't begin to imagine. The sound of his voice brought her back from the brink of despondency.

'I'll fetch Daisy for the milking. You go and rustle up something to eat. I'm starving.'

As she and Rob sat down to eat their meal that evening, it was as though they'd taken a step back in time. It felt surreal - and yet so normal. Normal. Isobel pondered over that word. Her life thus far had been anything but normal. It wasn't normal to have been engaged to your brother. It wasn't normal to have married your former university lecturer. And it certainly wasn't normal to be widowed at twenty four years of age. A pregnant widow at that - and she still hadn't told Rob.

While toying with her food, Rob's voice interrupted her thoughts. 'You really should try to eat something you know.'
'I'm pregnant.'
For a brief moment, there was complete silence. Rob then rose from the table, forsaking his half-eaten meal, and came to sit beside her.
'Then all the more reason why you should eat something,' he said softly as they embraced.
Isobel melted into the familiar comfort of his arms. Apart from John, Rob was the only man she'd ever bonded with. Perhaps, she mused, it was because they were siblings and alike in so many ways.
'Why don't we pay Gordon and Mairead a visit?' he said suddenly, 'Perhaps it would help to talk to another female.'
'I would like that very much,' Isobel replied and wiped the tears from her face. 'I'll get Máiri ready.'

The initial, horrendous shock of John's death was followed by a period of acceptance as far as Isobel was concerned. She couldn't quite comprehend the fact that she was still functioning on a daily basis in the immediate aftermath. Was it because she'd suffered the loss of a loved one before, she wondered. Then again, it may just have been the survival instinct kicking in. Prior to John's death she'd been unable to imagine a life without him. Recalling a conversation she'd had with her father as a child, he'd said: "It's a tough world out there and I have been trying to prepare you for life's journey".
Her arrogant reply had been: "I am already well prepared father".
How naïve she'd been. Tough and resilient as she was, nothing could have prepared her for this.
Isobel went through the daily ritual of eating, resting and carrying out the necessary chores her pregnant body would allow. Eventually, John's remains were released for burial. The official verdict recorded the cause of death to be a head injury inflicted by a blunt object – most likely – a charging bull. Consequently, Isobel finalised the funeral arrangements and notified friends and family.

****

Chapter 14

Isobel lay wide awake in her bed on the eve of John's funeral, just as she had every night since his death. There was much on her mind as she tiptoed silently towards the window - but sleep wasn't one of them. The very first time she'd set eyes on them, and at all times since, the mountains had been her source of inspiration. Gazing upon their majestic, moon-lit peaks, she wondered if they would inspire her to decide where to go from here. After all, the ageless mountains had watched over the inhabitants of the glen since time immemorial. Unlike the frailties and mortality of humanity though, they'd been blessed with perpetuity. Tonight, as always, the mountains were deploying their inimitable magnetism, which in turn, was having a profound effect on Isobel. As her eyes flitted over each individual snow-capped peak, the realisation that she was now a free spirit began to sink in. At this precise moment, Isobel Caldwell ceased to exist and Isobel Ferguson was reborn. For the first time since John's death, her mind began to function in a rational manner. She was a widow, alone and solely responsible for her future. She could revert to her childhood state of indifference. She could survive - or wallow - in her isolation, and she could succeed - or fail - in her independence. Since John had gone forever from her life, she no longer needed, or wanted, anyone else. Since her childhood dream of living at An Gleann Dubh had come true and nothing, or no-one could take it from her, she could live right here in the glen for the rest of her life. Isobel made a silent vow that no-one would ever take John's place in her heart, and, come hell or high water, nothing, except death, would separate her from An Gleann Dubh. With these thoughts in her head, she returned to bed and lay awake until the dawn broke.

John's funeral service took place in the small village church in Ardbuie. Apart from their wedding day, it was one of the few occasions when the entire Ferguson family were gathered together. Isobel walked behind the coffin with Máiri in her arms as the procession made its way towards the altar. She

72

then took her place in the front pew beside John's parents and his two sisters. As the minister read the eulogy, they sobbed quietly into their lace-edged handkerchiefs. Isobel, on the other hand, sat in a state of silent and dignified composure. She was lost in a sea of nostalgia as her eyes scanned the congregation, before coming to rest on John's oak coffin. It seemed only a short time ago that the same people had gathered here for their wedding. Reminiscing about their all too brief time together, her heart felt as if it would break in two. She recalled the day they met, by pure chance, on the bus. The first time they made love.... how could she ever forget her first mind-blowing experience of intimacy? Then, her eyes moist with unrestrained tears, she recalled their wedding day, when they'd made their vows in front of the altar, exchanging looks of adoration as they promised to love each other until separated by death. The inevitable had come much too soon. Now, the mourners were filing out of the church and mumbling words of condolence as they passed by. Isobel though, remained detached and unreachable inside her self-imposed cocoon of indifference.

At his widow's insistence, John was to be interred in the old graveyard in the Black Glen. Initially, the suggestion that he be buried there had caused a few raised eyebrows, a few questions over protocol, and a few minor objections. All of which, had led to a major family dispute. Isobel though, had stood resolutely by her decision. As usual, she got her way. She'd told family and friends alike that, while they were welcome to attend the funeral, if they chose not to, then they wouldn't be made welcome at the croft in the future. The locals had been horrified that Isobel was prepared to defy "The Curse of The Black Glen" by laying her husband's body to rest in such a highly controversial spot. She though, refused to be intimidated by the locals, or the curse for that matter, and stood by her decision - with one condition - only a chosen few would be allowed inside the graveyard.

The funeral procession of Dr John Caldwell was one of the most unorthodox anyone in the locality had witnessed for many a long year. Since it was impossible for the hearse to negotiate the three miles of track that led from the farm to

73

the croft, his coffin had been unceremoniously transferred, amid the quagmire of mud in the farm steading, from the hearse to the Land Rover. The final part of the journey had been undertaken on foot - a distance of just over a mile. This had caused a fair amount of inconvenience to some of the more "well-heeled" mourners. Until that is, the majority of them had removed their best Sunday shoes and walked barefoot. Kismet had been hitched to a small carriage and with Fly, Ben and Floss running alongside, had taken John's coffin to his final resting place. It was ironic, but unavoidable, that it just happened to be close to the spot where he had drawn his final breath. Isobel was in no doubt that her funeral arrangements didn't meet with the approval of John's family, however, she no longer cared what anyone thought.

Despite being laid to rest amid the rugged and remote mountains of the Scottish Highlands, a large crowd had turned out to pay their last respects. Among the mourners were neighbouring crofters, former colleagues from John's time spent lecturing at the universities of London and Dumlocher and several of Rob's new-found affluent acquaintances. Isobel was surprised, and if she were to be honest, slightly annoyed, to see the young vet from the practice in Drumevie among the local contingent; after all, he hardly knew John. Nonetheless, she remained calm and composed as the minister conducted the moving ceremony at the graveside. Despite there not being a breath of wind in the glen that day, just as the coffin was being lowered into the ground, a gust of warm air caught Isobel full in the face. She likened it to someone having exhaled a long, lingering breath, yet it had been powerful enough to waft her hair. Isobel lifted her head and slowly cast her eyes around the mourners that were gathered outside the perimeter fence. They stood in silence, heads bowed and motionless, like a hotchpotch of human statues in the ethereal stillness of a bleak, midwinter's afternoon.

****

74

Chapter 15

The following week, Gordon and Calum arrived at the croft to bring Torcall in from the hill. On the day of the funeral, a few of the local crofters had been passing judgement and saying that, if in Isobel's position, they would have him slaughtered, but she wouldn't hear of it. Torcall was a young bull with an excellent pedigree and Isobel was astute enough to realise that, from a financial point of view and from the breeding perspective, replacing him would be out of the question. Helen, who'd been staying at the croft since the day of John's death, had now returned to help Ruaridh with the running of their farm. Rob had returned to Inverculden, and family members on both sides had long since departed for home. Isobel was determined that, from now on, or at least until she'd given birth, it would be just her and Màiri at the croft. The never ending stream of visitors and media since John's death had reinforced her conviction that she could quite happily live out the rest of her life in solitude.

Torcall had been brought into the byre without incident and he was now housed in his stall, where he would remain until springtime. Gordon had voiced his concerns over a cup of tea one day about their ability to bring him in from the hill without incident. To their surprise though, he had sauntered in as docile as a lamb.

'I just don't feel happy about you being here on your own in your condition,' he remarked as they were leaving. Mairead and I had a wee chat and we agreed that Calum should move in with you. Purely for practical reasons,' he added with a grin.

While acknowledging the fact that she would need help with the running of the croft and that Calum would be more than happy to provide that help, at this moment in time, the last thing she needed was complications in her personal life.

'I'll be fine,' she replied. 'I'm perfectly happy on my own. Besides, I'm going to take Ben back to his kennel in the byre and bring Dileas into the cottage.'

'You're taking a chance, are you not?' Gordon responded with a frown. 'From what I've heard, that dog's a savage brute. It could attack you, or even worse, little Máiri.'

'We'll be just fine,' Isobel replied. 'I would appreciate Calum's help from time to time, but not on a daily basis.'

Winter was fast approaching and Isobel knew that, if last year's horrendous conditions were anything to go by she would have to be better prepared this time around. Since the day they'd returned from Dumlocher, she hadn't had time to listen to the radio, or even read a newspaper. One day, after seeing the post van pull up in the yard, she went out to meet the postman.

'Isobel, what can I say?' he began. 'I just don't know where to begin......'

Although the postman had only been acquainted with John for a short period of time, he and Isobel had known one another for many years.

'Have you time for a cuppa?' she asked, forcing a feeble smile.

'For you, I'll make time,' he replied eagerly.

While Isobel made her way to the cottage, the postman went to the van and reappeared a few minutes later with a large bundle of envelopes in his hand.

'I don't suppose you have a spare newspaper,' Isobel remarked as he handed her the mail.

He shook his head and said, 'No, but you can have mine.'

Isobel sighed and handed him his tea, saying, 'I've completely lost touch with the events in the big bad world.'

Máiri was still fast asleep when the postman left to resume his country deliveries and, after opening her mail, Isobel half-heartedly flicked through the pages of the daily newspaper he'd left behind. She skimmed over the headings of the various news items, none of which made the slightest bit of difference to her life here at the croft, until she reached the centre pages. The face depicted in a small, grainy photograph made her blood run cold. It was a chilling blast from the past - a face she recognised from her childhood years - one that would stay in her memory 'til the day she died. It was the boy that had almost ruined her life - the one who'd ruined Mary's life. Now though, he wasn't a boy, but a man of twenty five years of age, and he was missing. Isobel read the article again. Apparently, he had been missing for several weeks

76

after going hill walking in the Scottish Highlands. His name was Robert Thornton - a doctor's son - her former neighbour and classmate. He was the father of the illegitimate child Mary had been forced to give up for adoption. The last time Isobel had set eyes on him Robert walked with callipers due to the effects of the polio virus. She hadn't spoken to him after the episode with her best friend and the family had moved away from the housing estate in Dumlocher soon after. If he is the missing person the police have been searching for at An Gleann Dubh........ then it means that....... Dileas is his dog.

'No. It can't possibly be,' she muttered to herself. 'That would be too much of a coincidence.' Isobel didn't believe in coincidence.

She began to sift through her mail, most of which were belated condolence cards, until she picked up a letter with a London postmark. Nothing could stop the flood of tears at that moment as she recalled the eve of her and Helen's joint wedding day. On that occasion they'd both been in a state of euphoria. Each of them was marrying the man of their dreams the following day and had sat in this very kitchen sifting through the large pile of congratulation cards and giggling like a couple of school-kids. That day, there had also been a letter with a London postmark amongst the cards. Since neither of them knew anyone from London, they'd been intrigued - until Helen read that it was from Claire, their long lost sister. Claire had written to inform them that their mother had contacted her with information about the forthcoming family event. Consequently, Claire had travelled north for the double wedding. Neither Isobel nor Helen had seen her since that day. Perhaps the letter was from her?

The letter wasn't from Claire however, and Isobel's curiosity changed to disbelief as she scanned the contents.

"Dear Isobel,
We sincerely hope that, in time, you will come to understand our reasons for having returned to London."

The letter was from John's parents and Isobel read on, the words washing over her and not making much sense.

"Since John's death, there is nothing left for us in Scotland, apart from you and our grandchild of course; therefore, it is with much sadness that we have come to this decision."

The letter went on to say that, since An Gleann Dubh was much too remote and distant for them to visit on a regular basis, coupled with the knowledge that Isobel had no desire to visit Dumlocher, there was little chance of them seeing much of their granddaughter anyhow. The upshot was that they planned to consult an estate agent with a view to putting John's house in Dumlocher on the market.

Isobel was extremely upset to read of their decision. She was very fond of John and Mildred and their returning to live in London meant that, not only would she possibly never see them again, but they would never get to know their second grandchild. There and then, she replied to the letter and expressed her sentiments. She was also saddened by the fact that John's house was to be sold. It held many fond memories - and yet - while having enjoyed the years spent in John's beautiful suburban home, never had she felt the sense of belonging there that she did at the croft. It was with a heavy heart that she signed her name at the bottom of the page. As she licked the gum and sealed the envelope, it was almost like reaching the end of a chapter of her life. While acknowledging the fact that she had chosen to isolate herself from friends and family by coming to stay in the wilderness of the Black Glen, she had no regrets. What was more, although anything but happy without John in her life, at this particular moment, she was experiencing something far more conducive to her well-being. It was also one that had eluded her for most of her life – acquiescence.

****

Chapter 16

Now, it was the week before Christmas. Isobel had always loved spending Christmas at the croft, but this year, as far as she was concerned, there would be no celebrations. No presents would be bought, no tinsel would be hung, and no Scots Pine would be felled and decorated with baubles. In fact, she couldn't wait for the festive season to pass, quietly and uneventfully. Then she would hang up the calendar that signified the start of a new year - a year that would bring about a new beginning, a new life, and hopefully, a new purpose for her existence. She was now almost three months pregnant and still hadn't paid a visit to the doctor to have it confirmed. As far as she was concerned, there was no need. She'd known she was with child, just as she had with Máiri, from the moment of conception.

Calum had now taken on the day to day running of the croft and Isobel was more than happy to give him a free reign to do so. Their friendship spanned many years and despite having once dated, their current relationship was based entirely on a business footing. Gordon and Mairead, as always, were regular visitors to the croft and Rob and Helen visited when time allowed.

Due in part to nostalgic memories of happier times spent here, Isobel spent much of Christmas Eve in a state of melancholic depression. She and Máiri were alone in the cottage, and, since she was fast asleep, Isobel decided to check on Dileas. The fact that she was leaving Máiri alone for a short time didn't warrant a second thought. After all, she was safely tucked up in her cot and the two dogs were asleep in front of the range. After lighting one of the paraffin lamps, Isobel made her way towards the kitchen door. The dogs were watchful, however, sensing they weren't being summoned, barely lifted their heads as she left the kitchen and closed the door behind her. Floss had been running around in the yard all day, and Fly, now having reached the ripe old age of fifteen, spent most of the time asleep. Heeding Gordon's words, Isobel hadn't brought Dileas into the cottage and she was still kennelled in the byre. Tonight though, with the temperature plummeting rapidly, she'd decided to bring the two dogs into the cottage for the night. Although Ben and Dileas were kennelled in the byre, they'd never met face to face since the unfortunate incident at the graveyard. That day, their confrontation had resulted in each of them receiving horrendous bite wounds; therefore, the greatest of caution would have to be exercised when re-introducing them. The last thing she wanted on Christmas Eve was to have cause to summon the unsociable vet from Drumevie.

First, she released Ben and brought him down from one end of the byre to the other, where Dileas was kennelled. The initial signs were looking good. There was no snarling and Ben's body language showed no signs of aggression. As for Dileas, she was lying flat on her belly in a submissive pose. After unclipping the leash from her collar, the pair began to sniff each other from nose to tail. Isobel could do nothing more than watch, and pray. With no sight or sound of animosity between the two dogs, she began to walk towards the door. Glancing behind, she saw that Ben had followed, and, not far behind him, was Dileas. As she slid the door along, Dileas squeezed though the opening and took off at great speed towards the hayshed. Ben, obeying her command, stayed close by her side. Isobel was faced with the choice of taking Ben back to his kennel in the byre, or into the cottage. It would have to be the cottage she decided, that way, she could check on Máiri before going in search of Dileas.

Nearing the cottage, Isobel could see that the back door was ajar. She was puzzled, not to mention, concerned; she distinctly remembered having pulled it shut. An ominous sense of foreboding hung in the air as she entered the gloom of the porch. Fearing what, or who, may be lurking behind the kitchen door, she hesitated before opening it. The dogs ran towards her in a state of frenzy and were swiftly shooed aside as Isobel ran to Máiri's bedroom. Thankfully, she was still blissfully asleep in her cot. On her return to the kitchen, Isobel looked into the pantry to find that it had been ransacked. Never, in all the years she'd spent at the croft, had she any reason to feel afraid. At this precise moment though, she was in the grip of sheer terror.

For the first time ever, Isobel locked the back door to the cottage before going in pursuit of Dileas. The night was calm, still and moonlit. A million stars studded an inky velvet sky, but there was neither sight not sound of Dileas anywhere. Isobel was aware that she could be anywhere. She may even have returned to the hills, in which case, there would be no hope of finding her until daylight. It was the first time the dog had been off the leash since being rescued and Isobel feared she may have gone in search of her master. Just then, the chilling sound of someone calling out in pain, made her stop in her tracks. It had come from the direction of the hayshed. Isobel ran back to the cottage and grabbed the shotgun, knowing full well she may be forced to use it this time. Nearing the hayshed, the sound of snarling made her blood run cold. She quickened her pace, wondering what, or who, was on the receiving end of Dileas' ferocity this time. After loading a cartridge into the barrel, she placed the shotgun against her shoulder and entered the gloomy shed.

'Oh my dear Lord,' she cried out.

Dileas, with blood-spattered jaws and muzzle was standing guard over her victim.

'Oh Dileas,' she gasped. 'What have you done?'

Dileas responded by wagging her tail jubilantly as Isobel knelt beside the motionless body. She felt for a pulse and, with a combination of anguish and relief, found one. Dileas' victim though, had lost a lot of blood and was in a state of severe shock.

'Stay there and guard him with your life,' she commanded, before racing back to the cottage.

'Come in. Are you receiving me?' she called into the transmitter.

'Receiving you Isobel,' Gordon responded in a bewildered tone. 'What's the problem?'

'Dial 999. I need police and ambulance here without delay. No time to explain.'

Gordon, Calum and Mairead duly arrived at the croft within fifteen minutes of Isobel's call. Mairead volunteered to stay in the cottage with Màiri while Isobel and the two men made

81

their way to the hayshed. Aided by the beams from the torch, they could see Dileas dutifully guarding the casualty. Neither she, nor the man, had moved an inch. It wasn't long before they heard the sound of another vehicle pulling up in the yard.

'We've brought the medics with us,' the policeman said as he emerged from the vehicle. 'The ambulance is waiting at the farm.'

'Follow me,' Isobel called as she began to make her way to the hayshed.'

'We'll need more light,' another voice called out.

'I'll bring the Land Rover closer,' someone responded.

With the beam of the headlights illuminating the shed, the doctor and his assistant began to assess the patient's injuries. Meanwhile, Dileas stood guard, watching their every move.

'Is this the perpetrator?' asked one, glancing at her warily.

'Yes,' Isobel replied curtly. 'But the man's an intruder and a thief. He's been inside the cottage and raided my pantry.'

'All the same, the dog's attacked and severely injured him,' he responded. 'It's a dangerous dog and I would be failing in my duty if I didn't take it to the dog pound.'

'I forbid you to take my dog,' Isobel retaliated. 'As a guard dog, she would have been failing in her duty if she hadn't acted the way she did.'

The policeman gave a wry smile. 'Given the circumstances, I'll allow her the benefit of the doubt. Nonetheless, if anything like this ever happens again, we'll have no option but to impound her.'

Isobel heaved a sigh of relief. Although the dog had only been at the croft a matter of weeks, she'd become very fond of her – and the feeling appeared to be mutual. On that fateful day in the glen, she had spared the dog's life, and Isobel had a gut feeling that tonight, the balance had been redressed.

With the injured man now on his way to hospital, Gordon and Calum accompanied Isobel back to the cottage. Dileas followed close to Isobel's heel.

'Is *she* allowed in?' Gordon muttered, scowling at the dog when they reached the back door.

'Too right she's allowed in,' Isobel said emphatically. 'If it hadn't been for her, who knows what might have happened tonight.'

This had been a Christmas Eve like no other as far as Isobel was concerned. However, with Gordon, Calum and Mairead steadfastly refusing to leave her on her own, it meant that she wouldn't be spending it alone. While lying in bed, she began to relive the horrific events of the evening. It was then that the impact of her vulnerability hit home. She was three months pregnant and now solely responsible for the welfare of their young daughter. Her bank balance had hit rock bottom, and she had no transport. The tractors, her only means of accessing the track to civilisation, were of no use at present.

****

Chapter 17

Isobel was wide awake when dawn broke on Christmas Day - to be truthful - she'd been awake most of the night. As on many previous occasions, she rose from her bed and tiptoed across the floor towards the window. Perhaps the panoramic scene will help rationalise, and maybe even stabilise, my turbulent mind, she mused. A dusting of snow had fallen overnight and the sight that met her eyes momentarily gladdened her heavy heart; it did nothing though to relieve the feeling of utter desolation, isolation and futility at facing the rest of her life without John. Gazing moist-eyed through the tiny window pane, she caught sight of the shadowy outline of a hooded figure trudging through the snow. Her heart began to race. It was comforting to know that Gordon, Mairead and Calum were in the cottage. Had she been alone, goodness only knows how she would have felt. After dressing silently, she closed the bedroom door behind her. The dogs had been left in the kitchen overnight and they rose in unison to meet her as she entered.

'Ben, Floss, Dileas, come,' she urged softly while exiting the kitchen. Knowing they would have to move quickly to have any chance of catching up with the mysterious trespasser, she whispered, 'Fly stay,' as the old dog struggled to his feet. Conflicting thoughts ran through her head as she and the dogs made their way through the snow. Perhaps he is an accomplice of the man Dileas had apprehended last night. On the other hand, he could be just a rambler who has lost his way. The figure was now within sight and just a few yards ahead of them.

'Come by,' she called to Floss and Ben.

The two dogs ran ahead immediately, and, much to her surprise, Dileas followed in hot pursuit. Being much larger, and more powerful than either of the two collies, Dileas reached the figure ahead of them. Isobel could only watch with a combination of helplessness and concern as Dileas pounced from behind and took her quarry down. Isobel moved as fast as the conditions would allow, until she got within a few feet of the huddle of dogs that surrounded the prostrate figure on the ground.

Then she heard a gruff voice muttering the words, 'It's only me for goodness sake. Let me up.'

Isobel's feeling of relief was overwhelming. Not only because it was Calum who was struggling to his feet, but also because Dileas was wagging her tail and had made no attempt to attack him.

'Oh Calum,' she groaned, 'I'm so sorry. Are you all right?'

'I thought I'd be doing you a favour by bringing Daisy in for the milking,' he replied angrily.

On seeing that he was none the worse for his unfortunate incident, Isobel couldn't stop herself from smiling. Calum however, failed to see the joke and was glaring at her as if she was bordering on insanity.

'I'm sorry. I know it's not funny, but I'm just so relieved you're not a burglar,' she muttered in a feeble act of contrition.

'Since it's Christmas Day, I'll let you off,' he responded with a wry smile, before adding, 'I'll get Daisy.'

Under normal circumstances, Daisy would have been brought inside long ago, but with the weather being mild and the fact that Isobel had other things on her mind, she'd been left out in the meadow for the time being. Now though, with the first signs of winter being upon them, she would have to be brought into the byre until springtime.

Isobel began to make her way back to the croft with the three dogs running by her side. The winter sun was peeking its head over the horizon and reflecting off the pristine white, snow-covered landscape. As always, the beauty and wonder of nature in the raw made her heart skip a beat. The downside was that it also reminded her of happier times spent at the croft and tears of self-pity began to spill down her cheeks. Just then, she heard a familiar voice say, 'Isobel, are you all right?'

Due to the covering of soft snow on the ground, she hadn't heard Calum, or Daisy, approaching.

'I'll be fine,' she sobbed, wiping the tears from her cheeks. 'I'm just so lonely and miserable without John.'

'I'm going to move in with you, at least until springtime,'

Calum began in a solemn tone. 'And don't even think about arguing with me.'

Isobel had to admit to being comforted by the knowledge that Calum was moving in with her at the croft - albeit on a temporary - and purely practical, basis.

Christmas Day was a day Isobel had been dreading since John's death. Having no wish to celebrate, her plan was to spend it in solitude. Like so many times before though, the day didn't go according to plan. It began with Mairead insisting that she and Gordon spend Christmas day at the croft. Later that morning, completely out of the blue, Rob strolled into the kitchen and announced that he had a surprise for her. This puzzled her slightly since he wasn't carrying any gift-wrapped presents.

'It's outside,' he remarked casually upon seeing her bemused expression.

'Outside,' she repeated, her frown deepening.

Rob took her by the hand, saying, 'come with me.'

Isobel cast a glance of total bewilderment at the others, before being led from the kitchen.

Before opening the back door, Rob told her to close her eyes. She did as asked and he led her into the yard, saying, 'You can open them now.'

'Oh Rob,' were the only words she could utter before dissolving into a flood of tears.

'Merry Christmas Bella,' he said softly. 'I know it's going to be a difficult day for you, but perhaps this will make your life a little easier from now on.'

Isobel could only stare with a mixture of wonder and disbelief at the mud-spattered, but otherwise pristine brand new Land Rover parked in the yard.

'Would you like to take her for a trial run?' he asked.

'I would love to, but I can't abandon Máiri, or my guests.' Isobel replied ruefully.

'I'm quite sure they'll survive without you for half an hour,' he laughed.

In response to Rob's request, Gordon and Mairead insisted that they would be more than happy to babysit Máiri while

Isobel took her "new toy" for a spin. As for Calum, he'd already left with the dogs to check the livestock on the hills.
Isobel's solemn expression had now been replaced with the merest hint of a smile.
'In that case, I would love to go for a drive,' she replied.

Heading south and with no particular destination in mind, Isobel recalled the day she and John had travelled to Dumlocher shortly before his death. Rob, who had been sitting in silence until now, asked in a cynical tone, 'Are you planning to drive far?'
'Oh Rob,' Isobel replied despondently, 'If not for Màiri, I probably wouldn't stop driving until I ran out of fuel.'
'Pull over,' he said.
Rob's words were spoken in such a way that she wouldn't dare ignore them. After taking her foot off the accelerator, Isobel drove the Land Rover onto the grass verge and switched off the engine.
Rob turned in his seat to face her and took her hand in his saying, 'It's time we had a heart to heart. I realise now that I was being incredibly selfish when I said you should remain at An Gleann Dubh. I can see now that it's not in your best interests and I retract my earlier words of advice.'
Isobel sat in silence for a few moments. She was deep in thought, mulling over her brother's words, before saying in a clear and resolute tone, 'For most of my life, my dream was to live at An Gleann Dubh. It was you who made that dream come true and it was you who told me I had been sent there for a reason. I have to go back.'
Rob looked uneasy, his face etched with remorse as he spoke. 'I know, and I can only apologise for that. Please forget I ever said it. I'm also sorry for burdening you with the impossible task of running the croft single-handedly. Given the present set of circumstances, it would be best if I advertise for new tenants for An Gleann Dubh and you and Màiri come and stay with me at Inverculden.'
Isobel gazed intently into her brother's face before replying in a calm and assertive tone, 'I'm going home, and there I will remain until the day I die.'

Rob remained silent. He knew his young sister well enough to realise that arguing with her at this moment would be futile. Besides, Isobel had already started the engine and turned the vehicle around.

The return journey was spent in virtual silence. Rob spoke only once to say, 'I'm so proud to have you as my sister. As a child, I always knew you were extra special, but as a woman, you are extraordinary.'

Isobel smiled. She continued to drive in silence, her eyes firmly focused on the road ahead, yet deep in thought. As they approached the yard, Isobel could see another vehicle parked beside Gordon's Land Rover. It was one she didn't recognise. As she and Rob entered the cottage, the sound of lively banter could be heard coming from the kitchen. On opening the kitchen door however, the chatter faded away to a deathly hush. Isobel stood for a brief moment in a state of bemused silence, before saying, 'Claire, what a lovely surprise.'

'Merry Christmas Isobel,' she replied as they embraced. 'I can't begin to explain the reason, but I was overcome by a need to be with you today.'

'How long can you stay?' Isobel asked tentatively.

'How long can you put up with me?' Claire responded with a wry smile.

The unexpected visit from Claire had left Isobel in a state of shock, but as her eyes flitted around the room, she was in a state of further bemusement. During her and Rob's short absence, Mairead had prepared a Christmas banquet and the table was set for lunch. She had now taken on the role of "mine host" and was ushering everyone to take their seats at the table.

'Mairead.......' Isobel began in a tone of mock chastisement.

'Sit down,' came the stern reply.

Mairead's tone was one Isobel had seldom heard before and it momentarily took the wind from her sails. She was being downright domineering and Isobel didn't take kindly to being told what to do, especially in her own home. With Mairead though, she made an exception. For the duration of the meal, Isobel was treated as the guest and allowed to do nothing but

88

sit at the table and be waited on.

Later that afternoon, Mairead, Gordon and Calum announced that they were going home. They left in a happier frame of mind knowing that Isobel had family for company, not to mention, her very own transport for the first time.

That evening, three of the Ferguson siblings were together in the cottage at An Gleann Dubh. If only Helen was here, the four Ferguson siblings would be reunited at the croft, Isobel thought to herself. It was as though she'd rubbed the magic lamp and the Genie had appeared and granted her wish, because at that very moment, the door opened and Helen walked into the kitchen.

'Oh my dear Lord,' she exclaimed. 'My eyes must be deceiving me.' She crossed the room and threw her arms around Claire's neck, saying, 'What a lovely surprise. How long are you planning to stay?'

'How long is a piece of string?' Claire replied casually, 'I am in no hurry to return to London.'

'I'll put the kettle on,' Isobel remarked, casting a sidelong glance at Helen as she stood up.

Over an hour, and several cups of coffee later, Claire had completed her account of the real reason for having made the long trip north from London.

The second youngest of the Ferguson siblings, Claire had been estranged from her two sisters for many years. This was partly due to the fact that she'd chosen to remain in London and couldn't be traced. She and Isobel had met only once before, at her wedding to John four years earlier. As for Helen, until her wedding day, she hadn't seen Claire since they'd been separated at the onset of war in 1939. Claire was a child of three years old at the time, therefore, they knew very little about her. Claire went on to rectify this by giving her siblings a brief account of her life history to date.

Similar to Helen, she'd been evacuated during the war. Unlike Helen though, she had kept in touch with her parents throughout the war years. She'd been sent to stay with a family in rural Somerset, and, when the war was over, had moved with them to a house in Hertfordshire. It was at this time her parents had decided to return to Scotland. Claire was only three years old when she left Scotland and had little or no memory of her time there, or of her older sister Helen. She was happily settled with her foster family and they, in turn, were more than happy to unofficially adopt her. Later in life she had moved to London and attained secretarial qualifications at college. After spending a few years in a menial office job she had been offered a promotion - that of personal assistant to the company director. She went on to say that the relationship between them had begun on a professional level and had remained so for many years. He was a married man with two young children, and her only ambition in life was to further her career. The nature of the business necessitated them travelling abroad on business trips, but even on those occasions, the relationship had remained purely platonic. On returning from one of their trips however, Martin, her boss, had been informed by a reliable source that each time he was out of the country, his wife had been seen socialising with a variety of men. Utterly distraught and devastated, Martin had confronted her, with the result, she and their two children had moved out of their suburban home. During the following few years, the relationship between Claire and her boss blossomed, until eventually, it developed into one of intimacy. Ultimately, she had fallen head over heels in love with him. He, on the other hand, had been merely using her as a convenience. Nevertheless, he'd allowed her to stay rent free in a luxurious, suburban flat, showered her with gifts, and given her the use of a company car. She had accompanied him to many social events and revelled in the affluent lifestyle to which she was becoming accustomed. Assuming that marriage would follow just as soon as his divorce was finalised, her world had been turned upside down just a few weeks ago. Martin had announced, in a cold, callous and formal manner, that their relationship, in its present form, could no longer continue. Apparently, his wife had made contact and implored him to give their marriage a second chance.

"It's only for the sake of the children," Claire mimicked.

Thumping her fist on the table, she added irately, 'Men! Who needs them?'

Claire had said the words without thinking, and, seeing the tears welling up in Isobel's eyes, added hastily, 'Oh Isobel, I'm so sorry. I should have chosen my words more carefully.'

'Don't worry about it,' Isobel sighed. 'We can drown our sorrows together.'

****

Chapter 18

Christmas Day 1966 turned out to be nothing like the one Isobel had faced with dread and despair. Instead of spending the day alone, she'd been surrounded by her dearest friends and family. Claire's unexpected arrival was something she couldn't have foreseen in her wildest dreams. Following Helen's departure, the threesome left the croft in the new Land Rover to take Rob back to Inverculden. Upon first setting eyes on his stately pile, Claire's expression was one Isobel wished she'd caught on camera. Her older sister had been equally impressed, and slightly overawed, when taken on a guided tour of the mansion house and grounds. Returning to the lounge to find that Isla, the maid, had brought a tray of tea and cakes, she'd flopped into one of the large armchairs and exclaimed, 'I can see myself adapting to country life very quickly. Come to think of it, I really have no need to return to London – ever.'

It was at this moment Isobel realised Claire wouldn't stay more than a few days at An Gleann Dubh. Before leaving, Rob suggested that they join him for the Hogmanay celebrations at Inverculden. Glancing in Isobel's direction, he added, 'It's a family tradition as you already know.' He then turned to Claire and said, 'It would also give you a chance to meet some of the locals.'

Isobel frowned. The "locals" Rob hung out with these days were not the crofters he'd known in the past from the local agricultural shows and ceilidhs. He now mingled with the tweeds and brogues, shooting and fishing fraternity - in other words - the aristocracy. Instead of entering his rams into the local shows, he now travelled the length and breadth of the country to watch his racehorses compete. In place of the rowdy, foot-stomping ceilidhs, he now attended rather more sedate, society balls. Already, Isobel could see that Claire, having inherited the trait from their mother, had aspirations of grandeur. It was obvious she would fit perfectly into Rob's inherited lifestyle. Although Rob, and Helen likewise, had been accustomed to a much higher standard of living than Isobel, he was her brother, and, whether Laird of

Inverculden, or crofter at An Gleann Dubh, he was, and would remain forever, her dearest friend. Nonetheless, she had absolutely no intention of joining him and his snooty friends at the Inverculden Hogmanay Ball.

Her pensive state was rudely interrupted by Claire's excited outburst: 'Despite having reached the ripe old age of thirty years, I've never been to a traditional Scottish Hogmanay celebration. Wild horses couldn't keep me away.'

'That's settled then.' Rob remarked with a grin of approval. 'I'll arrange for your rooms to be made up for your arrival later in the week.'

The sky was black as pitch when the Land Rover came to a stop in the yard at An Glean Dubh and Isobel couldn't see Claire's face; nonetheless, she could sense her air of despondency. Threatening, black storm clouds obscured the moon and an ominous shudder ran up and down her spine as she made her way slowly and gingerly towards the cottage. As a child growing up in the city, Isobel had been petrified of the dark, and yet, since her very first visit to the croft, she had never, at any time, felt afraid here. She hadn't even been intimidated by the dark, shadowy silhouettes of the mountains. Nor had she given a second thought to what, or who, might be lurking within the barns and outbuildings. The deathly silence, once a source of comfort, only intensified the sense of foreboding that enveloped the croft at this moment. As her fingers fumbled along the window ledge in search of the torch, she couldn't help thinking that, since their last visit to the city, something had changed at An Gleann Dhubh, and the voice in her head was telling her that it wasn't for the better.

The following few days passed without incident and Isobel was pleasantly surprised by Claire's eagerness to help out with the daily chores at the croft. In a short space of time she'd become adept at milking Daisy and, petite as she was, insisted on lugging bales of straw and hay from the shed to the byre. Isobel was impressed. Although virtual strangers, she had an optimistic feeling that a bond was in the process of being forged between them. Isobel had also introduced Claire to the working collies, as well as to Dileas and Kismet.

Despite having been raised in an urban environment, Claire appeared to have been blessed with the Ferguson sibling trait, a natural empathy with animals, and couldn't wait to be taught to ride. Isobel, recalling her own initiation to horse-riding, only just managed to stop herself from saying, "Just throw your leg over the saddle and hang on for dear life".

Tossing and turning in bed one night, Isobel's mind, as always, was in overdrive. How bizarre, she mused, that Claire has turned up in my life just when I need her most. One of her father's old quotes also came to mind: "When one door closes, another opens".

The eve of Hogmanay duly arrived and, with a few reservations, Isobel packed some overnight things into a suitcase for her and Màiri. Celebrating and conviviality were the last things on her mind at this moment; however, for the sake of her beloved brother - and Claire - whose presence at the croft had been a godsend, she was prepared to make the effort. After all, it would only be for one night and Calum had promised to hold the fort until their return.

The hour-long drive to Inverculden was now familiar to Isobel and, while negotiating the narrow, tree-lined drive she was surprised to feel an odd sense of home-coming. Her flagging spirits were further boosted by the sight of the brightly lit mansion house as they drew up at the front door. Before they'd even had time to emerge from the Land Rover, Henry the butler had appeared and was offloading the luggage.

'I'm going to enjoy every last minute of this vacation,' Claire gabbled excitedly while following Isobel up the marble steps to the front door.

'Vacation,' Isobel exclaimed. 'It's an overnight stay, and you'd better make the most of it, because tomorrow, it's back to work for you and me.'

Rob met them in the entrance hall and welcomed them both with a brotherly hug, before saying, 'Helen and Ruaridh are coming to the ball this evening, which means that the four Ferguson siblings will be united for the second time in the space of a week.'

'Wouldn't it be wonderful if we could all meet up on a regular basis,' Isobel remarked without thinking.

As they made their way towards the drawing room, Claire, who had heard her, quipped, 'I don't see any reason why you can't. After all, the three of you live within an hour's drive of each other.'

'But you live in London,' Rob chipped in.

'*Lived* in London,' Claire responded, emphasising the first word. 'I intend to return only to collect my belongings before moving here on a permanent basis.'

'Here?' Rob gasped.

'Well, it's, not as if you don't have a spare room,' she responded with a beguiling smile. 'At the moment, I'm homeless, and I am your little sister after all.'

'You Ferguson girls have one thing in common,' Rob muttered as he decanted three glasses of sherry. 'An irresistible, and, I must add, extremely persuasive, smile. However, if you do come to live here, you'll have to work for your keep.'

'Oh Rob,' Claire cooed, draping her arms around his neck, 'I'm so lucky to have found you. I'll do anything you ask if you'll allow me to stay here.'

Rob and Isobel exchanged glances. For her part, Isobel had always known that Claire wouldn't survive the hardships and isolation at the croft for long. As for Rob, he could hardly believe his luck. Claire's timely arrival meant that he had someone with secretarial skills to help him sort out the mountain of paperwork that had amassed since inheriting the estate. Besides, he was looking forward to becoming acquainted with the third female Ferguson sibling.

Isla had been delegated to act as nanny during the Hogmanay party, which meant that, for the first time since John's death, Isobel was relieved of her mothering duties. It was with mixed emotions and a half-hearted attitude that she got ready for the celebrations that evening; memories of her two previous visits to Inverculden being at the forefront of her mind. On her first visit, she'd become engaged to Rob – long before finding out that they were siblings - and the second visit was for the funeral of Laird and Lady Inverculden. While closing the bedroom door behind her, Isobel said to herself: This time, I pray it will be uneventful, and tomorrow, I'll

95

return to the croft and resume my dull and boring life.

Isobel felt vulnerable, nervous and very much alone as she negotiated the long, winding staircase that led to the ballroom. Just then, something stirred inside her belly. Butterflies - she thought to herself. Then a fleeting smile played on her lips. The stirring within wasn't psychosomatic, but physical. It was the first sign of movement from her unborn child, and its timing was perfect. Placing her hand lovingly on her diminutive baby bump, she whispered, 'Thank you John.'

Although John, in person, was no longer with her, it was comforting to know that his progeny was slowly and surely developing within her womb. For six years, John had been her soul mate, and as far as Isobel was concerned, he would stay in her heart forever as the love of her life. With that thought in her head, and all the poise she could muster, she made her way towards the stirring sound of music.

'Good Evening,' a voice called out.

Turning her head sharply, she saw the young vet from Drumevie walking towards her.

With his arm extended, he went on to say, 'May I offer my condolences on the tragic death of your husband?'

Isobel, having been caught off guard, took the outstretched hand in hers and uttered a feeble, 'Thank you.'

Although their previous meetings had been fraught with hostility, Isobel's "old school" upbringing was preventing her from being anything but courteous – or was it – frostily polite?

'Although we've met previously on a few occasions, due to the unfortunate nature of them, we haven't been formally introduced,' he continued. 'My name is Tormod Seumas MacAlister.'

Isobel recalled their previous meetings. The first was when Ben was at death's door. The second was when he turned up at the croft unexpectedly to inspect Dileas' wounds, and the third was the day of John's funeral. On each occasion she'd been fraught with anxiety and his offhand manner had done nothing to endear him to her, in fact, it had only added to her angst. Other than that, she really had no justifiable reason to

96

feel animosity towards the young man. Perhaps I should give him the benefit of the doubt and reciprocate his effort to make amends, she mused.

Responding drily, she remarked, 'A good Gaelic name,' before adding with the merest hint of a smile, 'The old bull at the croft was called Seumas.'

His face lit up with delight and Isobel noticed that it reached his eyes this time as he asked, 'Do you have the Gaelic?'

'Tha, tha agam,' she replied curtly, before adding: 'S'mise Isobel Ferguson Caldwell.

Isobel couldn't understand the reason for having included her maiden name alongside her married surname. Perhaps, she mused, it was that she felt the need to resort to her pre-marital status. Prior to meeting John, she'd been completely independent and wholly self-reliant. It was imperative that she regain some of those inherent virtues – her very survival depended upon it. Without another word, she brushed past Tormod Seumas MacAlister, leaving him slightly bemused and extremely humiliated. Isobel's offhand manner had taken the wind from his sails and he realised that, had she not beat a hasty retreat, he would have struggled to continue the conversation. His brief encounter with Isobel Ferguson Caldwell had nonetheless, left him deep in thought. Although recently widowed, and obviously still in mourning, she radiated an air of self-assurance that he couldn't help but admire. What was more, her presence had penetrated deep within his soul. During their all too brief exchange of words he'd felt her hostile detachment strike at his heart like a dirk. And yet, from somewhere deep within that aloof exterior, there radiated a warmth and sensuality that gladdened his wounded heart. What prevailed amid her air of aloofness, apathy, and self-assurance though, and which he'd found most disconcerting, was her vulnerability. Tormod watched with conflicting emotions as Isobel Ferguson Caldwell flounced towards the ballroom - admiration, empathy, curiosity - but certainly not indifference. Since his arrival at the practice in Drumevie, he'd come to enjoy staying in this part of Scotland, and, for the first time since leaving his native West Coast Island felt a sense of belonging. Not only

97

had he been made to feel welcome by the local crofters - the recently bereaved female crofter from An Gleann Dubh being the exception - but he'd been the focus of attention among the young ladies in the locality. On the few occasions when he'd popped into the local pub for a beer after work, he was never without a group of young girls by his side. Since there was a dearth of eligible, wealthy bachelors in Drumevie, he was aware that they viewed him as a potential catch. Nonetheless, the well-meaning compliments from female admirers served to boost his male ego, and since Gaelic was spoken in these parts, no-one glared at him as if he was an alien in their midst when, on occasions, he spoke in his native tongue. All things considered, he'd settled well into the locality, and, second to his beloved island, now regarded Drumevie as home.

Isobel meanwhile, having spotted Rob, was making her way, rather hastily, towards him. Having witnessed the brief confrontation with the young vet, he mumbled the words in an apologetic manner as they embraced: 'I hope you're not angry with me for inviting the young vet from Drumevie. He's still quite new to the area and I thought it would be the ideal chance for him to get acquainted with the local gentry.'

'It's your party,' Isobel replied sharply. 'I have no right to vet your guests.'

Rob smiled at the fortuitous pun, before saying, 'I'm aware you don't have a very high opinion of him, but he is an excellent vet. On the occasions I've required his services, I have found him to be utterly dedicated and highly proficient.'

'Be that as it may,' she replied in an offhand manner. 'I have no issue with him as far as his professional credentials are concerned. However, on a personal level, I neither have any wish, nor any need, to regard him as an acquaintance.'

Just then, Claire appeared on the landing at the top of the staircase. As she and Rob turned to view the impressive sight, Isobel stifled a gasp of admiration. There was only one word to describe the manner of her descent, and that was, theatrical. Claire gracefully sashayed from step to step, glancing first left, then right with a degree of arrogance, as if eager to be noticed by the arriving guests. Claire would have given any of the current top models a run for their money. Despite making her feel like a fish out of water, Isobel was forced to admit that her older sister was elegance personified. Her shimmering, silver ball gown clung to her slender frame like a second skin. Isobel was conscious of the extra pounds that had gathered on her hips during pregnancy - and which she hadn't succeeded in losing. Not much hope of that now, she thought dejectedly. Over the past few weeks she'd noticed her former hour-glass figure becoming increasingly rotund. As for her hair, it hung straight and limp around her shoulders. Since John's death, she hadn't taken any interest in her appearance. She never wore make-up these days and it had made no difference to the devotion she'd received from her animal friends. Compared to her older sister, she felt plain, fat and frumpy - come to think of it - the way their mother once looked.

'Oh how I wish I hadn't come,' she muttered under her breath.

In complete contrast, Claire was in her element. She was obviously relishing the thought of mingling with the local aristocracy during the course of the evening. Isobel, on the other hand, would much rather have been sitting beside the log fire at the croft with the dogs by her side.

'Wow,' Rob exclaimed as he ogled Claire with unabashed admiration 'She's a dead cert for The Belle of the Ball award.'

Tormod MacAlister reached the foot of the staircase just as Claire completed her descent and the pair engaged in a brief conversation, before making their way towards them.

'You look absolutely stunning,' Isobel remarked while embracing her sister.

Rob meanwhile, was staring wide-eyed at the vision of beauty in their midst.

'I can see your presence at Inverculden being a beneficial acquisition in more ways than one,' he began. 'Not only will your secretarial skills be an invaluable asset, but you exude a charismatic quality that is even more valuable. I hereby ask that you accept the role of my late mother, Lady Inverculden, as Lady of the Manor and authorised representative of Inverculden Estates.'

Isobel's eyes filled with tears. Among her many vices, jealousy had never, as yet, reared its ugly head. At this particular moment though, she was experiencing more than a twinge of the "green-eyed monster". While having no wish to live at Inverculden and assume the role of "Lady of the Manor", it was as though she'd just been demoted to second place in Rob's list of favourite people. How could he do this to me, she fumed under her breath. Her self-esteem had never been this low since childhood. Not only that, but she was becoming increasingly agitated by Tormod MacAlister's presence. Above all though, her anger and irritation was directed at Claire and Rob. It was Rob who had helped to build her confidence as a child, and it was Rob who was now playing his part in undermining it. As for Claire, the estranged sister with whom none of them had been familiar until recently, she had waltzed into her life, invaded her space, and was about to stick her snooty nose into what she regarded to be, her domain. Despite being shocked by her feeling of hostility towards her sister, a voice in her head was screaming out: How dare she.

Apart from her lonely childhood years, Isobel had never been a wallflower at any social event. Normally the life and soul of the party, not to mention, never being off the dance floor, tonight was the exception. Despite being asked to dance several times, she firmly declined each offer and spent most of the evening alone. She had no reason to celebrate; besides, she had her unborn child to consider. Claire was, as Rob had predicted, Belle of the Ball and Isobel had observed that she and Tormod MacAlister had danced with each other more than once throughout the evening - not that it bothered her of course. Eventually, filling her with immense relief, the last waltz was announced and she could hardly wait to make a swift and discreet exit. Her plan, as usual, didn't materialise, because at that very moment, Rob took her by the hand, saying, 'I forbid you to sit out the last waltz on your own,' and gently pulled her to her feet.

Isobel forced a smile as he led her onto the dance floor, before moving slowly round the ballroom in his arms.

'It's a funny old world,' he sighed. 'Who would have thought when we became betrothed on New Year's Eve a few short years ago, that we would be in the situation we now find ourselves.'

'It's probably just as well we don't have a crystal ball,' she replied solemnly.

Just then, Isobel became vaguely aware of someone talking to Rob, before he excused himself and his place was taken by Tormod MacAlister.

'My apologies for the intrusion,' he said softly, 'but I know full well that, had I asked, you would have declined my request to dance.'

Despite every muscle in her body tensing up as Tormod took her in his arms, Isobel was aghast to find a degree of comfort from the proximity of his body. He was holding her at arm's length, their bodies apart, he wasn't encroaching on her personal space, and yet, there was a connection between them that she was at a loss to understand. The dance ended before either of them had the chance to say another word.

'Thank you,' he said politely, before escorting her off the dance floor.

The dancers were now forming a circle for the traditional "Auld Lang Syne ", when Tormod asked if she would like to join them.

'No thank you,' she replied curtly.

'In that case, I'll sit it out with you,' he responded with a smile, 'It'll probably end up in a stampede.'

'That's the last thing I need in my pregnant state,' Isobel remarked solemnly.

She'd said the words without thinking, but the corners of her mouth lifted in the faintest of smiles at the sight of Tormod's dumfounded expression.

'You have an endearing smile,' he said after a short pause, 'You should do it more often.'

Immediately realising his inappropriate choice of words, he apologised profusely.

'I'm so sorry Isobel. Each time we meet, I seem to open my mouth and put my foot in it.'

Isobel was aware that his attempt to make amends was genuine and couldn't resist smiling at the expression of

101

childish guilt on his face.

'We can't change the way we are,' she responded softly.

Rob, Claire and Helen had now joined them at the table, and Helen, having noticed the faint smile on Isobel's face, asked if she had enjoyed the evening.

'There would be no point in lying,' she replied solemnly. 'I have never felt so miserable in my entire life. I'm also heartbroken, frightened, and confused.'

Helen placed her arms lovingly around her young sister's shoulders and held her close. Isobel began to sob uncontrollably. As with every Hogmanay, it had been an emotional roller coaster of an evening. This one however, would go down as her worst ever.

Tormod MacAlister discreetly walked away, leaving the siblings comforting one another. Although the occasion should have been one of celebration, he couldn't quite understand his morose frame of mind at this moment. Perhaps, he mused, I've been influenced by the heartache I've just witnessed. He too, had suffered personal loss in his lifetime and could empathise with Isobel's grief and anguish. He was an outsider though and had no right to intervene; yet it didn't stop him wishing he could.

The following day, Isobel and Máiri returned to the croft. Claire, having decided to stay for the Ne'er Day shoot and the obligatory after party, wasn't with them. Her plan was to collect her meagre belongings from the croft the following day before returning to Inverculden to take up permanent residence. At some point in the near future, she would make the long trip south to London to finalise her affairs and collect the rest of her belongings.

Despite being where her beloved husband had lost his life, and no longer deluded by its beguiling magnetism, Isobel experienced the same sense of joy she did as a child on approaching the gate that led to An Gleann Dubh. The croft was in darkness as she pulled up in the yard in the early evening of New Year's Day 1967. Calum, who had foregone the Hogmanay celebrations to man the croft, was attending a

New Year's Day party at a croft nearby and wouldn't be returning until the following day – hangover permitting.

Máiri, having fallen asleep during the long journey, was still in the Land Rover as Isobel made her way to the cottage. The previous feeling of elation at her homecoming was suddenly replaced by one of despondency as she opened the back door. Inside, it was cold, dark and deathly silent. Isobel felt sick, both physically and emotionally as she fumbled in her jacket pocket for matches to light the paraffin lamps. Having established a dim and flickering degree of visibility, she looked forlornly at the black grate. While attempting to rekindle the flames from the residue of warm ash, she was thinking that the fire had long since died. Unlike the fire in her heart, it would come again though. The dying embers ignited and flickered before flaring up in her face as she stoked it with dry wood. Soon, its warm glow radiated round the room, affording a small degree of comfort.

That evening, as she sat by the ingle nook with only the dogs for company, Isobel was deep in thought. It was the first time in ages she'd been completely alone at the croft. It was also the first time she'd felt unnerved by the stillness, the silence and the sense of complete isolation. All the things she'd once dreamt of..... would they eventually drive her to despair - or even insanity - she wondered. Or, would they inspire her to achieve the unfulfilled part of her dream?

Until now, she'd survived all that life had thrown her way - her loveless childhood - a life-threatening miscarriage - bereavement, and the first festive season without John. The realisation that she'd successfully overcome another major hurdle in her life filled her with fresh hope for the future.

'No matter what the future has in store for me, I *will* survive', she whispered to herself.

Before going to bed that night, she made a point of ensuring that the back door was unlocked. In all the years she'd spent at the croft, it had never been locked. The cottage at An Gleann Dubh was an open house; had it not been, neither she nor Mairi would be here today. Not only for that reason, but because she would let no-one change or intimidate her way of life, Isobel made up her mind there and then that, for as long as she was tenant crofter at An Gleann Dubh, this is how it would remain.

It was the end of the first day of a new year, and before falling asleep that night, Isobel vowed to look upon it as the first day of a new life. Leaning forward to snuff the flame on the paraffin lamp, she caught sight of a shape at the bedroom door. It was Dileas. Unknown to Isobel, the big dog, who usually slept in the kitchen beside Floss and Fly, had followed her to the bedroom. Dileas lay down at the door and eyed her with a look that said: I'm here to stay.

Isobel couldn't begin to understand the reason for the sudden appearance of the dog at the croft – or indeed in her life. But then, she mused, it was just another of the many inexplicable things that happened in the Black Glen?

****

Chapter 19

Claire and Calum returned to An Gleann Dubh the following day; Calum, to resume his role as crofter, and Claire, merely to collect her belongings. After saying goodbye to Isobel, her parting words were: 'I'm so sorry for abandoning you. How I wish I could have stayed longer.'

Isobel wasn't taken in by her apologetic tone - or the meaningless words. She knew Claire was neither sorry to be leaving nor had any intention of staying at the croft. She bore her no malice though. As she'd said to Tormod MacAlister last night, 'We can't change the way we are.'

Whatever the season, daily life at the croft revolved around the stock, and despite it being mid-winter, there was an endless list of chores to keep Isobel and Calum busy during the first few weeks of January. The weather was exceptionally mild for the time of year and, as yet, there had been hardly any snowfall. One day, a buff coloured envelope with a London postmark was delivered by the postie. Isobel knew it was official because it had been stamped with a franking machine. On looking closer, she could see that it was from a lawyer and was curious, to say the least. She was also concerned that it may contain bad news about John's family; after all, since Claire was now living with Rob at Inverculden, she knew no-one else in London.

After making herself a hot drink, she sat down to open her mail, leaving the official envelope until last. It was fortunate she was seated as the letter was from John's lawyer requesting that she come to their office in London as a matter of urgency.

'London,' Isobel cried aloud. 'I can't go to London.'

At that very moment, Calum entered the kitchen muttering that he was in desperate need of a cup of tea and would she care to join him.

'No thanks,' she replied, 'I've just had one. What I need right now is something much stronger than tea.'

As Calum cast a questioning glance in her direction, she handed him the letter, saying, 'Read this.'

Calum took the letter from her and scanned the page, before

responding in a casual tone: 'What's the problem?'

Isobel glared at him in disbelief. There were so many, she didn't know where to begin.

'Calum, I can't just up sticks and dash off to London at a moment's notice.'

'What's to stop you?'

'I've never been to London before.'

'Well now's your chance.'

'I'm pregnant.'

'You'll still be pregnant when you get back.'

'I've got Máiri.'

'Take her with you.'

'I'm virtually penniless.'

'I'll lend you the money.'

'What about the croft?'

'I'll be here.'

The conversation continued to bounce back and forth between them in this manner, and for every obstacle Isobel came up with, Calum had a solution.

She finished by saying, 'I really wouldn't be happy about driving all that way on my own, besides I would probably get lost in London.'

'Then why don't you go with Claire,' he responded casually. 'That way, you wouldn't have to drive, you wouldn't be on your own, and, she knows her way around London.'

Isobel's face broke into a smile. 'Calum, you're a genius. Why didn't I think of that?'

She stepped forward and gave him a friendly hug.

'What was that for?' he asked with a sheepish grin.

'Just for being you,' she replied softly. 'You've been my rock since John died, and to be honest, I'm not sure if I could have coped without you.'

Calum kissed her gently on the cheek and replied, 'I'll be here for as long as you need me.'

Calum's presence at the croft was a great comfort to Isobel. He was the image of his mother in looks and character, small, stocky and kind. His mop of carrot-red hair was a perfect match for his ruddy and freckled complexion. Despite being the same age as Isobel, he had an old man's head on

106

his shoulders and was rather old fashioned in his ways. He was one hundred per cent reliable and honest as the day is long. As if those virtues weren't enough, he worked from morn 'til night, seven days a week to ensure that the croft ticked over smoothly. Now, he had surpassed himself by coming up with a solution to her current problem. Isobel had known for some time that Claire was planning to return to London, unfortunately, on a purely temporary basis, but it made sense that they should travel together. As Calum had so rightly pointed out, Claire knew her way around London like the back of her hand. Problem solved. All she had to do now was ask Claire for her travel plans before replying to the letter.

The following day, Isobel left the croft with the intention of travelling to Inverculden. While aware that phoning Claire from Mairead's would have saved her the trouble of a two hour round trip, today, she was in the mood for a drive. By the time she'd finished the morning chores and loaded the Land Rover, it was almost lunchtime. The sky was dark and threatening, the mountaintops shrouded in mist and low cloud as she made her way through the glen. With thoughts of the impending trip to London uppermost in her mind, a sudden gust of wind took her completely by surprise. It caught the Land Rover broadside on, causing it to veer towards the precipitous edge of the track. Wrenching the steering wheel in the opposite direction and with a gasp of relief, she managed to reposition the wheels inside the tyre tracks. By the time she'd reached the farm it was blowing a gale, and despite her earlier imprudent wish for adventure, Isobel was beginning to have second thoughts about the onward journey. Approaching the farmhouse, she was thinking to herself how much simpler it would have been just to stop and phone Claire, yet she drove on. The main road was just a short distance ahead, and by now, giant hailstones were beginning to swirl in the wind like miniature ping-pong balls.

'This is crazy', she muttered under her breath, 'I really should turn back.'

Isobel though, had made up her mind to drive to Inverculden, and when Isobel set her mind on something, nothing - except the forces of nature - could stop her. With the visibility now down to a few feet and a blanket of soft, powdery snow covering the tarmac, she was faced with two options. One was to keep going in a southerly direction in the hope that the snowstorm would fizzle out, the other, was to turn around and head back to the croft. Isobel was aware that the latter wasn't really a viable option. By now, the track to the croft would be impassable due to the snow, and thus her decision was to press on. The Land Rover had four-wheel drive and despite the horrendous conditions it ploughed through the deep snow with relative ease. The wind though, was causing a problem. It was whipping the powder fine snow into large drifts and once or twice Isobel had to veer across to the opposite side of the road to avoid them.

Fortunately, Màiri had fallen asleep in the Moses basket on the passenger seat, but Isobel was hit by a twinge of panic upon realising they'd been travelling for over an hour. To make matters worse, the road signs were obscured by snow, daylight was fading fast, and she had no idea of their location. Not only that, but no-one would know where they were. Since she'd intended to complete the round trip before nightfall, she hadn't told anyone of her plans. The weather conditions continued to deteriorate rapidly and the swirling snow was causing a complete whiteout. Isobel was blinded, mesmerised and hypnotised as the snowflakes danced in the headlights beams.

'Where am I? I can't see the road! What's that looming up ahead? Oh no...........'

The Land Rover slewed across the road, crashed into a bank of snow and came to a sudden stop. As it did so, the Moses basket slid off the seat and Isobel catapulted headlong into the rear view mirror on the windscreen. Her first concern being for Màiri, she leant forward to retrieve the Moses basket and felt a warm, sticky substance trickling down her face. Even in the dusky twilight, the bright, crimson red blood was visible on the white blanket. Màiri was now awake and whimpering, but thankfully, apparently unhurt. Isobel fumbled in the bag for a nappy to stem the flow of blood, before ramming her shoulder against the driver's door, but it was stuck fast. Isobel had been holding one of Máiri's nappies against her head, and in a short space of time it had become saturated with blood. She inhaled deeply. Although the current situation was dire, she realised that the worst thing she could do right now was panic. She must focus and think rationally. She had two options. One was to sit it out and hope that the snowstorm would pass, and the other was to try to exit through the rear flaps of the Land Rover. She was aware though, that even if she and Máiri were able to exit the Land Rover from the rear, any attempt to walk in these conditions would be complete madness. Her decision therefore, was to sit it out in the vain hope that another vehicle would come along soon.

With the engine turned off, the little amount of heat that was inside the Land Rover slowly began to diminish, and despite her several layers of clothing, Isobel began to shake. The combination of shock, severe blood loss, and the rapidly plummeting temperature, was now jeopardizing her safety. Recalling her frequent travels with her parents, she remembered that they never left home without a thermos flask. At the time, she'd thought they were old-fashioned skinflints. Now though, as with many of her parents' die-hard habits, she fully understood the wisdom of their ways.

Máiri was beginning to get fractious. She was obviously cold, and most probably hungry. Although being gradually weaned onto solids, she was still being given breast milk and Isobel lifted her from the Moses basket and cradled her to her breast. With the cot blankets wrapped around them to afford some heat, and Máiri now happily settled in her arms, Isobel closed her eyes and began to doze off. She was completely oblivious to the vehicle that had just pulled up behind them. When rudely awakened by a tapping sound at the window, followed by a torch beam directed at her face, she saw, with relief, that it was Tormod MacAlister.

'Are you all right?' he mouthed through the glass.

Isobel merely shook her head and held up the blood- stained nappy. Moments later, she could hear him scrambling about in the back of the Land Rover.

He reached into the front and detached Máiri from her breast, saying anxiously, 'Let's get you both out of here before you catch pneumonia.'

Never in her wildest dreams did Isobel think she would find herself thanking God for sending Tormod MacAlister to her rescue - but she did at that moment. The fact that he was here was nothing short of a miracle. The fact that he'd seen her naked breast in the beam of his torch was of little importance. Within minutes, Tormod had returned and helped Isobel clamber out through the rear of the Land Rover. He made one final trip to retrieve the Moses basket and the bag that contained Máiri's bits and bobs, before getting into the van beside them, when Isobel began to cry. There were many reasons for her outpouring of emotions at this moment; relief, shock, confusion and a feeling of utter helplessness, to name a few.

'I'll take you home,' Tormod said softly.

Assuming he meant home to An Gleann Dubh, Isobel was slightly surprised when, after travelling only a short distance, he pulled up at a small cottage that was set back from the roadside.

Noticing the bewildered expression on her face, he said, 'This is *my* home. I was on my way to an emergency call-out at a farm further south. Since your vehicle is blocking the road however, I'll have to postpone it. I heard on the radio that the conditions further north are treacherous and all roads in the area are closed for the rest of the day. I'm afraid that, like it or not, you have no option but to stay here.'

Isobel, with Máiri cradled in her arms, was taken into a dimly lit room that exuded sanctuary and warmth. The large armchair beside the dying embers of a log fire was beckoning. Tormod disappeared for a few moments and reappeared with a mug of steaming hot tea, by which time, Isobel had already sunk into the armchair and was basking in a combined state of fatigue and serenity. Tormod threw a few logs onto the fire, before taking Máiri from her arms. His tone was curt, almost domineering, as he said, 'Once you've finished your tea, I'm going to take a closer look at that head wound.'

Isobel forced a feeble smile and replied with the words, 'Did

110

you qualify as a doctor as well as a vet?

'Not quite, but the technique of closing an open wound is the same for both,' he replied with a smile.

As yet, Isobel hadn't seen her head wound, but knew by the amount of blood loss that it would require treatment. Máiri was now fast asleep in her Moses basket and Tormod returned to sit by Isobel's side. Similar to the night she'd danced in his arms, his closeness had a profound effect on her and she couldn't help but wonder why. Other than Calum, whom she thought of as a dear friend, no-one had been this close to her since John's death. Prior to this, she had felt repulsed by any man who dared to invade her personal space. There wasn't a shadow of doubt in her mind however, that the intentions of Tormod MacAlister were both professional and honourable and she found his closeness comforting.

The words, 'I'll fetch my bag,' interrupted her thoughts, before Tormod rose to his feet and left the room.

Isobel glanced around at her surroundings. The room was small and sparsely furnished - what she would call a bachelor pad - with no feminine touches. It was modest, slightly untidy, yet homely. In many ways, it reminded her of the cottage at the croft. How bizarre, she thought to herself - of all the places to spend the night - why here?

Tormod returned with his medicine bag and administered a local anaesthetic before drawing Isobel's gaping head wound together.

He then rose to his feet and said with a smile: 'That should stop the bleeding and allow it to heal without spoiling your beauty.'

Without glancing up, she replied with the words, 'I have every confidence in your ability. After all, I've already seen the quality of your work, but I doubt if you can perform miracles.'

Tormod simply smiled to himself as he cleaned up.

'How are the injured dogs doing?' he asked after a short silence.

'They've both made a full recovery,' she replied, 'but Dileas' owner is still missing.'

'Are you planning to keep the dog'?

'Yes. At least, I'm hoping to.'
Another awkward silence ensued. Isobel wasn't exactly in the mood for small talk. Due to the impact with the windscreen, the recently inserted stitches and the thoughts that were whirling around inside, her head was aching. As for Tormod, he'd never had a female in his house before - or indeed - in his life, and was simply at a loss for words. He glanced at Isobel, but she was asleep.

Meanwhile, back at the croft, Calum was frantic with worry. When he'd come in for lunch, Isobel was nowhere to be seen and now it was evening, pitch dark and she still wasn't here. Due to the snow, the road to the farm was impassable, and he couldn't begin to imagine where she and Máiri had gone. Apart from the radio link, he was completely cut off from civilisation and at this moment, said a silent prayer of thanks that Isobel had the foresight to install it. He contacted his parents at the farm to enquire if Isobel and Máiri were there.
'No, they're not here. I haven't seen them today,' his mother informed him in an anxious tone. 'I'll phone Rob and Helen.'
When it became apparent that neither Rob nor Helen had heard from Isobel, or indeed had any inclination of where she might be, the decision was taken to inform the police and organise a search.

Isobel awoke with a start and glanced briefly at the unfamiliar surroundings.
'Oh my head,' she groaned, rising too quickly. 'I have to phone Mairead.'
Such was her state of shock following the day's dramatic events that she'd completely forgotten to let anyone know that she and Máiri were safe and well.
Just then, a deep voice ordered, 'Sit down. I'll phone her.'
Isobel was so taken aback by Tormod's abrupt manner that she immediately sat down and gave him Mairead's telephone number.
'Tell her Máiri and I are safe and well and I'll see her tomorrow,' she called out as Tormod left the room. 'Weather permitting,' she muttered to herself.

Perhaps I've got concussion, she thought to herself while basking in a state of serene acquiescence. On the other hand, my mellow mood could be down to gratitude. Whatever the reason, she hadn't felt this relaxed since John's death. What was more, for the first time in ages, she felt safe.

Tormod returned and reassured Isobel that all communications had been taken care of. Mairead had promised to notify Rob, Helen and Calum of her whereabouts and let them know that she and Máiri were in safe hands. She would also contact the police so that they could stand down the team that were on the point of co-ordinating a search of the roads in the area.

Isobel yawned sleepily and murmured the words: 'Thank you.'

Tormod smiled and said, 'It's not me you have to thank, but good fortune. I just happened to be in the right place at the right time.'

While sinking into a blissful sleep, Isobel mouthed the words, 'It was kismet.'

****

Chapter 20

By some inconceivable quirk of fate, Isobel spent the night at the home of Tormod MacAlister. She lay awake into the early hours of the morning reliving the day that had turned out to be more of an adventure than she could ever have imagined. But there was much more on her mind than that. She couldn't quite believe the odd and wholly unforeseen set of circumstances that had thrown them together, her and the vet from Drumevie; the one she'd taken an instant dislike to. What she couldn't fathom was: Why did she dislike him so much? Why couldn't she just feel indifferent? Perhaps it was because he had a habit of turning up when she needed him most, she mused. Or, could it be that he was an excellent vet? He also had the Gaelic, and, come to think of it, he was quite attractive, in a rustic sort of way........

Isobel was shocked by her thoughts. John, her beloved husband and soul mate had been dead only a matter of months, and she was almost four months pregnant with his child.......

So too, did Tormod MacAlister lie wide awake that night, in the bedroom next to Isobel's. The thoughts running through his mind were of the extraordinary events that had led to him having a woman and child sleeping under his roof. The fact that it was the crofter from An Gleann Dubh, recently widowed following her husband's mysterious accident, was even more incomprehensible. He rose and gazed through the bedroom window. The snow had stopped falling and a full moon was casting its silvery light on the surrounding mountains like a welcoming beacon. For the first time since his early childhood, he felt cocooned in a warm glow of contentment. Suddenly, the reason for this hit him hard. In fact, he couldn't have been more shocked if he'd been hit between the legs by a badly aimed snowball - he yearned for a family. Since leaving his island home almost twenty years ago, he'd been a loner. His parents were dead and he had no siblings. Any surviving distant relatives had chosen to disown him, and now, out of the blue, he felt a deep longing to be part of a family.

Isobel had drifted into a shallow sleep and was awakened by the sound of Máiri whimpering. The time on the alarm clock told her it was 5am and it was dark as pitch. She fumbled her way towards the Moses basket, and, with Máiri now latched onto her breast, snuggled back under the blankets. It wasn't long before she heard the sound of Tormod moving about in the bedroom next door. Máiri had fallen asleep and she tucked the blankets around her before creeping silently towards the window. Through a chink in the curtains she saw two large headlights looming out of the inky blackness. As the vehicle trundled noisily by, she saw that it was a snowplough. She let out a gasp. Her Land Rover was embedded in a snowdrift in the middle of the road. She and Tormod emerged from their bedrooms simultaneously?

'Good morning. Did you sleep well?' he asked politely.

'I'd be lying if I said yes,' she replied curtly.

'Me neither,' he responded.

'The snowplough has just gone past. It's heading south and my Land Rover is blocking the road. The last thing I need is for it to be crushed by the front of a snowplough,' Isobel said anxiously.

'Fetch Máiri,' Tormod urged. 'I was about to head out to the appointment I missed yesterday.'

The plough had rendered the road passable, but as they followed in its wake, the compacted snow was making the journey almost as hazardous as it had been the previous day. The dawn was breaking when they came upon the stationery snowplough, ahead of which was the gigantic snow drift, and Isobel's Land Rover.

Armed with shovels, Tormod and the three man crew began to dig the Land Rover from the drift. With the vehicle now free and none the worse for its mishap, Isobel thanked the crew and left them to deal with the wall of snow that had blocked the road south. She also thanked Tormod, without whose help, she and Máiri would have been in a perilous situation.

'How will I know you've reached home safely?' he asked in a concerned tone.

'You won't,' she replied curtly. 'I have no telephone at the croft.'

Shaking his head in bemusement, he said, 'It takes a lot of guts to stay there alone - especially with no means of communication.'

'I'm not alone,' she responded curtly. 'I have Calum for company, and I do have a means of communication.'

Tormod scowled, before saying, 'Calum! I didn't realise you and he were co-habiting.'

'Not that it's any of your business,' Isobel replied frostily, 'but we're not. It's a working relationship, and what's more – it works – for both of us.'

On that note, Isobel drove off, leaving Tormod alone with his thoughts. He couldn't quite understand his emotions at that moment. Why did it feel as though she had lifted her hand and slapped him across the face? And why was he so annoyed at the thought of her sharing her life with Calum Fraser?

****

Chapter 21

Isobel's mood, as she drove back to An Gleann Dubh, was one of frustration and irritation. Her frustration was mainly due to the fact that she hadn't got to Inverculden the previous day, and for some reason, Tormod MacAlister had succeeded in irritating her once again. The concentration required to negotiate the rutted, snow covered road did little to ease her edginess as the Land Rover slithered along the track the snowplough had cleared. Nonetheless, she reached the road end that led to the farm and the croft much quicker than anticipated. It was then that it dawned on her she had only travelled a distance of about fifteen miles the previous day. She'd been a long way from her destination and was aware that, even without her unfortunate mishap, the chances of ever reaching Inverculden had been extremely remote. She pulled up at the farmhouse with the intention of phoning Claire, before attempting to undertake the three miles of treacherous, snow covered track through the glen.

As always, Mairead greeted them with a warm welcome and fussed over Máiri like a mother hen. She then reprimanded Isobel for her foolhardiness and stupidity, not to mention, the downright danger to which she had exposed Máiri by setting off in such conditions.

'You're worse than my mother,' Isobel retorted while flopping, in a state of extreme fatigue, into an armchair. 'We're fine.'

'Thanks to the young vet,' Mairead retorted. 'If he hadn't come along when he did.........'

Isobel had heard enough. She was weary and weepy. Her head was throbbing, and she was in no mood to be lectured over an imprudent decision made on a whim.

'Mairead, I don't want to discuss it. We're fine and that's all that matters.'

'What matters, is that you should be more responsible,' she scolded. 'It's not just yourself you have to think about you know. You are responsible for two other lives as well as your own.'

Despite closing her eyes, Isobel could still hear the incessant droning of Mairead's voice. Soon, it began to fade into the distance, and finally, all went quiet as she drifted into oblivion. Isobel woke with a start and glanced at the clock on the mantelpiece. It was ten o'clock.

'Mairead, you should have wakened me,' she cried in alarm, 'I have to go home.'

This time, it was Gordon who answered: 'You, young lady, are not going anywhere at this late hour. It's dark as pitch and far too dangerous to drive through the glen.'

Although knowing and accepting he was right, Isobel was anxious to get home.

'I wish I'd never set off to drive to Inverculden yesterday afternoon,' she cried in anguish. 'If only I'd phoned Claire from here, none of this would have happened.'

'Phone her now,' Mairead said softly. 'Perhaps it'll make you feel better.'

'Thank you Mairead,' Isobel responded with a smile of appreciation. 'I don't know what I would do without you and Gordon, or Calum for that matter.'

Isobel returned to the lounge in a happier frame of mind. She'd had a chat with Claire and Rob, both of whom had succeeded in lifting her flagging spirits. Claire had been surprised to hear about her business affairs in London, but didn't hesitate to affirm that she could accompany her on the journey south. In fact, her suggestion had been that, since she still had occupancy of the flat, they stay for a week and spend some time together; if only to make up for the lost years. Consequently, they planned to travel to London just as soon as the roads were passable.

The hours of darkness had brought about a rapid and unexpected thaw, and as she peered through the curtains next morning, Isobel was surprised to see that most of the snow had disappeared. After dressing hastily, she made her way downstairs to rustle up some breakfast for Máiri. Mairead was in the kitchen and greeted her in the usual cheerful manner:

'Good morning Isobel. Sun's up. Breakfast's up, and from what I can see, even the weather is looking up.'

After ushering Isobel to her place at the breakfast table, she promptly dished up a plate of sausage, bacon and eggs.

'Mairead, I came downstairs to get breakfast for Máiri,' Isobel began. However, her words had fallen on deaf ears; in fact, she found herself talking to the four walls as Mairead had disappeared. A few moments later, she reappeared with Máiri in her arms and sat down in the chair next to Isobel.

'I was thinking......' she began.

'Yes?' Isobel responded wearily.

'I don't know how you're going to take this, but.......'

'Take what?' Isobel prompted.

'London's many miles from here,' she began, while trying to force-feed Máiri some porridge.

'I'm well aware of that, and, as yet Máiri hasn't eaten porridge,' Isobel replied, looking on anxiously as she blew a mouthful of food into Mairead's face.

'It's about time she did then,' Mairead replied in a superior tone.

Isobel had the greatest respect for Mairead and was aware she was only trying to offer helpful advice. Nonetheless, as a mother she felt belittled, which prompted her to respond by saying, perhaps rather abruptly, 'She's only nine months old and I'm still breast-feeding her.'

'Oh dear,' Mairead remarked in a dejected tone. 'Bang goes that idea then.'

'What idea?' Isobel enquired with a sigh of exasperation.

'I was going to suggest that you leave Máiri with Gordon and me when you go to London.'

'What!' Isobel exclaimed. 'I couldn't do that. I wouldn't dream of leaving her for a whole week.'

'A week... I thought you were only going for a couple of days.'

'That was the original plan, but Claire has suggested that we stay for a bit longer.'

'All the same, Máiri would be much happier - and safer – if she were left with us,' Mairead responded in a patronising tone.

'Are you implying that I wouldn't take good care of her?' Isobel asked abruptly.

'You know that wasn't what I meant,' she replied, her stern expression transforming into a sympathetic smile, 'You deserve a break, and without Máiri, you would be able to relax.'

Appreciating that Mairead was acting in her best interests, Isobel asked for some time to think it over.

The outcome was that Isobel and Claire arrived in London the following week; Máiri having been left in Mairead and Gordon's care. Claire drove directly to the flat in the suburbs, the one she'd once called home, and Isobel was pleasantly surprised by its location. It was situated on the edge of Hampstead Heath, so Claire had informed her, and was in complete contrast to the mental image she had conjured up of the city of London. From her bedroom window she could see wide open spaces - not a bit like staying in a city - apart from when she scanned the horizon and saw domes and steeples dominating the skyline in every direction.

'I'm going to make the most of my city break', she said to herself before sliding between the sheets that night.

The following day, Isobel phoned John's lawyer and arranged a meeting for Friday morning, the day before they returned home. The days in between were going to be spent shopping and sightseeing. The highlight of the holiday, as far as Isobel was concerned, would be a trip to the cinema to see the current Elvis film. The title was "Easy Come, Easy Go" and, not only was it relevant to her current situation, but it brought back distant memories. The title of an earlier film, "Follow That Dream", had inspired her to reach her goal as a vet, not to mention, pursue her dream of staying at An Gleann Dubh. Now, as then, the title seemed to fit her situation perfectly. If her financial situation didn't improve soon, she would be in danger of losing her long sought after dream. Despite knowing that Rob would never ask her to move out, if she, as tenant, couldn't make it viable, then she would leave and make way for someone who could.

Isobel was enjoying her time in London so much that the week went past very quickly and Friday morning arrived much too soon. Claire was accompanying her to the lawyer's office and the letter that had initiated her trip to London was firmly clutched in Isobel's hand as they walked up the steps of the imposing office block. Having accompanied her thus far, Claire insisted on staying behind in the reception area as Isobel was ushered upstairs.

'Good Morning. Please take a seat,' the bespectacled, geriatric gent said in a gruff voice. 'Mr Bingham will be with you shortly. Can I offer you tea - or coffee perhaps - while you wait?'

'No thank you,' Isobel replied nervously.

Never in her short life had she been in such an austere, inhospitable and downright scary room. As well as radiating an atmosphere of doom and gloom, she detected a peculiar, nauseating smell. It was somewhere between stale pipe tobacco and Old Spice aftershave. As she waited, thoughts of all the traumatic and tragic tales that had been related across the solid oak desk were running through her head. She recalled Rob's meeting with his father's lawyer following his death and was deliberating on the nature of the terrible news that John's lawyer was about to reveal. Her thoughts were interrupted by the sound of a man clearing his throat. Turning in her seat, she saw a slightly younger version of the old gentleman walking towards her with his hand outstretched.

'Mrs Caldwell, my name is Mr Bingham. I'm your late husband's lawyer.'

Isobel's eyes filled with tears. She couldn't bear to hear her beloved John being referred to as her "late" husband. He was, and always would be, her husband, be it in the past, the present, or the future.

Observing her distressed state, Mr Bingham frowned and continued in a deep, formal tone, 'Mrs Caldwell, as few months before your late husband's untimely death, he came to see me and left instructions, in the event of his death, to read to you in person the terms of his last will and testament.

The shock made Isobel retch. It hadn't crossed her mind that John had drawn up a will. Just then, Mr Bingham began to read out the words contained in the document. When he finally stopped talking, Isobel sat in stunned silence. One by one, she went over the words in her head until they began to sink in. My entire estate, including my properties in London and Dumlocher, I hereby bequeath to my beloved wife, Isobel.

121

The revelation left her speechless. For one thing, she'd always believed that a will was made by old people. Besides, she had no knowledge of John ever having drawn up such a document. She wasn't even aware that he owned a property in London.....

Mr Bingham's voice interrupted her thoughts. 'Your husband's assets, which include shares, life insurance policies, notwithstanding the two properties, are worth close to two million guineas. With the addition of the properties in Bayswater and Dumlocher, it amounts to a rather considerable legacy. Obviously, it will take some time to get the paperwork in order, but I shall instruct my secretary to contact you to arrange a further meeting in due course.'

Claire, waiting in reception, couldn't fail to notice Isobel's ashen face, red rimmed eyes and stunned expression as she came downstairs.

'I hope it's not more bad news,' she said anxiously.

Isobel shook her head, before saying, 'Can we go for a coffee? I need to sit down, otherwise I'll fall down.'

Isobel left the office block in a state of shock and bewilderment. Had Claire not been with her, she would have become lost and disorientated and probably ended up wandering aimlessly around London for the rest of the day.

'I'm so glad you're here,' she murmured as Claire guided her along the busy streets towards a café.

When seated with their drinks, Claire urged her sister to spill the beans.

'The suspense is killing me,' she added impatiently. 'Tell me the good news.'

Her face expressionless and her tone without emotion, Isobel simply said, 'I'm a millionaire.'

'What!' Claire called out. 'That's not good news, that's great news. This calls for a celebration.'

'Let's buy a bottle of the finest champagne and go back to the flat and celebrate,' Claire urged.

'I can't,' Isobel replied, her voice breaking.

'How thoughtless of me,' Claire began apologetically, 'You're still in mourning. You won't feel like celebrating.'

'I am, and I don't,' Isobel responded. 'But that isn't the only

122

reason. I'm pregnant.'

'Pregnant!' Claire exclaimed loudly.

Isobel could feel a hot flush creeping up her neck and into her cheeks as she glanced around with embarrassment. It was obvious from the expressions on the faces staring in their direction that everyone within earshot had heard Claire's outburst.

'How did it happen?' Claire asked in a stage whisper.

'There's only one way I know of,' Isobel replied while suppressing a smile, 'I'm almost five months gone. And John didn't even know,' she added ruefully.

Claire rose from the table and hugged her young sister, while saying, 'That's wonderful news.' She then added with a smile, 'I'm going to buy that bottle of champagne. I don't mind having to drink it all myself.'

****

Chapter 22

The following morning, Claire and Isobel left London to begin the long and tedious drive back to Scotland. Although she'd had more than a few reservations about leaving Máiri behind, as they joined a queue of standing traffic, Isobel silently thanked Mairead for having such prudent foresight. Without Máiri, it had felt as though she was missing a limb. Nonetheless, it would have been difficult, for all of them, had she been here. During the week, Claire had made arrangements for her personal belongings to be transported to Inverculden, and before they left, deposited the key to the flat with the estate agent.

'That brings another chapter of my life to a close,' she remarked as the city slowly faded into the distance.

'You and me both,' Isobel responded drily.

'I wonder if a handsome husband awaits me in the next chapter,' Claire remarked dreamily.

'Certainly not for me,' Isobel retorted.

'At least you won't have to worry about finances ever again,' Claire replied.

'Happiness can't be bought,' Isobel retorted.

'Money sure brings independence and security though,' Claire quipped.

Except for a brief stop at a roadside café, Isobel slept for most of the return journey, and when next she opened her eyes, they had arrived at Inverculden.

'Are you coming in to see Rob for a few minutes?' Claire asked while helping to transfer Isobel's luggage to the Land Rover.

'No. I've missed Máiri and the dogs so much that I don't want to waste another minute. Tell Rob I'll catch up with him soon.'

Following a brief stop at Mairead and Gordon's to collect Máiri, Isobel drove the final lap of her epic journey. The sight of the croft brought tears to her eyes; whether they were tears of relief, happiness, or grief, she couldn't be sure. The Land Rover had no sooner stopped in the yard than the back door opened and Calum ran to meet her with outstretched arms.

The dogs however, beat him to it and were first to reach Isobel.

'Welcome home Isobel,' Calum said joyfully as he shooed the dogs aside. He then planted a sloppy kiss on her cheek, saying, 'I've missed you. It's not been the same without you here.'

'It's good to be home,' Isobel replied, forcing a feeble smile, 'but I'm totally exhausted. If you don't mind, I think I'll go straight to bed.'

First Rob, then John and now Calum, all emerging from the same door to greet me – how bizarre – she thought to herself, but there was something about Calum's greeting that had irritated her.

She brushed past him and made her way towards the bedroom. As she did so, he remarked in a tone of disappointment, 'Goodnight Isobel. I'll catch up with all your news in the morning.'

No, Isobel said to herself as she closed the bedroom door. You won't. Since they were, "cohabiting" as Tormod MacAlister had so offensively put it, she probably should have shared the news of her inheritance with Calum - but she wouldn't. Only her closest and most trusted friends would be told the news. As for Calum, he was becoming over familiar. It would appear that he thought of himself as a permanent fixture in her life now, and, in her vulnerable state, it would have been so easy just to go along with that – but she wouldn't – she mustn't. Isobel decided there and then that the relationship between them must be firmly established on a business footing. From now on, he must look upon her as the employer – the one who paid his wages. Perhaps, she mused, thoughts of the clandestine liaison between Claire and her boss were influencing her powers of reasoning at this moment. Her main reason though, was that she didn't want folk to think, as Tormod obviously had, that they were in a relationship.

'Calum,' she began in a solemn tone next morning. 'We need to talk.'

'That's what I was trying to do last night,' he began.

'I don't mean a friendly chat - I mean a professional one. A meeting,' she responded drily.

125

A meeting,' he echoed with a laugh. 'Are you serious?'

With a poker straight face, Isobel responded by saying, 'Do I look as though I'm joking? From now on, your role here will be solely as an employee.'

'Isn't that what I am at the moment?' he questioned in bemusement.

'No, you've been helping me out, as a friend, since John's death. I want to make it clear that this is purely a temporary position and will continue until such time as I am able to run the croft by myself.'

'I don't suppose I have much choice, other than to go along with it,' he replied solemnly.

'You do. You could seek employment elsewhere,' she said curtly. 'I can quite easily find someone to replace you.'

Calum was both shocked and confused. He'd known Isobel for many years, and although he'd been aware of her stubborn and independent streak, he had always found her to be warm-hearted and compassionate. Since returning from her trip to London however, she was behaving like a virtual stranger; a cold, surly and arrogant one at that.

Unlike the previous winter, the first few months of 1967 were relatively mild. Calum, having been raised on a farm, had adapted to the hardships of running a hill croft like a duck to water – unlike John – and so far, everything at An Gleann Dubh was running smoothly.

Now six months pregnant, Isobel was unable to hide her growing bump, and each time she shopped in Drumevie was acutely aware of the surreptitious whispers behind her back. Apparently, it was common knowledge that Calum Fraser had moved in with her at the croft and rumours were spreading like wildfire. Isobel held her head high and tried to ignore the idle gossip mongers. After all, she told herself, I have nothing to hide. Only Mairead, Gordon, Calum and her family knew the truth. Recalling her brief encounter with Tormod MacAlister on New Year's Eve, she added him to the list. But John's parents, who had returned to live in London, knew nothing of the impending birth of their second grandchild.

126

On the sixth of June 1967, Isobel gave birth to a baby boy. When first handed her infant son, she could only gaze at him with amazement and adoration. He was the image of John.

'Does this little chap have a name?' the midwife asked.

'Yes,' Isobel replied without hesitation. 'His name is Iain Seumas Ferguson Caldwell.'

'An excellent choice of names,' she replied, nodding her head in approval. 'He'll make you proud one day.'

'How can you tell?' Isobel asked, her voice choking with emotion.

The midwife took Isobel's hand in hers and turned it over, before gazing intently at her palm.

'Can you keep a secret?' she asked cagily.

Isobel hadn't time to reply before she went on, 'I am a Speywife. I have the gift of second sight.'

An involuntary shudder ran through Isobel's body as the two women gazed into each other's eyes. Despite being total strangers, Isobel had a distinct feeling they'd met before.

The midwife spoke softly as she added, 'You too, have the gift.'

Isobel remained silent, recalling the numerous paranormal events in the Black Glen - her gut feeling that Rob was her brother - her premonition of John's death – but long before that - the curse she'd bestowed on Robert Thornton for his deplorable treatment of her best friend Mary.

The midwife's voice interrupted her thoughts, 'Are you all right? Shall I call the doctor?'

'I'm fine,' Isobel replied, 'slightly confused, exhausted, but otherwise, fine.'

'Don't fight it,' the midwife whispered.

'Fight it?' Isobel murmured drowsily.

The midwife's reply seemed to reverberate around the room, 'Acknowledge the gift you were born with. It could work to your advantage.'

Isobel never saw the midwife again, and despite asking several of the staff during the remainder of her stay in hospital, no-one could tell her the name of the person that had delivered her infant son.

Iain weighed a healthy eight pounds and ten ounces and

127

from the minute he was born, Isobel was besotted with him. He was different from Máiri in every way. He was dark, while she was fair. He was strong and responsive, whereas Máiri had been delicate and slightly lethargic. In fairness to Máiri, she was a six weeks preterm baby and had come on in leaps and bounds recently; nonetheless, the bonding with her son had been spontaneous. Perhaps it was due to the fact that she had been allowed to hold him immediately after birth, or perhaps it was because he would complete her brood, she mused. Although once having longed to fill the cottage with children, without John, she realised there was no chance of that dream ever coming to fruition.

****

Chapter 23

The early summer months saw a few of the rams being entered into the local agricultural shows, and once again, lifting rosettes and cups. Calum, to his credit, proved to be an excellent stockman and both Rob and Isobel were delighted with his successes. At the back of her mind was the realisation that John, having no inherent farming knowledge, couldn't have filled Rob's boots with as much expertise. The Ardbuie show was being held the following Saturday and, following tradition, there was a dance in the village hall afterwards.

One evening, as she and Calum sat down together after work, he said, 'Isobel, I have a question for you.'

His manner was abrupt, his tone formal and it caught her slightly off guard.

'Fire away,' she remarked with a bemused expression.

'Would you allow me to escort you to the ceilidh after the show on Saturday?'

'No. It wouldn't be appropriate,' she replied immediately.

'It's almost nine months since John's death and you've hardly left the croft,' he began. 'It's about time you started living again......'

Isobel had heard enough. In her opinion, Calum had no right to be telling her what she should, or shouldn't, be doing. After all, he was merely an employee; therefore, she interrupted, saying, 'What I meant was, it wouldn't be appropriate for us to be seen together.'

'I can't believe you just said that,' Calum retorted. 'Who do you think you are? Just because your brother is Laird of Inverculden and I'm an employee, all of a sudden you think you're better than me. We've been friends since childhood and I remember the shy, caring, compassionate Isobel. I liked you then - loved you I suppose - but I don't like the high and mighty person you've become. I would even go so far as to say you've become a snob. Yes, that's what you've become, an upper class snob.'

Having struggled to remain silent during Calum's tirade, Isobel was thinking that he'd completely missed the point.

Clearly, he had taken her refusal to attend the ceilidh with him as a personal insult - which hadn't been her intention. She was angry with him. Perhaps it was because he'd called her a snob, the very trait of her mother's she detested, or perhaps it was due to the fact that he was beginning to encroach on her personal life.

'Have you finished?' she asked arrogantly.

'Yes. I *have* finished,' he replied, scowling, 'Finished for good. Tomorrow, I'll pack my bags and move out.'

Calum rose and left the room, leaving Isobel stunned, bewildered and infuriated; her anger now directed at herself as much as at him. One of her father's old phrases came to mind: "Don't cut off your nose to spite your face".

Appreciating the dire consequences of Calum quitting his job, she had to make a decision – and fast. The choice was between letting him go and trying to find a replacement - not an easy task - or offering him a grovelling apology in the hopes that he would stay. Grovelling, or apologising, was not something that came easily to Isobel though - if she was in the right - which in this case, she was. The gossip mongers would have a field day if Calum escorted her to the ceilidh. She could just hear them now: Has she no shame? Her husband's barely cold in his grave. She's given birth to another man's child and is flouting their relationship in public.

Isobel was adamant she wouldn't be attending the village ceilidh with Calum – or anyone else for that matter - and if he chose to terminate his employment and end their ten year friendship because of it, then so be it.

Isobel didn't apologise to Calum and he left the croft the following morning. Part of her was glad to see him go, while a tiny part of her was beginning to panic. The summer months meant long days working outdoors; hills to be tramped, hay to be mown, sheep to be clipped and dipped, not to mention, the fact that the rams were entered into the Ardbuie show in a few days time. 'What have I done?' she asked herself.

Later that morning, Isobel was in the yard when the mail van drew up; it wasn't the usual postman, but an unfamiliar, younger man.

130

'Good morning,' he called cheerily. 'I'm Donald.'

'Isobel Caldwell,' she responded, taking the outstretched hand in hers. 'What's happened to old Fergus?'

'Retired,' he replied. 'And not before time, he's pushing sixty five.'

Isobel recalled the days when, as a youngster, she'd run out to meet him to collect her comics, thinking at the time he was an old man.

Among the mail was a letter from John's lawyer, and she opened it first. It was to inform her that John's entire estate had been transferred into her name and a request for further instructions with regard to the two properties bequeathed to her in his will. Having no knowledge of property ownership – and not even having seen the house in London – Isobel was in a quandary over how best to deal with the problem.

'I'll have to phone Rob and ask his advice,' she said under her breath. This, of course, meant a trip to the farm.'

With a fifteen month old child and a young infant in tow, a three mile trip to the farm, or anywhere else for that matter, wasn't as simple as it once had been, and by the time Isobel got the children organised, it was early afternoon. She was met at the farmhouse door by Mairead, who, instead of her usual jovial greeting, muttered in a rather hostile manner, 'I'm disappointed in you Isobel. Not for one moment did I think you would fire Calum?'

'I didn't,' Isobel replied in the same tone. 'It was his decision to leave.'

'You'd better come inside,' Mairead muttered under her breath.

Making her way towards the kitchen, Isobel remarked frostily, 'I came to ask if I could use the telephone.'

'Yes, but make it a quick call,' Mairead replied in the same tone. 'The bills are increasing at an alarming rate these days and we don't all have wealthy brothers to help us out.'

'I'll pay for the call,' Isobel responded calmly.

Although outwardly unruffled, inside, she was seething. It took every last ounce of self-restraint to maintain her composure, but she adored Mairead and owed her life to her, therefore, had to tread carefully. Although her immediate response was to about turn and drive to Ardbuie, where there was a public telephone kiosk, it was no time for angry words or decisions made in the heat of the moment. Anyhow, her quarrel wasn't with Mairead. While dialling the number, Isobel realised her conversation with Rob would have to be cryptic as Mairead knew nothing about her inheritance.

Claire answered the telephone, and, following a brief chat, she asked to speak to Rob. Claire then informed her that Rob had left the previous day to fly to London on business.

'I wish I'd known that earlier,' Isobel remarked dejectedly, 'I could have gone with him.'

'Can I help?' Claire asked.

'Oh Claire,' Isobel replied despondently, 'I could certainly use some help. But I doubt very much if you could replace Calum.'

'Would it help if I came to see you? Then we could discuss it further.'

'I would appreciate that so much,' Isobel replied and replaced the receiver.

Returning to the kitchen, she said dejectedly, 'I'll have to go Mairead, I have a mountain of work to get through when I get back.'

Shaking her head, she replied, 'You'll never cope away up there on your own. Not with two youngsters to look after.'

'I'll just have to,' Isobel replied doggedly. 'In the meantime at least, until I find a replacement for Calum.'

On that note, Isobel beat a hasty retreat, but not before laying a shilling on the kitchen table to cover the cost of her phone call.

****

Chapter 24

On her return to the croft, Isobel felt as though she'd hit rock bottom. She sat in the chair by the kitchen range with tears of self-pity running down her cheeks. Máiri and Iain had fallen asleep in the Land Rover on the way back from the farm, and apart from the dogs, she was on her own. Floss, Fly and Dileas lay quietly by her side and six doleful, questioning eyes were fixed firmly on her face as she continued to sob noisily. Just then, the dogs barked in unison and ran to the kitchen door. Isobel sprang to her feet, wiping her tear-stained cheeks as she opened the doors and followed the dogs outside. The sight of a familiar white van parked in the yard, from which the young vet from Drumevie was emerging, left her flabbergasted.

'Hello Isobel,' Tormod remarked casually as he walked towards her. 'It can't be me that's upset you this time.'

Isobel merely shook her head and wiped the remaining tears from her eyes.

'Can I come in?' he asked softly.

She nodded, before walking towards the cottage, stopping briefly to check on Máiri and Iain while passing the Land Rover. Floss and Dileas had followed Isobel into the yard and hadn't paid too much attention to the unfamiliar visitor; however, as Tormod neared the cottage, Dileas placed herself between him and the door. Her eyes were firmly fixed on her mistress, as if awaiting a command.

'It's okay, he's a friend,' Isobel said while patting her head.

Reassured by her words, Dileas turned and ran inside with Floss, before taking up her place on the mat in front of the range.

'I consider it an honour to be regarded as your friend,' Tormod remarked with a faint smile.

Isobel didn't reply straight away, but filled the kettle and placed it on the gas stove.

'Have you time for tea or coffee?' she asked politely.

'Unfortunately not, this isn't a social call....'

Unwittingly, Isobel's face portrayed disappointment, which prompted him to add hastily, 'but I'll make time.'

Almost an hour later, Isobel and Tormod were still lost in conversation. He, being concerned about her distressed state, had asked if there was anything he could do to help, and she, being in desperate need of a replacement for Calum, had offloaded her current dilemma.

'I'll see what I can do,' he said as he left the cottage.

'Thank you,' Isobel responded politely.

As Tormod climbed into his van, she said with a faint smile, 'Once again, you turned up at the right moment.'

'Just coincidence,' he responded. 'Glad to have been of help. I'll call back some other time to discuss the real reason for my call.'

'I'll look forward to that,' she replied with the hint of a smile.

'What did I just say?' Isobel muttered while going to the Land Rover to check on Màiri and Iain. She was puzzled and confused - and yet - her previous mood of gloom and doom had been lifted slightly by Tormod's surprise visit. Since Màiri was awake, Isobel picked her up and was making her way towards the cottage when Claire's car pulled up at the gate. By the time she'd returned to the Land Rover to get Iain, Claire was in the yard.

'I met Tormod MacAlister on the track,' she began in a condescending tone. 'Thankfully, not on the part where's there's a sheer drop and no room to pass. What was *he* doing here,' she added, casting a suspicious glance in Isobel's direction.

'Not that it's any of your business,' Isobel began cagily, 'but he was here on business.'

Claire didn't pursue the matter but asked her to spill the beans about the reason for her phone call earlier in the day. Isobel proceeded to enlighten her about the lawyer's letter and Calum walking out and leaving her with no-one to tend the livestock or prepare the rams for Saturday's show – and that was only the short term problems – the long term ones didn't even bear thinking about.

'I can help you with one, but not the other,' Claire responded after listening intently.

'One, I can probably solve myself, but the other, I don't know where to begin,' Isobel said as if thinking aloud.

134

'My advice would be to keep the property in London and sell the one in Dumlocher,' Claire replied. 'As for finding a replacement for Calum, I wouldn't know where to start.'

Claire went on to say that a property in Bayswater would be a valuable asset in the future. It could be rented out and provide financial security for the rest of her life, not to mention, a legacy for the children. She finished by saying she would inform Rob on his return from London and arrange for the three of them to meet up to discuss it further.

'Thanks Claire,' Isobel replied and flashed a smile of gratitude. 'I just can't get my head around all of this at the moment.'

'Rob is due to return on Friday evening, why don't you come to Inverculden on Sunday,' Claire remarked.

'I would like that,' Isobel replied, before adding, 'Ask Rob to invite Helen, I would like to break the news of my inheritance to her personally.'

'That's a wonderful idea,' Claire responded. 'It'll be good for us all to meet up again.'

****

Chapter 25

With Claire gone, Isobel was alone once more. There was much on her mind as she set about preparing food for Máiri, the dogs, and finally, herself. Once that task had been successfully completed, there was an urgent and slightly more hazardous task to be undertaken – bringing the milking cow from the meadow to the byre. Daisy had recently come to the end of her productive life and her replacement was a dairy cow she'd selected, with Calum's help, at a recent stock sale. How she was going to get to the field with Máiri and Iain, not to mention, persuade the young cow to come into the yard and not go walkabout on the hill, she couldn't begin to imagine. Since Calum had already told her that the young cow was spooked by dogs, it would be pointless taking Floss and Ben. While deliberating over her present predicament, a vehicle drew up in the yard. Three visitors in one day, she mused, this is something of a record. The door opened and Gordon and Mairead walked in without uttering a word. Isobel was almost certain that Mairead's expression was one of guilt, while Gordon's was most definitely one of anguish.
'We need to talk,' he began.
'We're here to apologise,' Mairead added.
'I was just about to bring Bluebell in for milking,' Isobel interrupted.
'I'll get Bluebell,' Gordon offered.
'I'll put the kettle on,' Mairead added.
'I'll just sit down then,' Isobel muttered under her breath.
'I'm so sorry for being abrupt and tetchy with you earlier,' Mairead sobbed.
Isobel couldn't fail to notice the anguish etched on her face as she struggled to speak through her fits of sobbing. In fact, this wasn't the same Mairead she'd known for the past sixteen years. This was a completely unfamiliar Mairead, and it concerned her deeply. Mairead took a sip of her tea before continuing, 'We received bad news in the morning post and Calum coming out with the news that he had been fired from his job at the croft was just the last straw.'
'I'm so sorry to hear that,' Isobel responded. 'Just for the

136

record though, I didn't fire Calum. We had a difference of opinion and he decided to leave. Are you going to tell me about your bad news? Or is it personal?' she added in a sympathetic tone.

'It's very personal,' Mairead began. 'It's something I'd rather folk didn't know, but I suppose it'll come out soon enough, and when it does, the gossips in the village will have a field day.'

'Mairead, I'm completely baffled. I have no idea what you're talking about, but I'm sure you know that if there's anything I can do to help, you only have to ask.'

'Thanks, but unless you've come into a fortune recently, there's nothing you can do,' Mairead replied despondently.

'Can you elaborate?' Isobel asked with a look of concern.

'We've run into a bad patch financially,' Mairead sobbed. 'We've no money to pay the rent and Gordon's had to sell some of his prized Highland cattle just to keep the bank off our backs.'

'I can help you,' Isobel said softly.

'It'll break out hearts if we have to leave here,' she sobbed. 'I'm quite sure it would kill Gordon........ What did you just say?'

'I said, I can help you,' Isobel replied.

'Your situation here is almost as bad as ours,' Mairead responded in a bemused tone. 'How in heaven's name could you help? I won't allow you to borrow any money from Rob.'

'Mairead, just keep quiet for two minutes and allow me to speak. John has left his entire estate to me. I have more money than I'll ever be able to spend in my lifetime, and I want to help. I owe you and Gordon my life.'

Mairead rose from the chair, threw her arms around Isobel and the two women dissolved into floods of tears.

'Calum told us you had changed. He said you were cold and uncaring. He called you a snob for looking down on him because he worked for you,' Mairead blurted out between sobs. 'And for a short time, I was foolish enough to believe him.'

'Mairead, for as long as I live, I will never change,' Isobel began. 'And for as long as I live in the Black Glen, I will do

137

everything in my power to ensure that you and Gordon remain my nearest and dearest friends.'

Gordon walked into the kitchen at that very moment cursing under his breath and muttering that he had never encountered such a thrawn, awkward, and downright difficult milking cow as the one he'd just chased round the meadow.

'Don't worry Gordon,' Isobel remarked with a smile, 'Give me a few weeks with her and she'll be as docile as a lamb.'

Noticing the red-rimmed eyes on the two women, he asked sarcastically, 'Have you two been drinking?'

Mairead scowled. 'Don't make light of our dire situation,' she reprimanded.

Gordon tutted, before saying, 'Well, one of us has to keep a sense of humour. It's all doom and gloom around these parts at the moment. John's dead. A man's vanished into thin air. Isobel is without a crofter, and you and I are on the brink of bankruptcy. What else could possibly go wrong?' he added scathingly.

'Nothing,' Isobel responded. 'From now on, everything will be just fine,'

She went on to tell Gordon about the terms of John's will, and finished by saying, 'Some of the funds have already been transferred into my bank account. In addition, I'm planning to sell the house in Dumlocher. Tell me what sort of figure you need in the short term and I'll arrange for it to be transferred into your bank account.'

Gordon sank into the armchair beside the range and buried his face in his hands. 'I can't let you do that,' he muttered.

'What's stopping you?' Isobel asked

He shook his head and said, 'Pride.'

'Then why not come and work for me. That way, we'll be helping each other.'

Since first befriending the tenants of the farm at the foot of the glen, Isobel had been aware that Gordon, Mairead, and Calum had bent over backwards to assist their neighbours at the croft, and now, she could reciprocate their generosity.

Suddenly, Isobel had a purpose in life again. She was overjoyed at the thought of being able to help her life-long friends in their time of need. Not only that, but with Gordon helping out on the croft, there would no longer be any personal encumbrances in her life. That night, for the first in ages, she went to bed and slept like the proverbial log. Gordon had promised to help get the rams ready for the Ardbuie show on Saturday, and on Sunday, she planned to travel to Inverculden to meet up with her three siblings.

Making her way to the byre the following morning, Isobel was surprised to see a car pull up in the yard. Two dark-suited men emerged from the vehicle and asked her name before enquiring if she could spare them a few minutes of her time.

Before reaching the back door of the cottage, the men introduced themselves as officers from the Dumlocher branch of the CID. Isobel was suspicious to say the least and insisted that they produce proof of identity. Once satisfied, she invited them into the cottage. The officers then went on to explain that they were co-ordinating an investigation in conjunction with the local police force. This was in regard to a recent bank robbery in Dumlocher and subsequent murder enquiry. Isobel's confusion was growing by the minute. What had all this to do with her?

'Information gleaned from witnesses on the day of the robbery suggests that four men were involved in the crime,' one began. 'It is our belief that we have one of the suspects in custody. We've also been informed that he was apprehended here. Due to injuries inflicted by your dog, we have been unable to question him until now.'

'He is a known criminal,' the other began, 'and at the moment, we have no evidence to link him to the robbery, unless of course, the murder weapon – or the stolen cash – turns up.'

'What can I do?' Isobel asked nervously.

'Keep your doors locked at all times and report any prowlers without hesitation,' one replied.

'And if you happen to find a piece of ground that looks as if it's been disturbed recently, do likewise,' the other added.

With that, they departed, leaving Isobel in a state of bewilderment, anxiety and confusion. How could this remote, tranquil and idyllic haven be connected to a murder investigation?

The day of the Ardbuie agricultural show duly came around and was one of mixed emotions for Isobel. Despite her best efforts to enjoy the carnival atmosphere that prevails on such an occasion, memories of previous years weighed heavily on her mind. As always, it was a family day out and she met up with Ruaridh, Rob, Helen and Claire. The icing on the cake though, as on previous years, was that two of her rams picked up prizes and one was awarded best in show. Claire, never having experienced the excitement of a rural agricultural show, was positively bursting with enthusiasm. Isobel recalled having experienced exactly the same feeling on previous occasions, except that this year, she was alone.

'There's a ceilidh in the village hall tonight,' Claire enthused, 'I'm not missing that for anything.' Glancing at Isobel, she added, 'You must come.'

'I'm not going to the ceilidh,' Isobel responded solemnly.

'Party pooper,' Claire scoffed.

Her memories of previous ceilidhs spent with John were still raw and Isobel was determined her sister wouldn't cajole her into attending.

'Have a good time, I'll see you all tomorrow,' she called before leaving the showground.

The following day, Isobel drove to Inverculden. The main purpose of her visit was to talk things over with Rob. Hopefully, this would allow her to make an informed decision on the London property. While appreciating Claire's attempt to advise her on the issue with the two properties, and having given some thought to her advice, Rob was the one whose opinion she would most likely heed. After a lengthy discussion, Rob, like Claire, had strongly advised that she hold on to the property in London, while leaving the decision on the property in Dumlocher to Isobel. Rob also suggested several ways of investing her fortune to ensure that it paid lucrative dividends in the years to come.

Isobel was enjoying the day with her siblings, especially the respite she'd had from looking after Iain and Màiri. Isla had taken them for a short walk, and upon their return, Helen had taken over for much of the time. Isobel was concerned about Helen though. As a child, she'd looked upon her eldest sister as a role model and the pair had shared a close affinity since that time. The two sisters had been blessed with a strong, indomitable character, but today, Isobel was concerned to find Helen rather downcast and subdued.

'Are you all right?' she asked when they had a brief moment alone.

'Not really, but I can't say any more at the moment,' Helen replied despondently.

As for Claire, her incessant chattering was beginning to get on Isobel's nerves; the ceilidh the previous evening being her main topic of conversation.

'I *have* been to a ceilidh before,' Isobel snapped in frustration.

'Yes, but you weren't there *last* night,' Claire jibed.

'I was quite happy with my canine companions,' Isobel responded casually.

'I was more than happy with *my* companion,' Claire retorted with a smug expression.

'Oh, did you find a handsome husband,' Isobel teased.

'He would do,' Claire replied. 'He ticks most of the boxes. Young, unattached, property owner, reasonably handsome, professional.....'

'I can't think of anyone around here who fits that description,' Isobel remarked with a wry smile. 'Do I know him?'

'Yes, but from what he told me last night, you and he don't get on', she replied brusquely.

Isobel, now in no doubt about the identity of her sister's suitor, wondered why she was becoming more infuriated by the minute.

'I can't begin to fathom the reason for you disliking Tormod,' Claire rattled on. 'He's polite and kind, and what's more, we have a date next Friday evening.'

'I only hope he doesn't disappoint,' Isobel responded drily.

Before leaving Inverculden that day, she arranged to meet up with Helen in the near future for a heart to heart. During her meeting with Rob, he'd suggested that they fly to London

141

together. Isobel had agreed, albeit with reluctance. For one thing, she hadn't flown before. There was also the problem of leaving the croft, the animals and the two children.

****

Chapter 26

The working arrangement between Gordon, Mairead and Isobel was proving to be advantageous to all concerned. Isobel was enjoying having the cottage to herself again, minus Calum at least, and Gordon was helping out at the croft on a part-time basis. On the numerous occasions that Mairead accompanied him, she doubled up as a child minder. They were each paid generously for their labours and looked upon the extra cash as a godsend. In fact, Isobel was surprised when Gordon, not a religious man by any means, had come out with a phrase her father often quoted: "God works in mysterious ways".

The current arrangement also enabled Isobel to ease herself gently back into crofting – the job she and John had originally come here to do. On this particular day, since Mairead was in the cottage with Iain and Máiri, Isobel decided to ride out to the graveyard in the Black Glen. As yet, she hadn't erected a memorial to her beloved husband and decided that, since she could now afford to, this would be given top priority. Given the remote location, similar to the ones she'd placed at the graves of her collie Meg and her mother Moss, the memorial to John would have to be easily transported.

As she and Kismet approached the ruined cottage, they met a group of climbers. Following a brief conversation, they went on their way towards the foothills and it was then that another idea, one she'd harboured since her early visits to the croft, came to mind. It was an idea she'd once put to Rob, and which he'd regarded to be both impossible and ridiculous. Isobel though, had never let his opinion dissuade her from pursuing it when the time was right. Now, she said to herself, is the right time. She had always known that her childhood dream of establishing a mountain rescue centre at the croft was achievable; now though, it was a step closer to being within reach. One of the stumbling blocks, as far as Rob was concerned, had been the cost involved. "Who would fund it?" he'd asked. Another question had been: "Who would set it up?" Now, she had the funds and was perfectly capable of organising it herself. There was just the minor problem that none of her current dogs were trained in search and rescue. Fly, once a proficient tracking dog, was nearing the end of his life. Both Moss and Meg, once equally adept at finding missing climbers, were dead, and Floss had never been given the opportunity. As for Dileas, the dog she didn't even own, she hadn't been out on the hills since the day she'd savaged the flock. That, she said to herself, will have to be rectified, and soon. Now, Isobel had a mission, albeit a challenging one, but one she was determined to see come to fruition.

On reaching the graveyard, Isobel dismounted and looped Kismet's reins loosely over the metal railings. Recalling a previous, rather fraught visit to the ruined croft with Kismet, she could hardly believe how biddable her little pony had become. Kismet dropped her head and began to graze on the unfamiliar fodder at her feet. Isobel noticed that the reins had become detached from the railings but let the pony wander off.

After scaling the metal fence, Isobel walked towards the burial ground. With each and every carefully placed step, her heart-rate changed up a gear. The tiny graveyard behind the ruined cottage had held a special fascination for her long before it had become the resting place of her two beloved pets, and more recently, her husband. For over three hundred years it had been the sacred burial ground of four young children, their charred remains having been carried from the burnt out shell of the nearby cottage by their heartbroken parents. It was their callous murder that had given rise to the legend of the curse of the Black Glen. Over the years, death and tragedy had befallen all those who'd dared to set foot on the hallowed ground, John included. Isobel though, for a reason as yet unknown, hadn't fallen victim to the curse. While scattering a few wild flowers on the grass covered tombs of the deceased, she recalled the words of the midwife: "I have the gift of second sight."

Apart from the distant bleating of an anxious ewe calling to her lamb, the silence in the glen was almost tangible. Just then, the mournful sound of weeping cut through the eerie stillness like a knife. Only this time, there was no mysterious source. Isobel's tears were for all those who had fallen foul of the curse of the Black Glen, but today, she wept mainly for herself.

Now mounted on Kismet's back, the pair ambled slowly back to the croft. The leisurely pace combined with the silence and serenity of the glen, gave Isobel time to mull over the thoughts that were spinning around inside her head. She had so many unanswered questions, but today, unlike her childhood days when Rob had provided all the answers, there were none.

****

Chapter 27

Gordon arrived for work the following day with a message from Rob. Apparently he'd phoned the farmhouse the previous evening asking that Isobel contact him at her earliest convenience. My days are so full at the moment, he may have to wait, she thought to herself while feeding the chickens. On second thoughts, she could kill two birds - or several in this case - with one stone, and make a few phone calls. One call would be to John's lawyer to arrange a meeting. One would be to Helen to arrange a meeting. One would be to Rob, and the other, to the local joiner.

However, a vehicle drawing into the yard as she was about to leave the croft, scuppered her well laid plans. The occupants of the car were an elderly couple, and as they emerged from the vehicle, Isobel couldn't help thinking that they looked familiar.

The man greeted her with the words, 'Good Day. I do hope we're not intruding. I must apologise for our unexpected visit, but we've come to see the dog.'

'The dog,' Isobel repeated in a questioning tone.

'I believe you have my son's dog,' he began. 'I'm sorry, I should have introduced myself, my name is Dr Thornton.'

'Isobel Caldwell,' she replied, shaking his outstretched hand. 'You would know me better as Isobel Ferguson.'

The woman, who'd remained silent until now, piped up in a tone of surprise, 'You must be Robert and Nancy Ferguson's daughter. Well, well, well, isn't this a coincidence.'

Coincidence! Isobel mouthed the word, while thinking - that word again. How many times has it cropped up in my life? And yet, each "coincidence" has marked a significant event, or turning point, in my life.

'Would you care to come inside for a cup of tea?' she asked politely.

'That's very kind of you,' Dr Thornton replied, 'but if you don't mind, I would rather see the dog.'

Isobel's head was in a spin – for many reasons. The first one was Dileas, the dog they'd come to see. She'd grown so attached to her that she couldn't bear to think about being

146

parted from her now, and the feeling was reciprocated. She was also aware that, as the parents of the dog's legal owner, they had the right to take the dog from her if they so wished. Another reason for her turmoil was the chance meeting with two of her former neighbours in such bizarre circumstances. Being conscious of the fact that Máiri and Iain were in the Land Rover, Isobel insisted on taking them into the cottage before going to the byre, where she'd left Dileas.

'I'll stay with the children if you like,' Mrs Thornton suggested. 'I never trusted that dog. I have no wish to see it again.'

With the children happily settled in the cottage, Isobel led the way to the byre. She had to stifle a snigger on turning her head to see Dr Thornton wading through the mire in his polished shoes.

'Dileas you have a visitor,' she called as they entered the gloomy shed.

'Her name is Freya,' Dr Thornton corrected while wiping his shoes on the straw.

'She answers to Dileas now,' Isobel replied drily.

Now unleashed, Dileas came to sit at Isobel's feet. She wagged her tail in recognition of the man beside her mistress, but bared her teeth and snarled as he took a step towards her.

'It's my son's dog without a doubt,' Dr Thornton began. 'But I can't understand her change of temperament. She was always so friendly.'

'We are completely in the dark as to what happened,' Isobel began. 'All I know is that she is extremely lucky to have survived and is happily settled here.'

She went on to give Dr Thornton a detailed explanation of the circumstances, and finished by saying, 'What do you plan to do with her?'

'The police are no nearer to solving our son's mysterious disappearance,' he began. 'My wife and I have given up hope of ever seeing him again and are now resigned to that fact. Because of the polio he suffered as a child, his legs never regained their full strength and we fear he has fallen to his death. The only question we would like answered is, where?

Had his remains been found, at least we would have closure. My wife and I thought that by seeing the dog and ascertaining that it was indeed Robert's, we would know the proximity of his final resting place.'

'I've not been out on the hills for almost two years,' Isobel began, 'mainly due to the fact that I have given birth to two children in quick succession. Prior to that, me and my collies were on the hills every day and between us, found many unfortunate victims. Some, we were able to rescue - others, we couldn't. I'm hoping to establish a mountain rescue centre here very soon though.'

'I fear it will be too late for Robert,' Dr Thornton remarked with a wry smile. 'Is the offer of tea still open?'

'Yes, of course,' Isobel replied. 'Dileas, come.'

'Is she allowed inside?' Dr Thornton enquired as Dileas walked towards the cottage at Isobel's side.

Isobel laughed. 'Dileas is by my side all day long and at night, she sleeps beside my bed. She was only in the byre because I was on my way out when you arrived.'

Floss came to meet them as they entered the kitchen, before going to lie on the mat in front of the log fire beside Dileas.

Dr Thornton took a sip of his tea, looked at his wife and said, 'Darling, I've changed my mind about taking Freya home with us. She is obviously very happy here, and has an excellent home.'

'Thank goodness for that,' she sighed. She then turned to Isobel and continued, 'Soon after we left Dumlocher, we lost our youngest son Benjamin to meningitis, and so, we have no grandchildren. Richard thought that by having Robert's dog, it would fill the gap in our lives. I though, have never liked dogs, they scare me to death. Especially that one,' she added, glancing warily at Dileas.

'You have two beautiful children,' Mrs Thornton remarked before leaving. 'Your parents are truly blessed to have grandchildren. I do hope they appreciate them. Alas, there is no chance of us ever becoming grandparents now.'

Isobel suddenly had a flashback to her childhood, when she, Mary and Robert were fifteen years old. Robert was the father

148

of the illegitimate child that Mary had been forced to give up for adoption, and the words came tumbling out,
'You *have* a grandchild....'
 If only she could have bitten her tongue, but it was too late.
Mrs Thornton fell back into the seat she'd just vacated. 'I don't know what you are talking about,' she gasped.
Dr Thornton stood in silence, the colour draining from his face by the minute.
'Have *you* any idea what she's talking about?' his wife asked accusingly.
'I think I need another cup of tea', he muttered under his breath.
By this time, Iain was demanding to be fed and Isobel made her stupefied guests another cup of tea, before excusing herself to breastfeed her baby.
She returned to the kitchen to find Mrs Thornton sobbing her heart out.
'All those years,' she wailed. 'You have known for all those years and I didn't know.'
Her words were directed at her husband, who by this time, was also on the verge of tears.
'I couldn't be sure,' he began. 'Robert always denied being the father.'
'There was never any doubt in my mind,' Isobel interrupted drily. 'Or my best friend Mary's for that matter. She has never recovered, and probably never will, from having to give her firstborn child up for adoption.'
'Mary Anderson,' Mrs Thornton began slowly. 'I remember the scandal in the cul-de-sac. She was only fifteen years old when she got herself pregnant.'
'Yes, she was,' Isobel cut in. 'She was also my best friend. Still is I may add, and it takes two to make a baby, in case you had forgotten.'
Isobel's anger was rising. It wasn't directed at his parents, but at Robert Thornton - the missing man, owner of Dileas - the schoolboy she had bestowed a curse on all those years ago.
Mrs Thornton's anguished voice interrupted her thoughts. 'Has Mary any idea who adopted our grandchild?'

'We never discuss it,' Isobel replied quietly, 'but if she did, I'm sure she would have told me.'

'He'll be eleven years old now,' Mrs Thornton remarked with a faint smile.

'Mary was never told if it was a boy or a girl she'd given birth to,' Isobel responded rather sharply. 'All she did was sign the adoption papers; under duress as I understand.'

Isobel recalled the hatred she'd felt for Robert Thornton at the time. She could still see the anguish etched on Mary's face when telling her that Dr Thornton had come to the house to discuss the options of abortion or adoption with her parents. Mary hadn't even been consulted, or given the chance to say what *she* wanted. She'd also been asked by her parents, in front of Dr Thornton, to name the baby's father. When confronted by his father and asked to reveal the truth, Robert, of course, had denied it. He even went so far as to call Mary a liar and a slut; his father, of course, had believed him. Following Mary's departure from the cul-de-sac, Robert had gloated and boasted to his school friends that, once again, he hadn't been caught; until he was struck down with polio that is. They were only fifteen years old at the time and Mary, unlike Robert, was naïve, gullible and deeply in love. Isobel knew that the ache in her heart and the gap left in her life by losing her baby to adoptive parents would be carried to the grave.

'We must find our grandchild,' Mrs Thornton said in a solemn tone.

'We can't do that. We have no rights,' Dr Thornton responded.

His wife merely continued in the same tone, 'He, or she, is our grandchild, our flesh and blood and the only person in the world to whom we can bestow our estate.'

With a look of humiliation, Dr Thornton glanced at Isobel and remarked, 'I must apologise. We shouldn't be discussing this in front of you. After all, we only came here to collect the dog.'

'I thought you weren't taking her,' Isobel cried out in anguish.

'I've changed my mind,' he began apologetically. 'As my wife has just said, we have nothing, or no-one left in our lives now. At least if we take the dog, we'll have something

150

belonging to Robert. And, if he does turn up safe and well, his dog will be at home waiting for him.'

'Where, exactly, is home?' Isobel asked, trying to hold back the tears.

'I'll leave our contact details,' he replied. 'Can I ask that you notify Mary of our visit and give her our kindest regards,' he added.

'I will,' Isobel mumbled while attaching a leash to Dileas' collar.

It was a slightly confused and hugely reluctant canine passenger that left An Gleann Dubh with Dr and Mrs Thornton that afternoon. As for Isobel, she returned to the cottage and wept buckets of tears. Although only a short time had elapsed since the stray dog appeared in the glen, she had grown extremely fond of her. Glancing at the address on the slip of paper through tear-filled eyes, she gasped, 'I don't believe it. They're taking Dileas to London.'

****

Chapter 28

Isobel busied herself around the cottage in the hopes that by doing so it would take her mind off the empty space on the mat beside Floss and Fly; but to no avail. Every few minutes, her shoulders would heave as another fit of sobbing engulfed her body. The sound of someone knocking at the kitchen door made her jump. She ran to the door, hoping against hope it was the Thorntons bringing Dileas back, and was mortified to see Tormod MacAlister standing there.

'I'm so sorry,' he began. 'I knocked on the outer door, but you obviously didn't hear..... Are you all right?'

Next moment, she was in his arms.

'This is becoming a habit,' Tormod said softly as he held her close.

'Your visits - or me being in your arms,' Isobel responded nervously.

'Both. And the fact that, each time we meet I find you in tears.'

Isobel found herself relating the bizarre events of the afternoon to the young vet, without understanding, or even caring about, the reason. During the conversation he informed her that his visit was business related and explained further that he had come to discuss some new government rules that applied to all sheep-breeders in the area.

'That was the reason for my last visit, and which I didn't get time to discuss,' he continued.

'I believe you're dating my sister,' Isobel remarked casually while placing the kettle on the stove.

'It's nothing serious,' he responded hastily, 'just a visit to the cinema. A new Elvis film I was eager to see is showing in Drumevie and Claire told me she was a fan of his on the night of the ceilidh.'

Liar, Isobel said to herself. Claire has never liked pop music.

With all the restraint she could muster, Isobel replied casually, 'I didn't know he had a new film out. I've seen all the others.'

'It's called "Double Trouble",' Tormod replied.

152

Isobel smiled at the irony. Once again, the name of the film was applicable to her current situation....... Or perhaps not. With Dileas her protector gone, having let the cat out the bag about the Thornton's grandchild, the quandary over her two newly acquired properties, and the latest, her conflicting feelings for Tormod MacAlister, her current troubles had multiplied. Not only was her long-held dislike for the young vet rapidly diminishing - but worse than that - she was actually beginning to like him.

The sound of his voice brought her back to reality.

'If I'd asked, would you have come with me?'

'To the cinema,' she gushed, 'Probably not.' While at the same time, wondering why she was fibbing.

'What would my chances be next time?' he continued with a mischievous grin.

'That depends,' she replied demurely.

'That's not an answer,' he chided.

'I'm sorry. I can't give you an answer at the moment.' Her voice tailed away - her expression forlorn.

'Isobel, forgive me,' he began in a solemn tone. 'I shouldn't be adding to your problems. I appreciate the fact that you are recently bereaved and have no interest in socialising.'

In a voice that was little more than a whisper, she began by saying, 'As a child, I dreamt of living here for the rest of my life. I'm living my dream. Who would have thought it would turn into a nightmare.'

'Is there anything I can do to help?' he asked gently, 'If so, you only have to ask.'

Isobel could think of no rational or practical reason for proceeding to burden Tormod MacAlister with her present dilemma over the two properties bequeathed to her in John's will, but she did.

'Claire has advised me to keep the property in London and sell the one in Dumlocher,' she added.

'Have you seen either of the properties?' he queried.

'Not the one in London,' she replied.

She went on to tell him about her and John having stayed in the house in Dumlocher and that she and Rob were planning

153

to fly to London soon to collect the keys and view the other house.

'That's another problem,' she said shamefully, 'I'm too embarrassed to admit to Rob that I'm scared to fly.'

'But not to me,' he quipped.

Isobel smiled. She hadn't thought about it like that.

'I like you when you're smiling,' he said softly.

'Does that mean you don't when I'm not?' she asked coyly.

Tormod looked away and avoided the question.

'I could make a suggestion,' he began, 'though I don't know how you'll respond.'

'If you don't ask, you'll never know the answer,' she replied with a faint smile.

'I have a week's holiday coming up quite soon. My experience of travelling to date has been extremely limited and I wouldn't mind spending a few days in London. We could travel there together..... by road.'

Although taken aback by his suggestion, Isobel's initial thought was that it would solve a few problems. Despite beginning to find the idea quite exciting, she replied demurely, 'I would need some time to think it over.'

'Take all the time you need,' he replied while glancing anxiously at his watch.

'I really have to go. I've got evening surgery in less than an hour.'

It had been yet another eventful day for Isobel. One that had brought with it a whole host of roller coaster emotions. Although having felt a degree of pity for Dr and Mrs Thornton, she also felt that they, or at least he, had brought their heartache upon themselves. She was also heartbroken about Dileas, the dog whose life she'd saved and was now on her way to London. But the strangest emotion was the one she'd experienced when Tormod MacAlister had been here. It was one of safety and serenity. She'd been aware of an ambience in the cottage that had been missing for many years. It was one she associated with more pleasant times spent here as a child.

****

Chapter 29

For the second time this week, Isobel left the cottage with the intention of visiting Helen and Rob. This time, she was hoping to get further than the yard. A few days had passed since her surprise visitors had scuppered her plans and it was imperative that she speak with Rob. Tormod's suggestion that they drive to London together was quite tempting. With flying becoming ever more popular as a means of commuting these days, Isobel had added it to her list of phobias and vowed never to become airborne. The other reason for her eagerness to leave the croft was to talk to her sister Helen and find out what was troubling her. Although the siblings shared a close bond, she couldn't begin to imagine what it could be. Since their very first meeting almost sixteen years ago, Isobel had known her eldest sister to be tough and resilient. The two sisters also shared the common trait of being indifferent to anything that didn't revolve around their own family unit.

Driving up the track that led to the farm, she spotted Helen in one of the fields and stopped the Land Rover. Helen, having seen her, jumped down from the tractor and began to walk across the field towards her.

'Hi. What a lovely surprise,' she called, 'I'll hitch a lift to the farm with you.'

After removing her dungarees and wellingtons, Helen washed her hands before making a mug of coffee for Isobel.

'Are you not joining me?' Isobel asked.

'In a minute,' she replied. 'Once I've hugged my little nephew.' Helen lifted Iain from the Moses basket, saying, 'I hope you don't mind me picking him up.'

'Of course not - why should I?' Isobel replied.

'Babies are so fragile. If he were mine, I wouldn't let anyone pick him up.'

Helen and Ruaridh were married on the same day as John and Isobel, almost six years ago, and Isobel was surprised that they hadn't made a start to their family before now. The subject had often been discussed during their girly chats and Helen, being more maternal than Isobel, had confided that she hoped to conceive straight away and go on to have a large family. With this thought in mind, Isobel remarked casually, 'One day soon, you'll have a baby of your own to cuddle.'

Helen fled from the room in tears, leaving Isobel completely bewildered. She returned a few minutes later, blowing her nose into a handkerchief.

'Forgive me Isobel, but Ruaridh and I have just been told that we'll never have children of our own.'

'Oh Helen,' Isobel began ruefully. 'It's me who should be apologising. Do you feel like talking about it?'

'I'll be driven to despair if I don't talk to someone soon,' she replied despondently. 'Neither of us has told anyone yet, and now, Ruaridh won't even discuss it with me.'

For the next hour or so, Isobel doubled up as "Agony Aunt" while Helen poured out all her troubles. She also confided that the stress of the situation was causing a rift between her and Ruaridh. For as long as Isobel could remember, she'd known Helen and Ruaridh to be inseparable. They worked together on the farm from morn 'til night, socialised together and shared their life as husband and wife and best friends. Recently though, according to Helen, Ruaridh had begun to go out alone in the evenings, sometimes not returning home until the early hours of the morning. Rumours were rife among the locals that he'd been seen with a young girl from the village.

She finished by saying, 'I am absolutely heartbroken. I married the man of my dreams, and now, I feel as though I'm losing him.'

Helen's words brought tears to Isobel's eyes.

'You and me both,' she said softly. 'I married the man of my dreams that day, and I've lost him too.'

The two sisters hugged and consoled each other until jolted from their state of mutual mourning by the sound of Máiri crying. Isobel bent down and picked her up.

'You don't know how lucky you are to have been blessed with two beautiful children,' Helen said tearfully.

Recalling Mrs Thornton's words to the same effect a few days earlier, Isobel replied, 'I do. I truly do.'

Helen rose and put the kettle on the stove, before laying the kitchen table with crockery and cutlery.

'It's almost lunch-time, Ruaridh will be here soon. You may as well join us,' she said.

'I can't stay very long. I'm on my way to Inverculden,' Isobel replied while helping her sister set the table for lunch.

Ruaridh walked into the kitchen at that moment and appeared surprised and slightly embarrassed to see Isobel. Although previous visits to the farm had always been jovial and light-hearted, lunch was eaten in a strained and unusually sombre atmosphere that day. No sooner had Ruaridh finished his lunch than he rose from the table saying he had a hayfield to mow before nightfall. While clearing the table, Isobel asked her sister if she'd considered adoption.'

'Adoption!' she exclaimed. 'Raising someone else's child could never compensate for having one of my own.'

Isobel reminded her that Rob had been adopted by Laird and Lady Inverculden and they'd been loving and devoted parents. She then went on to tell her about the visit from Dr and Mrs Thornton.

Similar to Rob, Mary's child had been given up for adoption. It was due to the prevailing circumstances at the time and not because she was unloved or unwanted. Just as our parents felt about Rob, there isn't a day goes by that Mary doesn't dream of finding her lost child.

'It just wouldn't be the same,' Helen said tearfully.

'All the same, it's something to think about,' Isobel replied.

Leaving the farm in a despondent and sombre frame of mind that day, Isobel's thoughts as she drove south were focused not on her own problems for a change, but on those of her beloved sister Helen.

Máiri and Iain were soon fast asleep and the journey south to Inverculden was a time of quiet reflection for Isobel. Helen's world, similar to her own, had been turned on its head. They'd both been faced with a completely different set of life-changing circumstances, yet each having the same outcome. Their once idyllic little world had been shattered and they could do nothing more than pick up the pieces and try to rebuild their lives.

There were many things on Isobel's mind as she drove the

last few yards towards the mansion house of Inverculden that day. The purpose of her visit was twofold. One was to seek Rob's advice on the London property, and the other, was to let him know that she wouldn't be accompanying him on the flight to London. The reason for her decision to travel south with Tormod MacAlister was a question she couldn't answer at that moment.

'Bella,' Rob called out in delight while running down the steps to meet her. 'My favourite sister, come inside and have afternoon tea.'

Isobel smiled. It was comforting to know that she hadn't been demoted from top place in her brother's affection by the irresistible Claire. As for having afternoon tea, it was less than an hour since she'd eaten lunch. Glancing at her watch, she saw that it was four o'clock. When Gordon had asked how long she would be away, she'd told him she hoped to be back in time for the afternoon milking. There was little chance of that now though.

Rob and Isobel, with Claire frequently butting in, discussed the best long term options regarding the two properties bequeathed to her in John's will.

Rob now frequented the city of London on a regular basis for social and business trips and was well qualified to give informed advice. Subsequently, he told Isobel that, in his opinion, she shouldn't sell the London property. He told her further that the rental market in London was on the rise, and in particular, the Bayswater area where the house was situated. As for the house in Dumlocher, unoccupied since John's parents returned to live in London, he advised her to sell it. Claire agreed wholeheartedly and remarked in a superior tone, 'That was my advice exactly.'

Rob glanced at Isobel and rolled his eyes upwards. Perhaps he is beginning to tire of Claire already she gloated, and returned his wry smile.

Rob's lifestyle was now far removed from his years spent in the back of beyond. The crofter from An Gleann Dubh, who at one time hadn't left the isolated croft for six years, was now jetting around the globe and living the life of a socialite as Laird of Inverculden. Once, his only aspiration in life was to be recognised locally as a reputable breeder of blackface rams. These days, he was gaining national acclaim as a breeder of champion hurdlers.

While driving back to the croft, Isobel had much on her mind; thoughts of Helen being uppermost. In second place was her forthcoming meeting with John's lawyer. While driving past the cottage where she'd spent the night, loosely speaking, with Tormod MacAlister, the impending trip to London with him as her companion also occupied her thoughts. The local gossips would have a field day when they found out. Now though, the snide remarks being whispered behind her back didn't matter in the least to Isobel. She stopped at the farmhouse before negotiating the last three miles of track through the glen. One reason was to telephone the lawyer's office in London and arrange a provisional date for the meeting, following which, she would phone Tormod.

****

Chapter 30

The date for the trip to London had now been confirmed. In two weeks time, Isobel, Tormod and the two children would travel south in the mini. Before then, Isobel had to find a local joiner.

The nearest joiner's business was in Drumevie and Mairead had offered to look after Máiri and Iain while she went off on her whimsical mission. Having put forward her proposal to both Gordon and Mairead, they, like Rob had thought she was crazy. Granted, with Dileas gone, she only had one dog, or at least one that was capable of being trained in search and rescue.

At the joiner's yard, Isobel was greeted by a youngish man with white hair. Once he'd run his hands through it and removed the sawdust, she observed it was actually blonde.

'Mrs Caldwell,' he said, dusting sawdust from his clothes. 'What can I do for you?'

It hadn't escaped Isobel's notice that his eyes had a mischievous glint while being fleetingly cast over her body.

Choosing to disregard his ambiguous greeting, she proceeded to explain in detail the idea she'd run past him in her telephone call - her idea of constructing two wooden shelters high up on the mountains in the Black Glen - and asked if he thought it was possible.

'If you set your mind to it, anything's possible,' he replied with a roguish grin.

A man after my own heart, she thought, and returned his smile.

He went on to say, 'I'm quite sure I could do something for you. Obviously, I would have to make a site visit.'

Isobel laughed and responded by saying, 'A site visit. What's your hourly rate?'

'I charge three pounds an hour, but I don't usually charge for my first visit. Give me your address and we can arrange a suitable date.'

Isobel explained that, given its remote location, the "site visit" would probably take up the best part of a day. To which he replied: 'I'm free all day Sunday.'

'Do you work on a Sunday?' she asked in dismay.

'Not normally, but I won't look upon it as work,' he teased. 'I'll consider it to be leisure – and hopefully - pleasure.'

Isobel was slightly bemused as she left the joiner's yard. While aware that the young man had been flirting with her, she was surprised to feel flattered. He was rakishly good-looking and oozed charisma, slightly roguish, but incredibly likeable. Although still mourning for John, a tiny part of her was beginning to yearn for male company. She would never consider entering into a serious relationship, but an innocent friendship wouldn't go amiss. Being a young widow, she was aware that some men would perhaps look upon her as being desperately lonely, and therefore, easy prey. She was also aware that if news of her inheritance became public knowledge, she could be courted for all the wrong reasons. Isobel Caldwell wasn't one to be taken in easily though. She had a sensible head on her shoulders. As for her heart, it would belong to John until the day she drew her final breath.

Today was Sunday and Mairead was already at the croft to mind the children while Isobel accompanied the joiner onto the hills. Having enough previous experience of the hazards facing mountaineers during blizzard conditions, she had two ideal locations for the bothies in mind. Whether or not her plan could be put into practice, was something she was about to find out.

Emerging from the pick-up, the young man apologised for not having introduced himself at their previous meeting. 'I'm Andrew MacLennan,' he said while shaking Isobel's hand, 'known to my friends as Drew.'

'Do I fall into that category?' she teased.

'I would like to think we could become friends,' he replied with a sly smile, 'What do you think?'

Avoiding both his gaze and his leading question, Isobel said hastily, 'I hope you don't mind if I take my dogs along.'

'By all means, I'm a dog lover myself,' he replied.

Isobel made her way to the byre with a slight spring in her step and unleashed Ben. She then returned to the cottage to get Floss. If only Dileas were here, she said to herself. It

161

would have been the ideal opportunity to take her onto the hills and re-introduce her to sheep.

As they scaled the rock strewn lower slopes of Beinn Ghlas, Drew suddenly stopped in his tracks.

'I have a horrible feeling that I may have to eat my words,' he said between gasps.

'Why is that?' Isobel asked with a bemused expression.

'Last time we met, I told you that anything is possible if you set your mind to it,' he began. 'Not only is the construction of a wooden shelter around here impossible, it would be bordering on insanity.'

'I hadn't thought of erecting it here,' Isobel replied indignantly, 'there's a plateau just a bit further up.'

'Further up,' he gasped in disbelief,' 'how much further up did you have in mind?'

'This is the easy part,' she quipped, smiling at his horrified expression. 'Until recently, I walked these hills every day. Not so much nowadays though. I fell pregnant and got a pony,' she added ruefully.

Drew stifled a laugh before saying, 'Let's rest awhile,' and sat down on a large boulder.

With Isobel now perched on another boulder, Floss and Ben came to lie by her side. It was a warm, balmy day with just the hint of a breeze and the conditions for hill walking were near perfect. The view from the spot they'd chosen to rest was spectacular and Isobel found herself lost in a moment of nostalgia. She had so many wonderful memories of being out on the hills on a day like this. If only, she said to herself.

The sound of Drew's voice made her jump. 'You truly are a remarkable young woman.'

'I beg your pardon,' she replied curtly.

He didn't respond straight away, but continued to gaze intently into her face. Isobel was aware of being mentally undressed, garment by garment, as his eyes slowly scanned every inch of her body.

'It takes a very special person to survive in such challenging conditions – alone - and with two young children, without the added complication of planning the construction of two mountain bothies.'

Her cheeks now burning with embarrassment, Isobel was glad of the distraction of being able to offer an explanation.

'Many years ago, I found two casualties out here,' she began ruefully, 'sadly, they didn't survive. Over the years, many climbers have become stranded, been injured, or lost their lives, and, as the pursuit of mountaineering becomes ever more popular, the need for shelters will become even greater. Establishing a mountain rescue centre is one of my unfulfilled childhood dreams,' she added wistfully.

'And the other?' he probed.

'My other dream died along with my husband,' she replied solemnly.

'Come on,' he said, pulling her to her feet. 'Show me this plateau.'

Drew kept a tight hold of Isobel's hand as they climbed higher up the rocky mountainside. She didn't withdraw it because he'd told her it was to make sure she didn't lose her footing. She didn't let on that, due to her familiarity with the terrain, her feet were as sure as a mountain goat's. In fact, if truth be known, there was more chance of him slipping. Perhaps it was for his benefit he was holding my hand, she mused. Whatever the reason, for the moment, she was happy to play along.

When at last they reached the plateau, they stopped for a second time.

'This is it,' Isobel remarked casually.

Much to her surprise, Drew's customary devil-may-care expression had been transformed into one of incredulity. As his eyes drank in the panorama before him, he said with complete sincerity, 'I'm so glad I came. Even if I don't get a job out of it, I wouldn't have missed this for the world.'

On the descent, as before, Drew kept a tight grip of Isobel's hand. By the time they'd reached the croft, they'd been gone for over three hours and Mairead was in the yard to meet them.

'I have to get back to the farm,' she shrieked. 'Gordon called me on the radio. He's had an accident.'

'I'll come with you,' Isobel called out as Mairead ran towards the Land Rover.

163

'Stay here. I'll call if I need you,' she responded anxiously.

The Land Rover disappeared in a cloud of dust and Mairead hadn't even stopped to close the gate. Isobel crossed the yard with the intention of closing it, and then changed her mind. After all, Drew would be leaving soon and she would close it once he'd gone. However, instead of heading towards his pick-up as Isobel had anticipated, Drew was making his way towards the cottage.

'I don't know about you, but I could murder a beer,' he began. 'I'm not used to all this exercise on my day off.'

Now, Isobel was beginning to feel guilty. After all, he'd given up his leisure time for her benefit and wasn't charging for it. The very least she could do was oblige. Therefore, against her better judgement, she ushered him inside.

Máiri was in her playpen and Iain was asleep in his Moses basket when they entered the kitchen and Isobel went to the pantry to fetch a can of beer. She was slightly annoyed to find Drew sprawled on the sofa on her return to the kitchen but managed to suppress it. Nonetheless, his over familiarity in what was once John's domain, didn't sit well with her.

'Come and sit down,' he said patting the empty space on the sofa beside him, 'you must be exhausted.'

'I'm fine,' she replied curtly, 'I have to feed my baby.'

Iain was now awake and beginning to whimper, which, as far as Isobel was concerned, was a relief. She couldn't bear the thought of sitting next to Drew on the sofa where she and John used to snuggle up together.

A brief moment of serenity followed her irritation as she lay on the bed with Iain latched onto her nipple. It was quickly replaced by a moment of panic when it dawned on her that she had left Máiri in the kitchen with a complete stranger. Despite having no grounds for concern, it suddenly struck her that she knew absolutely nothing about the man she and her children were alone with. Her thoughts were interrupted by the sight of Drew standing in the doorway.

'That's something I haven't seen before,' he said with a smile. 'It's the first time I've seen a woman's breast being used for the purpose it was intended. It puts the female body into a completely different perspective. I'll have to go,' he went on.

'Things to do. I'll come back and check out the second location another time.'

With that, he left, and Isobel let out a long sigh of relief. Returning to the kitchen with the intention of calling Mairead to enquire about Gordon, she spotted a highland cow sauntering past the window. This in itself wasn't unusual, except that, it wasn't one of her cows. It was then followed by another and another.......

'Oh no!' she cried in alarm. 'Drew hasn't closed the gate and Gordon's cattle have come in.'

This, she knew, could lead to disaster. If they couldn't be rounded up, and soon, they would make their way onto the open hills where her cattle were grazing. Apart from the fact that the two folds would become intermingled, it was breeding season. Torcall had more than his fair share of cows to service without Gordons' to boot. Silently thanking herself for having installed the two-way radio link, she made a frantic call. When Mairead picked up the receiver, Isobel blurted out the potentially disastrous situation she was facing at the croft.

'I can't help you,' she replied in an anxious state. 'I'm waiting for the ambulance to arrive. I think Gordon's leg is broken.'

'Can you call Rob - or anyone?' Isobel pleaded. 'I can't do anything on my own.'

Isobel then dashed from the cottage and closed the gate, but by this time, half the fold had already got through. The others, including the bull, were now bellowing in anger and frustration at the other side of the gate. As for the cattle that had got in, they were now disappearing into the distance towards the Black Glen.

Isobel was powerless to do anything. Leaving Iain and Máiri alone in the cottage to round up cattle would have been reckless, even by her standards, not to mention, totally irresponsible. There was nothing for it but to wait in the hopes that Mairead had been able to contact Rob. Almost an hour later, the sound of a vehicle stopping in the yard made her heart skip a beat with relief. Thinking it would be Rob, she was slightly bewildered to see Helen emerging from the pick-up.

165

'Did Mairead phone you?' Isobel asked with a look of confusion.

'Mairead. No. Why would she?' Helen replied with a similar expression.

'Then, why are you here?'

'I've left Ruaridh,' she replied in a sombre tone.

'Left him?' Isobel gasped.

'Yes. I walked out on him. Can I stay here?'

Isobel was shocked to say the least. Her thoughts were still on Gordon's cattle integrating with hers - and on Rob's impending arrival.

'Well?' Helen asked anxiously.

'Of course you can stay here,' Isobel replied. 'I'm sorry, I was miles away.'

Helen went on to say that she'd had to chase the cattle away from the gate before opening it.

'What's going on? In all the time I stayed here, never once did I see them milling around the gate.'

'I've got something of a problem,' Isobel began.

She proceeded to tell Helen about her trek out to Beinn Ghlas with the joiner from Drumevie, and why the gate had been left open in the first place. The sound of a vehicle drawing up outside interrupted the conversation and Isobel ran to the door to find Claire and Rob emerging from a brand new pick-up.

'Sorry for the delay,' Rob began. 'I received the urgent phone call from Mairead but had to collect my new set of wheels first.'

On seeing Helen, he frowned and said, 'What are you doing here?'

'I'll explain later. Let's see if we can round up Gordon's cattle first.'

After glancing scathingly at Claire's apparel, Isobel remarked, 'One of us will have to stay here with the children, and you're certainly not dressed for the outdoors.'

Claire, although obviously not amused at being left to mind the children, had little say in the matter. Her three siblings were already making their way towards the outer door.

Fortunately, the cattle had stopped to graze just beyond the

166

big meadow, approximately half a mile from the croft. Between them, Isobel, Rob and Helen coaxed and cajoled them into heading back the way they'd come. With the potential nightmare scenario now resolved, the trio made their way to the cottage.

'Well, at least that's the cattle sorted out,' Rob began. Looking directly at Helen, he went on, 'Now, are you going to explain why you're here?'

'Since when was it a sin to visit my young sister on a Sunday?' she responded in an exasperated tone.

'It's not a sin by any means,' he replied. 'It *is* a sin to tell a lie though. For a start, you would normally have brought Ruaridh along and I lived with you long enough to know when something is troubling you.'

'I'll put the kettle on,' Isobel muttered under her breath.

Meanwhile, Helen had begun to pour out her troubles to Rob and Claire. The additional piece of information, which was news to Isobel, was that, under grilling him about his affair, Ruaridh had confessed that it was true.

'Men!' Claire fumed. 'They're all tarred with the same brush. They want to keep their cake, but still savour the icing on the top.'

Isobel smiled and remarked, 'Well, I've heard lots of sayings, but I haven't heard that one before.'

Helen meanwhile, was sitting with her head in her hands and staring blankly at the floor.

'Have you left him for good?' Rob enquired.

'I'm not sure,' she murmured, 'I just need some time on my own to sort things out in my head.'

Now, the cogs were beginning to grind slowly into motion in Isobel's head. An old saying of her father's had come to mind: "It's an ill wind that doesn't blow somebody any good".

Helen's heart-breaking predicament could actually work to her advantage. She was planning a trip to London. Due to his broken leg, Gordon was incapacitated. Helen had asked if she could stay at the croft and was in need of some peace and quiet - Eureka! Helen had helped Rob with the running of the croft for many years; therefore, she could be trusted implicitly to take charge in her absence.

Just then, Claire's irritating voice interrupted her thoughts. 'On second thoughts, not all men are nasty and devious. My current boyfriend has a heart of gold and I trust him implicitly.'

'You have a new boy-friend already,' Helen exclaimed. 'I'd have thought you would want to be foot-loose and fancy free for a bit longer - especially after your last disastrous experience.'

'For a start, this one's not married,' Claire began. 'He is also sincere and trustworthy and is taking me to a posh restaurant in Drumevie later in the week.'

'A posh restaurant in Drumevie,' Rob repeated scornfully. 'I didn't know there was such a place.'

'It's not posh by your standards,' Claire retorted. 'Or Isobel's either for that matter. But then, Helen and I are the unfortunate siblings who didn't inherit their dearly departed relatives' fortune.'

Rob and Isobel were visibly shocked and upset by Claire's comment. Helen, on the other hand, was furious.

'That was totally uncalled for,' she snapped. 'Rob has been kind enough to provide a roof over your head. A fairly substantial one at that,' she added. 'As for Isobel, her love for John was true. I'm sure she would return every last penny in exchange for his life.'

'True love,' Claire said scathingly. 'I wouldn't know the meaning of the words.'

Isobel couldn't hold back her tears and began to sob quietly. Helen went over to her young sister and hugged her; Rob meanwhile, glared at Claire while saying, 'It's time we were heading back to Inverculden.'

As they were leaving, Helen asked Claire if her new boyfriend was someone they knew.

'Yes,' she replied smugly. 'You've met him. His name is Tormod MacAlister, the new vet from Drumevie.'

'I hope it works out for you this time,' Helen replied.

Isobel didn't respond. Once again, her emotions were in a state of confusion.

Following Rob and Claire's departure, Helen and Isobel sat down together on the sofa and began to wallow in their mutual anguish.

'Oh Isobel,' Helen sighed. 'Why is life so cruel?'

'There has to be an explanation,' her young sister replied philosophically. 'Although we can't make sense of it at the moment, there must be some justifiable reason for it.'

'You are so down to earth,' Helen remarked. 'But then, you've always had an old head on your shoulders.'

'We'll be fine you and I,' Isobel replied with a feeble smile. 'We don't need men in our lives.'

'You're right,' Helen agreed. Then added in a forlorn tone, 'but at least you have your children. I have no-one.'

'You have me,' Isobel replied.

'Thank the lord for that. I'm so pleased we finally found one another.'

'Hmm,' Isobel muttered, 'I'm so pleased I found you and Rob, but I'm not so sure about Claire.'

'I have to admit, she's not a bit like us,' Helen agreed.

The two sisters chatted about many things that evening, but mainly about old times, happier times, and what the future held in store for them. Helen, knowing of Isobel's inheritance, asked if she'd made any headway regarding the two properties. It was the opening Isobel had been waiting for.

'Actually, I'm planning a trip to London next week,' she began. 'Due to Gordon's accident though, I was hoping that perhaps you could fill the void here.'

'You want me to man the croft in your absence?' Helen asked with a quizzical smile.

'Yes, that's exactly what I want,' Isobel replied, returning her smile.

'I would love to be back in charge of An Gleann Dubh,' Helen responded, 'Albeit on a temporary basis.'

'It can be as temporary or as permanent as you want it to be,' Isobel replied.

'Time will tell,' Helen said with a wistful smile.

Isobel went on to say that Tormod MacAlister was accompanying her on the trip, but as yet, they hadn't decided on a date for travelling.

'What has Claire got to say about you swanning off on holiday with her boyfriend?' Helen asked with a note of

169

cynicism.

'We're not exactly going on holiday together,' Isobel began. 'The reason I'm driving to London is because I'm scared to fly.'

She went on to explain that Rob was flying down on business beforehand and they would meet up at some point before the meeting with John's lawyer. Prior to that, she would visit the property and come to a decision on whether or not to sell it.

'Where will you stay?' Helen asked.

'I did think of contacting John's parents to ask if I could stay with them.' Isobel replied, before adding, 'I'm not sure how they'll respond though. I haven't been in touch with them for some time.'

'I'm sure they would love to see their grandchildren,' Helen remarked.

Isobel paused for a moment. 'I haven't told them about Iain,' she said with a guilty expression.

Helen, visibly shocked, responded in a solemn tone, 'Then you must phone them immediately and let them know.'

Isobel had always felt guilty about the fact that John's family were unaware of Iain's birth. The encounter with Robert Thornton's parents had endorsed that, and now, the fact that Helen would never be able to have a child of her own, made her realise the significance of regeneration. It also highlighted the importance of maintaining family ties.

****

170

Chapter 31

With the running of the croft left in Helen's capable hands, Isobel and the children set off one morning to drive to London. Heeding her sister's words, Isobel had made contact with Mildred who'd insisted that she and Máiri stay with them whilst in London. Isobel had also revealed the news about the birth of their grandson. Mildred's initial outburst of surprise on hearing the news was promptly followed by one of elation at the prospect of seeing him very soon.

Isobel had arranged to pick Tormod up en route and, since the tiny mini was filled almost to capacity, could only hope that he was travelling light. Negotiating the short track that led to his cottage, she recalled the night she'd spent here during the blizzard. She also recalled how, on their first few meetings, a mutual frostiness had existed between them. How bizarre, she thought while parking the car, that we've become friends and are about to set off on an epic journey together. Even more bizarre, was the fact that her sister Claire was now dating him. It's a funny old world right enough, she said to herself.

Tormod emerged from the cottage carrying only a rucksack, for which Isobel was relieved. His explanation for travelling light was that he intended to stay in a youth hostel while in London.

The long journey was broken up by a few stops at roadside cafes, and further south, where parts of the road had been converted to motorway, they were able to cover the miles much faster. Driving on a motorway was a completely new experience for Isobel, but one she considered preferable to flying. Driving in London was also a first for her, and with a city map for guidance and Tormod acting as navigator, she drove to a pre-arranged rendezvous point to meet up with John's parents.

The meeting was a joyful, albeit tearful, reunion; their last being at John's funeral. Mildred glanced at Iain fast asleep in his Moses basket and said between sobs, 'He is the spitting image of his father at that age.'

Isobel followed their car through the streets of London to

their destination. Their house, in the district of Hyde Park, was much larger than Isobel had envisaged and was just a stone's throw from Kensington Gardens. Although by no means a city lover, her thoughts as she entered her late husband's family home was that she may indeed keep her inherited property if it was as grand as this one. Mildred's voice interrupted her thoughts, 'And where are you staying?'

Her words were directed at Tormod and it suddenly occurred to Isobel that she hadn't even introduced them.

'I'm so sorry,' she began. 'This is Tormod MacAlister, our local vet. He is hoping to find youth hostel accommodation and plans to spend the next few days taking in the sights of the city.'

As Tormod shook hands with Mildred, John senior glanced at her and remarked, 'We could quite easily put him up here. We've been rattling around in this empty house since returning from Dumlocher. It's much too big for us now that we're on our own.'

Isobel and Tormod exchanged glances, his expression was one of uncertainty as he stammered, 'I couldn't possible impose on your family reunion to that extent.'

Isobel's response was an immediate, 'I have no objections.'

She was certain Tormod's smile was one of relief as he said to John, 'In that case, I accept your kind offer with gratitude, but insist on paying for my stay.'

First, they were shown to their rooms, following which, Mildred took Isobel on a guided tour of the rambling, three storey property. With its five bedrooms, two public rooms and large kitchen, Isobel fully understood the reason for John's elderly parents finding the size of the house overwhelming.

'John's house in Bayswater is only half this size,' Mildred remarked as they returned to the kitchen. 'It was the one he shared with Jennifer until she died.' Her voice breaking, she added, 'and now, they're both gone.'

'I.....didn't know they lived there together,' Isobel began hesitantly. 'I presume you know that John left the property to me.'

'Yes, we know,' she replied solemnly. 'We know that he also left the property in Dumlocher to you. She paused for a few

172

moments before adding, 'It's as it should be. We have no need for them. We've already discussed selling up and moving to a smaller residence.'

Isobel lay wide awake in her bed that night. As on previous occasions, sleep was the last thing on her mind. What *was* on her mind though was the fact that, for a second time, by another strange twist of fate, Tormod MacAlister was asleep in the room right next to hers. Also, Mildred had revealed that the property she'd inherited from John, and had considered keeping, was the one he'd shared with Jennifer. If not for her tragic and untimely death, she and John would most probably have spent the rest of their lives together in that house. As a consequence of life's unpredictable twists and turns, both were now dead. Realising that it would only open up wounds that were beginning to heal, Isobel suddenly had no wish to see the house. It would be a permanent reminder of the life John may have led, had they not met.

During breakfast that morning, Isobel told John's parents of her decision to put the property in Bayswater on the market. The purpose of her long trip south had been to view the property with Rob and thereafter come to a decision. Now though, without even having seen it, her mind was made up. Mildred's eyes suddenly widened with new found inspiration as she exclaimed, 'Why don't we exchange houses?'

'You can't be serious!' Isobel exclaimed. 'I'm quite sure this house is worth twice as much as John's.'

'Perhaps so,' John senior replied, 'but it would be given to you as a legacy for our grandchildren. In the meantime, it'll be yours to do with as you wish.'

On the morning of the meeting with John's lawyer, John senior suggested that he drive her to the office. Although relieved that she wouldn't have to find her way there alone, Isobel had concerns about taking Máiri and Iain along.

'That's very kind of you,' she replied, 'but I had rather hoped you and Mildred would look after the children for me.'

It was then that Tormod, having overheard the conversation, stepped in. 'I can quite easily forego a morning's sight-seeing to look after Máiri and Iain.'

Isobel suppressed a laugh. Tormod had no previous

experience of looking after young children and she wouldn't dream of leaving her precious children in his care; therefore, she politely declined his offer. Tormod though, wasn't put off by Isobel's negative response and insisted that it was the least he could do to repay her for the transport she'd provided to and from London, not to mention, the hospitality received from her in-laws. John and Mildred agreed with Tormod and thought it was the ideal solution. Isobel was forced to admit that a solicitor's office was no place for a tearaway toddler and a baby of just a few months old, and with reluctance, was persuaded to leave them in his care. Before setting off, she began to give Tormod a few last minute instructions.

'Don't you trust me?' he asked cagily.

Isobel paused for a few moments, before saying,

'Once upon a time, when we were complete strangers, I trusted you with Ben's life and you didn't let me down. Does that answer your question?'

'I'm so pleased you no longer regard me as a stranger,' he replied with a warm smile. 'Good luck.'

Rob was waiting in the reception area of the lawyer's office when Isobel arrived. They embraced with unconcealed delight and Isobel proceeded to tell him, without going into detail, of her decision.

'You must wait and be guided by the lawyer on this matter Isobel,' he responded in a stern, but brotherly tone.

'I will be guided only by my heart and my mind is made up,' she replied doggedly.

As on many previous occasions, Rob realised there would be little point in trying to dissuade his young sister; nonetheless, he suggested that they go for lunch after the meeting to discuss the pros and cons in more detail.

Following the meeting, Rob, now familiar with the trendy places to eat in the city, introduced Isobel to a recently opened restaurant, where they ordered lunch. The convivial ambience of the bistro was a welcome change from the tense and traumatic meeting with the lawyer and it wasn't long

174

before the weight began to drop from her shoulders. The brief respite from motherhood, the pounding beat of the pop music in the background, and perhaps the effects of a large glass of wine, all played their part in the process of her unwinding. Observing that most of the other customers were young courting couples, Isobel was enjoying being part of a twosome again. The fact that her male companion was her beloved brother was as guilt free as it was comforting. Emerging from the bistro into the autumn sunshine, Rob suggested that they spend the remainder of the afternoon together and take in some of the city's highlights. It was a tempting offer. Since she'd no intention of traipsing around London on her own, her thoughts were that this may be her only chance to do a spot of sightseeing. The downside was that, by now, John and Mildred would have returned to take over the baby-sitting duties from Tormod and the last thing she wanted to do was take advantage of their kindness.

Rob's voice interrupted her thoughts, 'Well, have you come to a decision?'

'I would love to spend the afternoon with you,' she replied, while thinking that the extra time with him would provide an opportunity to explain her true reason for deciding against keeping John's London property.

During the meeting and subsequent lengthy discussion with John's lawyer, Isobel had instructed him to market the property in Dumlocher. She had further instructed that, as soon as the title deeds had been transferred into her name, he should arrange the leasing of John and Mildred's property. Then Isobel began to explain her reasons for reaching her decision. She told him that John and Mildred were planning to move into their son's former home in Bayswater and were gifting their house in Hyde Park to her and the children.

She finished by saying, 'I neither have the time, nor the need to maintain two city properties.'

Rob shook his head and responded by saying, 'I think you're making a big mistake.'

The discussion was now closed. Each had conflicting views and it was decided to leave it at that. Rob then changed the subject by asking Isobel what tourist attraction she would

175

most like to see. She had no hesitation in giving him her answer. As always, Rob went the extra mile - or miles in this case - to ensure she got her wish. Hailing a cab, he instructed the driver to take the shortest route to Trafalgar Square. Despite her aversion to cities, Isobel had to admit to being thrilled by the sights as they strolled through Trafalgar Square and made their way towards The Mall. The long walk also provided an opportunity to reveal the true reason for her reluctance to set foot in her husband's former home. Rob mulled over her words for a few moments before saying, 'It's only bricks and mortar - extremely lucrative bricks and mortar at that. It would fetch a good deal more than the property in Dumlocher.'

She frowned, before replying, 'John and I were happy there. It has no ghosts.'

Isobel glanced at her watch and realised she'd been away from the house for over five hours.

'Doesn't time fly when you're having fun?' she remarked. 'I have to go back.'

'And I must dash to the airport,' Rob responded. 'I have a plane to catch.'

With one arm frantically hailing a passing cab, he fumbled in his pocket with the other, before pressing a crumpled note into Isobel's hand.

'What's that for?' she asked with a puzzled expression.

'Your taxi fare,' he replied as a hackney cab performed a U turn in the street.

'I don't need your money,' she chided. 'I'm not destitute anymore.'

'I can't quite get my head around the fact that we are both millionaires,' he remarked as the cab pulled up at the kerb.

A familiar voice calling her name made Isobel turn her head sharply.

Tormod waved, before greeting them with the words: 'Well, isn't this a coincidence?'

'Coincidence,' Isobel repeated with a laugh. 'A chance in a million, I would have said.'

Rob interrupted, saying, 'A lucky chance for me.......must dash.'

176

After planting a kiss on Isobel's cheek, he jumped into the black cab. Meanwhile, Isobel and Tormod were left on the pavement in a state of bemusement. After an awkward silence, she asked about the children.

'They were good as gold,' he began. 'But I have to admit to being relieved when John and Mildred returned. Fortunately, they appeared to be relishing the thought of taking over the baby-sitting duties.'

'Be that as it may,' Isobel responded, 'but I have to get back as a matter of urgency.'

'I'm sure they won't mind being left in charge for another couple of hours.' Tormod replied. 'We could visit the palace, or take a stroll to the Houses of Parliament.'

Isobel was thinking that, much as she would love to go along with his suggestion, she was beginning to experience extreme discomfort. This was due to the fact that she was breastfeeding Iain and seven hours had passed since his last feed. Despite having made up a bottle of powdered baby milk as a stand-by, it was imperative that she return immediately for her own sake. After apologising for having to decline the invitation, and for a reason she couldn't begin to understand, told Tormod the reason. His response left her gobsmacked. 'In that case, I'll come with you.'

'I can't let you do that,' she argued. 'Then your entire day will have been ruined because of me.'

Tormod smiled wryly and replied, 'As my dear departed father used to say, "Tomorrow is another day".

As the taxi snaked between the stationery traffic, horns honked incessantly and Isobel felt like the proverbial fish out of water. She'd always preferred the solitude of the countryside to the hustle and bustle of the city and travelling alone in unfamiliar territory would have been quite daunting - even for Isobel the fearless. Yet, with Tormod beside her, she was surprised to find herself enjoying sharing the sights with him. Until now, their conversation had been restricted to pointing out various places of note on their route, when, out of the blue, he asked, 'Would you like to come with me tomorrow?'

'I can't,' she replied dejectedly.

'Why can't you?' he asked abruptly. 'Don't you want to?'

His forthright manner had, once again, taken Isobel by surprise. For one thing, she wasn't used to being put on the spot like this and found it unsettling.

'You seem to have forgotten that I have two young children to consider,' she replied brusquely.

He laughed, before saying, 'How could I forget, I spent the entire morning with them.'

Her tone softened as she replied: 'Thank you. I really do appreciate you doing that.'

'I would be very happy to include the children in my invitation to join me tomorrow,' he said softly.

For the first time since early childhood, Isobel was dumbstruck. She couldn't possibly accompany him tomorrow, and yet, since he'd included Mairi and Iain, she had no feasible excuse. Her heart was telling her that she would love to spend the day in his company; her head though, was screaming out that it would be so wrong. Just then, the cab came to a stop. They'd reached their destination and while Isobel had been rummaging in her handbag for her purse, Tormod had already handed a note to the driver.

'How much do I owe you?' she asked as they walked towards the house.

'It is I who should be asking you that question.' he responded with a warm smile.

'You don't owe me anything,' she said, deliberately avoiding his gaze.

'Then you owe me the chance to express my gratitude,' he said softly.

For the first time since meeting him, Isobel had the distinct feeling that Tormod MacAlister was gaining the upper hand. His previous offhand manner had been a source of annoyance to her, but then, it had given her the excuse to retaliate in a curt and brusque manner. Now though, his mild-mannered approach was as alien as it was disconcerting. After deliberating how best to deal with the situation, she decided to reciprocate his courteous approach by replying, 'How can I do that?'

178

'By accompanying me tomorrow,' he said with a smile.

'I'll sleep on it?' she replied as they walked up the steps together.

****

Chapter 32

While lying wide awake in bed that night, the cogs in Isobel's head began to grind into motion. A plan was forming in the depths of her brain. Whether it would materialise or not, remained to be seen. Each and every day since the Thornton's unexpected arrival at the croft, the dog, whose life she'd saved, had been on her mind. Since both she and Dileas were in London, the chance of seeing her again, just to put her mind at rest, was too good an opportunity to miss. Even if she were to accept Tormod's invitation to accompany him on a sight-seeing tour the following day, it would still leave one free day before they set off on the long drive north. The slip of paper with the Thornton's address and telephone number was in her handbag and in the morning, she planned to ask Mildred if she could use the telephone. With just the hint of a smile on her face, she drifted into a deep and restful sleep.

During breakfast the following morning, Tormod, seated across the table from Isobel, asked if she'd come to a decision about accompanying him on a sightseeing trip that day. John and Mildred exchanged glances of mutual surprise. Most surprised however, was Tormod when she replied, 'Since I have nothing else planned for today, I would be delighted to accompany you.'

'Your reply would suggest that you have something planned for Friday,' he responded with a questioning smile.

Casting her eyes across the table towards John and Mildred, she remarked cagily, 'That depends.'

Tormod didn't pursue his questioning, mainly due to the fact that he was still treading on thin ice with Isobel. Despite having known her for some time and for a reason he was at a loss to understand, he had a habit of upsetting her. He concluded that it was probably because he'd had no previous experience of dealing with the complexities of the female mind. Even so, Isobel was something of a challenge. One minute, all sweetness and smiles, and the next, she would cut him dead with a mere glance.

After breakfast, John and Mildred rose from the table;

Mildred, on the pretext of checking up on her grandchildren, and John, for a tobacco break. They're either being extraordinarily perceptive, or exceptionally discreet, Isobel thought to herself. The conversation between her and Tormod had ended rather abruptly, but now that they were alone, she told him about her plan for Friday.

'Would you like me to come with you?' he asked.

'It's still in the planning stages at the moment,' she began. 'I haven't asked Mildred if I can use the telephone, and besides, the Thornton's may not be at home.'

Later that morning, Isobel dialled the number on the slip of paper she'd kept since the day of the Thorntons' visit to the croft. As the dialling tone rang out, millions of butterflies fluttered inside her stomach.

'Good Morning, Dr Thornton speaking.'

'Good morning Dr Thornton, it's Isobel Caldwell here. I'm staying in London for a few days and wondered if I may visit you tomorrow to see Dileas before returning home.'

A slight pause caused Isobel's butterfly sensation to be replaced by one of nausea. Similarly, Dr Thornton's curt tone was replaced by one of despondency as he said, 'I'm afraid that won't be possible.'

Isobel's heart sank to her feet.

'Freya didn't settle here at all,' he began. 'She became very edgy and my wife was in fear of her. Only last week, she insisted that we have her put to sleep.'

'No,' Isobel cried out.

'The very next day, I put Freya in the car and told my wife I was taking her to the vet to be destroyed. While driving there, my head was filled with thoughts of Robert. I recalled seeing him in his sick bed, a helpless child, crippled by polio. Then I thought of Mary, a naïve, slip of a girl who carried our son's child for nine months and was forced to hand the baby, our grandchild, over for adoption. I thought about the joy we felt when Robert regained the use of his legs, and later, when he was fit enough to take up hill walking. If by some miracle he is still alive, I thought about his reaction to the news that I had callously taken the life of his beloved and devoted companion. It was then I knew that I couldn't go through

181

with it. Perhaps it was my profession of saving lives that came into play. I can't be sure. Whatever the reason, I just couldn't bring myself to snuff out the life of a healthy animal that, in truth, had done nothing to warrant the death penalty.'

He paused for a moment and Isobel, who'd been hanging on to his every word, was mentally urging him to continue.

'In the end, I found myself taking a different route, towards Battersea Cat and Dog's Home.'

Isobel let out a sigh of relief, which prompted Tormod to mouth the words, 'What's going on.'

She shook her head as Dr Thornton continued by saying, 'Before leaving Freya at the dog's home, I gave the kennel maids a detailed account of the unfortunate circumstances surrounding her recent past and warned them about her uncharacteristic displays of aggression. Their reply was that they would monitor her behaviour over the next few weeks before finding a suitable home for her. If, in their opinion, she was unsuitable for re-homing, they would have her humanely destroyed.'

'Thank you so much for your time,' Isobel said politely, before adding, 'and for the information.'

After replacing the receiver, she continued to stare blankly into space, until the sound of Tormod's voice made her jump.

'Would you like to share it with me?'

'Dileas has been taken to Battersea Dog's Home,' she began slowly. 'Apparently, she didn't settle and Mrs Thornton insisted that she be put to sleep. Dr Thornton though, decided to spare her life.'

'Would you like to go there today?' Tormod asked.

'To Battersea?' she exclaimed. 'I thought you'd planned to go sightseeing today.'

He smiled, and this time, Isobel couldn't help but notice that it was a warm, natural smile; his eyes displaying a hint of mischief as he replied by saying, 'We'll go sightseeing on Friday.'

Mildred returned to the dining room cradling Iain in her arms. Máiri toddled behind, sucking her thumb and dragging her security blanket. A mother's instinct told Isobel that she'd been wakened from a deep slumber.

'I really don't mind looking after the children while you and Tormod go sightseeing,' Mildred began enthusiastically. 'After all, once you leave, I probably won't see them again for some time.'

Furtive glances were exchanged between Tormod and Isobel before she replied, 'Well, actually, there's been a change of plan. I have an appointment today.'

'Are you meeting with John's lawyer again?' Mildred asked with a frown.

'No. We're going to Battersea Cat and Dog Home,' Isobel replied with a wry smile.

'A strange location for a day's outing,' Mildred responded in a tone of bemusement.

Isobel sighed, before giving her a brief account of the impending mission, to which she replied: 'I do hope you're not planning to bring the dog here.'

Isobel laughed. 'No, I'll not be bringing her here. For one thing, there would be no room in the car. If I'm allowed to reclaim her, I'll make arrangements for her to be transported home to the croft.'

The croft.......! Home......!

The words were music to Isobel's ears. Her spirits soared and a feeling of well-being engulfed her mind, body and soul. Although she'd enjoyed her short break in London, as far as she was concerned, Saturday couldn't come soon enough. To add to her joy, there was a slight chance that Dileas would be coming home in the near future.

Later that morning, equipped with a City of London route map, Isobel and Tormod set off to drive to Battersea Cat and Dog Home. Tormod had kindly offered his services as map reader and route finder, but as it turned out, his navigational skills left a lot to be desired and they became completely lost. Whether by accident or design, Isobel stopped outside a small hotel to consult the map and Tormod suggested that they go inside and ask for directions. Was it by chance, Isobel asked herself as her empty stomach rumbled, that lunches were being served at that very moment. They were given directions to Battersea Dog's Home by the friendly barman and, rather dejectedly, Isobel turned and began to make her way back to the car. Just then, the sound of Tormod's voice stopped her in her tracks:

'I don't know about you, but I'm starving. Would you like to have lunch before we go?'

With all the restraint she could muster, she replied, 'We may as well.'

While relaxing with a glass of cold beer in his hand and waiting for lunch to be served, Tormod briefly touched on his unhappy childhood. Isobel listened intently as he told her that, not long after he'd left the island to further his education on the mainland, his parents had died as the result of a terrible accident.

He stopped abruptly, saying, 'I'm sorry, I can't believe I told you that. I have never spoken about it to anyone. '

'There's no need to apologise.' Isobel began. 'I can relate to an unhappy childhood.'

'Let's not get melancholy,' he responded with a smile. 'We are on holiday after all and it was wrong of me to bring up the past. We should be talking about the future.'

'My future will revolve around the croft, my dogs and my children,' Isobel replied resolutely. 'What about you?'

He smiled. Isobel, now intrigued by the mystery of his unhappy past, was heartened to see that, for the second time since they met, his smile was spontaneous and sincere.

'My future,' he began dreamily, 'will revolve around my practice on the island of my birth.'

'I wasn't aware of you having your own practice,' Isobel remarked with a bemused expression.

He laughed, before saying, 'I don't. Not yet at least. It's a childhood dream. Until that day comes, I'll never know true happiness.'

Isobel remained silent. She was reminiscing about her own childhood dream. It did come true and, for a short time, had brought happiness. It was capricious and transient though and had left her bereft and bewildered.

Lunch was eaten amid a strained atmosphere and immediately afterwards, Isobel rose from the table saying, 'I think we should go. I'm anxious to see Dileas.'

Although that was the case, she had used it as an excuse to hide the true reason for her haste. She was determined not to become involved in Tormod's personal life. In fact, she had no intention of becoming involved with anyone - especially him. After all, he was dating Claire. Without saying another word, Tormod rose and strode towards the bar, where he paid the bill.

'Let's go,' he said curtly while making his way to the door.

Oh dear, Isobel thought to herself while following him to the car. It's always one step forward and two steps backwards with him. Just when I think I've made a breakthrough, he becomes cool and detached at the flick of a switch. Likewise, Tormod was deep in thought as he made his way towards the car. His normally placid, bordering on apathetic, persona was becoming agitated. Why was he allowing Isobel Caldwell to get under his skin? Until now, he'd felt nothing but complete indifference for his fellow man – and more especially - woman.

The remainder of the journey was spent in virtual silence. Tormod spoke occasionally, but only to say, 'Take a right here,' or, 'Straight on at the roundabout.'

Her heart now thumping erratically, Isobel finally pulled up outside Battersea Cat and Dog's Home, hardly daring to believe that in a few minutes, she and Dileas would be reunited. Was that the only reason for her pounding heart though? Or could it be that, once again, the rift between her and Tormod was like a gaping chasm?

As she opened the car door, her moment of elation at the thought of seeing Dileas was replaced by a feeling of despondency as Tormod remarked sulkily, 'I'll wait in the car.'

Isobel slammed the car door in frustration and made her way towards the entrance of the rescue centre. Following a few preliminary questions she was told that Dileas would be brought from her kennel into the exercise yard. Thereafter, depending on the dog's reaction, a decision would be made as to whether or not she would be allowed to reclaim her. A moment of panic ensued. She'd only had the dog in her possession for a few months and wasn't sure how she would

185

react. Nonetheless, her irritation changed to unconcealed delight as a young man led Dileas into the yard. Then, all hell broke loose - or rather - Dileas did. Yanking the leash from his hand, she bounded across the yard and launched herself into Isobel's open arms. She then completed a few laps of the yard in frenzied excitement, all the time yelping with sheer jubilation, before coming to lie at Isobel's feet.

'I'm amazed,' the young man exclaimed. 'It's the first time she has shown any emotion since coming here.'

'I agree,' one of the kennel maids piped up. 'She has cowered in her kennel in a state of depression, hardly eaten, and has never barked during all the times I've handled her.'

The outcome of the joyous reunion between dog and mistress was that Isobel was asked to complete a reclaim form which included her name, address, telephone number, and the contact details of her local vet. After filling out her own details, she duly entered the name: Tormod Seumas MacAlister MRCVS, and had to bite her tongue to stop herself from saying that he was sitting in the car. It never even occurred to her to disclose the fact that she was a vet. It was irrelevant. At this very moment, nothing else mattered except that she was being allowed to take Dileas home to An Gleann Dubh. Then no-one, not even Robert if he turned up safe and well, could ever separate them again.

Isobel made her way back to the car with a heavy heart. Her eyes were brimming with tears at the thought of Dileas being led back to her kennel in a state of bewilderment and confusion. There she would remain until arrangements could be made to transport her home to An Gleann Dubh. Nearing the car she could see Tormod leaning against the passenger door. Conscious of the fact that her eyes were still moist, she kept her head down on approach; but to no avail. Noticing her glum expression, Tormod frowned, before saying, 'Is it bad news?'

Isobel couldn't speak for fear of bursting into tears, but when Tormod took her in his arms, she was powerless to stop them. So too, was she powerless to stop herself from melting into his arms. The stolen moment was over all too soon and, while gazing into each others' eyes, unspoken words hung in the air.

Tormod broke the silence by saying, 'Tell me what happened.'

Isobel gave a faint smile. 'It went very well. I'm just so unhappy at having to leave Dileas in London until I can organise her transport to the croft.'

There was another awkward silence and Tormod was deep in thought. His frown then changed to a smile as he began, 'Why don't we go home tomorrow? I don't have to be back at work until Monday. I could travel back here on Saturday, stay overnight and collect Dileas on Sunday.'

Isobel was speechless. Tormod's suggestion was ludicrous - impossible - insane even. It was a round trip of over 1,000 miles. Why on earth would he put himself to all that trouble for a dog?

****

Chapter 33

It was yet another sleepless night as far as Isobel was concerned. Although physically exhausted, her overactive mind was preventing her weary body from shutting down. Excitement at the thought of going home the following day was partly to blame. The realisation that in three days time Dileas would be returning to the croft, occupied some of her thoughts; but there was another, more disturbing reason for her insomnia. It had something, or perhaps everything, to do with the fact that she couldn't erase Tormod MacAlister from her mind. That brief glimpse of his roguish smile was etched on her brain like an image created in indelible ink. Smiling didn't come easily to Tormod. He was a loner, ill at ease in company - especially female company - and yet she was conscious of the fact that there was another side to him – one she was privileged to have been given a glimpse of. Despite previously having no knowledge of, or interest in the reasons behind his staid persona, now, she was intrigued.

Having explained the reason for their premature departure to John's parents, the following morning was spent packing. Before leaving, Isobel hugged John and Mildred and promised to return soon. Despite having no wish to return to London in the foreseeable future, it was a promise she intended to keep. The long, tedious drive north was a daunting prospect as they joined the queuing traffic, but before long, the city of London had been left far behind. They were heading in a northerly direction and thoughts of home kept Isobel's spirits high as the little car sped along. Her three passengers had fallen asleep and she drove on autopilot, her thoughts everywhere but on the job in hand. After three hours on the road and in need of a break, she drew into a roadside café. The comfort break included relieving herself of breast milk; which meant having to rouse Iain. As it turned out, there was no need. As soon as the car came to a stop, all three passengers stirred.

'Are we home already?' Tormod asked sleepily.
'Unfortunately not,' Isobel replied curtly.

188

It wasn't that she'd meant her reply to be abrupt, but she was weary, uncomfortable and therefore, irritable.

By now, Ian was wailing pitifully in his Moses basket on the back seat of the car.

'Why don't you feed him before going into the tearoom,' Tormod remarked.

'What – here - in the car?' Isobel replied indignantly.

'It's more hygienic than feeding him in a toilet cubicle,' he replied in the same manner.

Appreciating that his suggestion made sense, and urged on by the sound of Iain lungs reaching a crescendo, Isobel joined the children in the back seat of the car before lifting Iain from the Moses basket and cradling him to her breast.

Tormod reached into the car, took Màiri by the hand and began to lead her towards the tearoom. For some unexplained and ridiculous reason, it all felt so normal. To anyone observing the sequence of events, it would appear to be a typical family outing – with Tormod as the doting father. Any previous feelings of animosity towards him were rapidly being replaced – but by what?

The remainder of the homeward journey was uneventful and by the time Isobel drew up at Tormod's cottage, it was dusk.

'Would you like to come in for a cup of tea?' he asked politely after retrieving his rucksack from the boot of the car.

'No thank you,' Isobel replied in an equally stilted manner. 'I'm eager to get home before darkness falls.'

'Actually, I'm relieved to hear that,' he began. 'I was planning to go straight to bed. I'll be leaving for London at the crack of dawn.'

Isobel was lost for words. She just couldn't find the right ones to convey her gratitude to Tormod for offering to drive to London and collect Dileas from the dog's home. On impulse, she leant forward and kissed his cheek.

'What did I do to deserve that?' he questioned with the roguish smile that had interfered with her sleep the previous night.

'More than you'll ever know,' she whispered.

After parking the mini in the barn, Isobel transferred the luggage – and the children - to the Land Rover before

189

negotiating the last lap of her epic journey. Her heart was pounding in her chest with excitement as she drove the last few miles to the croft. The feeling of elation was intensified by the knowledge that Helen would be there to welcome them home. Her joy though, was short lived. The expression on Helen's face as she entered the cottage, told her that something was amiss.

Almost afraid to ask, she blurted out the words: 'What's wrong?'

'It's Mary,' Helen replied solemnly.

'*Mary?*' Isobel repeated.

'She's taken an overdose.'

'Oh my God,' Isobel cried out. 'Is she......?'

'She's alive,' Helen responded, 'but her family have been told that she's brain dead and there's little or no hope of recovery.'

'I have to see her,' Isobel gasped.

'Isobel, you can't possibly drive to Dumlocher tonight.....'

But Isobel wasn't listening. Instead, she was buzzing around like a demented bluebottle in preparation for the long drive south.

'Helen, I need you to take care of Máiri and Iain for just one night,' she called out, while darting back and forth like a whirling dervish. 'I'll be back tomorrow before nightfall.'

The two suitcases had been emptied in the short time Isobel had been scurrying around, and one of them was now packed with overnight necessities for the impending trip. Before leaving, she expressed some breast milk into a bottle and gave Helen instructions for making up the powdered milk kept as a standby for Iain.

Helen sighed, before commenting, 'Isobel, it's exactly the same as making up the lambs milk supplement.'

'Just be sure not to get the two mixed up,' Isobel responded with a wan smile.

Helen embraced her young sister and whispered in her ear, 'I'll not sleep a wink tonight.'

'Iain and Máiri will see to that for sure,' she responded.

'Take care. I love you,' Helen called out as Isobel closed the back door.

Retracing the route she'd taken earlier that evening, Isobel's thoughts were focused on her dearest childhood friend. Mary, whose life now hung by a thread, was only twenty five years old. Why would she want to end her life? She had a daughter the same age as Máiri and a wonderful husband in James. Throughout her own grief and heartbreak, never, at any time had she contemplated taking her life. She valued life. It was a precious gift, and should be lived to the full - no matter what sorrows and challenges fate may throw your way. By now, Isobel was approaching Tormod's cottage. It was surreal to think that she'd dropped him off here less than a couple of hours earlier. Assuming he'd be fast asleep in preparation for his long drive to London, she was surprised to see the light from his bedroom window shining out like a beacon in the inky blackness. Turning into the drive, it was as if alien forces had taken control of her actions. Within minutes, she found herself pulling up outside the front door of Tormod's cottage. Even as she knocked hard on the wooden door, the situation seemed surreal. Tormod, pyjama clad, opened the door and stared at her as though she was an apparition. He'd gone to bed and was trying, unsuccessfully, to fall asleep, but couldn't because Isobel was consuming his mind. For a split second, neither one spoke.

'Are you..... coming in?' he asked hesitantly.

'I really shouldn't. I'm on my way to Dumlocher,' she stammered while following him inside.

'Dumlocher!' he mumbled drowsily. 'What takes you there at this unearthly hour?'

The emotions Isobel had perfected the art of keeping in check – apart from when in his presence - ran free at that moment, and floods of tears spilled down her cheeks. Lifting her head to meet his gaze, their lips met. The kiss was clumsy and fleeting - yet for Isobel it was a revelation. She'd always hated being kissed on the lips – John being the exception – and since his death, had vowed that no-one would ever do so again.

Tormod, with a look of boyish embarrassment, apologised profusely. 'I'm sorry. I shouldn't have done that,' he stammered.

'My sentiments exactly,' Isobel muttered.

191

'Can you stay awhile?' he asked.

'Not for long I'm afraid. I'm on my way to see my second best friend.'

His confused expression prompted her to offer an explanation.

'Mary is my dearest, childhood friend and I have to be with her. I can't tell you any more at the moment.'

'You can fill me in with the details when I bring Dileas home on Sunday,' he replied.

Isobel arrived in Dumlocher just as the dawn was breaking. Robert's expression upon finding his youngest daughter on the doorstep was one of complete bewilderment. Once inside, Isobel explained the reason for her visit.

'I can't believe Mary would do such a thing,' he began. 'She has everything to live for.'

Isobel's impromptu visit to her father's house was brief, staying just long enough to down a mug of coffee and a slice of toast, before making her way to the hospital.

Only family members are being admitted, she was told by a nurse on arrival. But fate intervened. Just at that moment, she caught sight of James walking along the corridor.

'Isobel,' he gasped, upon seeing her. 'I'm so glad you're here.'

They embraced briefly and, as they began to walk along the dimly lit corridor, Isobel enquired about Mary.

With tears in his eyes, James murmured, 'We've been told there's no hope.'

Isobel could see that James was beside himself with grief and in no fit state to talk, therefore, they continued to walk in silence towards the darkened side ward, where Mary lay. Isobel stifled a gasp as she gazed upon her dearest childhood friend. Many thoughts ran through her head in the few moments she stood, head bowed, in silence. She'd only ever seen Mary's face this pale once before, when, at only fifteen years old, she'd been given the news of her pregnancy. Now, Mary was barely recognisable as the youthful, carefree child she'd once known. The troubled expression on her beautiful face would be her death mask.

'Oh Mary,' Isobel cried in anguish. 'What have you done?'

192

James' face broke into a smile as Mary's eyes flickered momentarily. The familiar sound of Isobel's voice had registered somewhere deep within her drug induced coma. The brief moment of semi-consciousness had given false hope though. A mere second later, the bloodcurdling sound of a rasping breath chilled her two dearest childhood friends to the bone. Isobel's shrieks resounded round the room. In contrast, James stood rooted to the spot in stunned silence while gazing in disbelief at the corpse of his young wife.

****

Chapter 34

As the croft came into view, the effects of driving almost two hundred miles without a break began to take their toll on Isobel. It was Sunday morning and she'd driven overnight from Dumlocher. No more could be done for her dearest, childhood friend. As for James, he wished to be left in solitude to come to terms with the death of his wife. Today, Tormod was bringing Dileas home to the croft. It was a day she had dreamt of for so long. Now though, her heartache over Mary's death overshadowed the excitement of Dileas' homecoming.

Isobel was greeted at the door by Helen, and, sobbing with grief and overcome by exhaustion, she collapsed into her arms. Such was the close bond between the two sisters that Helen knew straight away Mary's troubles were over. They made their way indoors, following which, Isobel excused herself and went to her bedroom. No sooner had her head hit the pillow than sheer fatigue overcame her state of mental anguish, and within minutes she was fast asleep. The sound of a man's voice awakened her from a deep slumber.

'Isobel, wake up. I've brought someone to see you.'

Opening her eyes, she saw Tormod bending over her. Her actions made no sense whatsoever as she flung her arms around his neck and clung to him for dear life. For a few moments, neither of them spoke. It was little more than a comforting embrace and at this particular moment, just what Isobel needed. Tormod was now a familiar figure in her life - a friend in time of need – and at this moment, she needed him more than ever before. As for Tormod, he was on unchartered territory. He'd been a loner for most of his life. Since the death of his parents, he'd needed no-one - and no-one had ever needed him.

'What can I do?' he asked gently.

'You can open the door and let Dileas in,' she replied tearfully.

Tormod opened the door and left the room. Meanwhile, Dileas bounded across the floor and leapt on the bed. While hugging her devoted, four-legged friend, Isobel was confused by her

194

emotions. Although nothing could detract from the joy of being reunited with Dileas, she couldn't help thinking it would have been nice to have had Tormod share the moment with her.

Making her way along the passageway to the kitchen, Isobel could hear the sound of chatter. However, the conversation between Helen and Tormod stopped abruptly as she crossed the floor and came to sit beside them at the table.

'I was just filling Tormod in with the details of your trip to Dumlocher,' Helen began with an expression that conveyed a mix of guilt and sympathy.

'Do you feel like talking about it?' Tormod asked gently.

'Not right now if you don't mind,' Isobel replied, averting his gaze.

'I'll be ready to listen when the time is right,' he replied tenderly.

Dileas had followed Isobel to the table and was lying at her feet. When Tormod left to return home, she followed close to her heel as Isobel accompanied him to his van.

'You've acquired a friend for life,' Tormod quipped.

'In you.....or in Dileas?' she responded in the same tone.

'I was referring to the dog,' he replied, his face poker straight. With that, he drove off, leaving Isobel, once again, at odds with her emotions.

'Tormod's an agreeable and sincere young man,' Helen remarked as Isobel entered the kitchen. 'If he and Claire continue their relationship, I for one, will be more than happy to welcome him into our family'.

Since Isobel didn't respond, Helen changed the subject by suggesting that she would take care of the croft, and the children, to allow her to attend Mary's funeral when the time came.

****

Chapter 35

The following week, Isobel returned to Dumlocher for Mary's funeral. It had been previously arranged that she stay overnight at the home of her father and Stella, and, as she lay in bed on the eve of the funeral, sleep was evading her. Each time her eyes closed she could see, as clearly as if they were here in the room beside her, the death masks of Mary and John. It was almost beyond belief that she'd lost her beloved husband and dearest childhood friend in tragic circumstances within the space of nine months. What was more - she had seen each of them immediately after death - the images of which would never be erased from her memory. 'Why have they been taken?' she cried out. 'What did they do wrong'?

James had told her that, since the birth of Jessica, Mary had suffered from acute depression. Rather than help get over the loss of her adopted child, Jessica's birth had served only to accentuate the guilt. Such a tragedy; and one that could have been avoided, Isobel thought desolately, if only she'd been allowed to keep her first-born child. In the vain hope of drifting into oblivion, Isobel squeezed her eyes shut, but to no avail.

In the weeks that followed Mary's death, Isobel's routine fell into a daily pattern of chores, child-care, eating and sleeping. Helen was still staying and working at the croft, and apparently, since notifying Ruaridh of her whereabouts, had made no further contact with him. According to Mairead, the rumour was rife in the neighbourhood that the young girl he'd befriended had taken up residence at the farmhouse. In conversation one evening, Helen mentioned that she was planning to talk to a solicitor about divorce proceedings.

'Aren't you being a bit hasty?' Isobel asked.

'Hasty!' Helen exclaimed. 'We've been living apart for three months and he hasn't even bothered to make contact. He's obviously preoccupied with his floozy,' she added scornfully.

'You can't always believe what you hear,' Isobel began. 'Why don't you go and see him and give him the chance to tell his side of the story.'

'There's no smoke without fire,' Helen retorted.

Isobel knew by the dogged expression on her sister's face that the discussion was over; besides, Helen had changed the subject.

'Have you given any more thought to setting up the rescue centre?' she asked.

'I haven't, but not through choice,' Isobel replied. 'I've had more than enough on my plate during the past few months.'

For much of the night, Isobel tossed and turned in her bed. As on many previous such occasions, her head was filled with conflicting thoughts. Helen's off the cuff question had stimulated the need to fulfil her ambition of providing a place of shelter for mountaineers, and perhaps, even the setting up of a mountain rescue centre. Now that she had time on her hands, not to mention, adequate resources, she resolved to continue her pursuit of a long held ambition. Then her thoughts turned to James. Like her, he had lost his soul mate. As for Helen, she had suffered the same fate, but in a different way, though no less painful.

Helen was also lying awake in bed. She too was grieving, though not for the death of her soul mate; her grief was for the demise of her marriage. It was dead. Now, it was time to bury it. There and then she decided that, first thing tomorrow morning she would visit her solicitor in Drumevie and instruct him to commence with divorce proceedings. Like Isobel, Helen was a proud, stubborn and totally independent woman. Whether her husband's transgression was the result of a casual fling, infatuation, or true love, it made no difference. As far as she was concerned, their marriage had come to an end and there was no going back. She had no qualms about the prospect of remaining here at the croft for the foreseeable future. For some unexplained reason, the remote croft in the Black Glen had always held the same allure for her as it did for Isobel. It was here she felt a true sense of belonging and, now that her marriage was over, where she would remain for the time being. Similar to her young sister, she considered herself to be a one-man woman and no-one would ever replace Ruaridh as the love of her life.

It would make sense therefore that, in the meantime at least, they share the workload at An Gleann Dubh. Although the croft was owned by Rob, Helen was aware that Isobel could now afford to buy it from him if she so wished.

Although Helen thought the world of her siblings, if truth be known, she was slightly envious of Rob and Isobel's wealth. For one thing, it afforded them complete independence, although sadly, it had taken two tragic quirks of fate to bring this about. The four Ferguson siblings, once estranged by war, were alike in many ways. Although each had their own identity, they shared a common trait; they were single. There, the similarity ended though. Two of them were wealthy landowners, while the other two were penniless and homeless. Claire though, had landed on her feet. She was living a life of luxury in the mansion house at Inverculden, waited upon by servants, paid an adequate wage for her secretarial skills and had the added advantage of being allowed to fraternise with Rob's influential associates.

Early next morning, Helen left the croft with a bee in her bonnet. Her destination was Drumevie and her mission was to make an appointment with a solicitor. Isobel left soon after, on a different mission. Her destination was also Drumevie, but she was planning to revisit Drew, the joiner, to ask him when he could make a start to erecting the bothies.

****

Chapter 36

In the evening, the two sisters sat down to discuss the day's events. The children were asleep, the three dogs lay peacefully on the mat in front of the log fire, the Tilley lamps had been lit and the kitchen of the cottage at An Gleann Dubh radiated a sense of tranquillity and reassurance, and yet, Isobel felt that something was missing. Helen looked at Isobel and she returned her gaze.

'How did your meeting go?' she asked.

'I have an appointment with my solicitor on Friday morning,' Helen replied. 'How about yours?'

'Drew's coming here on Sunday to discuss the possibility of erecting the bothies.'

'Your future is all sorted and you have to rely on no-one to make it happen,' Helen remarked dolefully. 'What am I going to do about mine?'

Noting that she was on the verge of tears, Isobel replied reassuringly, 'You can stay here for as long as need be.'

'I appreciate that, but I can't stay here forever,' Helen responded solemnly.

The two sisters went on to discuss many topics that evening. They spoke about their past, their present and their future. They smiled while discussing the past, reminiscing about a happy, carefree, bygone time. The present they discussed with sorrow, heartache and regret. As for the future, it was uncertain, especially for Helen. Other than the croft, she had no place to call home. Unlike Isobel, she had no qualifications, and therefore, no career prospects. Isobel, on the other hand, had no concerns over her home or career - yet her future was also filled with doubt. She had two young children to rear and their welfare was her priority. As their needs changed, she would have to adapt her lifestyle to suit. Although the lives of the two siblings were in complete contrast to one another, the two sisters were unanimous in their decision. No matter what the future held for them, neither of them would consider remarrying.

Helen then changed the dreary and depressing subject of their present dire situation by asking Isobel about her plans for replacing Fly as a working sheepdog. He was failing fast and could no longer accompany Ben and Floss onto the hills. Isobel replied by saying that she had given some thought to advertising Ben as a stud dog; that way, she could have pick of the litter instead of charging a stud fee. The alternative, to take a litter of pups from Floss, she wouldn't even contemplate. Memories of losing her beloved Meg during whelping were still raw, and Floss and Ben were her only legacy.

Sunday morning duly came around and Drew had arrived to walk out with Isobel to Beinn a' Bhròin, the pinnacle of the mountain range. On his previous visit, he and Isobel had scaled Beinn Ghlas as far as the plateau. On their return he'd voice his opinion that, because of its remote location, not to mention the rugged terrain, he was dubious about the possibility of erecting any kind of shelter there. Beinn a' Bhròin was even more remote, and the terrain even more treacherous, therefore Isobel didn't hold out much hope of him agreeing to take on the job. Nonetheless, such was her dauntless spirit and perpetual optimism, it was a case of, nothing ventured - nothing gained.

Since Helen had kindly offered to mind Màiri and Iain, Isobel decided to leave Floss and Ben behind, but she would take Dileas. It would be the first time Dileas had left the croft since being brought here almost ten months ago and so much had happened in that time. On reflection, Isobel could hardly believe that the first anniversary of John's death was drawing near.

Dileas was on a long leash as the trio set off to walk to Beinn a' Bhròin. Isobel was conscious of the fact that they would be passing by the graveyard and through the narrow pass of the Black Glen. It was near to this spot that she'd found Dileas lying in a corrie, though how far she'd travelled, was anyone's guess.

She and Drew chatted while they walked, mostly idle chit-chat, but at one point, Drew looked at Dileas and commented that he hadn't seen her on his last visit.

'They're my favourite breed of dog,' he added. 'What made you decide to buy an Alsatian?'

Isobel's reply was a casual, 'I didn't.'

'Was she given away free to a good home?' he asked.

'No,' she answered with the hint of a smile.

'Ah, then you must have got her from the Cat and Dog Home,' he concluded with a smug expression.

'You're partly right. On the other hand, you're still wrong,' she responded with a smile.

All the while, Dileas, never having walked on a leash with Isobel, was acting as if this was an everyday occurrence.

Drew responded by saying, 'She's obviously been very well trained.'

Knowing that Drew's interest in Dileas's past was genuine, she decided to satisfy his curiosity by telling him the story of how she came to be in her possession.

****

Chapter 37

By the time Isobel had related the story from start to finish, they were approaching the graveyard. Isobel was concerned to see that Dileas' hackles were rising along the length of her spine and her body language had changed significantly. Apart from a few stragglers from the flock, there was not a living thing in sight. Although slightly puzzled by her bizarre behaviour, Isobel was also pleasantly surprised to see that Dileas had made no attempt to chase after the ewes. They had taken to their heels and were now mere dots in the distance. It was here Dileas had attacked the sheep and consequently been set upon by Ben. Perhaps that was the reason for her panic attack, Isobel thought to herself. Following her brief account of the history of the grave-yard, Isobel suggested to Drew that, since time was of the essence and they had a few miles to cover before even reaching the foothills, they shouldn't hang about. Not long after they'd left the vicinity of the ruined cottage, Dileas settled down. Now, they had reached the rocky slopes of Beinn a' Bhròin. Neither sheep nor cattle were in sight, and Isobel, aware that she was taking a huge risk by doing so, let Dileas off the leash. As she and Drew scrambled upwards over the uneven terrain, Dileas stayed close beside them. On the occasions when they stopped to rest, she obediently lay down at their feet. On one such occasion, Drew voiced his opinion that, while not meaning to shatter her dream of erecting a bothy in this location, to do so would be completely untenable.

'Having said that, I wouldn't mind coming out here again, if only for the walk,' he added.

Isobel glanced down at her feet and realised that Dileas had disappeared.

'I should have known better than to let her off the leash,' she cried in despair.

Despite scanning the horizon in every direction, there was neither sight nor sound of Dileas anywhere.

'She'll come back in her own time,' Drew remarked optimistically.

'And if she doesn't..........?'

Isobel couldn't even bear to contemplate the consequences of Dileas not returning. Her livestock roamed free on these hills. A large dog living wild among them would not only cause chaos and fear, but with winter fast approaching, she wouldn't survive for long in this harsh environment. Daylight was now beginning to fade and Dileas still hadn't reappeared.

'Hadn't we better head back to the croft?' Drew asked anxiously.

'I'm not going anywhere without Dileas,' Isobel replied abruptly.

'Are you crazy? We can't stay out here any longer. It wouldn't be safe.'

Isobel retaliated by saying, 'It would be, if we had a bothy.'

Drew laughed. 'You are one of a kind,' he muttered while shaking his head. 'I'll stay with you for another ten minutes. If she hasn't come back by then, I'm off.'

Isobel called on Dileas. She continued to call her name for another ten minutes, by which time, Drew had begun his descent. Just then, Dileas appeared out of nowhere and came straight to her side. While clipping the leash onto her collar, even in the twilight, Isobel could see that her muzzle was covered in mud. In fact, her entire body was mud-splattered.

'Where have you been?' Isobel murmured.

It was irrelevant. Dileas was here. Safe, if slightly muddy - but not bloody. Whatever she'd been doing in her absence, at least she hadn't come to any harm; and, equally important, she hadn't inflicted harm on anything- or anyone - else.

Isobel finally caught up with Drew and they completed the precarious descent from the mountain before the last glimmer of daylight disappeared. From here on, she was familiar with the terrain and the route. She had either walked or ridden this route so many times that she felt as though she could find her way back to the croft blindfolded if need be. They had now emerged from the narrow pass and were approaching the ruined croft, when Drew, lagging a few paces behind, let out an agonising scream.

'What have you done?' Isobel called out.

'Broken my ankle I think,' was his pained reply.

Oh no, Isobel muttered under her breath. As if that wasn't

bad enough, Dileas, now beginning to get edgy, was pulling on the leash and almost yanking her off her feet. As they retraced their steps towards the sound of Drew's agonising groans, Dileas stopped pulling on the leash. For some unknown reason, something about the area surrounding the graveyard was spooking her. Drew was lying on the ground and writhing in pain when Isobel reached him.

'Can you hobble to the shelter of the ruined croft?' she asked.

'Be better than lying out here I suppose,' he groaned.

Supporting Drew as they slowly made their way towards the burnt out shell of the old croft, Isobel had no alternative but to let go of Dileas' leash, knowing as she did so that, if she were to run off, she would be powerless to stop her. Much to her surprise and immense relief however, she followed close to her heel.

'I'll be back as soon as I can,' she called to Drew after propping him against one of the broken walls.

As she and Dileas made their way back to the croft, a pale moon lit up the night sky. Almost a year had passed since John's death and yet Isobel could remember the day as if it were yesterday. Soon, the welcoming glow from the paraffin lamps in the windows became visible. The croft was now in sight. Dileas had run ahead, and long before she reached the yard, Isobel could hear the sound of her high-pitched barking. Helen's face, as she stood in the doorway with a paraffin lamp in her hand, portrayed bewilderment and concern.

'I was on the point of calling a search party,' she began anxiously.

'Call Gordon and ask him to dial 999. We have to get a doctor out to the ruined cottage as a matter of urgency,' Isobel gasped. 'I'll explain later.'

Isobel tacked up Kismet and packed a thermos flask, blankets and a powerful torch into the saddle-bags before heading towards the Black Glen. This time, Dileas had been left in the safety of the cottage. In a relatively short time, they reached the graveyard. Her small but sturdy highland pony was familiar with the route, as sure-footed as a mountain goat, and much faster than the Land Rover. After dismounting, Isobel ran towards the ruin to find that Drew had lapsed into a state of semi-consciousness. The temperature had dropped sharply and, being conscious of the risk of hypothermia setting in, she tucked the blankets tightly round his quivering body. She felt his brow. It was cold and clammy. Then she felt his pulse. It was alarmingly faint and irregular. She lay beside him and wrapped her arms around him in an attempt to diffuse some of her body heat. With the blankets now shielding both their frames from the icy blast, she moved her body closer to his.

'Have I died and gone to heaven?' he whispered.

'Thankfully, you're still with us,' she replied softly.

Drew and Isobel lay in each other's arms for what seemed like an eternity, until the sound of the Land Rover could be heard approaching. Stepping from the shelter of the ruin, she could see Gordon, Helen and the local GP emerging from the Land Rover. At that moment, she let out a sigh of relief. At least the curse of the Black Glen hadn't claimed Drew as a victim. He was speedily diagnosed as having broken his ankle and given a shot of pain relief, before being manhandled into the Land Rover and taken back to the croft. Isobel mounted Kismet and reached the croft ahead of them.

As Gordon was about to leave to transport Drew to the hospital in the Land Rover, Isobel heard him calling her name.

Upon opening the vehicle door, Drew took her hand in his, saying, 'Thank you for saving my life. Just as soon as I'm mobile, I'll be back to discuss the erection of the bothies.'

'Get well soon,' she responded teasingly and squeezed his hand.

Isobel smiled to herself as they left the yard...... She was a step closer to achieving her other childhood dream. But it had taken a near tragedy to convince Drew of the need for a place of shelter on the unforgiving mountains.

The following day, Isobel walked out to the Black Glen with Dileas, Floss and Ben. The reason was two-fold. One, she was curious to see whether Dileas would react in the same

205

peculiar manner at the graveyard as she had the previous day, and two, while they'd been lying together in the shelter of the ruin, Drew had told her the reason for his fall. Apparently, he had stumbled over a large metal object. As they strolled along, Floss and Ben ran ahead as usual, while Dileas, being on the leash, walked by Isobel's side. As they approached the graveyard however, she stopped in her tracks and refused to move. Floss and Ben, tongues hanging from their mouths and glad of the chance to rest, were now lying in wait by the metal railings. Taking one tentative step at a time, Isobel persuaded Dileas to inch forward towards the waiting collies. For some unknown reason, Dileas was filled with fear. Yet the fact that the other two dogs were oblivious to anything untoward, left Isobel completely baffled. Similar to the previous day, as soon as they'd passed the graveyard, Dileas settled down and resumed her confident stride. Not far from the graveyard was the spot where Drew had stumbled, and, as they approached, Isobel could clearly see an object lying in their path. From a distance, it looked like a spade. As they got closer, a spine-chilling tingle shot through her entire frame. It was the spade John had used to bury the dead ewes. But why was it lying here she wondered? One by agonising one, Isobel went over the events of the last few days of John's life.

While out checking the stock one day, Dileas had appeared from nowhere and killed some of the ewes. Ben too, had been attacked and injured by Dileas. Dileas herself had been injured in the fight with Ben and Isobel had saved her life. The following day, John had gone to the Black Glen to bury the dead ewes. After doing so, he came across a young ram trapped by the horns in the metal railings. He dropped the spade and entered the graveyard to free the ram and returned home without the spade. Soon after, John had been killed by the bull..........

Isobel couldn't stop the tears from falling. In a few days time it would be the first anniversary of John's death and her heart still ached for him. His remains lay in the graveyard nearby and she retraced her steps towards the ruined cottage, leaving the spade in situ. Knowing that the last person to touch it had been her beloved husband, she couldn't bring herself to go near it. Dileas hung back as they approached the graveyard and Isobel let go of the leash before scaling the fence. She went over to the mound under which John's remains lay and knelt on the damp grass. Floss and Ben lay patiently on the other side of the fence, while a short distance away, Dileas hung her head and whimpered pitifully.

If only I could read her mind, Isobel said to herself. She knows something that I can't even begin to comprehend. Isobel continued to gaze straight ahead at the small headstone she'd erected in John's memory. She then began to read the inscription to her beloved husband: Here lie the remains of Dr John Caldwell...... but that wasn't all she was seeing. An image had appeared in front of her eyes. It was depicted on the headstone as if projected onto a cinema screen and the words were now imprinted across the face, making it almost impossible to recognise. Closing her eyes, Isobel drifted subconsciously into a state of meditation. The words began to fade and the image became crystal clear......... 'It can't be', she murmured. Isobel was bewildered and traumatised by the vision she'd seen so vividly depicted on the headstone. Then she recalled the words of the midwife. Is it possible that I really do have the gift of second sight, she asked herself.

****

Chapter 38

Isobel was deep in thought as she and the three dogs made their way back to the croft. Helen had stayed behind in the cottage with Máiri and Iain, the plan being that upon her return, Isobel would relieve Helen of the baby-minding duties so that she could check the stock on Beinn Ghlas. On entering the yard, Isobel was rather surprised to see Ruaridh's pick-up parked there. What could have prompted his visit, she wondered. After all, he'd known for almost three months that Helen was staying here. The raised voices she'd heard from outside stopped as she entered the kitchen. After a brief and awkward silence, Ruaridh said rather sheepishly, 'Hello Isobel.'

'You're not welcome here anymore,' she retorted.

'I didn't expect to be welcomed with open arms, but then, I didn't come here to see you, I came to talk to Helen. In private,' he added brusquely. 'Would you mind leaving us please?'

Isobel was struggling to control her anger. After her harrowing morning, all she longed for was to relax in solitude in the sanctuary of her own home. Ruaridh however, had made it clear that her presence was neither required, nor welcome.

'The cheek of him......' she fumed silently. Turning up unannounced and more or less ordering me out of my own home.

Isobel called on the dogs and left the cottage to check the flock on Beinn Ghlas. By the time she returned, Ruaridh had gone. Helen was preparing lunch when she entered the kitchen, albeit a late lunch since it was now mid-afternoon. She appeared composed and in a happier frame of mind than Isobel had been expecting; perhaps she and Ruaridh had sorted out their differences.

'Ruaridh has saved me the trouble of proceeding with the divorce,' Helen began as Isobel cast a questioning glance in her direction.

'Are you going back to him?' she asked expectantly.

'No never in a million years. He has already instructed his

solicitor to serve the divorce papers on me.'

'On what grounds,' Isobel exclaimed in disbelief. 'After all, he's the adulterer.'

'Irretrievable breakdown, apparently,' Helen replied nonchalantly. 'Let's drown our sorrows.'

Helen added two wine glasses to the place settings on the table, and, after filling both with champagne, lifted her glass and proposed a toast: 'To the future. The past is dead and buried. May the years to come bring love, luck and lasting happiness.'

'To the future,' Isobel echoed while raising her glass.

The present brought about a few milestones for the four Ferguson siblings. For Isobel, it saw the passing of the first anniversary of John's death. For Helen, it was the beginning of the termination of her marriage to Ruaridh. As for Claire, now running the estate of Inverculden, she appeared to have taken to her aristocratic country life like a duck to water. Having been given carte blanche by Rob to diversify as she saw fit, she was pursuing an enterprising venture that had been suggested by a guest at one of the recent social events she'd hosted.

As for Rob, he was gaining the reputation of being a successful breeder of steeplechasers and was more often jetting around the globe than at home.

The beginning of 1968 saw daily life for Helen, Isobel and her two children fall into a familiar pattern that suited all concerned. For the first time in many years, the croft was proving to be a viable business and providing a steady source of income. As part of John's legacy, the proceeds of the sale of his house in Dumlocher had been deposited into Isobel's bank account. His parents had now moved into John's house in Bayswater, leaving their own property, which they'd gifted to Isobel, unoccupied. Isobel planned to lease this property, that way it would provide yet another source of income.

Because of his excellent pedigree, having been bred from national champion sheepdog stock, Ben had been advertised as a stud dog in a farming magazine. The outcome of this was that several local crofters had responded and requested his services. Although the income from this was negligible in comparison to her vast wealth, it was all the more appreciated by Isobel because the idea had been hers alone. Another idea she'd had up her sleeve for some time was to acquire one of Ben's progenies to replace Fly as a working sheepdog. However, until now, and although she'd vetted all the litters he'd sired, none had taken her eye.

Helen's long-standing knowledge of crofting was proving to be invaluable in the running of the croft, as was her contributions of needlework and home baking. Having lifted the winner's cup many times at the local agricultural shows for her handicraft skills, Isobel suggested one day that she utilise them in a professional manner. Helen asked what she meant by her remark.

'Why don't you open a shop in Drumevie?' Isobel replied.

'Much as I'd love to, I don't have the resources,' she replied solemnly.

'But I do,' Isobel quipped. 'I'll provide the finances and the premises and leave the rest to you. That way, it'll be a joint venture.

'What a wonderful idea,' Helen replied dreamily. 'It's exactly the challenge I need to restore my confidence and provide a purpose to my existence. You are a wonderful sister and I thank God each day for reuniting us.'

'It was kismet that brought us together,' Isobel whispered as they embraced.

****

Chapter 39

The weeks rolled into months. The relatively trouble free winter had passed uneventfully and now, it was the summer of 1968. Isobel was twenty six years old and Helen, thirty four. Despite the two sisters being comparatively young women mourning their lost loves and shattered dreams, their daily workload meant they hadn't time to dwell on their heartache. Both siblings looked upon this as a blessing and had launched themselves into a gruelling routine of shift patterns to ensure that Máiri and Iain didn't suffer as a result. The two sisters had been blessed with the virtues of acquiescence, optimism and resilience, which stood them in good stead for dealing with life's challenges. Claire on the other hand, having been raised in a completely different way, was capricious, easily disillusioned, and workshy. On a whim and as a result of a casual remark made by someone she regarded as a rival, she'd decided to establish a riding school and livery yard at Inverculden. Tourism in the Highlands was beginning to flourish and at one of the social events she'd attended, she had eavesdropped on a conversation. The topic being discussed was the lucrative venture of establishing a pony trekking centre in the area. It was at that moment the seed was implanted in her head and the more thought she gave it, the greater the possibilities grew. The local scenery was magnificent, yet the finest views could only be reached off road. The extensive but challenging terrain was ideal for the sturdy, indigenous ponies. As far as the livery was concerned, Inverculden had adequate grazing pastures and the estate boasted a large, but at present unused, stable block. Despite her fortunate position of running the estate of Inverculden in Rob's absence, not to mention, the affluent lifestyle she'd acquired, Claire wasn't content with her lot. She was envious, perhaps even jealous, of Rob and Isobel's wealth. The scheme hatching inside her head was that, if the business venture was successful she could cream off some of the profits, little by little, to feather her own nest. After all, Rob had more cash than he could spend in a lifetime. He would never miss a few thousand pounds here and there.

The only drawback as far as Claire was concerned was that she wasn't a horse lover, or indeed, an animal lover. Despite the fact that Isobel had shown her how to tack up, mount and dismount, and even remain in the saddle in between, she had no intention of becoming involved in the physical practicalities of running an equestrian establishment. Her role would be purely in a managerial capacity.

One afternoon, Claire arrived unexpectedly at An Gleann Dubh. It was her first visit to the croft in over a year and Isobel was under no illusions that there would be an ulterior motive. Nonetheless, ever polite, she welcomed her sister with a friendly hug and the words, 'Claire, how nice of you to pay us a visit.'

Helen and Isobel exchanged glances as Claire responded by saying in a patronising tone, 'I was so concerned about my two sisters struggling to survive in this archaic, dilapidated, little cottage that I just had to check up on you.'

Isobel, always one to shoot from the hip, couldn't stop herself from responding with the words, 'But the real reason for your visit is.......?'

Claire smiled sweetly and replied, 'Plug in the percolator and I'll explain over a coffee....' before adding with a feigned gesture and a condescending smile, 'How silly of me. I'll settle for instant.'

Isobel filled the kettle and placed it on the gas stove, however, as she turned the tap on and held a match to the ring, it wouldn't ignite.

'Damn!' she cursed. 'The gas cylinder is empty and we don't have a spare.'

'So much for that idea then,' Claire muttered sarcastically.

'Fortunately, we have the means to improvise in our archaic, dilapidated, little cottage,' Helen responded in a similar tone.

Meanwhile, Isobel had brought out the sooty, old kettle, filled it with water and placed it on the hob at the side of the range. Before long, the water had boiled and coffee was served.

'Now, where was I?' Claire began as she sipped her piping hot, if slightly smoky flavoured, coffee.

Isobel butted in, saying, 'Make it snappy. I'll have to drive to Drumevie and pick up a gas cylinder before closing time.

Claire then rattled off her proposal to her two sisters, who meanwhile, had sat in silence, engrossed and deep in thought.

'That's a fantastic idea,' Isobel remarked enthusiastically.

Helen endorsed her remark by saying, 'I agree wholeheartedly. But what is it you want from us?'

'Quite a lot actually,' Claire replied. 'In fact, I don't know where to begin.'

For the next hour, the three sisters traded ideas and discussed the pros and cons of entering into the world of chiefly male dominated commerce. The outcome of the discussion was that Isobel would provide the necessary financial backing for Helen and Claire's businesses and assist Claire in the preparatory work. Once established, each would then take sole responsibility for their individual ventures. Isobel excused herself and left to make a quick dash to Drumevie to pick up a cylinder of butane gas, leaving Helen and Claire in charge of Màiri and Iain. Claire had promised to hang around until she returned, if only to get a decent cup of coffee before returning to Inverculden.

While struggling to heave the cumbersome canister into the rear of the Land Rover, Isobel heard a familiar voice calling out, 'Let me help you with that.'

She turned to see Drew MacLennan standing beside her.

'Too late,' she responded with a smile, while fastening the rear flaps of the Land Rover.

'The story of my life,' he joked.

Isobel's puzzled expression prompted him to add, 'I'm married.'

'Me too,' she responded with a mischievous grin.

They hadn't met since Drew's unfortunate accident, and, noticing that he appeared to have fully recovered, Isobel asked if he had given any more thought to taking on the work of erecting the bothies at An Gleann Dubh.

'If you've got half an hour to spare, we could discuss it over a coffee,' he replied.

Isobel couldn't begin to understand her reason for answering in the affirmative. It wasn't as if she had nothing better to do.

Back at the croft, Claire was beginning to get anxious. She'd promised to wait until Isobel returned and she'd already been gone over an hour. Isobel too, was anxious. Why, she asked herself, was she sitting in a café in Drumevie and engrossed in conversation with a married man. According to Drew, the purpose of the meeting was to discuss business, yet thus far the conversation had been rather one-sided. Isobel, well known for her ability to hog a conversation, hadn't been given the chance to speak. Drew had talked non-stop and bombarded her with questions. He wanted to know all there was to know about Isobel Caldwell.

'I dream about you,' he said, gazing intently into her eyes. 'I can't erase the memory of your body next to mine.'

Isobel was speechless. It was flattering to know that she was still desirable, yet at the same time, hugely embarrassing. She could feel the warmth of his knee touching hers under the table, and now, he had reached across and laid his hand on hers. Conscious of the fact that they weren't strangers in town and a few of the locals were seated nearby, Isobel withdrew her hand sharply.

'Drew, you're a married man,' she gasped. 'I really have to go.'

As luck would have it, the veterinary practice directly across the street was due to open for evening surgery as she and Drew emerged from the café. Isobel groaned silently when she spotted Tormod walking directly towards them, while at the same time thinking - why do I wish that the ground would open up and swallow me? On the other hand, she argued, I have no reason to feel guilty. I've done nothing wrong. Tormod was, after all, only an acquaintance. Yet, judging by the look on his face as they met, it was as though she'd committed the ultimate crime.

After a mumbled apology to Drew, Isobel beat a hasty retreat and headed for home. Her emotions were all over the place as she drove along the familiar route from Drumevie. Her main concern was that Tormod may have jumped to the wrong conclusion about her being with Drew. Then again, why should she care what he thought? Her powers of concentration were everywhere but on the road ahead, and at one point, the words John had instilled on her first driving lesson came to mind. "Let nothing distract you and never,

214

ever, take your eyes off the road, even for a moment". It was at a notorious bend not far from here that he'd learnt that lesson many years ago. Isobel though, was an experienced and confident driver. Besides, she knew the road like the back of her hand and could negotiate the hairpin bends like a racing driver. Unfortunately, the lorry heading in the opposite direction couldn't, and didn't. Even as she hit the brakes and yanked the steering wheel, the collision was inevitable. On impact, the gas cylinder shot through the Land Rover like a wayward missile, striking Isobel's head as it passed.

Claire, who'd given up waiting for Isobel, was heading back to Inverculden when she met a police car with a flashing blue light on its roof. Next, she encountered an ambulance, followed by a fire engine. Both had sirens blaring and blue lights flashing. Must have been an accident further north, she thought to herself while continuing on her way.
In Drumevie, Tormod and Drew heard the wailing of the local fire station siren but thought nothing of it. After all, a chimney fire in the locality was a common occurrence.
At the scene of the accident, the Land Rover was ablaze. The gas cylinder was lying on the road just a few feet away. The driver of the lorry, shocked, dazed and traumatised by the horrendous consequences of his momentary lack of concentration, staggered from the cab. He could see that a woman was trapped inside the burning vehicle; whether she was dead or merely unconscious, he couldn't tell. Then he spotted the gas cylinder. Due to the intense heat, it was in danger of exploding and the woman was trapped inside the burning vehicle. He pushed the gas cylinder with his foot and it began to roll down the road, then he ran to the Land Rover. He yanked the driver's door, but it was jammed against the side of his cab.
'Please God, will somebody help me,' he called out.
The fire engine from Drumevie, approaching from the north, was first to arrive at the scene. Within minutes, the firemen had extinguished the flames that had engulfed the canvas covered sides of the Land Rover, but Isobel was still slumped, motionless, across the steering wheel. Without knowing the

extent of her injuries, they daren't move her until the medical team arrived. Now, a small group of spectators had gathered at the scene, one being the person who had driven to Ardbuie and called the emergency services from the village kiosk.

'Get back, there's nothing you can do', they were told by the firemen.

'I recognise the Land Rover's registration number,' someone called out. 'It's the widowed crofter from An Gleann Dubh.'

Just then, two police cars and an ambulance arrived on the scene. Since the two crashed vehicles were completely blocking the road in both directions, the drivers of all stationery traffic were instructed to about turn and find an alternative route.

Back at the croft, Helen was frantic with worry. Isobel had been due back with the replacement gas cylinder over an hour ago. The fact that she'd no gas to cook the evening meal was an inconvenience, but her main concern was for Isobel. It was completely out of character for her to be late - or thoughtless. Perhaps she's had a puncture, or a breakdown, or........The sound of a vehicle drawing up in the yard made her heart skip a beat. That'll be her now, she said to herself while rushing to the back door. Helen could see that it wasn't Isobel, but a neighbouring crofter with whom she was vaguely familiar. Before she had a chance to speak, he blurted out the words, 'There's been an accident.'

'Isobel......?'

'Yes, I'm afraid so. It looks bad, really bad,' he said solemnly.

'Where is she?' Helen asked, the colour draining from her face. 'I have to see her.'

Nodding towards the pick-up, he said, 'Jump in. I'll drive you there.'

'I've got Isobel's two children here,' Helen gasped, 'I'll go fetch them.'

Helen bundled Iain and Màiri into the pick-up and they began to make their way down the track towards the farm.

'Stop here for a moment please,' Helen said as they approached the farmhouse, 'I'll leave the children with Mairead and Gordon.'

216

Mairead was inconsolable by the time Helen had finished briefing her. 'Call me the minute you've any news,' she cried out tearfully as they sped off.

They'd only travelled a short distance along the main road when Helen spotted the flashing blue lights through the trees. Her stomach was heaving so much she feared she would vomit in the pick-up as it came to a stop behind the rear of the lorry. Opening the door to take a gulp of fresh air, all she could smell was burnt fabric and acrid smoke. Helen just couldn't stop herself from throwing up on the grass verge. She felt a comforting hand on her shoulder and heard a voice say, 'When you're ready, I'll come with you.'

The crofter, his arm now reassuringly around her waist, guided Helen towards the burnt out shell of the Land Rover. The fire crew were still cutting through the twisted metal in an effort to free Isobel.

'Stay back,' a policeman ordered.

'Helen's her sister,' the crofter retaliated while pushing his way past.

Isobel had now been freed from the tangle of twisted metal and the medical team were assessing her injuries. Helen was told that her sister had sustained multiple injuries, but most concerning, since she'd remained unconscious throughout, they suspected that she'd also suffered an injury to the brain. When the nurse had finished taking some personal details from Helen, she could only watch with increasing despair and futility as Isobel was placed on a stretcher and carried to the waiting ambulance. Since the nearest hospital in Drumevie wasn't well enough equipped to deal with the severity of her injuries, it was decided to take her to a city hospital some forty miles away.

'Please let me go with her,' Helen pleaded. 'I'm her next of kin.'

Helen was told that, while she would be permitted to come to the hospital, she would have to make her own way there. The rear doors closed and the ambulance sped off with lights flashing and siren wailing. Helen stood in the middle of the road like a petrified statue. She was in a state of shock, trembling, horrified and made worse by the fact that she couldn't take her eyes off the burnt out shell of the Land Rover. She was rooted to the spot, apparently inconspicuous as a police officer interviewed the lorry driver and others surveyed the crash site. It suddenly dawned on her that she was alone, with no money or transport. Making her way aimlessly from the crash scene, her eyes fell on an object at the side of the road. It was the gas cylinder Isobel had picked up from Drumevie. Helen began to sob hysterically. Then she heard a familiar voice say, 'I'll drive you to the hospital.'

Helen turned to see the crofter standing beside her, the one she didn't know by name, but had been kind enough to summon her and drive her here.

'Thank you, but I can't take up any more of your valuable time. I would really appreciate a lift to the farm though,' she replied tearfully.

Helen climbed into the pick-up and was driven the short distance to the farm by the crofter she knew by sight, but not by name. Isobel occupied her thoughts throughout the journey as they travelled in silence. She'd only been a few minutes' drive from the road end into the farm when she met her fate. Helen reprimanded herself for thinking the worst. She's not dead. She's alive.......At least, she was.

As they drew up at the farmhouse, Helen mumbled the words, 'Thank you so much. I don't even know your name, or where you're from.'

Her Good Samaritan's tone was soft and lilting as he replied, 'My name is Dùghall MacKintosh. I run the croft over the hill from yours - in the neighbouring glen to An Gleann Dubh.'

The words went over the top of Helen's head. All she could think about right at this moment was Isobel.

****

Chapter 40

In Drumevie, the rumour was spreading like wildfire that the crofter from An Gleann Dubh had been killed in a horrific road accident, just a few miles south of the town. It was only a matter of time before the news reached the ears of Tormod MacAlister and Drew MacLennan.

Needless to say, they were both deeply affected by the awful news. Drew's emotions were of sadness and guilt. After all, he'd known Isobel was in a rush to get back to the croft and it was he who'd delayed her. From the moment they met, he'd been intrigued by the feisty, young widow from An Gleann Dubh. He'd been looking forward to meeting up with her over the summer months to discuss the bothies – and perhaps get to know her better. As for Tormod, he was in shock and utterly devastated. He'd only ever felt this way once before, when he'd lost his parents. He'd been in the midst of evening surgery when he'd overheard two of his clients discussing the tragic accident in the waiting room. With their two canine patients still to be seen, he'd taken the decision to close the surgery.

'What can I do?' he muttered to himself as he began to make his way home. 'Who can I contact?'

Tormod's homeward journey took him past the scene of the accident and by the time he got there, the lorry had been moved to the side of the road to enable single file traffic to pass. The Land Rover's charred remains however, were still in situ. While taking his foot off the accelerator on approach, Tormod couldn't take his eyes off the wreckage. His van was now stationery and he was staring at the Land Rover's burnt out remains in disbelief when a police officer appeared at the window.

'Can't stop here,' he told him. 'Keep moving.'

'I'm a friend of Isobel's,' he stammered. 'Was a friend, I should say.'

'She was alive when they cut her free,' the officer began in a solemn tone, 'must have died on her way to hospital.'

'Alive!' Tormod exclaimed.

'Aye, in a bad way, but still alive,' the officer said. 'Move on now.'

Tormod drove on, and for a reason he couldn't explain, found himself driving up the drive that led to the farm of Mairead and Gordon. As he pulled up at the farmhouse, Helen and Gordon were emerging from the door. He could see that Helen had been crying, and Gordon, big and brawny as he was, had matching red-rimmed eyes. Tormod emerged from his van with the intention of enquiring about Isobel, but was completely tongue-tied. The words just wouldn't come out.

'Hello Tormod,' Helen began. 'Isobel's been involved in an accident. We're on our way to the hospital.'

'I heard.....' Tormod began. 'I heard about it in Drumevie. I'd like to come with you if I may?'

Helen and Gordon exchanged glances.

'There's no point in us all going,' he began. 'If Tormod's going with you, I'd be better staying here and holding the fort at the croft 'til you get back.'

Helen glanced at Tormod expectantly. 'If Tormod doesn't mind driving me to the hospital, it would solve a few problems.'

Helen jumped into the passenger seat and she and Tormod set off on the long drive to the hospital. As they travelled, Helen filled him in with the details of the accident and as much as she'd been told about Isobel's condition. Apart from that, the journey was spent in complete silence.

Upon reaching the hospital they were advised that Isobel was in theatre and, following surgery, only her next of kin would be allowed to see her for a brief moment.

'You may as well go home,' Helen said to Tormod as they sat in the waiting room.

'I'm not going anywhere until I've seen Isobel,' he replied adamantly, and within deliberate earshot of the nurse.

Helen was slightly taken aback by the uncharacteristic outburst from the mild-mannered young vet. Even Tormod himself was taken aback by his aberrant determination that he wasn't leaving until he'd seen Isobel.

'You'll be allowed five minutes maximum,' the nurse warned him.

Helen managed a faint smile. It was comforting to be in the

company of someone with whom Isobel was familiar, and especially someone who thought so highly of her.

'Please God, don't let her die,' Tormod murmured.

For someone who'd never prayed in his life, he was clutching at straws. Yet, he had to hang on to something, and what was there but hope, faith, and........love.

'I love her,' he whispered.

Helen laid her hand on his and said softly, 'You and me both.' Helen leant her head against Tormod's shoulder and closed her eyes. It was now eleven o'clock in the evening and Isobel was still in theatre. She'd been there for over five hours. Just then, a nurse appeared, glanced at Tormod and asked, 'Are you Isobel Caldwell's next of kin.'

Helen's heart skipped a beat. 'No. I am,' she said nervously.

'You may come and see Isobel for a few minutes.'

Tormod followed on as Helen walked behind the nurse, who then stopped in her tracks and asked rather sharply, 'Are you a relative?'

'Yes,' he stammered, 'we are...... planning to get married.'

Tormod's uncharacteristic behaviour thus far tonight was causing him some confusion. For the first time in his life he had raised his voice in public. He had offered a prayer to God, and now, he had just told a whopper of a lie.

The nurse led them into a brightly lit room filled with weird apparatus and noisy machines, to which a patient was hooked up. Helen stifled a gasp as she gazed down at the bed. She'd never seen a corpse before, but right at this moment was convinced that this person, whom she'd been told was her sister, had just passed away. The reassuring beep at regular intervals from the machine monitoring her heartbeat was the only sign that Isobel was still in the land of the living. Her face was bruised and swollen, her head swathed in bandages, rendering her unrecognisable. The thought crossed Helen's mind that, had Isobel died and she'd been asked to identify her, she would have struggled to do so. Her stomach began to heave. She was praying she wouldn't throw up in here. The room began to spin. As she slumped to the floor, a buzzer sounded and two nurses entered the room. Helen was carried off on a stretcher, leaving Tormod in the

221

room with Isobel. So engrossed in reading the data on the machines was the nurse, that Tormod thought he must be invisible. However, she turned sharply as he asked, 'Is she going to be okay?'

'It's too early to tell,' the nurse replied. 'The surgeon has removed a blood clot from her brain and she has suffered severe blood loss from her internal injuries. She'll be kept in an induced coma for as long as is necessary. Tormod buried his face in his hands. His conflicting thoughts were addling his brain. A voice brought him back to reality. 'I'm afraid you'll have to postpone the wedding.'

His head shot up.

'I was told you were planning to get married soon.'

Just then, a doctor entered the room and asked Tormod to leave. He went in search of Helen and found her in a small cubicle. Having merely fainted due to dehydration and the effects of shock, she'd come round after being given fluids. It was time to go home.

That same evening, many miles away in London, Dr and Mrs Thornton were in a state of shock and despair. They knew nothing about Isobel's accident, but had received an old copy of the Dumlocher Weekly Herald in the post. Occasionally, one of their old neighbours forwarded it when she'd finished reading it. Dr Thornton had been scrolling down the list of obituaries, when, out of the blue, he'd let out a gasp of surprise. His wife had looked up from her knitting and asked, 'What is it?'

'Mary Anderson is dead,' he'd replied solemnly. 'We must write to Isobel Ferguson at the croft. Once we have an address, we must contact Mary's family and send our condolences. After all, she was the mother of our grandchild.'

****

222

Chapter 41

Six months had now passed since Isobel's horrific accident and she'd remained in the city hospital in an induced coma for that time. The family had been told that it was impossible to establish the extent of her brain damage until she'd regained a degree of consciousness. They'd been told further that the trauma suffered as a result of the gas cylinder striking her head had been horrendous and her best chance of recovery was complete rest. During her stay in hospital, her only visitors, on Doctor's orders, had been her closest family members. Helen had visited when time allowed, but due to her being in sole charge of the croft, not to mention caring for Máiri and Iain, it hadn't been as often as she would have liked. Rob too, had visited, as had Claire and their father. Nancy, Isobel's mother, couldn't be contacted; her whereabouts being a mystery to all at present. Tormod, being betrothed to Isobel, at least as far as the hospital staff was concerned, was allowed to visit daily. Despite it being a round trip of eighty miles, he had carried this out as often as his workload would allow.

Although Tormod was now virtually running the place single-handedly, the veterinary practice was still owned by the old vet who'd hired him to help out in his semi-retirement a few years ago. One day, he summoned Tormod to a meeting. Tormod was slightly concerned by this. Perhaps he was about to be reprimanded for taking so much time off work to visit Isobel in hospital, he mused. On the other hand, it could be worse than that, perhaps he'd decided to replace him. It was with much relief and surprise that he was asked by the old man if he would be interested in taking on the practice single-handedly. Tormod replied that he would like nothing better, if only he had the capital. The elderly vet sat in thoughtful silence. He was aware that the local crofters had taken to the young vet. Tormod had an inborn and unique gift of handling animals, both great and small. He was equally as adept at calving a cow on a remote hillside as he was at calming the fears of an elderly pet owner in the surgery. He was a true professional and completely dedicated to his vocation. After a lengthy discussion, they came to an amicable agreement. Tormod would continue as before, the only difference being, that instead of receiving a weekly wage he would retain the income for himself. Any profit accrued could be used to buy the business little by little. The pair shook hands on the deal and parted company.

As Tormod drove back to his cottage, he was mulling over the commitment he'd just made. The more he thought about the idea, the more he liked it. It was the only veterinary practice in Drumevie, actually, it was the only one within a ten mile radius. The number of domestic animal patients attending evening surgery was slowly but steadily on the increase and the local crofters were currently experimenting with imported breeding stock. All of which meant more business for him. How could he possibly fail?

For the first time ever, Tormod was in an extremely positive frame of mind as he entered the empty cottage that evening. If only he'd had someone to share the good news with...... or even someone to run it past for a second opinion. Isobel would have been the ideal person, he mused. She would have voiced her opinion in no uncertain terms. Just then, the shrill ring of the telephone jolted him back to reality.

'I'm phoning from the hospital. I have to get in touch with Isobel Caldwell's next of kin...,' the female voice began.'

Fearing the worst, Tormod's blood ran cold.

'Yours is the only telephone number we have on file,' she added.

'What's happened?' Tormod asked frantically.

'Isobel has regained consciousness,' she replied.

Tormod could feel tears welling up in his eyes as he whispered, 'Thank God,'

'She has been asking for Màiri, Mòrag, and Seumas,' the voice went on. 'Are they your children?'

Tormod, realising he was in a bit of a predicament, responded by saying, 'One is Isobel's child from her first marriage. I don't know the others. Can I see her?'

'Yes, of course. I'll let her know you are on your way.'

The handset at the other end of the line was promptly put down and Tormod stared straight ahead for a few moments, before replacing his in the cradle. His emotions were all over the place. He was ecstatic at the news that Isobel had regained consciousness and, from what he'd been told, appeared to be coherent. He would have to get a message to Helen and let her know the good news. Then he would make his way to the hospital before the end of visiting time. He hadn't even had time to eat, or wash, and........he couldn't even be sure how Isobel would react upon seeing him. After all, he really had no right to be there. He'd been told she was only being allowed two visitors, and even then, only for a short time. Rob should have had precedence over him. He dialled the number he'd found in the directory for Gordon and Mairead. It was Mairead who answered and she promptly burst into tears when told the good news.

'Mairead, I have to go,' he said urgently. 'Can you get a message to Helen?'

Tormod's heart was thumping erratically as he walked along the familiar corridor that led to Isobel's side-ward. During his many visits over the summer months he had merely sat in silence by her bedside. Occasionally, when a nurse was present, he'd held her hand - he was her fiancé after all - but today, he had no way of knowing what awaited him. As luck would have it, Isobel was being attended to by a nurse when he entered the ward and she turned her head as he approached the bed.

'I'll leave you two lovebirds alone for a couple of minutes. You'll have a lot of catching up to do,' she said with a wink before leaving the room

'Hello Isobel.'

There was no response and Isobel merely gazed at him with a vacant expression.

'How are you feeling?' he asked.

'I've felt better,' she replied feebly. 'Do I know you?'

'I'm Tormod MacAlister, the local vet.'

It was obvious that Isobel was struggling to make sense of the situation, her response being slow and laboured, 'I've been told I'm in Locherton City Hospital, forty miles from my home. It's good of you to come all this way to see me.'

Tormod smiled and said reassuringly, 'If Helen gets my message, she'll be here soon.'

Isobel's face remained expressionless as she focused her eyes on his face and said in a forlorn tone, 'Do I know Helen?'

Just then, the nurse entered the room and said, 'I'm sorry, but Isobel needs to rest now.' Following Tormod from the room, she added, 'The consultant would like a word with you.'

Tormod was taken to the consulting room of the hospital's senior neurosurgeon.

'Take a seat,' he said, motioning towards a large armchair. 'I'm led to believe that, apart from her immediate family, you are next in line as far as family goes.'

'I.... I..... suppose I am,' Tormod stuttered.

The surgeon carried on regardless. 'Although I am delighted with her truly remarkable recovery from what was potentially a life-threatening injury, she's not out of the woods yet. Since regaining consciousness, Isobel has had a few lucid moments, however..........'

He paused, and Tormod was conscious of the rumbling sound coming from his stomach. Partly, it was due to nerves, but also, he was ravenous. Primarily, it was down to apprehension about what was to come. His prime concern had been that Isobel would have enlightened the staff about him not being her fiancé, but nothing could have prepared him for what came next.

'When Isobel regained consciousness, the first question I asked was, 'What is your name.' She replied without hesitation: "My name is Ishbel MacKenzie."

'*What?*' the word came out like a bullet from a gun.

'That's not all,' the surgeon went on. 'I asked if she could remember her date of birth, and again she replied immediately, 23rd July, 1710.

Tormod was beginning to feel slightly uneasy.

Our main concern is that we have no conception of what's going on inside her head. It's early days of course, but it would seem that, somewhere in the deep, dark depths of her mind, she has taken on the identity of someone else - even more bizarrely, someone who lived during the eighteenth

226

century. She also mentioned the names, Màiri, Mòrag and Seumas.

'Màiri is her daughter. Seumas was the name of a bull at the croft, but I have no idea who Mòrag is,' Tormod remarked while shaking his head in bewilderment.

'Perhaps you could try to find out,' the surgeon responded.

They stood up simultaneously and Tormod asked, 'What happens now?'

'She'll stay in hospital for a few weeks. We may transfer her to Drumevie to convalesce. If she is still suffering from delusions, we'll refer her to a psychiatrist.'

Tormod's head was reeling as he walked along the corridor. A psychiatrist, he muttered to himself. Isobel is only suffering from amnesia for goodness sake. She doesn't have mental health issues. As he was leaving the hospital, Helen barged through the door and they literally bumped into one another.

'Oh Tormod, isn't it wonderful news,' she began excitedly.

'It is...... and then again - it isn't,' he replied with a frown.

'I don't understand,' Helen exclaimed anxiously.

Tormod hesitated - after all - perhaps Isobel would recognise Helen. He hadn't eaten since lunchtime and knew that, right at this moment, he was in no fit state to drive.

'I'll wait for you in the café,' he said wearily. 'I'll explain then. If you haven't found out for yourself,' he added when Helen was out of earshot.

Tormod's hunger had now been satisfied and his hands were wrapped round a mug of strong black coffee when Helen walked into the café. Her face was ashen and she appeared on the point of collapse as she approached the table.

'Sit down,' he said gently, 'I'll get you a coffee.'

Helen sat down and sighed wearily. Her eyes were red and swollen from crying.

'Didn't she recognise you either?' he asked sympathetically.

She shook her head and said despairingly, 'Oh Tormod. What are we going to do?'

'We're going to try and find out what's going on inside her head,' he replied resolutely.

It was the week before Christmas when, during a hospital

visit, Tormod was told that his fiancé had recovered sufficiently from her physical injuries to allow her to be discharged from hospital. Tormod was delighted to hear this; however, there was a downside. He was told further that Isobel was being allowed home for a brief visit over the festive period, following which, she would be referred to a psychiatrist. This would necessitate her being institutionalised to allow the obligatory tests and assessments to be carried out. Three weeks had now passed since awakening from her coma and she had no recollection of her present life to date. In the hopes that it would jog her memory, Màiri and Iain had been allowed a brief visit, but to no avail. The children hadn't seen their mother in six months and Màiri had clung to Isobel like a limpet. Isobel had been told they were her children and although she acknowledged them as her own flesh and blood, had remained coolly detached. It almost broke Helen's heart to see the expressions of confusion on the children's faces. Isobel had always been a loving and devoted mother and now, she was behaving like a total stranger. Perhaps, she thought optimistically, once back home and in familiar surroundings, her memory will begin to return.

It was on Christmas Eve that Tormod travelled to the hospital in Locherton to bring Isobel home. On the return journey, the atmosphere between them was strained, with neither knowing what to say. As far as Isobel was concerned, Tormod was a complete stranger, and yet, she'd been told they were engaged to be married. Her mind was befuddled anyhow, but she couldn't understand why she was already wearing a wedding ring on her finger. She gazed at the two rings on her left hand and began to fidget with them. Without looking up, and with no emotion in her voice, she said, 'I believe you are my fiancé.'

Tormod was taken unawares by her unexpected remark and it took a great deal of effort to maintain his concentration on driving.

Without taking his eyes off the road, he responded by saying, 'I have a great deal of explaining to do. But it can wait until you're feeling better.'

Gazing vacantly out the window as they passed the farmhouse, there wasn't a flicker of recognition on Isobel's face. However, as they began to negotiate the winding track through the glen, she sat up in her seat and looked around with interest. At the croft, Helen and the children were eagerly awaiting their arrival. Màiri had helped Helen to decorate the Christmas tree and hang the tinsel. Rob had returned from his travels abroad and he too had come to welcome Isobel home. Against his better judgement, but at her insistence, he'd brought Claire along. Tormod and Isobel were approaching the gate into the yard, when Isobel gasped and exclaimed, 'I recognise this place. I've been here before.'

Tormod sighed with relief. Perhaps there was a chance that her memory would return after all.

The moment the van stopped in the yard, the back door of the cottage opened and the welcoming party emerged. As Isobel stepped from the van, the first ones to greet her were Ben, Floss, and Dileas – sadly, Fly had passed away during her absence. She bent to pat the dogs before staring at Rob and Claire.

Rob stepped forward and held her close, before greeting her with the words, 'Welcome home little sis, it's so good to have you home.'

Isobel responded by saying, 'You must be Seumas.'

'No Bella, I'm Rob, your beloved brother,' he replied with a look of confusion.

Claire then stepped forward, 'And I'm your older sister Claire.'

'My brother's name is Seumas and my older sister's name is Mòrag,' Isobel responded with a frown.

'Let's go inside,' Rob interrupted, 'before we all freeze to death.'

Isobel smiled as she entered the spacious kitchen of the little whitewashed cottage; here, she felt some connection. There were no blinding, artificial lights. It felt warm and homely instead of clinical and alien. The logs spat and hissed inside the ingle nook, sending sparks and multicoloured flames dancing up the chimney. A couple of flickering candles adorned the mantelpiece and the smell of oil from the lamps in the window recesses pervaded the room. In the corner, the

229

Christmas tree shimmered and sparkled with brightly coloured baubles and silver tinsel, and three large dogs lay peacefully on the mat in front of the hearth. Despite feeling completely detached from any of her companions, for the first time since wakening from her nightmare, Isobel had a feeling she was in familiar surroundings.

Later that evening, Rob and Claire left the croft to return to Inverculden. Before they left, Claire glanced at Tormod and said with a hint of sarcasm, 'Perhaps you'll have some time for me now that Isobel has come home. Would you care to join us for Christmas Day lunch at Inverculden?'

Tormod declined the invitation, making work commitments his excuse. Once again, he was telling a little white lie. Despite being on stand-by for any emergencies, Tormod had no surgery appointments the following day and had envisaged a day of complete rest. For the past six months he had juggled his life between work and hospital visits. Now that Isobel was home, albeit temporarily, he was looking forward to a brief respite from travelling; besides, he had no wish to spend Christmas Day with Claire.

In the evening, as he sat by the roaring log fire, Tormod could feel himself dozing off. He couldn't remember a time when he'd felt so relaxed. Helen had taken Màiri and Iain to the bathroom to get them ready for bed, and Isobel had gone to her bedroom to unpack. His repose was interrupted by Helen saying, 'Would you like to stay overnight and have Christmas Day lunch with us?'

'Much as I'd like to, I can't. I'm on emergency stand-by,' he began sleepily. 'Besides, you, Isobel and the children have some catching up to do and, much as I'd like to be, I'm not part of the family.'

'I'll never be able to thank you for your moral support during the past few months,' Helen replied. 'During that time, I've come to think of you as part of the family and I would love you to share Christmas Day with us.'

Tormod and Helen shared a common bond - their genuine concern and love for Isobel. He'd enjoyed being part of their family for the past six months and suddenly, the thought of

230

spending Christmas Day alone was quite depressing. There was something about this little croft he felt an affinity with. It reminded him of his childhood, the only time - apart from right at this moment - he'd ever felt truly happy.

'You've twisted my arm,' he responded with a smile.

Helen excused herself saying she would make up the bed in the loft. 'It used to be Isobel's favourite room,' she added.

Isobel returned to the kitchen and knelt beside the dogs on the mat in front of the fire. Even though she didn't recognise them, she began to stroke each of them lovingly.

'What are their names,' she asked.

Tormod, recalling the stressful and traumatic times Isobel had endured with both Ben and Dileas, not to mention the devotion she felt for all her dogs, found it almost incomprehensible that it had all been completely wiped from her memory.

He smiled sympathetically as he named each dog in turn. The three dogs couldn't hide their pleasure at having their beloved mistress home and were vying for closest position.

'Kismet will also be pleased to see you,' Tormod remarked casually.

'Kismet,' Isobel questioned.

'Your Highland pony,' he explained.

'I have a pony?'

'Yes. I'll take you to the stable tomorrow.'

'Are you coming back tomorrow?' she asked.

Tormod couldn't stop himself from laughing at her bemused expression, and replied, 'No. I'm staying here overnight.'

Helen popped her head round the door to say that the bedroom in the loft was ready for use, she was going to bed, and would see them in the morning.

'I can't begin to understand why I don't feel any emotions,' Isobel said as she gazed, trance-like, into the flames. 'I'm like a robot. No feelings, no heart, no soul and no personality.'

'You suffered a serious head injury. You are extremely lucky to be alive.' Tormod replied.

'If we are engaged to be married, shouldn't I be in love with you? ' she asked.

Tormod's heart went out to her at that moment. Her

expression was forlorn, confused, vulnerable and childlike. How could he go on deceiving her?

'Isobel.....' he began.

'Kiss me,' she said softly, draping her arms around his neck.

Their lips touched lightly. Tormod had no previous experience of kissing anyone properly.

'That's not a kiss,' she whispered, and their lips met again. This time, she ran her tongue around the inside of his mouth and he could feel the softness of her hands against his skin.

Tormod had never experienced a sensation like this before. He was trembling. His reactions were purely instinctive as he reciprocated her kiss, his hands now caressing her naked skin. He was nervous, excited, and burning up with desire, yet he recoiled as if he'd been electrocuted.

'What's wrong,' she murmured. 'We are betrothed.'

'Isobel, we are not betrothed.'

'I don't understand. Why are you trying to confuse me?'

Tormod was struggling to find the right words. How could he explain the reason for having deceived her without becoming deeper involved. He hadn't set out to mislead her. It had all been caused by a white lie told on the spur of the moment.

'Where is my husband?' she asked abruptly.

Tormod looked up sharply.

'I'm wearing a wedding ring.'

'You were married once,' Tormod replied in a sympathetic tone.

'Am I divorced?'

'No. You are a widow.' he replied softly.

Isobel frowned and bowed her head. Tormod thought that, from somewhere deep within, there was a flicker of light, but her reply scuppered that conclusion.

'Are we a couple?' she asked.

Tormod gave a wry smile 'No. Unfortunately, we're not even that.'

'Are you married?' she asked with an innocent expression.

Tormod shook his head.

Isobel stood up saying, 'I'm going to bed. Goodnight.'

****

232

Chapter 42

Tormod didn't sleep a wink that night. Although he'd previously imagined that he would fall asleep as soon as his head hit the pillow, he was wide awake and thinking that he should really be at home waiting for the telephone to ring. He couldn't get his head around the fact that, this is where he wanted to be, not just for one night, but forever. Isobel was a lost soul and he was the only person, apart from Helen and the hospital staff, with whom she'd communicated since awakening from her coma. She had three weeks in which to regain her memory – or at least – some degree of recollection. If not, she would be locked away beside patients with serious mental health problems. The nearest asylum was some thirty miles away, and despite mental health issues now being regarded as a curable illness, there was a stigma attached to anyone that had been a patient in an asylum. Perhaps, he thought, if he could spend some time with her, he could prevent that from happening. What he mustn't do, was stand back, do nothing and allow it to happen. He lay awake and wracked his brains to come up with a solution. Then he had an idea. He could advertise for a temporary locum to cover the practice for the next few weeks. Then again - perhaps not - there wasn't enough time for one thing. Perhaps his predecessor would come out of retirement for a few weeks? There was no harm in asking.

In the stillness of the night, Tormod thought he could hear footsteps on the stair ladder. He'd left the door slightly ajar, and although the room was in complete darkness, he could sense that someone had just entered.

'Tormod,' a voice said softly. 'I'm scared of the dark.'

'I'm right here,' he replied. As she snuggled up to him in the single bed, he held her tightly and whispered, 'I'll always be here.'

They lay in each other's arms until daybreak. Even here, in the room that held so many precious childhood memories for Isobel, it was like being here for the very first time. Next morning, as they entered the kitchen together, Helen and the children were opening their presents from under the

Christmas tree.

'Merry Christmas,' Helen said as she rose and greeted Isobel. 'Your gifts are under the tree.' She then gazed at Tormod apologetically and said, 'I'm afraid I don't have anything for you.'

'I have all I need right here,' he responded tenderly while placing his arm around Isobel's shoulders.

Isobel smiled and leant her head on his shoulder.

'I'll have to go...' he'd begun to say, when Isobel looked at him wide-eyed and said imploringly, 'Please don't leave me here alone.'

'I thought you were staying for lunch,' Helen added.

Tormod kissed Isobel's cheek and said, 'I'll be back in time for lunch, I promise.'

The two sisters spent the morning preparing lunch, while Màiri and Iain played contentedly with their new toys. Each time Màiri asked a question, she directed it at Helen rather than her mother. Not that this bothered Isobel in the least. She accepted that they were part of her family, yet oddly, still felt completely alienated from them. So too, did she feel detached from her bizarre existence. It wasn't that she was unhappy here, but there was something about this place, somewhere in her mind, that was troubling her. If only she could remember what it was? While helping her sister set the table, Isobel was puzzled by the fact that Helen was fastidiously setting out twelve places.

'Who are we catering for?' she asked in bemusement.

'I've arranged a surprise for you,' Helen replied with a wink. 'You'll find out soon enough.'

Unknown to Isobel, Helen had invited their father, Stella, their daughter Anna, Mairead, Gordon and Calum. Surely, she had thought to herself when the idea first came into her head, of all the most important people in her life, Isobel would recognise one of them. The other person she'd invited, this one a complete stranger to all, but one she wanted Isobel to meet, was the Good Samaritan from the day of her horrific accident. The crofter had been a tower of strength to Helen that day and had kept in touch over the summer months. He had even lent a hand during the haymaking and had followed

234

Isobel's progress from day one. Helen had learned that he lived alone on the croft in the neighbouring glen. He, like them, was a tenant crofter, the land being part of Inverculden Estate. He and Helen had become firm friends, and although there was no romantic involvement between them, he had provided a willing shoulder for her to cry on. Helen's divorce from Ruairidh was well underway, and strangely, she could hardly wait for the day to come when the decree would become absolute. Since meeting him many years ago, there hadn't been a time when she imagined she would ever feel this way, but she accepted that, times and circumstances bring change.

The first ones to arrive at the croft were Mairead, Gordon and Calum. Since none of them had been allowed to visit Isobel in hospital, this was their first reunion since before the accident. Most of the injuries Isobel suffered had been internal, and, apart from a large scar on her head from the operation, which her hair was now covering, Isobel hadn't changed a bit – at least on the outside. As Mairead gazed at the vacant expression on the beautiful face she knew and loved, tears filled her eyes. 'Isobel,' she whispered, hugging her tight, 'Surely you must remember me.'

'I believe you're Mairead,' Isobel replied in a matter-of-fact tone. When introduced to Gordon and Calum, they each received the same response. Tormod arrived next – as the bearer of good news. While home, he'd phoned the old vet in Drumevie. He'd put forward the proposition to him and his reply had been that, since he was twiddling his thumbs and finding retirement rather boring, he would be more than happy to relieve Tormod of his duties until further notice.

'Which means,' he said, glancing knowingly at Isobel, 'I have some time on my hands to spend here with you.' Isobel smiled radiantly. Her familiar and infectious smile lifted the air of despondency and Gordon called out, 'This calls for a celebration.' He produced the customary bottle of malt from his jacket and asked Helen for six glasses.

Next to arrive was Robert, Stella and Anna. They were hardly inside the door before Gordon handed Robert and Stella a glass filled with single malt. The party had begun and the

235

inhabitants of the cottage were in festive mood. Despite being among virtual strangers, Isobel was happy to join in the revelry. There was much hugging and kissing as family members met for the first time in ages. Isobel was happy to hug and kiss Robert and Stella, although oblivious, until enlightened, of their relationship. Anna and Màiri seemed to hit it off straight away and were happy to share each other's toys. Baby Iain wasn't left out as his doting grandfather, seeing his grandson for only the second time, took great delight in getting reacquainted with him. Now, there was only one guest to arrive before they could sit down to lunch. After answering a knock at the door, Helen returned to the kitchen accompanied by a man with whom none of them was familiar.

Helen had just begun to say, 'Let me introduce.......
when Isobel cried out, 'Dùghall MacKintosh.'

You could have cut the air with a knife as everyone fell silent and all eyes focused, first on Isobel, and then on the stranger in their midst.

Dùghgal looked nervous, agitated and embarrassed as he stammered, 'We've never met before.'

For the first time since regaining consciousness, Isobel was agitated, emotional, and anything but indifferent as she said accusingly, 'You've no right to be here.'

'Perhaps I should leave,' he stammered.

'No, you must stay,' Helen responded adamantly. 'You are my guest. Isobel has obviously mistaken you for someone else,' adding almost inaudibly, 'she's very confused at the moment.' Raising her voice again, she called out, 'Sit down everyone. Lunch is about to be served.'

While Helen and Mairead served the meal, Tormod, seated next to Isobel, laid his hand on hers and gave it a squeeze. She turned her head towards him and gazed into his eyes. He returned her gaze, and for a brief moment they were lost in a world of their own. Her eyes were moist with unshed tears. Tormod likened them to deep, dark pools of cobalt liquid. They were penetrating his soul, imploring him for answers – fearful, yet at the same time - lucid and sane. Whatever was going on inside her head, Isobel's fears were rational and genuine. How easy it would be though, he thought to himself, to categorise her as deranged.

For the duration of the meal, convivial chatter and laughter filled the large kitchen. Tormod, being unfamiliar with most of the guests, politely took part in as much of the conversation as possible; Isobel however, sat in morose silence. As coffee was being served, she glanced up at Tormod and whispered, 'Would you take me to the stable to see Kismet?'

'Yes of course,' he replied with a smile.

After excusing themselves from the table and changing into outdoor clothing, Tormod led the way to the barn. On the way, Isobel linked her arm through his and snuggled up to him.

'Are you cold?' he asked in a concerned tone.

Nodding her head, she replied, 'A bit. But also, I feel safe when I'm with you.'

Tormod gently placed his arm around her delicate frame and drew her closer to him.

'This is Kismet,' he said as they entered the gloomy barn where Isobel's pony was being stabled for the winter.

Isobel gasped with unconcealed delight, 'She's a beauty.'

'Yes. She sure is,' Tormod replied in agreement. It wasn't Kismet he'd been gazing at as he spoke though, he'd been gazing adoringly into Isobel's eyes.

Although being a complete novice in the courting game, Tormod had very quickly mastered the art of kissing, and this time, it was he who was the instigator. Isobel reciprocated his rather cautious, but affectionate approach. There was no frenzied passion conveyed in the kiss – rather - just a mutual, loving communication between kindred spirits. As they drew apart, Tormod couldn't help but notice how radiant Isobel looked. In fact, he couldn't remember a time when she'd looked so beautiful. Previously, each and every time they'd met, Isobel had been beleaguered with problems, trauma and tragedy, all of which had been wiped from her mind since the accident, rendering it a clean slate.

'Can I ride her?' she asked excitedly.

'I don't know,' Tormod replied teasingly. 'Can you ride?'

Her giggle was childlike as she said, 'I can't remember, but I'd like to find out.'

Tormod watched with a combination of admiration and concern as she adeptly tacked up Kismet and climbed on her back.

'Isobel, please take care,' he called as Kismet left the yard and immediately broke into a canter.

Heart in mouth, he leaned against the gate into the meadow and watched the impressive display of unison between horse and rider. It was obvious that Isobel was a skilled rider and even more obvious that the pair shared a unique bond as Kismet walked, trotted, cantered and popped over the small jumps at Isobel's command. Nonetheless, he was conscious of the fact that Isobel was supposed to be convalescing after undergoing major brain surgery. If she were to fall off.........
The consequences didn't even bear thinking about.

'Okay,' Tormod called to her. 'So you've proved you can ride.'

Isobel turned Kismets head and the pony trotted towards him.

'Can you though?' she asked, eying him with a challenging expression.

'Though I've often treated them for ailments,' he replied solemnly, 'I must confess, I have never sat on one in my life.'

'Then now's your chance,' Isobel replied with a wry grin.

Tormod was now seated in the saddle and Kismet was standing stock still.

'What do I have to do to get her to move,' he asked.

Isobel gave a wicked laugh and slapped Kismet on the rump, whereupon, she took off down the field in a canter. Isobel was in fits of laughter as she watched them complete a circuit of the small paddock. Tormod did manage to stay in the saddle, but only by hanging round Kismet's neck. Isobel was still laughing when Kismet returned to stand at her side. Tormod's dismount was as ungainly as his posture in the saddle and he staggered against Isobel while struggling to regain his feet. Isobel wrapped her arms around him, saying, 'I can't remember a time when I laughed so much. But then again, I can't remember anything at all.'

It was a light-hearted moment, yet tinged with serious

238

undertones. As far as Tormod was concerned, part of him was now hoping Isobel wouldn't regain her memory. Her grief over John's death had been erased from her mind and she was happy and carefree again. Tormod also knew he was falling deeply in love with her. In complete contrast to her former indifference and frostiness towards him, it would appear that she now had some romantic feelings for him.

As for Isobel, she so desperately wanted to remember her past life, if only to recall all the happy memories of her time spent at this idyllic place. She had loved every minute of being on Kismet's back, but had no recollection of acquiring the pony or ever having ridden her. The dogs were obviously devoted to her, as were her children and family, but she had no recollection of any of them. As for Tormod, the man to whom she once believed she was betrothed, but since had been told different, it was difficult to tell where she stood. Her heart was telling her that his devotion was genuine. This in itself meant a great deal to her. She'd been told that he'd visited the hospital regularly month after month, just to sit by her bedside. He must be a very special person indeed, she mused.

Isobel, with Tormod walking alongside, led Kismet back to the yard.

'I was thinking,' he began. 'Since I have some time off for the next few weeks.......'

Isobel was listening intently, hanging on to his every word and urging him to continue.

'Yes, go on,' she said brusquely.

'If I bought a pony, perhaps you could teach me to ride. We could spend some time on horseback, explore the hills together and.......'

'And.....'

'Get to know one another again,' he said softly.

'I would like that very much,' she replied, and dropped a kiss on his cheek.

Isobel was in a light-hearted frame of mind on her return to the cottage that day. Everyone was left wondering what had caused the sudden change, but was afraid to ask. Not that it mattered. They were all too relieved to have been given a brief glimpse of the fun-loving, care-free Isobel they remembered from former times.

Later that evening, once the guest had departed, Isobel, with Tormod's assistance, bathed Màiri and Iain and read them a bedtime story, before tucking them up for the night. Dùghall, having downed too many drams of Gordon's whisky, was slightly inebriated and Helen had recently left to drive him home. Isobel and Tormod sat down together on the sofa in front of the range. Gordon had left the dregs of his bottle of single malt and Isobel poured the residue into two glasses.

'Happy Christmas,' she said, touching glasses. 'To the best Christmas Day I can remember.'

'I'll drink to that,' Tormod replied.

The pair sat in virtual silence, each with their own thoughts, but serene in each other's company. Tormod slipped his arm round Isobel's shoulder and she nestled against his body. Tormod felt like purring. Never since childhood had he experienced a feeling of such complete contentment.

For her part, Isobel was thinking to herself, No matter how happy I was in my previous life, nothing can compare with the way I am feeling right at this moment. Tormod kissed the top of her head and whispered, 'I love you.'

****

Chapter 43

Tormod was aware that he had three weeks in which to jolt the cogs of Isobel's brain into gear. Which key would unlock the past though, was anyone's guess. At Helen's suggestion, he'd taken up residence at the croft, and today, he and Isobel were travelling to view a Highland pony that had been advertised for sale. Although proficient at naming every part of its anatomy and diagnosing any ailment, he couldn't tell a good horse from a bad one. Their destination was a croft some thirty miles north of Drumevie and they were now approaching the accident black spot of Isobel's crash. While driving down the track and passing though the farm steading, Isobel had been talking non-stop, asking this question and that question. Tormod had answered them to the best of his knowledge, until they approached the notorious double bend; the scene of the accident. At first, Isobel fell silent and stared out the window. Then, as if a light had been switched on inside her head, she exclaimed, 'I remember something about this bit of the road.......'

'Can you remember what it was?' Tormod asked gently.

'An accident.......' she muttered under her breath.

'Yes. This is where you had the accident,' Tormod said sympathetically.

'It wasn't me who had the accident,' she argued. 'It was someone else..... a long time ago. Oh, if only I could remember his name.'

The light had been switched off again and it was obvious that whatever was locked away in the depths of her mind would remain there for the time being. Presently, they reached their destination and were taken to a small paddock where a Black Highland pony was grazing. After a lengthy inspection of every inch of its body, Isobel said to Tormod, out of earshot of the sellers, 'It's a good one.'

'How can you tell?' he asked in amazement. 'Is it because of your veterinary experience?'

'My *what*!' Isobel exclaimed.

Tormod had spoken without thinking and he explained that, like him, she was a qualified vet.

'No-one ever told me *that*,' she retorted. 'Anyhow, it's because I like the look of her, but I would need to ride her to know for sure.'

Tormod shook his head. 'Is that wise? What if she's not as docile as Kismet?'

'What if?' she replied with a mischievous grin while sitting astride the pony's back.

There was no saddle on its back and only a flimsy rope halter on its head, but by now, they had disappeared from sight.

'I hope she's an experienced rider,' someone remarked solemnly.

'We'll soon find out,' said another.

'Why?' Tormod asked.

'The pony's not long broken.'

'High spirited too.'

Tormod and the others could do nothing but watch and wait. Presently, the pony and her delicate cargo reappeared, apparently unscathed.

'I love her,' Isobel exclaimed jubilantly as she slid gracefully from the pony's back. 'Her colour is so unusual, and so beautiful.'

'Would you recommend that I buy her?' Tormod asked cagily.

'Let's just say, if you don't, I will,' she replied.

The deal was done. Tormod handed over the cash, a slip of paper was signed and the new acquisition loaded into the horse-box.

'I'll have to think of a name for her,' Tormod remarked as they drove home to the croft.

'Have you thought about where you'll keep her?' Isobel asked.

'Well,' he began hesitantly. 'I was hoping to keep her at the croft. That way, you get to ride her whenever you want.'

'My two very own Highland ponies,' Isobel whispered. 'Kismet and....' She paused for a second before announcing with a jubilant smile, 'Karma.'

Tormod could feel Isobel's hand on his leg. He glanced sideways and saw that she was gazing at him intently.

'What is it?' he asked.

'I don't know. I only wish I did.'

242

One day, Tormod and Isobel saddled up the two ponies and left the yard. Their plan was to accustom the two ponies to riding out together, but also, this would be Tormod's initiation to riding. Sitting astride Karma, Isobel was leading the way. The reason for this was that Kismet was a safer ride for a complete novice. The pace was slow and leisurely as the two ponies cautiously picked their way over the uneven ground. The riders were engaged in idle chit-chat, much of it enthusing about the benefits of viewing the picturesque landscape from the back of a pony. Tormod surveyed the landscape with a sense of awe, and, judging by the expression on Isobel's face, it was as though she too was seeing it for the very first time. Presently, the outline of the ruined cottage became visible in the distance. The two ponies were walking side by side and Tormod could see that Isobel's carefree expression had changed to one of trepidation.

'I don't like this place,' she cried out without warning. 'I want to go back.'

'Can you remember why you don't like it?' Tormod asked gently.

Isobel had brought Karma to a halt and she was now standing stock still. Kismet automatically stopped alongside, when Isobel began to sob. It was her first real display of emotion since regaining consciousness, and therefore, a breakthrough as far as Tormod was concerned.

They returned to the croft to find an unfamiliar pick-up parked in the yard. Tormod read the name on the driver's door - Andrew McLennan.

'You have a visitor,' he remarked with a hint of annoyance.

'Do I know him?' Isobel asked innocently.

'It would appear so,' he replied abruptly.

'I'll have to see to the ponies first,' she responded in a solemn tone. 'Ask him to wait please.'

Tormod's mood was one of irritation as he made his way to the cottage. He'd no way of knowing the extent of the relationship between Isobel and the joiner from Drumevie, but he'd seen them together in the town just before her accident. He was also aware that Drew was a married man. By the time he'd reached the back door, suspicion and jealousy had been added to his mood of frustration and annoyance. Upon entering the cottage to see Drew sprawled on the sofa, his mood changed to one of anger.

'Hi Tormod,' Helen called from the pantry. 'How was your ride?'

'Eventful,' he replied curtly.

'Have you two met?' she asked upon entering the kitchen.

Drew stood up and held out his hand, 'Drew McLennan, a friend of Isobel's.' he said while smiling warmly.

'Tormod MacAlister. I'm also a friend of Isobel,' he replied drily.

'Tormod has been my rock during the past few months,' Helen gushed enthusiastically. 'I couldn't have coped without him. Coffee?' she asked, glancing at Tormod.

He smiled and replied, 'Thanks. A coffee would go down very well.'

Just then, the door opened and Isobel strode into the kitchen. She was still wearing her jodhpurs and riding boots and her cheeks glowed with a natural blush that can only be achieved from being embraced by the invigorating, outdoor air.

'Isobel,' Drew murmured as he embraced her warmly. 'You look amazing.'

'You'll have to forgive me,' she replied apologetically. 'I don't recognise you. I'm.....suffering from amnesia.'

'You and I had something on the go before you met with your accident,' he replied furtively.

Isobel flopped onto the sofa and held up each foot in turn so that Tormod could remove her boots. Her smile, as she thanked him, conveyed much more to Drew than its innocent intent.

'My acquaintances, and in fact my entire life prior to my accident have been completely erased from my memory,' she began. 'Therefore, as far as I'm concerned, my recollection of life began on the day I was discharged from hospital. Whatever, or whoever, came before, will remain locked in the past forever.'

'What about the bothies?' he asked with a frown. 'Have you forgotten about them?'

244

Isobel frowned. 'Bothies,' she repeated. 'Why would I want bothies?'

'For the mountaineers to shelter in,' he replied with a look of bemusement.

'I don't know what you're talking about,' she responded brusquely. 'The only mountaineers on these hills are sheep and goats.'

Drew glanced at the clock on the mantelpiece and said edgily, 'It's time I was heading for home.'

Once he'd gone, Isobel asked Helen and Tormod if they had any knowledge of the bothies. Treading cautiously and diplomatically, they explained to Isobel the childhood dream she'd nurtured and had set in motion just prior to the accident. Isobel sat in thoughtful silence for a few moments before remarking that the cost for this undertaking would be enormous, and asked who had been going to foot the bill.

Tormod and Helen exchanged glances. That information would have to be kept for another time. There was only so much information her injured brain could absorb.

****

Chapter 44

Each day brought progress as far as Isobel was concerned. She now accepted that Iain and Màiri were her offspring from her marriage to John, who was now dead. During Isobel's hospitalisation, Helen had looked after the children as if they were her own flesh and blood, but it didn't lessen the joy she felt each time she saw Isobel spending time with them. Helen longed to have children of her own, but was resigned to the fact that it wasn't to be. Mairead continued to visit the croft, and although Isobel had no recollection of their unique friendship over the years, felt an empathy with her that she couldn't begin to comprehend. One day, Mairead arrived at the croft with a message from Rob. He'd invited them to join him for the Hogmanay celebrations at Inverculden the following evening. Isobel had been eavesdropping with a bemused expression.

'The Inverculden Hogmanay Ball,' Helen began by way of an explanation. 'Surely you've not forgotten that. It's the society event of the year, attended by all the toffs for miles around. You've been many times before.'

Although it hadn't been Helen's intention to be disparaging, her words had left Isobel frightened and bewildered. She obviously had no recollection of her beloved brother Rob inheriting the estate of Inverculden, or any of the previous Hogmanay celebrations she'd attended there.

'I can't go,' she cried in alarm. 'I won't recognise anybody and everyone will think I've gone mad.'

'You've lost your memory, not your mind,' Helen said gently, 'no-one will blame you for that.'

'Have I anything suitable to wear?' Isobel asked anxiously.

During the past two years since John's death, Isobel had refused to socialise in public. Helen recalled that her last social event was the Inverculden Hogmanay Ball, two years ago. At the time, she'd only recently been bereaved and was four months pregnant with Iain. She told her, as tactfully as possible, that in her opinion, she would need a new dress.

'Would you drive me to Drumevie?' Isobel asked, glancing at Tormod.

246

'Of course,' he replied without hesitation.

As before, Isobel showed little emotion as they traversed the once familiar track. Nor did she express any recognition as Tormod drove through the farm steading and along the tree-lined drive towards the main road. However, as they passed the scene of her accident, she asked casually, 'Was my husband killed in a car crash?'

Tormod knew nothing of John's unfortunate accident at the same location many years ago, therefore, was momentarily dumbstruck. He then explained that the bull at the croft had been responsible for her husband's death.

Drumevie, the town she'd visited since childhood, was also unfamiliar to Isobel. If not for Tormod, who guided her to the appropriate shops, she would have struggled to find her way. People in the street had stopped to speak to her. They'd asked how she was feeling and remarked how well she looked, but all were complete strangers as far as Isobel was concerned.

'I'd like to go home now?' she said despondently as they emerged from yet another shop without a suitable dress.

Tormod smiled sympathetically and took her hand as they made their way to the car park. While driving back to the croft, Isobel said anxiously, 'I really don't want to spend Hogmanay at Inverculden.'

Tormod knew just how much Isobel meant to Rob, and likewise, how devoted Isobel was to her brother. The problem was that, since losing her memory, Rob and his friends were as alien to Isobel as the strangers in the streets of Drumevie.

'Would you like to spend Hogmanay somewhere far away, where no-one knows who you are?' he asked tenderly.

Isobel's expression, as she turned to look at him, was one of relief. It was as though a huge weight had been lifted from her shoulders. With a broad smile, she replied, 'I would like that very much.'

'Was your mission successful?' Helen asked upon seeing their beaming faces as they entered the kitchen.

'Let's just say, it had a positive outcome,' Isobel replied surreptitiously.

247

'Show me your ball gown then,' Helen said excitedly.

'I didn't find a dress,' Isobel began slowly. 'I'm not going to the ball. Tormod is taking me away to a secret location for a few days.'

'Are you taking the children with you?' Helen asked cagily.

Isobel glanced at Tormod. He shrugged and said, 'I have no objections to Màiri and Iain coming with us.'

Helen was visibly relieved as she went on to say, 'It's just that, I've invited Dùghall here for lunch on New Year's Day.'

Isobel frowned. For some inexplicable reason she was irked at the thought of Dùghall coming here on New Year's Day – or any other day for that matter – but right now, she couldn't justify her feelings.

The following day was New Year's Eve and Tormod, Isobel and the two children left An Gleann Dubh. Their destination, to all but Tormod, was unknown. He though, had already made up his mind where they would spend Hogmanay.

****

Chapter 45

As Tormod drove into the ferry terminal, Isobel gasped with unconcealed delight. Apart from An Gleann Dubh, she hadn't seen anywhere quite so idyllic. Stretching as far as her eyes could see was a vast expanse of azure blue sea - she couldn't remember ever having seen the sea before – and the blurred outlines of some distant islands were barely visible through a veil of mist. Despite it being mid-winter, palm trees flourished in the gardens of several whitewashed cottages nearby. The silence was broken only by the gentle lapping of the waves and the incessant call of seabirds wheeling overhead. Tormod stopped the car and turned off the engine. Placing one arm lovingly around her shoulder he pointed straight ahead with the other and said, 'Can you see the landmass in the distance?'

'Yes,' she replied eagerly, though straining to see clearly. 'It looks beautiful. Is that where we're going?'

He shook his head. 'Where we're going, is paradise on earth.'

Just then, the ferry rounded a headland and came into full view. At that moment, Isobel experienced her first real emotions since regaining consciousness. She was excited, elated - dare she say – ecstatic.

'Oh Tormod,' she murmured joyfully. 'This is going to be such an adventure, and much more fun than the Hogmanay Ball at Inverculden.'

Tormod gave a wry smile. This was a trip he'd planned since childhood. One that, for many years he had looked forward to, yet at the same time faced with a sense of dread. He was returning to his beloved island home for the first time since leaving it as a child. It would be a bittersweet and emotional journey; his first pilgrimage to the final resting place of his beloved parents.

Once aboard, and having left Tormod in charge of the children, Isobel set off to explore the ship. She leant over the railings at the stern as the powerful engines roared and black smoke belched from the funnel as the ferry reversed from the pier. As it began to pick up speed, she walked along the starboard deck towards the bow. The icy wind played havoc with her hair and whipped colour into her cheeks, but she was happy, exhilarated, and at this moment, so very glad to be alive. 'Thank you Lord,' she whispered, 'If my life has been spared just for this moment alone, thank you from the bottom of my heart.'

Isobel went inside and found Tormod and the children in the passenger lounge on the lower deck. The children were asleep and Isobel was slightly concerned that Tormod, in contrast to her mood of elation, was unusually subdued.

'Are you all right,' she asked softly.

Tormod heaved a long sigh as his eyes flitted over Isobel's face. He couldn't help but notice how joyful she looked. He noticed that her expression was one of childish innocence, expectation and unparalleled contentment. But then, he mused, Isobel was living in a world of oblivion. The tragic events of her recent past had been obliterated from her mind, and at this moment in time, she knew nothing of the fate that awaited her, should she continue to assume the identity of Ishbel McKenzie, whoever she may be. How could he possibly shatter her world of utopia?

'I'll be just fine,' he said reassuringly.

After sailing for almost three hours, the ferry approached the pier and as she gazed through the portholes, Isobel could see two lines of cars waiting to board to cross to the mainland. Tormod was now driving along a potholed, single track road and Isobel was slightly bewildered by the fact that he appeared to be familiar with the road. After travelling only a short distance, they reached a small village and Tormod turned into the car park of a hotel.

'Have you been here before?' she asked with a puzzled expression.

'Many times,' he replied with a dazzling smile.

They were barely inside the hotel when a voice called out, 'Well if it isn't Tormod MacAlister then it's his double.'

'Fergus MacSporran,' Tormod responded as the two men hugged each other.

Now, a large crowd had gathered around them.

'Allow me to introduce Isobel Caldwell,' Tormod said while

250

placing his arm reassuringly around her waist.

Fergus looked Isobel up and down, before casting his eyes over Màiri and Iain.

'Aye Aye,' he remarked with a sly grin. 'You've obviously done well for yourself on the mainland.'

Tormod simply smiled in reply. The moment wasn't right to explain the true circumstances to his old school chum. It was Hogmanay after all and the hotel was filled to capacity. The party had already begun and they hadn't even checked in. Tormod excused himself, but not before telling Fergus that he would have time to catch up with him before leaving the island.

'I'll see you both later at the ceilidh in the village hall,' Fergus called as they made their way to reception.

'I have a reservation in the name of MacAlister,' Tormod informed the receptionist.

Her head shot up and she cried out with unconcealed delight, 'Tormod MacAlister. Welcome home.'

'Dolina?' he probed.

She nodded.

Home? Isobel, standing behind Tormod with the children mouthed the word.

Dolina emerged from behind the desk and threw her arms around Tormod before kissing him on both cheeks. Her delighted expression turned to one of embarrassment upon noticing Màiri and Iain standing quietly beside their mother.

'I'm sorry,' she began in a lilting tone, 'I didn't realise you were married and had children.'

Ignoring her words, Tormod said, 'I have two rooms reserved.'

Dolina's smile didn't go amiss as far as Isobel was concerned. Her gut instinct told her that she may have a rival for Tormod's affection.

It wasn't a large hotel by mainland standards, however, Isobel's suspicions were further aroused by the fact that, when given their keys, Dolina told them, with an air of superiority, that the rooms were on different floors.

'I'm so sorry,' she began. 'Because yours was a late booking, those were the only available rooms. It is Hogmanay after all.'

Tormod carried Isobel's luggage to a room in the basement,

251

before leaving her alone with the children.

'I'll meet you in the dining room in half an hour,' he said while closing the door.

Isobel glanced round the room with apprehension. While she hadn't been expecting anything on a grand scale, she wasn't sure if she could spend a night here. The room was without windows and dark and dingy. It also smelt of mould and sweaty feet. A single bed, a chest of drawers and a bunk bed were crammed into a space not much bigger than the loft Tormod had slept in at the croft. Suddenly, she felt claustrophobic, nauseous and stricken by fear and panic. She collapsed onto the single bed and began to analyse her present situation. Her previous feeling of elation had rapidly been replaced by a deep sense of despondency and depression. Although having been brought here by Tormod, the reality was that she was alone and stranded on an island in the middle of the ocean, among strangers. She glanced at the two toddlers in the room beside her. It was the first time she could remember being alone with them. They were her offspring - hers' and John's - so she'd been told, but as far as she was concerned, they too were strangers. Màiri, she'd been told, was almost three years old, and Iain, almost two. Certainly, she could see the resemblance between herself and Màiri, but was at a loss to feel any connection with Iain. As for Tormod, the man she felt a unique bond with, he was in familiar surroundings among friends and family. Now feeling extremely vulnerable, she began to cry. A loud rap at the door made her jump with fright, before Tormod entered the room. Without uttering a word, she threw herself into his arms and began to sob uncontrollably.

'Isobel, what's the matter,' he asked while gently caressing her hair.

'Please don't leave me here alone,' she cried imploringly.

Tormod hung about just long enough for Isobel to tend to Màiri and Iain, before picking up the suitcases and heading for the door.

'Where are we going?' Isobel asked as she followed him from the room.

'We're going to spend the night in my room, and tomorrow....

252

well, I'll keep that as a surprise.'

Isobel heaved a sigh of relief as she closed the bedroom door behind her and began to follow Tormod upstairs. His room, in complete contrast to hers, was spacious, bright and had a large double bed as well as two single beds.

'Take your pick,' he said, motioning towards the beds.

'If you would rather sleep with the children in the double bed, then I'm happy to sleep in one of the single beds.'

Isobel smiled as she replied, 'I don't know about you, but I'm starving. Let's eat first and decide later.'

Isobel began to relax as she dined with Tormod and the children. The dining room was filled to capacity, mainly families from the mainland taking a few days vacation, and they blended in almost unnoticed. Once they'd eaten, she remarked that she would take the children upstairs and get them ready for bed and would probably have an early night herself.

'Hold on a minute,' Tormod responded in mock horror.

Isobel stopped in her tracks. Tormod's tone of authority had taken her by surprise. He disappeared for a few minutes and on his return, was accompanied by an elderly and rather matronly looking lady.

'I'd like you to meet Sine,' he began. 'She's an old friend of the family and has offered to babysit Màiri and Iain for us tonight.'

'For us..... to do what..... exactly?' Isobel asked hesitantly.

'To allow us to go to the ceilidh in the village hall,' he replied. 'It's the highlight of the year and not to be missed.'

Tormod wouldn't take no for an answer and Isobel had no option but to go with the flow. The "flow" consisted of several childhood friends of Tormod's, one of whom suggested that Isobel should be given a traditional island welcome. In the hotel bar, she was told to cast her eyes over each of the bottles of single malt on the top shelf and select her ten favourites in order of preference. She had no recollection of any of the brands, even though she'd previously sampled each and every one of them several times over, thanks to Gordon's love and knowledge of the finest single malts. In keeping with the convivial mood of the evening, and desperate not to offend the locals, she selected a brand - then another - followed by another. After downing her tenth dram, Tormod called out, 'Okay lads, she's passed the initiation test, Isobel can now be classed as an islander.'

'Not until she's passed the final test,' a drunken voice called out. 'She's got to stay on her feet long enough to dance the drops o' brandy.'

Tormod was now beginning to get slightly concerned. The island Hogmanay ceilidh was a cordial, but sometimes rowdy event. Uisge-Beatha, the water of life, not only lived up to its name, but flowed like its namesake. The inebriated revellers danced in their tackety boots, swung their partners around like rag dolls, and at times, lifted them completely off their feet. Isobel was still convalescing after her traumatic head injury. Perhaps it was time to call it a night. Isobel though, wouldn't hear of it. She was determined to pass the final test and thereby assert herself as an islander.

'Lead me to the ceilidh,' she responded defiantly.

Tormod was aghast. This was the first time he'd seen her so resolute - at least - for many years. Tonight, for the first time since John's death, he'd caught a glimpse of her former feisty and indomitable character; the one he'd been intrigued by when first they met.

'Shouldn't I take you to bed,' he asked in a concerned tone.

'Later,' she replied with an alluring smile.

Isobel was led onto the dance floor by first one crofter, and then another. She performed every dance like a true professional, thanks to her former Scottish Country Dance lessons, and Tormod, who hadn't any experience of dancing, watched with a mixture of surprise and admiration; he'd never realised she was such an excellent dancer. Just then, the band stopped playing and someone announced that it was one minute to midnight. Suddenly, the crowded hall fell silent as the bells of the town clock began to strike twelve o'clock.

'A Happy New Year to one and all.' The call resounded round the hall. 'Take your partners for the first waltz of 1969.'

As the throng in the village hall shook hands with one another and engaged in much hugging and kissing, suddenly, Isobel felt as though she was in familiar surroundings. Deep within the dark recesses of her mind, there was a flicker of light. Tormod had asked her to dance and she was now gliding round the floor in his arms. Never before had he been so affected by the feeling of her body so close to his. She was gazing adoringly into his eyes and running her fingers through his hair. This was a side to her he hadn't seen before and he wasn't quite sure how to deal with it. She was taunting him, though for what reason, he couldn't begin to understand.

'Is the invitation still open?' she whispered seductively.

He frowned and gazed at her with a look of confusion, prompting her to add, 'Earlier, you offered to take me to bed.'

'I think you've had just a little bit too much Uisge -Beatha,' he replied with a smile, 'but I'd be more than happy to escort you to our room.'

With Tormod's arm steadying her, Isobel reached the hotel without mishap. Sine was relieved of her duties and, after wishing them both a Happy New Year, bade them goodnight. Tormod eyed the three beds with a sense of dismay. Iain was in one of the single beds, while Màiri was in the other and both were fast asleep. He turned to speak to Isobel and saw that she had flaked out on the double bed. Although daybreak was only a matter of hours away, Tormod realised that, if he was to have any sleep at all, he would have to squeeze into the remaining space beside her. The rather bizarre sleeping arrangement hadn't been in the original plan, and although exhausted, he couldn't sleep. For one thing, he was conscious of the unfamiliar sounds coming from the single beds. He was used to sleeping alone, having his own space, and Isobel had now turned to face him and was snuggled against his body. Instinctively, protectively, or for whatever reason, he found himself draping his arms around her. She moaned softly and murmured the words, 'I love you John.'

Tormod drifted into a troubled sleep, and after what seemed like only a matter of minutes, was awakened by the sound of Iain whimpering. He found him lying on the floor - he'd obviously rolled from the bed - and Tormod picked him up

255

and comforted him before returning to bed. Both Màiri and Isobel slept on regardless. Eventually, Iain drifted off to sleep and Tormod dozed until awakened by the sound of Isobel's voice.

'Oh my poor head,' she groaned while attempting to sit upright.

Tormod raised his head off the pillow and glanced in her direction. He'd expected her to be shocked by the fact that the three of them were sharing a bed, but she simply smiled sweetly and said,' Good Morning. Thank you for a wonderful evening.'

Tormod continued to gaze at her in silence. Her hair was slightly dishevelled, her face showing signs of too much alcohol and too little sleep, but as far as he was concerned, she was beautiful.

Taking his silence the wrong way, she said in a tone of embarrassment, 'I must look a mess.'

'I was just thinking how beautiful you are,' he replied softly.

'Thank you,' she replied, avoiding his gaze.

In contrast to her behaviour last night, Isobel had now reverted to her timid, coy and anxious demeanour.

After breakfast, Tormod remarked that he would settle the bill and check out of the hotel. Isobel was bewildered and disappointed. If truth be known, she was concerned that he'd decided to cut the holiday short and return to the mainland. However, upon asking him why they weren't staying at the hotel for another night, she was relieved by his reply,

'Because,' he began slowly, 'tonight, I have a surprise in store for you.'

Isobel smiled to herself. Despite only having arrived on the island the previous afternoon, she'd already fallen in love with it.

The single-track road from the village followed the coastline and Isobel observed that Tormod was glancing from side to side as he drove. Dotted along the way were tiny, whitewashed crofts, each with their peat stacks by the door and tiny tractors and outdated machinery in their topsy-turvy yards. Isobel gazed in silent wonder at the breathtaking scenery. On the right hand side of the road, rippling waves gently kissed the pristine white sand. The foaming breakers from which they'd formed were the end result of hundreds of miles of surging ocean. On the opposite side, fertile, green pastures rose gently towards the hills beyond. Straight ahead, huddles of blackface ewes casually lounged on the tarmac, each eying the approaching vehicle defiantly before moving at the very last minute, in a leisurely and laid-back fashion, to the side of the road. Tormod had now slowed down almost to a standstill. Was that tears she could see in his eyes? She followed his gaze. Apart from the burnt out shell of a small croft, there wasn't much to see. Just then, the sound of a piercing scream shattered the morose silence. Tormod, rudely awakened from his moment of nostalgic reflection, turned his head sharply to see that Isobel's face was deathly white. Her eyes were glazed, staring, penetrating his soul, yet looking straight through him.

'Isobel, what is it?' he asked gently.

'The roof…. It's ablaze,' she gasped. 'We're all going to die. I can't breathe……'

How could she possibly have known about the fire, Tormod asked himself? He'd never told her. He hadn't told anyone on the mainland.

'It's over. It happened a long time ago,' he said softly. 'We must forget about the past and move on.'

Tormod drove on slowly, but kept his gaze on the little croft he'd once called home. A short distance along the road, he stopped again. After parking the car in front of a little whitewashed croft that was intact and situated just a few yards from the shoreline, he remarked with a feeble smile, 'Our destination.'

'Who lives here?' Isobel asked in dismay.

'For the next few days, we do,' he replied. 'I had a word with Sìne last night, explained that the hotel wasn't suitable for our needs, and she kindly offered to stay with her sister for a few days and let us have the use of her croft.'

The glimmer of a smile crossed Isobel's previously trouble face as she surveyed the idyllic setting.

'There's a downside,' Tormod said with a frown.

'What's that?' she asked in bemusement.

257

'Motioning his head towards the cow in a field on the other side of the road, he said, 'That's our milk supply, and the eggs are free range.'

Isobel giggled with unconcealed delight. 'I love it. I could quite happily stay here forever.'

'We have three days before we must return to the mainland,' Tormod responded solemnly. 'And back to the unknown,' he muttered to himself.

****

Chapter 46

The island croft consisted of a jumble of wooden sheds, a byre and a rather dilapidated cottage that looked as though it had been caught in a time warp. Despite its rather off-putting exterior, indoors it was homely, comfortable and as far as Isobel was concerned, much preferable to the hotel. It had the added advantage of having a view to die for - and a private beach. Today was the first day of a brand new year and she'd already made a resolution that she must go forward into the future without knowing anything about her past. If only, she thought to herself, the recurring flashbacks would stop interfering with my desire to move on.

Tormod and Isobel unpacked their suitcases before deciding to take the children for a stroll on the beach before dusk. Neither Isobel nor the children had walked on sand before today, and despite a cool breeze blowing in from the ocean, it was an experienced they enjoyed immensely. They scavenged the beach for seashells, explored the rock pools and were brave enough to dip their toes into the icy waves. Isobel had rolled up her trouser legs, and, giggling like a schoolgirl, waded knee-deep into the rushing waves until forced to abandon her show of bravado due to the freezing temperature. The four returned to the croft damp, tired, but exhilarated. Needless to say, the children were ready for bed earlier than usual that evening and were soon fast asleep. Tormod had stoked the fire with peat and was now settled on the sofa with a book, when Isobel began to raid the cupboards in search of food. Tormod had earlier made scrambled eggs for the children, but now, Isobel was beginning to feel ravenous.

'Would you like me to cook dinner?' she asked with a degree of apprehension. Not having cooked a meal since her release from hospital, she wasn't sure if she could remember how to.

Without looking up from his book, Tormod replied, 'No need. We've been invited out for dinner. Sine offered to babysit for us.' Glancing at the clock on the mantelpiece, he added, 'She'll be here in half an hour.'

Isobel looked down at her salt-stained and soggy trousers,

before making her way towards the bedroom.

'I'm going to change into something more suitable,' she called to Tormod.

'Perhaps I should do likewise,' he said, rising from the sofa.

Tormod changed in the bathroom, leaving Isobel the privacy of the bedroom. She eyed the double bed in the room and, conscious of the fact that the children were asleep in the other bedroom, wondered about tonight's sleeping arrangements. Having no recollection whatsoever of the previous night, she resolved to limit her alcohol intake tonight and remain in control of her actions.

Sine duly arrived and Isobel and Tormod left the croft for a destination as yet unknown, at least to Isobel. After following the shoreline for a few miles, the road took a sharp left hand bend, before climbing steeply into the hills. A pale moon lit up the night sky and the landscape was bathed in its soft, blue light. Isobel gazed in awe through the window at the seascape below as the road continued to climb steeply. Tormod then turned off the road and onto a rutted track, at the end of which, was a large farmhouse.

A few other vehicles were parked in the yard and Isobel quickly realised that they wouldn't be dining alone. A sense of panic, and a twinge of disappointment, engulfed her at that moment. Actually, she'd have been much happier spending the evening alone with Tormod at the croft. Just then, Tormod placed his arm around her shoulder and said, 'Fergus and Dolina invited us to join their Ne'er Day dinner party. You met them last night, remember.'

Of course she remembered Fergus and Dolina! But she hadn't realised that they were married to each other.

The party consisted of four other couples, all of whom had been childhood school friends of Tormod. As the evening wore on, they reminisced about the past, discussed the present, and speculated about the future. It was then that Tormod announced his plan to move back to the island in the future and establish a veterinary practice. Isobel could feel the colour draining from her cheeks. She couldn't begin to imagine her life without Tormod; he was now her best friend - at least - the only one she could remember. Dolina

260

interrupted her thoughts by saying, 'And will you be coming with him?' A devious smile had crossed her face as she spoke.

'Tormod responded immediately by saying, 'Isobel has commitments on the mainland.'

Isobel's head was reeling with confusion. She knew of no "commitments" as Tormod had put it. Much as she wished she could forget her past and concentrate on the future, it was obvious that, for the benefit of the present, it was essential that she uncover the truth about her past.

Each in turn voiced their opinion about Tormod's plan to return to the island. All were in agreement that his prowess as a vet would be much appreciated by the crofters. Fergus asked how he would feel about being reminded of his parents' tragic death each time he passed the old family home.

'That's something I still have to come to terms with,' he replied solemnly. 'But no-one can run and hide forever.'

****

Chapter 47

Tormod looked at his watch, 'It's time to go,' he remarked while glancing at Isobel.

'I'm ready,' she replied sharply.

If truth be known, she'd been ready to leave ages ago.

'Thank you for a lovely evening,' Tormod remarked as he shook hands with Fergus. 'It was good to catch up.'

'Aye, and once you move back here, we'll fill in all the gaps,' he responded with a knowing smile.

The journey back to the croft was spent in silence, at least, apart from Tormod asking Isobel if she was feeling all right. Isobel merely replied that she was tired and couldn't wait to climb into bed.

Sine left, and Isobel, desperate to get her head down, enquired about the sleeping arrangements. Without hesitation, Tormod offered to sleep on the couch and let her have the use of the double bed. Isobel though, decided that this wouldn't be fair. After all, since they'd both had a disturbed sleep the previous night, Tormod's need for a decent night's sleep was on a par with her own; therefore, she replied that she had no objection to him sleeping beside her, as long as he kept to his side of the bed. Tormod was thinking to himself that she had conveniently forgotten about, or was oblivious to, her advances the previous night. After undressing in the dark, the pair climbed into bed from opposite sides. The silence was tangible - an awkward silence - which neither of them quite knew how to break. Each lay awake with similar thoughts in their heads and a corresponding yearning in their hearts.

Tormod murmured the words, 'Goodnight,' but there was no reply.

The sound of someone weeping wakened him from a deep sleep and he lay for a moment in silent confusion. It was dark as pitch and he was struggling to think clearly. The sobbing sound was coming from the bed.

'Isobel,' he whispered, reaching out to touch her, 'what's the matter?'

'I had a bad dream,' she murmured sleepily.

262

Despite taking her in his arms to comfort her, she continued to sob pitifully.

'Hush. It's okay, I'm here,' he said softly while stroking her hair.

Isobel was trembling. Not only had she had a recurring nightmare, but her heart and her head were in conflict with each other. Although her heart was telling her she longed to be part of Tormod's life, a voice in her head was telling her that it wasn't to be.

'Promise me you'll always be here,' she said between sobs.

'I can't promise,' he whispered, 'but I'll do my best.'

She moved on top of him and began to kiss him passionately. He returned her kisses eagerly, his previous feeling of compassion now rapidly turning to desire.

'Please don't do anything you may regret in the morning,' he whispered.

Even in the semi-darkness, Tormod could see the solemn expression on Isobel's face as she replied, 'I never do anything without accepting the consequences.'

Tormod was trembling, partly with excitement, partly due to nerves. He'd dreamt of this moment for so long and yet......he was on edge. Despite nearing twenty seven years of age, he hadn't lost his virginity and was clueless in the art of lovemaking. Isobel, in complete contrast, had experienced a brief recall from her past. He moaned with unbridled passion as she kissed every inch of his naked body.

'Isobel......please stop........'

Was she taunting him to see if he could resist her advances? If so, she was pushing his powers of self-control to the limit. Never in his entire life had he experienced an emotion such as this. Having now entered into the spirit of her little game, he decided to take control by moving on top of her, but to no avail. She was still in control. Isobel wrapped her legs tightly around his torso and pulled him closer. She wanted him, of this he was in no doubt, but what of the consequences of them becoming lovers rather than friends. Isobel was still grieving for John and, had she not been suffering from amnesia, wouldn't have allowed him, or any other man for that matter, to make love to her. He couldn't, and wouldn't,

263

take advantage of her.

'Isobel, I can't do this,' he began forcefully.

'Can't, or won't, she asked woefully. Don't you want me?'

'My darling, I want you more than I've ever wanted anything in my entire life.......'

'Then take me. I'm all yours,' she murmured, 'I need you......I want you.......I love you.'

'And I love you.'

Tormod's powers of reasoning had now fallen by the wayside. His primal lust superseding logic, a heady surge of intoxication consumed his entire body as his manly flesh was consumed by her soft, moist, warmth. Isobel had succeeded in her quest to take him to the point of no return. Whatever the consequences, there was no going back. Adrenalin was coursing through his veins. His heart was pounding with pent up desire, yet his head was telling him that he must remain in control. Isobel was kissing him passionately and moaning rapturously. Without warning, he lost control and let out a long, shuddering cry of fulfilment. It was at this moment Isobel began to cry softly.

'Have I hurt you?' he asked anxiously.

She didn't reply, but was clinging to him, kissing him passionately as if afraid to let him go. For some absurd reason, it was as though a barrier from her past had been broken down.

Now asleep in each other's arms, they remained that way until awakened by the sound of Iain whimpering in the bedroom next door.

Tormod kissed her forehead. 'Go back to sleep,' he whispered, 'I'll see to him.'

Isobel smiled with sheer contentment and snuggled under the blankets before drifting into a deep and blissful sleep. She was awakened by the sound of rain lashing against the window panes and the aroma of bacon and eggs pervading the bedroom. Glancing sleepily at her watch, she saw that it was ten o'clock. While dressing hastily, the events of the hours of darkness filled her mind. It had begun with a nightmare. She'd had a vision of a decomposing corpse in a shallow grave high on a hillside. Following that, she'd had another dream, a pleasant one this time. In this, she'd made love to Tormod. Or had he made love to her? Her head was so mixed up, she really couldn't remember. She drew back the curtains and stood in stunned silence. A storm was brewing out at sea and giant waves were crashing relentlessly against the rocks. The sound she'd heard and thought was rain was actually the spray being thrown up by the gigantic waves. The sky was dark, and heavy with ominous, storm clouds. Just then, Tormod entered the room to tell her that breakfast was ready. Isobel sat down at the table beside Màiri and Iain, while Tormod dished up bacon, sausage and eggs and carried on as if nothing had happened between them last night. Had it been a dream after all? Her memory was still playing tricks on her and sometimes she struggled to differentiate between fantasy and reality.

Due to the ferocity of the storm, the tour of the island Tormod had planned for today would have to be postponed. As it was, there was nothing for it but to batten down the hatches, remain indoors and sit out the storm.

'The weather forecast is reporting gale force winds and torrential rain for the next couple of day,' Tormod began in a solemn tone. 'It's moving inland from the Atlantic and the Western Isles are predicted to be the worst affected. Ferry services will undoubtedly be disrupted, therefore we could be here for a bit longer than planned.'

Isobel smiled.

'It's not funny' he chastised.

'I think it's wonderful,' she replied dreamily. 'What could be better than being marooned on an exotic island with my lover.'

Despite avoiding her gaze, Tormod's expression of guilt told Isobel that they had indeed made love last night.

The inclement weather meant that it wouldn't be safe to venture very far from the croft that day. Tormod battled against the elements to bring the cow in for milking and managed to find a few eggs in one of the barns. They lunched on scrambled eggs on toast and spent much of the time listening to the weather reports on the radio. It reported that parts of the coastal road on the island were under several feet of seawater and ferry service to the mainland had been cancelled until further notice. In the afternoon, with the children in bed for a catnap, Isobel snuggled up to Tormod on the sofa and asked him to tell her about his island childhood and the tragedy that had befallen his parents. She sat in silence, engrossed by the tale of his happy and carefree childhood. She could empathise with that, it was exactly the same as she remembered hers to be...... How could she possible remember her childhood if she was suffering from amnesia, she reflected.

Tormod went on to tell her about his sadness at having to leave the island to further his education. Then he fell silent. Isobel was surprised and distressed by the fact that he had tears in his eyes and she kissed him lovingly.

'Not long after I left the island,' he went on, 'the croft.......' he paused and buried his face in his hands.

In a hushed tone, Isobel finished the sentence. 'The croft was burnt to the ground.'

Tormod gazed into hers eyes, murmuring in a tone of disbelief, 'How did you find out?'

'I was there,' she whispered. 'I saw it.'

Her eyes had a faraway look as she returned his gaze. They were staring straight through him, glazed and hypnotic.

She *is* crazy, he said to himself. She has completely lost her mind. Perhaps it'll be for the best if she's admitted to the asylum when we return to the mainland. Due to the impending storms however, when that would be, was anyone's guess.

'The body is lying face down in a shallow grave on a hillside,' she murmured. Although the words were coming from her lips, it didn't sound like Isobel's voice.

'Whose body is it?' Tormod asked warily.

'I can't tell you,' she replied resolutely.

'Can't, or won't,' he probed.

Isobel's face then broke into a strange smile. Tormod was bemused to see that it was shrewd and smug; in fact, almost one of retribution. What was she hiding in the deep recesses of her mind? Confused and bewildered, he rose from the sofa and put the kettle on the gas stove. Returning to sit beside

266

her, Isobel continued to gaze at him with a peculiar, rather unsettling, expression.

****

Chapter 48

Tormod settled down on the sofa with his book and his coffee while Isobel went to check on the children. Apart from being unusually quiet and pensive on her return she appeared to have reverted to her normal self - at least - her post-accident state of normality.

'Do you love me?' she asked out of the blue.

'Yes. Of course I love you.'

'Did you love me when I was married to John?'

Tormod frowned. 'Is this going to be a question and answer session?' he asked.

Her tone and expression were solemn as she replied, 'Just answer truthfully.'

'No, I didn't love you then. Actually, we didn't get along very well in those days,' he responded with a wry smile. 'But I've grown to love you very much.'

After a short silence, she asked, 'Why did you pretend to be my fiancée?'

'Because,' he began slowly. 'I so desperately wanted to see you after the accident, and the hospital would only admit your nearest and dearest.'

Isobel smiled warmly. 'I was told that you sat by my bedside for days, weeks, and then months on end,' she said softly. 'That was very sweet of you.'

Tormod's response was made under the assumption that if, and when, Isobel's memory returned, she would regret their intimate liaison and end their relationship.

'I'll be here for you until you get your life back on track.'

Isobel gazed at him despondently. 'Then what?' she asked in a sombre tone. 'Will you return here without me?'

He sighed. 'Who knows Isobel? Only time and Karma know the answer.'

'Let's go to bed.'

Tormod gazed at her in disbelief.

'You mean, right now?'

'Yes,' Isobel responded with a shrewd smile.

She took Tormod's hand and began to lead him towards the bedroom. Her recollection of their love-making last night was hazy. This was due in part to her recurring nightmare, and also because of her confusion between fantasy and reality. Now, she was wide awake and in a more coherent frame of mind. Something in her subconscious was telling her that, by giving herself willingly to Tormod, it may help to unlock the past - and perhaps keep him from seeking his pleasures elsewhere.

Tormod closed the bedroom curtains in a futile attempt to shut out the storm, before snuggling under the blankets next to Isobel. Outside, the hurricane was raging, while inside, the tempest was gathering momentum. Isobel began by kissing Tormod in a way that served to stimulate his simmering desire. Then, slowly and seductively she began to undress him. Once again, she was calling the shots and setting the pace. Although a newcomer to the game, Tormod recalled the gratification he'd experienced last night and was eager, perhaps over eager, to replicate the sensation. His body temperature now at boiling point, he threw back the covers and stripped Isobel of her clothing without further ado. Isobel was slightly bewildered by the stark contrast from her memories of the gentle, compassionate lover from last night. Had she only dreamt it after all? He was astride her now and stark naked. Her eyes fleetingly scanned his muscular physique and suddenly, she felt extremely vulnerable. Tormod was holding her arms above her head, his body-weight pinning her to the bed and she was powerless to resist as he took her by force. The intercourse was frenzied, sadistic and painful.

'Tormod, please stop,' she cried out in anguish. But her cries served only to accentuate his desire.

'I can't stop, he gasped. 'You know you don't want me to. I want you so much....'

'I want you, but not like this.....'

The force of his lips on hers silenced any further protests. Despite writhing underneath him and fighting him off with all the strength she could muster, her strength was no match for his. Her excruciatingly painful ordeal seemed to go on for hours, until suddenly, after letting out a rapturous groan, he lay completely still. Isobel too, stopped struggling. She lay rigid as Tormod, soaked in perspiration and panting heavily, held her in a vice-like grip. If he would only move off her, she thought to herself, she would check on the children. But Tormod didn't move off her. Instead, with her arms pinned by her sides, he began to kiss every inch of her naked body. Isobel was now crying softly. Tormod, recalling her tears during their lovemaking last night, took this to indicate her reciprocation of his fervour. Although never having any previous tendencies towards sadism, the sense of power, his victim rendered helpless and totally under his control, had taken Tormod by surprise. Nonetheless, it was one he would remember, and eagerly anticipate, in future. This time, his rampant lust now satisfied, his advances were tender and loving. As far as Tormod was concerned, Isobel now belonged to him alone and that served to increase his desire to augment his prowess; she would become his experimental plaything. As far as Isobel was concerned, this was her initiation to lovemaking, all previous recollection of such having been wiped from her memory. With a feeling of utter helplessness and realising the futility of resisting his advances, this time, she was wholly submissive and allowed him to use her body as he wished to whet his rampant sexual appetite. The strange thing was, this time around, she shared his passion with reciprocal pleasure.

Tormod, never having experienced feelings this intense before, knew that he could never let Isobel go.

After all, he'd waited a lifetime for this moment. No matter the outcome of their return to the mainland, he couldn't live without her in his life. As for Isobel, something strange had happened during her sexual encounter. She'd had to stop herself from crying out the name, John, and yet, she had no recollection of her late husband. As they lay in each other's arms, basking in mutual sexual fulfilment, the storm outside was reaching hurricane force. Suddenly, a calamitous noise made them leap from the bed and run to the window. A monstrous wave had swamped the yard and reduced the log shed to a plethora of floating matchsticks. Not only that, but the flood water was creeping towards the front door.

'Oh my God,' Isobel gasped.

270

'We'll have to get out of here,' Tormod called frantically.

After dressing hastily and wrapping blankets round the children, they bundled them into the car. The sea was thundering and crashing all around them as they set off along the coastal road. The car was being buffeted by the wind, drenched by wave upon wave and Tormod struggled to remain in control. At times, the road and the sea appeared as one.

'Where are we going?' Isobel shouted above the din.

'We'll try and make it to higher ground,' he replied. 'If we can make it as far as the turn off to Fergus' farm, we'll take refuge there.'

'Oh no,' Tormod gasped as the wipers cleared another deluge of seawater from the windscreen.

'What is it?' Isobel asked anxiously.

'The road up ahead is under water,' he muttered.'

The car slowed down almost to a standstill as Tormod drove into the salty floodwater. The engine spluttered and coughed before cutting out. Tormod tried desperately to restart it, but to no avail. Daylight was fading and Màiri and Iain were whimpering in the back seat. The sea was boiling, heaving relentlessly, and wave upon wave surged over the roof of the little car.

'Consumed first by fire and then flood,' Isobel muttered. Tormod, having heard her, responded by saying, 'Don't say that. You're not destined to die just yet.'

'Why did you say that?' Isobel called out with a startled expression.

Tormod gave a wry smile. 'I have absolutely no idea. Just a gut instinct I suppose.'

No sooner had he said the words than the sound of a vehicle could be heard above the storm. This was followed by an array of headlights appearing on the other side of the submerged road. Men kitted out in oilskins and carrying lifejackets now surrounded the car. One of them motioned for the passenger window to be wound down just far enough to allow the children to be passed through. Once Màiri and Iain had been taken to safety, the men returned to the car. Isobel wound the passenger window down a little bit further to allow her to squeeze through and as she did so, a deluge of seawater gushed inside the car. She was grabbed by her rescuer and carried to one of the waiting vehicles. Tormod though, was still inside the submerged car and was in danger of being swept into the boiling cauldron of the raging ocean. Powerless to go to his aid, Isobel's voice, screaming out his name, could be heard above the hurricane.

She and the children were driven off by strangers to an unknown destination. The children were soaked to the skin, scared out of their tiny minds, and fretful. As for Isobel, she was disorientated, distraught and in a state of shock and disbelief. She couldn't quite get her head around the events of the last few hours. How could her short vacation, which had begun so pleasingly, have turned into such a nightmare? A voice in her ear made her jump.

'We'll drop you and the children off at the hospital and head back to see if we can help find your husband.'

Hospital...... Husband...... What hospital, she wondered. As for her husband, she'd been told he was dead. Why are those people, whoever they are, trying to confuse me, she asked herself.

Her head was throbbing.... spinning..... Then suddenly, she had a vision of Tormod being dragged, lifeless, from the sea.

****

Chapter 49

Hospital staff met the ambulance at the entrance and Isobel and the children were taken to a small cubicle where they were checked by medical staff for the effects of shock and hypothermia. When asked her name, Isobel had replied, Ishbel MacKenzie. When asked if she had any friends or relatives on the island, she'd replied that she knew no-one. When asked if there was anyone she would like them to notify, she'd replied that, although she had family on the mainland, she couldn't remember their addresses or telephone numbers. The doctor was concerned to say the least. Despite there being no specific medical reasons for doing so, he made the decision to hospitalise her and the children overnight. He'd been briefed on the circumstances surrounding her admission, but was more concerned about her mental state than her physical one.

Later that evening, a victim of drowning was brought to the mortuary. Although he'd been carrying no means of identification, one of the rescuers had recognised him from the ceilidh in the nearby village on Hogmanay. It wasn't long before the news spread round the island that the victim's name was Tormod MacAlister, an islander by birth but now living on the mainland.
A nurse came to Isobel's bedside to break the terrible news that her husband Tormod, had drowned.
Isobel gazed vacantly into space as she replied, 'I don't know what you're talking about. My husband's name is Dr John Caldwell.'
'You were staying at Sine MacPherson's croft with Tormod and the children,' she said gently. 'Was Tormod a relative of yours?'
Isobel continued to stare straight ahead. She couldn't think clearly. There was too much was going on inside her head. Too many thoughts...... too many images..... too much heartache to bear.

News of the tragedy spread quickly round the small island

and it wasn't long before it reached the ears of Fergus, Dolina and Sìne. In a state of disbelief, shock and distress, they made their way to the hospital. Since Isobel was in no fit state to identify the body, and due to the fact that she'd denied all knowledge of him, Fergus was asked to confirm Tormod's identity. There was no doubt in his mind whatsoever that the corpse that lay in the morgue was that of his childhood friend, Tormod Seumas MacAlister.

Following this, he made his way to the ward where Isobel was being detained. He'd been briefed that, although she'd suffered no physical injuries, her mental state was unstable.

Not knowing quite how to deal with the bizarre situation, he greeted her with the words, 'Hello Isobel..... Remember me?'

She stared at him for a moment, her face expressionless.

'Hello Fergus,' she replied in a monotone. 'Where are my children?'

'Màiri and Iain are just fine,' he replied softly. 'They're in good hands.'

Dolina had suggested that she take the children back to the farm and care for them until Isobel was well enough to be discharged from hospital. Dolina adored children, but despite longing for motherhood, due to Fergus having a low sperm count, it was doubtful if she would ever have children of her own. Tormod hadn't enlightened them of the relationship between him and Isobel, but it had been apparent from seeing them together that they were in a relationship. It was obvious that he adored the children; therefore, she assumed Màiri and Iain to be the offspring of her childhood sweetheart.

Fergus found his visit awkward, traumatic and distressing. Isobel hadn't asked about Tormod and he couldn't bring himself to mention his name. He was still in a state of shock himself and trying to come to terms with the tragic and wholly inconceivable death of his former schoolmate. Leaving the ward, he was approached by a nurse who asked him to come into the office. Despite being quizzed over her identity and next of kin, Fergus was unable to reveal any information whatsoever about Isobel. On Hogmanay, Tormod had introduced her as Isobel Caldwell, so why, he wondered, was she insisting that her name was Ishbel MacKenzie?

It was decided that, due to the unusual circumstances surrounding the case, the police be informed. Unfortunately, the island didn't have a resident policeman and the ferries were grounded until further notice. The decision was made that Isobel would be kept in hospital until her true identity was established. It would be the following week before the storms abated and the ferries resumed their service. During that time, Sine had been asked to search the cottage for any further clues about the patient's identity. Due to the fact that the cottage had been under several feet of seawater for the past few days, any papers found in Isobel's belongings had been rendered illegible.

Back on the mainland, Isobel's family were beginning to have concerns over the whereabouts of Isobel, Tormod and the children. Tormod hadn't given any indication of the duration of their stay, or in fact, their destination. Nonetheless, they were aware that the Outer Hebridean islands had experienced severe storms over the past week. They could only hope and pray they were safe and well.

One day, the story of Tormod's death appeared in the daily newspaper. It was the old vet from Drumevie who saw it first. The article mentioned that the police were urging relatives of Tormod or his female companion to contact them as a matter of urgency. He was aware that Tormod had no relatives on the mainland. As for the identity of his female companion, Tormod had once told him he was dating Claire Ferguson from Inverculden. He duly picked up the phone and dialled 999. After speaking to a police officer, he consulted the telephone directory for the number of Inverculden Estate office. He dialled the number and waited.

'Good morning, Inverculden Estate, Claire Ferguson speaking. Can I help?' said the formal voice.

'I.....I....my name is Hamish Davidson,' he began hesitantly. 'I'm the vet from Drumevie. I believe you were acquainted with Tormod MacAlister.'

'I *am* acquainted with him....' she replied curtly.

275

Denying her the opportunity of going any further, he interrupted, saying, 'I'm afraid I've got some bad news. Tormod has drowned on his native island.'

Silence, followed by the sound of sobbing prompted him to add, 'Is there anything I can do?'

'No, nothing at all,' she replied curtly. 'Thank you for the information'

The news of Tormod's tragic death was subsequently relayed to Isobel's friends and family. Hamish had informed Claire that, according to the newspaper article, his female companion was safe and well in the small island hospital, awaiting identification. There was no mention of any children, but relatives were being urged to contact the police with information.

Helen was now on her way to the local police station in Drumevie, where she would pass on the relevant details about Isobel and seek further information about Tormod's tragic accident.

Later that day, Helen and Rob made arrangements to travel to the island on the next available ferry.

Back at the hospital, the doctor had come into the ward to talk to Isobel.

'Hello Isobel,' he began. 'Contact has been made with your next of kin. Your brother and sister will arrive on the morning ferry and I have decided to discharge you today so that you can return to your home on the mainland.'

Isobel had been hospitalised for over a week now and during that time, her only visitors had been Fergus and Sine. She'd asked about the children several times and now knew that they were being cared for by Fergus and Dolina. Not once though, had she mentioned Tormod's name, until now.

'Where is Tormod's body?' she asked.

Her question went unanswered, but the doctor asked with an odd expression, 'How well did you know Tormod?'

Isobel merely shook her head, before saying despondently, 'I can't remember anything prior to my accident, but apparently I've known him for some time.'

276

'Accident?' he questioned.

'A car crash,' Isobel responded and drew back her hair to reveal the scar.

'That goes some way to answering some of my questions,' he muttered to himself.

Isobel, having heard him, asked, 'What questions?'

He gazed intently into her face and said in a gentle tone, 'You didn't answer my question in the way I had hoped.'

'Now you're confusing me again. Too many questions,' Isobel said as her eyes filled with tears.

'I want to help you,' he began slowly. 'To do that, I need to know the answer to only one question. What was the relationship between you and Tormod MacAlister.'

'We were friends when we arrived on the island,' she began hesitantly, 'but we became lovers on the day of his death.'

He frowned, before asking, 'Were you compliant?'

'I don't understand the question,' she responded with a look of childish innocence.

Dr MacIntyre frowned deeply, but didn't respond.

The following day, Isobel was discharged from hospital and Fergus had come to collect her. He was taking her to the farmhouse to meet up with Dolina and the children and await the arrival of Helen and Rob the following day. Isobel's emotions at the thought of returning to the mainland were mixed. Fergus had told her that, since Tormod had no surviving relatives, he had been delegated to arrange his funeral on the island. Just as soon as it had been established that his death was nothing more than a freak accident, his body would be released for burial and he would be laid to rest in the local cemetery beside his beloved parents.

Following Isobel's discharge from hospital, the doctor received a telephone call. It was from the neurosurgeon at Locherton City Hospital on the mainland. He began by expressing his concern over Isobel's well-being and explained that she had merely been discharged from hospital for the festive period and was still under medical supervision. The island doctor was relieved to have been briefed on her medical condition and promised to keep an eye on her until she left the island.

He'd planned to visit her before she left the island anyhow, hoping that by then he would have the results of some tests he'd run.

The reunion between Isobel and her children was a joyous occasion. Máiri especially, had been severely traumatised by the separation from her mother and couldn't conceal her delight at seeing her again. As for Isobel, she too was happy to be among familiar faces once more.

That night, Isobel and the children slept together in a double bed at the farmhouse. Isobel though, didn't get much sleep. She was turning things over in her mind and trying to analyse her emotions – the few she had left. At this moment, they were mainly grief, sorrow and heartache. Her thoughts were that she couldn't possibly leave the island until after Tormod's funeral. It wasn't as if she had anything to rush back to the mainland for - she was still convalescing after all. The only problem she could envisage was financial. Somehow, she would have to get money to pay for accommodation for her and the children for a couple of weeks.

****

Chapter 50

Helen and Rob sailed to the island on the morning ferry and it docked at the pier just before mid-day. They'd been given directions to the farmhouse of Fergus and Dolina and were now approaching the small township of Portnashiel. They decided to stop for lunch at the hotel, unaware that this was where Tormod and Isobel had spent their first night on the island. In the bar, they found the locals to be inquisitive, and blunt to the point of being downright rude. When asked who they were and what had brought them to the island, Rob replied that they were Isobel Caldwell's next of kin and had come to take her back to the mainland.

'Aye, such a tragedy,' one muttered in response.

'Poor Tormod,' another opined with a shake of his head.

'First, his parents in the fire, then him in the flood,' said yet another.

Rob and Helen agreed that the death of Tormod was as unbelievable as it was horrific, especially for Isobel. Helen added that she was concerned for her state of health.

'It was all her fault from what I've heard,' someone piped up.

'I heard a rumour that she's lost the plot completely and can't remember anything about it.'

'Aye, conveniently,' another added sarcastically.

Rob and Helen, who hadn't been given any details of the circumstances surrounding Tormod's death, were in a state of shock and dismay. Their lunch was duly served, but by now, neither of them had much appetite.

After leaving the hotel they followed the shore, passing the burnt out croft of Tormod's parents. Then they passed Sine's croft, and finally, the spot where Tormod's car had been swept into the sea. They were completely oblivious to all this of course; they were only following directions to the farm on the hill. It was a cold but pleasant January day and the raging ocean of the past week had taken on a beguiling, picture postcard state of tranquillity. Similar to the day of Tormod and Isobel's arrival, the rippling waves gently kissed the pristine white sand as they met.

'It is absolutely beautiful here,' Helen remarked in awe as

Rob began the steep climb that took them into the hills. Similar to her sister, she'd never seen the sea before and had been oblivious to the contrast between the islands and the mainland.

As they turned into the drive that led to the farm of Dolina and Fergus, butterflies began to flutter in Helen's stomach. Although eager to see her beloved sister again, she was nervous and apprehensive. Isobel had come such a long way since being discharged from hospital for the festive period. It was mainly due to Tormod's genuine affection for her that this had come about. But with him gone, and from what she'd been told by the locals in the village hostelry, what awaited her was anyone's guess.

Fergus opened the door and welcomed them warmly before inviting them inside. Helen was greeted by screams of delight from Màiri and Iain who came running towards her, before clinging to her legs. She scooped them up, one in each arm, and kissed their tiny, smiling faces all over.

Isobel meanwhile, stood in the background, silent and morose. Rob walked towards her, before taking her in his arms and holding her tightly.

'Bella,' he began tearfully, 'I just don't know what to say.'

Had his beloved sister not been suffering from amnesia, their reunion would have been less formal, but she had no recollection of their closeness, their intimacy from the past. As far as Isobel was concerned, her beloved brother was, in effect, a stranger. Helen, with whom she'd spent some time at An Gleann Dubh prior to coming to the island, was less so, and they embraced with a little more affection.

'I've got tickets for the afternoon ferry tomorrow,' Helen began in an effort to make conversation.

Isobel didn't reply immediately, but went on to tell her sister that she was toying with the idea of staying on the island for a bit longer so that she could attend Tormod's funeral. If I can afford it, she'd added tentatively.

'We're staying at the hotel in Portnashiel tonight,' Helen replied. 'Why don't we meet later for dinner? We can discuss it then.'

Rob and Helen stayed for afternoon tea, following which they

280

left to return to Portnashiel. They hadn't long gone, when another visitor arrived to see Isobel. It was Dr MacIntyre from the hospital. He began by informing her of the telephone call from the neurosurgeon, then went on to explain his concerns over her physical, as well as mental, health. He then told her that, for the duration of her stay on the island, she would remain under his medical supervision. He finished by saying, 'The results of your pregnancy test came back today. It's positive.'

Isobel's jaw dropped and it looked as though she would collapse. The doctor reached out and caught her in his arms as her legs buckled.

'No. I can't be,' she protested. 'I would never be unfaithful to John.'

From somewhere deep within had been a tiny glimmer of recollection of her wedding vows.

'Isobel, you haven't been unfaithful, your husband is dead,' the doctor responded sympathetically.

'Tormod is dead too. They're both dead because of me.'

Isobel's shoulders began to heave as she sobbed pitifully.

'Under the circumstances, I could arrange for you to have an abortion,' Dr MacIntyre said gently.

'Abortion,' Isobel whispered the word. 'I couldn't even begin to contemplate aborting my own flesh and blood.'

Before leaving, Dr MacIntyre had made Isobel promise to let him know the outcome of her decision to extend her stay on the island.

That evening, Fergus drove Isobel to the hotel. Even as she entered the small reception area, the muted voices and blatant stares from the male customers in the bar were apparent. She couldn't hear what they were saying, but she could guess.

She felt sad about Tormod's death, but yet not devastated as one would expect. She couldn't justify her feelings, just as she couldn't do anything to change them.

For Isobel, the dinner date with Rob and Helen was a pleasant and welcome respite from the traumas of the past two weeks. It was apparent that they shared a close bond, and even though she had no recollection of them growing up

281

together, felt a connection with them. The discussions over dinner covered several issues, most of which had been kept from Isobel due to her fragile state of mind, one of them being the inheritance from her late husband. Isobel had remained in a state of shocked silence while digesting the news. Many things were now coming to light that would make a significant difference to her present situation. Isobel asked to be told the value of her inheritance and informed Rob and Helen that she would like to access her account.

'Rob has been appointed your attorney during your rehabilitation,' Helen began in a sympathetic tone. 'If you need any funds, or cash to settle bills, you only have to ask.'

Rob then added, 'In answer to your other question, you have a substantial sum in an investment account. You also own a property in London.'

'I believe I am also a qualified vet,' Isobel added with a knowing smile. After a short pause, she added, 'In that case, I've decided not to return to the mainland with you tomorrow. I'm going to stay on here for a few weeks and would like you to transfer £10,000 into my personal account.

Following Isobel's departure that evening, Rob and Helen were left wondering what their young sister was planning to do with £10,000.

They left the island the following morning, but not before promising to deposit the funds into Isobel's bank account and insisting that she keep in touch. Helen had given Isobel her assurance that she would continue to run the croft in the meantime. Nonetheless, it would only be on a short term basis. She now had other plans for the future.

****

To be continued

282

Also published by Llanerch:

THE WHITE TOWER
Liz Whittaker

THE CELTIC CHRISTIANITY
OF CORNWALL
by Thomas Taylor

A WEEK AT THE LIZARD
by C A Johns

SCILLY AND ITS LEGENDS
By Rev. H J Whitfield

WHAT IS NORMAL ANYWAY
The story of an Aspergers Relationship
by Annie Sheridan

TOMBS OF THE KINGS
By John Marsden

THE SACRED TREE
By J H Philpot

BROADSIDE BLACK-LETTER BALLADS
By J Payne Collier

For a complete list of small-press editions
and facsimile reprints of books on traditional
music, Celtic interest, early history, archery
mysticism, Anglo-Saxon interest and Literature
of Llanerch Press Ltd
publications, please visit our website:
www.llanerchpress.com
or alternatively write to:
Llanerch Press Ltd, Little Court, 48 Rectory Road
Burnham-on-Sea, Somerset. TA8 2BZ